Sniper's Honor

Center Point
Large Print

Also by Stephen Hunter and available from Center Point Large Print:

The Third Bullet
Soft Target

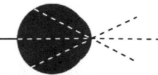

Sniper's Honor

A BOB LEE SWAGGER NOVEL

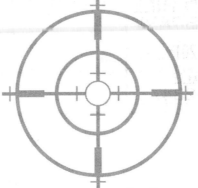

Stephen Hunter

CENTER POINT LARGE PRINT
THORNDIKE, MAINE

This Center Point Large Print edition
is published in the year 2014 by arrangement with
Simon & Schuster, Inc.

The text of this Large Print edition is unabridged.
In other respects, this book may vary
from the original edition.
Printed in the United States of America
on permanent paper.
Set in 16-point Times New Roman type.

ISBN: 978-1-62899-134-5

Library of Congress Cataloging-in-Publication Data

Hunter, Stephen, 1946–
  Sniper's honor : a Bob Lee Swagger novel / Stephen Hunter. — Center
point large print edition.
    pages ; cm
  Summary: "Washington Post correspondent Kathy Reilly taps her
friend, former marine sniper Bob Lee Swagger to find information on a
World War II female sniper. As they travel to Russia and the Carpathian
Mountains, someone is determined to stop them at any cost"—Provided
by publisher.
  ISBN 978-1-62899-134-5 (library binding : alk. paper)
  1. Swagger, Bob Lee (Fictitious character)—Fiction.
    2. Women soldiers—Fiction. 3. Snipers—Fiction.
    4. Missing in action—Fiction. 5. Women journalists—Fiction.
    6. Large type books. I. Title.
PS3558.U494N56 2014
813′.54—dc23
                                                        2014016078

For Kathy Lally, who invented me twice.
In 1981 as a film critic.
In 2013 as a Ukrainian partisan.
She gets around.

"I came across time for you, Sarah."

REESE (MICHAEL BIEHN)
THE TERMINATOR (1984)

Sniper's Honor

PROLOGUE

Ostfront

1942

It was a balmy November day in Stalingrad, 14 below, twelve feet of snow, near-blizzard conditions. Another twelve feet were expected soon and tomorrow would be colder. At the intersection of Tauvinskaya and Smarkandskaya streets, near the petrol tanks, not far from the Barrikady Factory, the boulevards were empty of pedestrian or vehicular traffic, though arms, legs, feet shod and unshod, hands gloved and ungloved, even a head or two stuck out of the caked white banks that lined them. A dead dog could be seen there, a dead old lady here. The sky was low and gray, threatening; columns of smoke rose from various energetic encounters in the northern suburb of Spartaskovna a few miles away. A ruined Sd. Kfz 251, painted frosty white for camouflage, lay on its side, its visible track sheared, a splatter of steel wheels all over the street. Its crew had either escaped or been long since devoured by feral dogs and rats. Farther down rusted away a T-34 without a turret, a relic of warmer months, as was presumably its crew. On either side of either street for blocks on end, the buildings had been reduced to devastation and resembled a maze, a secret puzzle of shattered brick, twisted steel, blackened wall, ruptured vehicle. In this labyrinth, small groups of men hunted each other and now and then would spring an ambush and a spasm of rifle or machine-gun fire would erupt, perhaps the blast of a Russian or German grenade. Occasionally a plane would roar overhead, a Sturmovik or a Stuka, like a predator bird looking for something to kill and eat.

But for now, the intersection was quiet, though a riot of snowflakes floated downward, swirling in the wind, covering bloodstains, human entrails, fecal deposits, muffling the screams of men who'd lost legs or testicles, the whole panoply of total, bitter war fought at very close quarters in frozen conditions, under a gossamer surface of silky frost.

One man, however, was quite warm and comfortable. He was prone-positioned in what had been Apartment 32, 27 Smarkandskaya Street, a model Soviet worker's building, which now had no roof and few walls. He lay belly-down on three blankets, under three blankets. His face was smeared with zinc ointment as a protection against frostbite, his hands were twice gloved, a white hood engulfed most of his head, and a scarf sheathed his mouth and nose, so that only the eyes, dark behind snow goggles, were visible. Best of all, every half an hour, a private would slither up the stairs and slip a hot water bottle under the blankets, its contents freshly charged from a boiling pot two flights below.

The prone man was named Gunther Ramke and he was a feldwebel, a sergeant, in the 3rd Battalion of the Second Regiment of the 44th Infantry Division in XI Corps in the Sixth Army under Paulus, facing the 13th Guards Rifle Division of the Soviet 62nd Army under Zhukov as the heavy fighting of Operation Uranus echoed in the distance. Zhukov was trying desperately to encircle Paulus as a preliminary to destroying him and his three hundred thousand colleagues. None of that mattered to Feldwebel Ramke, who had no imagination for any kind of pictures save the one he saw through his Hensoldt Dialytan four-power telescopic sight, set in a claw mount on his Mauser K98k.

He was a sniper, he was hunting a sniper. That was all.

The Russian had moved in a few weeks ago, a very talented stalker and shooter, and already had eliminated seven men, two of them SS officers. It was thought that the fellow had worked the Barrikady Factory zone before that, and possibly Memomova Hill. He liked to kill SS. It wasn't that Ramke had any particular investment in the SS, which struck him as ridiculous (he was farm-raised and thought the black costumes were something for the stage or cinema; additionally, he knew nothing of politics except that the Fatherland had been starved into submission in '18, then gotten screwed in the Treaty of Versailles), but he was a good soldier, an excellent shot (twenty-nine kills), and he had an assignment and meant to bring it off. It would keep his captain happy, and life was better for everyone in the company, as in all armies that have ever existed anywhere in the world at any time, if the captain was happy.

He knew this game was of a dimension he had not yet encountered. Normally you stalk, you slither, you pop up or dip down, and sooner or later a fellow with a Mosin-Nagant or a Red tommy gun comes your way, you settle into position, hold your breath, steady the weapon on bones not muscles, watch the crosshair ooze toward center body, and squeeze. The fellow staggers and falls; or he steps back and falls; or he simply falls; but it always ends in the fall. Plop, to the ground, raising dust or snow, followed by the eternal stillness known only to the dead.

But the character on the other side of the street was too good. So the new rules were, you never moved. You emulated the recently deceased. You never looked up or about. Your field of vision was your battlefield, and it covered about thirty feet at 250 meters. You stayed disciplined. The rifle was loaded and cocked so there was no ritual of bolt throw, with its bobbing head and flying elbows, either of which could get you killed. The name of this game was patience. The opponent would come to you. It was a question of waiting. Thus, Gunther was perfectly constituted for the job, being barely literate and lacking any ability to project himself in time or space. He was the ideal sniper: what was, was; he had no need for speculation, delusion, curiosity, or fantasy.

He was set up to cover the fifth and sixth floors of a much-battered apartment building across the street and the traffic circle that marked the intersection, with the knees of a statue of someone once important to the Russians still standing on a pedestal. If the enemy sniper was in that tightly circumscribed universe, Gunther would make the kill. If he was a floor lower or higher, or a window to the left or right, they'd never encounter each other. Tricky business. Wait, wait, wait.

And finally the ordeal seemed to be paying off. He was convinced that within the darkness of the rear of the apartment whose interior was defined by his sight picture lay a patch more intense and more shaped than had been there in previous hours. He convinced himself he saw movement. He just wasn't quite sure, and if he fired and hit nothing, he would give this position up, and he'd have to start anew tomorrow.

He didn't want to stare too hard through the glass. Eyestrain and fatigue led to hallucinatory visions, and if he let himself, he'd see Joe Stalin sitting in there, eating a plate of sardines and wiping his filthy peasant hands on his tunic. Realizing this as a trap, he closed his eyes every few seconds for some rest, so that he cut down on the pressure. But each time he opened them, he was certain there was a new shape in the shadow. It could have been a samovar on the floor, or the frame of a chair that lost a fight with a mortar round, or even the body of the occupant, but it also could have been a man in prone, hunched similarly over a weapon, eye pressed similarly to the scope. It didn't help that discriminations were made more difficult by reason of an occasional sunbeam that would break through the clouds and throw a shaft of illumination into the room just above the suspected enemy. When this happened, it broke Gunther's concentration and ruined his vision, and he had to blink and look away and wait until the condition passed.

But Gunther felt safe. The Ivan snipers used a 3.5-power optic called a PU, which meant that even if his enemy were on him, the details would be so blurry that no sight picture could be made, not at 250 meters, which was about as far as the Mosin-Nagant with that scope was good for. So he felt invisible, even a little godlike. His higher degree of magnification gave him enough advantage.

He would wait a little while longer. That low sun

would disappear and full dark would come. Both opponents, if there was another opponent, would wait until that happened and then gradually disengage and come back to fight tomorrow. But Gunther had decided to shoot. He'd been on this stand a week, and he convinced himself that he was seeing something new, having moved in at about three in the afternoon, and it could only be—

He closed his eyes. He counted to sixty.

"Not much time left, Gunther," came the call from his *Landser*, leaning out of the stairwell behind him. "Need more hot water?"

"Shhh!" said Gunther.

"You're going to shoot! Maybe we can get out of here early!"

Then the soldier disappeared, knowing further distraction was to nobody's advantage. Gunther, meanwhile, prepared to fire. He carefully assembled his position behind the rifle, working methodically from toes to head, locking joints, finding angles for his limbs, making nuanced adjustments, building bone trusses under the seven-pound 7.92mm rifle resting on a sandbag, pushing the safety off, sliding his trigger finger out of the sheathing of the two gloves via a slot he'd cut in each. He felt the trigger's coldness, felt his fingertip engage it, felt it move back, stacking slightly as it went, until it finally reached the precise edge between firing and not firing. At this point he committed fully by opening his eyes to acquire the picture through the glass of the Hensoldt Dialytan, four times larger than life, and settled the intersection of the crosswires on its center. He exhaled half his breath, put his weight against the trigger, feeling it just about to break, and then saw the flash.

The round hit him on a slightly downward angle at the midpoint of his right shoulder, breaking a whole network of bones, though missing any major arteries or blood-bearing organs. It was not fatal. In fact, it saved his life; his shoulder was so ruinously damaged that he was evacuated from Stalingrad that night, one of the last to escape the Cauldron, as it came to be called, full of Paulus's unhappy men. Gunther lived to be eighty-nine years old, dying prosperous and well attended by grandchildren on his farm in Bavaria.

However, at the point of impact it felt like someone had unloaded a full-swing ten-kilo sledgeweight against him, lifting him, twisting him, depositing him. He was aware that he had fired in reaction to the trauma but knew full well that the shot, jerked and spastic, had no chance of reaching the target.

Dazzled by the shock, he recovered quickly and tried to cock the rifle but found of course that the arm attached to the now-destroyed shoulder no longer worked. Still, on instinct, his face returned to the stock, his eye returned to the scope, and it so happened that his opponent, having delivered the shot, had risen to depart just as one of those errant sunbeams pierced the interior of the room. As the figure rose and turned, the hood fell away and Gunther saw a cascade of yellow hair, bright as gold, reflect in the sunlight. Then the sniper was gone.

Men raced to him, tourniquets were supplied and applied, a stretcher was brought, but Gunther said to anybody who would listen, "*Die weisse Hexe!*"

The White Witch!

CHAPTER 1

Outside Cascade
The Homestead
THE PRESENT

He was an old man in a dry month. Swagger sat on his rocker on the porch, hard, stoic, isolate, unmelted. Nothing much engaged him these days. Indifferently, he watched sun and moon change, he watched the variations of the clouds, the flocks of birds, the far prairie dog, occasionally the antelope on the horizon. He watched the wind blow across the prairie, and saw the mountains in the distance. It meant nothing.

He drank the coffee his wife left brewed every

morning. He played with his laptop until he got bored, and then he watched the wind in the grass until he got bored. He sat, he rocked. He was lonely.

Jen gone most of the day, one daughter a TV correspondent in Washington, D.C., the other at a summer riding program in Massachusetts where she would try to turn her western grace into eastern swank, his son the assistant director of the FBI sniper training school in Quantico, Virginia, Swagger spent most of his time on the porch in the company of ghosts and memories.

Dead friends, forgotten places, calls too close to call close, long shots paying off, luck by the ton, a lost wife, a found son, a murdered father, some justice here and there, all of it purchased with enough scars to carpet a house, the smell of fire and gun smoke eternally in his nostrils: it didn't seem like anything that could be called an odyssey, just one mess after another.

"You are depressed," said his wife.

"I got everything I ever wanted. I have friends, a fine wife, wonderful children. I survived several wars. Why would I be depressed?"

"Because you never cared about any of those things. Getting them is incidental and meaning-less. You cared about something else. You cared about pleasing your goddamned father because he died before you could, and it has never left you. That is why you are depressed. You haven't pleased him lately. You will never please him enough. You have issues. You need to see somebody."

"I am fine. I ride every day, I don't eat too much and never collected a gut, I can still put a bullet near anyplace I can see. Why would I be depressed?"

"You need a mission. Or a new young woman to fall in love with and never touch. I notice those things seem to come together. You need a war. You need someone to shoot at you, so you can shoot back. You need all those things, and as beautiful as this place is and as much as it's everything a man could want, it's not enough. For most, maybe. Not for Bob Lee Swagger, sheriff of dry gulches and high noons every day of the week."

But then an e-mail had arrived that actually had been authored by a human being: J. F. Guthrie, an ex–British service armorer who had made a career writing books about sniper warfare through the twentieth and twenty-first centuries and had approached Bob about telling the Bob story. Bob turned him down flat cold—he had no urge to refight old fights, since he visited them every night in his nightmares—but the man was so charming that a friendship had developed and the Internet allowed it to blossom.

Dear Swagger, *wrote "Jimmy" Guthrie,* thought I'd invite you to the British Gun

Club's annual WWII Sniper Match, to be held this coming October at the old British service range at Bisley. You'd have a fine time. The admirers and fan boys would know enough to keep their distance and you'd also meet some fellow tradesmen, Brit style, for a nice spot of shop talk. Everybody loves shop talk.

I'll be shooting my treasured Enfield No. 4 (T), of course, and I'd be happy to loan you either a Garand M1D or a Springfield with Unertl for yourself from my collection. Or you could bring an M40 of your own, if you care to do a dance with our antiquated customs.

Know you'd get a cheer-up, know the real boys would love to rub shoulders with the Nailer himself. Details if you're interested. Do consider.

Jimmy

It would be fun. It would be a goal, something to organize and prepare for. It would reengage him in the world, and prove to him that at sixty-eight, he still had some fuel left in the tank.

But: it would also put him into contact with people who were drawn to the killer. He knew, he understood. Certain folks, though they might never admit it, dreamed of killing and in some unsavory way were powerfully attracted to an artist of the craft, which Swagger certainly was. Not for sex, not for wisdom, not for fantasy or even, really, friendship; just in some soft-vampire way to feed on his aura. Maybe Jimmy himself was such a man; maybe if so, he hid it better. Swagger always felt a little debased by such transactions, not that there was any ill spirit in them, but they just felt wrong. They made too much of the killing, as if the killing itself were the point, when the truth was nobody could last in the profession for the killing alone. You had to believe in something bigger, and in service to that—duty, honor, country, the kid in the next foxhole, the will to survive, to win, something never clearly understood called the Big Picture, something never talked of called honor—you could persevere, even occasionally flourish. Whatever it was, it was not shared easily, particularly since he had made the big mistake of reading way too much on the subject and understood he possessed a dangerous amount of data that opened him up to the horror of self-knowledge.

He made his typical decision on Jimmy's invite: I'll think about it.

Oh, hello, another e-mail, a nice long one from his daughter Miko at riding camp in the Berkshires, where she'd gone because everyone said she was so smart it was wrong not to send her to an eastern school and open a new life for her, and it followed from that that if she had eastern-style riding in her background, it would make entrance easier and give her a culture to belong to.

He took pleasure in the long answer he sent her, but when it was gone, he was still on his porch, his hip still ached (it always did), the wind still blew across the prairie, and it was time for another cup of coffee.

He fetched it, returned, tried to imagine where he'd ride this afternoon, contemplated maybe getting up earlier tomorrow for breakfast at Rick's in Cascade, a ritual he always enjoyed, listening to the boys talk about Boise State football or the Mariners. Otherwise, not much seemed to be going on. And then there was.

That's how it happens sometimes, just that fast. A new message from Kathy Reilly, off in Moscow, where she was the correspondent for *The Washington Post.* They'd had a Moscow adventure some years back, and found themselves simpatico, and stayed in touch. She had that dry humor, a needler and subtle provocateur like he was, and smart, and they liked to prod each other.

Swagger, what would a Mosin-Nagant 91 be? I know it's some gun thing but I just get confused every time I Google it.

What the hell? Never in hundreds of e-mails had the subject of firearms come up, and maybe that's why he liked her so much. The possibilities more or less tantalized him, and for a time he thought it was a kind of joke. But no, she wasn't joking about the Mosin.

He played it straight, or as straight as he could with Reilly.

It's the rifle used by Russian troops from 1891 until, roughly, 19AK-47. Long, ungainly thing, looked like something the guards would carry in "Wizard of Oz," but solid and accurate. Bolt action. Does Reilly get bolt action? "Handle" which has to be lifted, pulled back, pushed forward, then down again to fire. I could tell you why but you'd forget in three minutes. Trust me. It's 7.62mm in diameter, shooting a cartridge that's confusingly called "Mosin-Nagant 7.62," though sometimes they add a "54," which is the cartridge length in mm. Roughly a .30-caliber military round, the equivalent of our .30–06, not that Reilly knows what a .30–06 is. It was OUR WWI and II cartridge. What on earth does Reilly need with this information? Is she going on a reindeer hunt? Good eating I hear, especially the ones with the red noses.

He waited, but the clarification was not forth-coming. Soon it was time to ride, and he got his lanky frame up, went to the barn, saddled up a new roan called Horse—he called all his horses Horse—and rode south, then west, then north again, three hours' worth. It felt good to have Horse under him and the rolling meadows around him and the purple mountains on three sides blurring the horizon. You couldn't feel sorry for yourself on a horse or you'd fall off. It was hot and sunny and that always improved his mood, and it helped that his imagination locked itself on the Mosin-Nagant and reviewed what he knew about it, what he thought he knew about it, what he assumed he knew about it. He knew, for example, that he had been shot at with it. First tour, platoon sergeant, Vietnam, 1964–'65, the later flood of Chinese AKs hadn't begun so the VC were using anything they could get their hands on, and the Mosin from the Chinese was prominent. But they learned their lesson fast, realizing that the old warhorse, with its five-round mag and its slow bolt, was no match for the M1 carbines the southerners used, nor his own M14. Slowly the AKs and the SVDs began coming in, and you could feel the guerrillas learning the new tactical possibilities of the modern weapons. Good news for them, bad for us.

He got back, put up Horse, took a shower, and

repaired to his shop. Current project: a round called 6.5 Creedmoor, from the Hornady shop, super-accurate. Possible future sniper round? That filled his mind, as it always did, saved him from the self, gave him something to plan and anticipate. He reloaded 150 cartridges, using five different weights of powder (varying by .1 grain); he'd shoot groups to find the best through a custom 6.5 a gunsmith in Redfield, Washington, had built for him. Then he showered, greeted Jen, who had arrived, and they had a light dinner. He didn't get back to e-mail until the sun had fallen.

Reilly again.

Okay, that's the rifle, but what about in conjunction with something called a PU 3.5? What would that be? What place is this, where are we now?

He got the ref to "Grass," part of his World War I project from years back. Carl Sandburg: "I am the grass; I cover all. Pile the bodies high at Austerlitz and Waterloo. . . . Two years, ten years and people ask the conductor, 'What place is this? Where are we now?'" She didn't know how appropriate it was and how not a joke.

The place is sniperland, the place is Russia, and I can even tell you the time:

1939–1945. That's the Soviet telescopic sight they mounted on their Mosin-Nagants, turning it into what I believe was a pretty good sniper rifle. The Russians really believed in the sniper as a strategic concept and sent thousands of them out against the Nazis. Much killing. The scope (3.5 means a magnification of 3.5) was solid, robust, primitive, nothing like the computer-driven things we have today. Range probably limited to under 500 meters and more usually way under that. Anyhow, if you see Mosin-Nagant 91 in conjunction with PU 3.5 in conjunction with any year between '39 and '45, you are most definitely in the sniper universe. I have to ask: What is Reilly doing in the sniper universe? It ain't her usual neighborhood.

It didn't take long for the reply. Five minutes.

That helps a lot. Thanks so much. It's beginning to fit together. As to why, well, long story, work-related. I'm on deadline now, get back to you tomorrow with a long explainer.

So another full day passed, then at last came word from Reilly.

Let me apologize now. It's really dull. Nothing to get excited about, just a feature. They're always interested in feminist heroes, you know, the crooked lib press pro-feminist anti-male meme and all that stuff, so I pitched something to them and they bought it, and it gets me off the *&^%$))&! Siberian pipeline beat. I was in the Moscow flea market a few weeks back and I bought a pile of old magazines. I do that, looking for story ideas. I got one from 1943 called *Red Star*, a war thing, all agitprop as hell, all the pro-Joe stuff to make you throw up. Anyway there were four women on the cover, arms locked together, all in uniform tunics festooned with medals. Three looked like Pennsylvania Dutch lesbian cow milkers but the fourth was— you didn't hear this from me—really a doll. As in knockout. She just blew the poor other three gals away. I read the story and the four were Russian snipers. Many kills, as you say, in Leningrad, two in Stalingrad, one in Odessa and all this stuff about the Mosin-Nagant and the PU 3.5. Anyhow got their names and the looker was called "Ludmilla Petrova" and she was the Stalingrad babe. Hmm, new to me. So I Googled "Russian

29

women snipers" and got all kinds of dope and names—4,000 snipers, over 20,000 Germans killed, that sort of thing—but not a mention of Ludmilla Petrova. So I looked into it more and more, and though the other three survived the war and got fame and fortune, communism-style, out of the deal, there wasn't a whisper about Petrova, whose nickname, from the '43 mag article, was "Mili," not "Luda," as Ludmilla usually yields. So I dug deeper and deeper and indeed, sometime in mid-1944 it seems, Mili just disappeared. Not only as a person but as a personage. She ceased to exist. In fact, I found several other copies of the *Red Star* photo but she'd either been cropped or painted out. The Stalin people disappeared her. It happened back then. Orwell, remember: "He who controls the past controls the future. He who controls the present controls the past."

So now I'm interested. I'm poking around. Be neat to find out what happened to Mili, what she did to so infuriate the Red bosses that they redacted her from history. So that's the piece, though I'm not having much luck with it, but in my dull Ohio way, I keep chipping away. I may have more sniper questions for you as I progress. Is that okay? Oh, and click on the attachment, I've scanned in that cover for you to see her.

He did as instructed, looked carefully at the woman.

Then he called his wife.

"I'm going to Moscow as soon as the paperwork clears," he said.

Then he went to Amazon and bought about six hundred dollars' worth of books on the Eastern Front.

CHAPTER 2

Moscow
On the Way to Red Square
JULY 1944

I know it's hard to believe, looking at me," the major said, "but I am an expert on beauty."

Outside, the undamaged city rolled by, as the 1936 ZiL limo cruised down broad avenues under a scorching sun. Everywhere: neatness, tidiness, order, citizens about their business. Food seemed plentiful, the leaves of many trees rustled in a breeze, the sky was bright.

To her, cities were landscapes of ruins, inhabited mainly by corpses and rats and scrawny men crusted in filth. Survival was figured in units twenty-four hours long. The capital, by contrast, lay unscathed, though a few bombs had fallen in long-ago 1941. The Germans had gotten within eighteen miles and then the winter arrived, assisted by the 15th Guards Army. Not so Stalingrad, where she had spent the full six months of the battle. It was hard not to hate Moscow. One hated all headquarters towns, it was the soldier's right and could not be helped in any case. Its wholeness was offensive. But such is war. Some survive, soldiers or cities; some do not.

"What is surprising," he continued, "is that much beauty is banal. Yes, I know. An astonishment! Yet many a well-formed country girl is disheartened to discover how commonplace she is. When I was at Mosfilm—well, not professionally, but nevertheless there on semi-official business and not without influence, I don't mind telling you, no, not without influence, I knew many key people. The point is, when I was there, every day, just like in Hollywood, beautiful girls from everywhere would show up. They believed their faces were their ticket to fame and, frankly, escape from the Motherland. Yet most ended up as prostitutes or mistresses. Do you know why?"

If he expected an answer, she did not give him one. The one star on his shoulder boards said

32

major, and the blue piping and blue visor on his cap said secret police, night visits, disappearances, NKVD, but his face said what so many men's faces said: I want you, I need you, I yearn for, dream of, hope and plan for you. It was a familiar message, and she had heard it many times in many formats. But in the hierarchy of men and women, she was a thousand ranks above him, no matter that she wore the insignia of only a sergeant. By laws older than politics, she did not have to answer.

Instead, she considered another matter. Was this about Kursk? Did he know? Did NKVD know?

"Because the camera tells a truth," he went on hopelessly. "Or rather, too much truth. It does not enjoy the commonplace and will not linger for long. It finds openness offensive. It wants to be teased, seduced, tricked. I don't know why this is, but even among beauties, only one face in ten thousand has the features the camera admires. That kind of beauty is quite rare."

The car passed Lubyanka, where this fool presumably labored, and it was nothing but a huge block of concrete, nine stories tall, the color of a piece of cheese. But she didn't see it. She saw Kursk. Burning men, burning tanks, a field of wreckage that seemed biblical in proportion, death in all its forms everywhere.

She had done the wrong thing at Kursk. But it

still felt like the right thing, try as she had to convince herself it had been wrong.

Is this about Kursk?

"You see, I mention this," said the idiot, "because I feel that yours *is* that special beauty. Your eyes, though large and deep and firm of purpose and focus, are occluded. They do not give up their meaning easily but suggest careful consideration, seriousness of purpose, lack of foolishness. And your record itself speaks of lack of foolishness. Sergeant Petrova is not a foolish woman."

Another mile around the walled perimeter and at last the limousine turned left, through medieval gates, and onto the Kremlin grounds and the cobbles of Red Square. Though Moscow had never been truly violated, every one hundred yards or so on the broad parade ground, anti-aircraft guns pointed skyward, planted in nests of sandbags, and a fleet of barrage balloons tethered to their thousand meters of cable floated over-head, casting drifting blots of shadows. The faces of the Motherland's great heroes hung from the buildings on immense banners, obscuring the architecture and suggesting the men were more important than the buildings. Comrade Stalin's wise and benevolent features dominated, behind a mustache as large as a tank and eyes the size of a heavy bomber. Since he had murdered her father, she was not impressed.

Now and then a Yak-3 pursuit ship howled overhead at three hundred miles an hour, on some training mission, for now the war was far away. The airplane reminded her of the one man whose face had expressed not want but only kindness, her husband, Dimitri, crashed and burned somewhere in Belarus.

She blinked. She could not dwell on Dimitri. Or Papa or Mama or her brothers, Gregori or Pavel. Or Kursk.

The car pulled to an entrance guarded not only by the anti-aircraft crew but by four men in tunics with chestfuls of medals, whose easy carriage of their tommy guns suggested much experience.

"And so, my dear, I wanted to put it to you. If you let me, I can make certain phone calls on your behalf, arrange certain meetings. This war will not last beyond 1946, and with your record— I imagine the other girls who've performed as you have all look like peasant horsefaces!—and the right training, it seems as if you might have a future, a nice future, a future of travel, of luxury, a future no Soviet woman would dare dream of, it's within your reach with my assistance, and you have only to—"

"I am the sniper," she said. "I want to be alone."

CHAPTER 3

Moscow

THE PRESENT

It was the same city he remembered from a couple of years back: capitalism, dust, a throbbing rhythm, construction everywhere, Porsches and Beemers everywhere construction wasn't, new skylines poking up all over the place, people in a hurry. He checked in to the Metropole, because he knew it, and had a nice room not far from the restored and gilded dining room and the ornate cage of the elevator.

A shower, a nap, then another shower, and he met Reilly at a restaurant that specialized in meat, where they had meat appetizers, meat entrees, and—no, not meat desserts but some kind of cherry tart whose red custard looked like glistening protein.

Same old Reilly. Smart, tart, and funny, she listened fully and considered an answer without any urgency to fill the air with noise, then came up, always, with the best one. She had an interrogator's clear blue eyes that compelled confession, and a kind of secretly dry delight in the follies of the day. She saw through anything and everything.

No hooch for a dry old coot, and finally, after

chatter of children and possibilities, jokes about politics, newspapers, the insanity of the North Koreans, they got to business.

"Why are you here?"

"It's complicated."

"It always is, isn't it?"

"I saw something in her face I liked."

"She was beautiful, no doubt about it."

"Yeah, sure. But something else. Reilly, I want to know more about this girl. I really do."

"I used to think heroes were always an illusion, a PR stunt. But you proved me wrong, so maybe she's not an illusion. Wouldn't that be nice? Let's go after her hard. Let's find out what was done to her and why."

And by who? Swagger thought, though he didn't say it.

"Here's today's news. I've found a woman sniper," said Reilly. "Very old, as you might imagine. She talks to me, but she's in and out. I have trouble staying with her. And I really don't know enough to engage her. Maybe if you came along, I could introduce you as a famous sniper, a comrade in arms, and if you asked her technical things, it would get her focused. What do you think?"

"I can't think of no better idea," he said.

At ten the next morning, in the shadow of a vast building of no identifiable architectural style except to communicate mass—it was built by engineers, not architects, like so much of the Stalinist legacy—Swagger found himself with Reilly and Katrina Slusskya. Slusskya, in her mid-nineties, lived in a ward in this veterans' home in a far Moscow suburb. She sat in a wheelchair under a birch tree, shielded from the sun, while the two Americans sat across from her, all of them drinking tea.

Slusskya had a photo in her hands. When she was told that the Great Swagger was a sniper hero of America, she proudly passed it to him.

He looked. It was clearly her, in some war year, beaming in pride. It was black and white, so the color was unknowable, but she wore a high collar similar to that of the Marine Corps dress-blue tunic, with a row of brass buttons down the front.

"Look at her medals," Reilly said. "She's very proud of them."

An array of decorations hung on her left breast in the photo, under her square, earnest, duty-to-death face.

"She should be," said Swagger.

"This man has medals, too," said Reilly in Russian.

Guessing the content, Swagger asked Reilly to add, "But not as many. You must be a true hero. I was just a lucky fellow. Can you ask her what the medals are?"

Reilly narrated: "Hero of the Soviet Union, the Order of Lenin, the Order of the Red Banner, the Caucasus Defense Medal, two orders of the Red Star, and the Order of the Patriotic War."

"That's a lot of combat she saw," he said.

"She says she'd do it again, not for Stalin, whom she loathed and is finally seen as the monster he was, but for Russia and its millions of good and decent people."

"I salute her."

The old lady smiled and reached out and touched his hand.

"Okay, we'll try shop talk. Tell her in Vietnam I worked with a spotter mostly. But the ranges were longer and finding targets more difficult. I'm wondering if, in the city battles, a spotter was necessary."

Slusskya considered, then answered.

"She says not only not necessary but not practical. We girls, she says, we were scrawny little rats and could squeeze into odd spots where no man could, and bend ourselves into positions no man could. In those circumstances a spotter would have been a hindrance. She also believes women have naturally more patient temperaments. She said she once waited three and a half days for a shot on a German colonel."

"She made the shot, I take it?"

Slusskya tapped herself on her forehead to mark where she hit him.

"The Mosin 91, did she find it an adequate rifle?"

"She loved her 91. Later in the war, they tried to take it away. She was given a rifle of an automatic nature called an SVT-40, with a telescope. She didn't like it as much. It squirted bullets, but of what use is that to a sniper?"

"I agree," he said. "I used a bolt-action."

"She said she had fifty-nine targets eliminated. How many did you have?"

"Fifty-eight," said Swagger.

The old lady laughed.

"She says that is a very good answer even if she bets you're lying to be polite."

"Tell her I'd never lie to a lady as sharp-eyed as she is. And I wouldn't gamble against her, neither. She'd get everything but my undershorts."

Again she laughed.

"She says you remind her of her first commanding officer. He was a wonderful man, very funny, very brave. Dead in Bagration. A great loss."

Swagger knew Bagration was the Russian offensive against Army Group Center in mid-1944, north of the Pripet Marshes, that drove the Germans out of Belarus.

"I've lost many, too," he said. "If you haven't lost, it's hard to understand how far the pain goes and how long it lasts."

She nodded, touched his hand.

"In that war," he said, "women were very brave."

"We were fighting to survive. Everybody had to fight. Even beautiful girls, who might normally marry a commissar or a doctor, they had to fight."

"I'm sure all the woman snipers were beautiful."

"That's the story, at any rate. Myself, I was always a plain girl. I had no expectations and so no disappointments. I married a plain man and had plain children. All turned out well. Beauty, it can be a curse. Too much light is on the beautiful, too many are watching. Belayavedma was cursed that way."

She began to chatter on about this Belayavedma and Reilly lost the thread.

"Bob, go to Petrova," she said in English.

"Ma'am, we want to remember all those valiant girls, especially one of them. My friend here wants to write her story. We believe she was killed. Beautiful girl, according to the picture. Ludmilla 'Mili' Petrova. Does that mean anything?"

The old woman stirred, shook her head. She was clearly disturbed.

"The names, they come and go. No, no Mili, no Petrova. I do remember a Ludmilla," and from there she launched into a long story of the other Ludmilla, the not-Mili Ludmilla, and Reilly struggled to stay with her and couldn't and soon was saying to Bob in quiet English, "I'm completely lost now. I thought we were in Belarus, but suddenly it's the Baltics."

And on it went for another couple of hours, with Reilly and Swagger feeding her eager eye-cues and judging when to laugh by the tone and timing in her voice. Names came and went, stories mingled, battles were transposed. Reilly tried to keep up but couldn't stay with it. But she heard more and more about this Belayavedma, who seemed to have come from nowhere.

She disappeared after being sent to Moscow, the story went, and it was a third- or fourth-hand story, as Slusskya had never seen Belayavedma herself.

"If she was as beautiful as I hear," the old lady said, "a plain girl like me, I would have remembered it the rest of my life. But no, she was gone before I even became active."

"Do you have a year?" asked Reilly.

"It's all run together. My memory, it's like I got hit in head by the bullet, not the German colonel. I can't even—" She paused as some old thought poked her. "I don't know why. Somewhere I heard someone say they sent Belayavedma to Ukraine and she never came back."

"When you say 'they'—"

"Bosses. The bosses ruin everything. We would have won the war fine without the bosses."

She told a long story about hiding in the trees

while thousands of young infantrymen walked across a field into German fire and were cut down like hay. The boss kept sending them, row after row after row. At the end of the day, the field was strewn with bodies, all those fine young men wasted by this boss who wanted to impress his boss.

She shook her head. "I am very tired now, my friends. Slusskya must sleep. It is not your fault, but I had forgotten all those young men, and now I remember them. I need to sleep again."

A nurse had been standing by and intervened to wheel Slusskya out, but not before she kissed each of them and grasped their hands with her firm old talons.

They watched as she was pushed up the ramp and disappeared behind the doors of the bleak institution.

It didn't happen right away. These things can't be scheduled. But somewhere in Reilly's mind the fog lifted and a shaft of light revealed that which was clear but not yet clear. They were in *The Washington Post*'s Chevy, driving back from their chat with the old sniper, trying not to get hit by moguls in Ferraris, when it broke through.

"Belayavedma! Ah! No, no, I'm such an idiot, I forgot that there are no articles in Russian so there wouldn't have been an equivalent to *Die*, as in *Die weisse Hexe*, the German nickname, remember, for Mili. But Belayavedma, it's really *belaya vedma*, two words. The two words in English: *white witch*. That's who she was talking about at the end."

"Not bad," said Swagger, which was as close as he got to admitting admiration.

"It was before Slusskya's time," Reilly continued, riding her insight to the end, "but it was part of the collective memory of female sniper culture, USSR, 1944 to '45. The women would talk and tell stories that weren't in the official record, pass them along, one to the other. There's always a real history that never gets into the books or the newspapers."

"Okay, we have some testimony on where they sent her. Fragile, from memory, otherwise unvalidated, but nevertheless, a place to look at."

"Sure, we'll check out Ukraine. But first let's think about who would have the power to pull her from duty wherever she was in Russia, give her a special mission, and send her on it with the whole apparatus making it happen. Who would have that much power?"

CHAPTER 4

Moscow
The Kremlin
EARLY JULY 1944

It was largely empty, like a museum, and her boots clacked against the marble tiles, echoing against the eighteen-foot ceilings. They must have polished the marble floors every night and dusted the pictures and statues of long-vanished gods. It still spoke of tsars and dukes, not commissars. At last they led her to a conference room; she entered to find three high NKVD officers sitting in awkward obeisance next to a man in civilian clothes who had the diffident posture of a duke among dungsweepers.

"Krulov," he said, rising and nodding, not extending a hand or any welcoming gesture.

Krulov's name conveyed enough information on its own. He was called the boss's right hand, in some circles the boss's steel fist. Where trouble lurked, Krulov was dispatched, with his sharp eyes and handsome features, with his brutal charm and steel will, and he handled whatever that difficulty might be, whether it was a hang-up in machine gun deliveries or the recalcitrance of a certain general officer in the

Baltics. He was a fellow known to get things done.

But she thought: Why would a big shot be so interested in a matter like Kursk?

"Comrade Sniper," he said, "I see from reports that your leg has healed, I see that you have been serving dutifully in a staff intelligence position under General Zukov for a few months as you healed, and he says extremely encouraging things about your heroic duty in the Stalingrad shithole. And he requests again your commission to lieutenant."

"The general has treated me well," said Petrova.

"He should. After all, you have killed several dozen of his enemies for him. Do you have an exact number, Comrade Sniper?"

"No, sir. I never kept count."

"The reports put your score well over a hundred. I would have thought a competitive athlete such as yourself"—she had been a tennis player, a champion, a thousand years ago—"would like to mark her place against the others."

"It is death," she said. "I don't enjoy it. I do it because it helps the nation, it helps our leader, and most of all because when a German goes still through my sight, I know he won't kill that boy I saw in the mess line this morning."

"Yes, it's true and well put. It's that boy, after all, for whom we are fighting."

The three officers nodded sagely. They had the

blue NKVD piping on their tunics and appeared to be two colonels and a lieutenant-general. They had the uniform, they had the shoulder boards, on the table they had the hats, all lined with blue. You could not miss it. But if you did, they had something yet more powerful: they had NKVD faces—she'd seen them in the the blocking battalions NKVD placed behind troops about to assault—which were blunt, sealed, small to the eye, and prim to the mouth. You did not want to stare at them too hard, however; as career secret policemen, they did not like to be stared at. In this circumstance their only task was to express ardent admiration to Krulov. After all, he could have them disappeared at the blink of an eye. What was more, everyone in the room, from Krulov himself to the sniper sergeant, knew this to be the case.

Krulov lit a Maxopka cigarette from a red and yellow pack, taking his time as if to express the idea that the world waited for him, not he for it. When he had the cigarette lit and had exhaled a huge billow of smoke into the room, he stared at her directly. He wore a dark civilian suit on his beefy frame and a tie without color and too much design. Nothing fit because nothing had to fit.

"Ludmilla Petrova, a hard question. I put it to you directly out of respect for your considerable accomplishments."

Here it came. Kursk at last.

But then it didn't.

"In the matter of your father, I must ask if you have anger still, and if so, whether that might cloud your judgment."

Petrova kept her eyes hooded and noncommittal. The first idiot was right, that was a true gift. Her eyes expressed only when she wished them to. Others leak their emotions into the world without care or caution. Petrova showed nothing.

"The state did what it thought was necessary," she said, willing herself to suppress the memory of the arrival of the Black Maria in 1939 and the removal—forever, as it turned out—of her father, a professor of biology at the University of Leningrad. "I trust that it acted in good faith, in the interests of the people. Once the war came, I endeavored to serve the people totally. I allowed myself to fall in love for one week, and to get married. My husband went back to duty and died shortly thereafter. I will serve as long as I am physically able. My death means nothing. The survival of the people is what counts."

"An excellent response," said the commissar, and his acolytes nodded. "Entirely fictitious, I am sure, but delivered with heartfelt if fraudulent sincerity. You lie well, and I appreciate the effort it takes. It's not so easy, as any commissar knows. I'm sure your father's opinions on wheat yield had their own logic, and he believed them sincerely, and whatever they were, they did not warrant the fate that befell him. A warning in his file, a withheld promotion, perhaps, but death? Such a pity. The regime has made many mistakes, even the boss himself will be the first to admit. But he hopes, and I do, too, that after the war, when we get everything sorted out, rectification of some sort can be made. In the meantime, though I know the wound to be still bitter, your patriotism is without question. Do any of my colleagues from the intelligence section have questions for Comrade Sniper?"

Here it comes, she thought. Kursk at last. Then it's off to Siberia for me.

But the questions were few and mild, and Petrova handled them easily enough. Born Leningrad, 1919, happy, athletic child of a professor, then his arrest, then the war, then Dimitri and her two brothers in the first two years, her poor mother gone early to a shell during Leningrad's siege, and her own condition, now stronger, the two shrapnel wounds having healed.

Nothing about Kursk or her assignment to the Special Tasks Detachment.

She did not let her eyes betray her.

Finally Krulov seemed satisfied. Glancing at his watch, he signified that it was time to move on; he had his usual eighteen-hour day and dozens more duties before him.

"Comrade Sniper, please open the folder before you."

CHAPTER 5

Moscow
Offices of *The Washington Post*
THE PRESENT

H ere's how I found this guy," said Reilly, sitting at her office computer in the annex to her apartment, both belonging to *The Washington Post.* "I Googled 'Stalin's Harry Hopkins.' Up comes the name 'Basil Krulov.' I've checked into him. Of Stalin's intimate circle, he is the only one who seemed to have the power to designate missions like that. He was Stalin's troubleshooter, the way Hopkins was FDR's."

From his long-ago immersion in the events that put his father on Iwo Jima in February 1945, Swagger knew of Hopkins, one of the powerful men who made—in good faith, it was hoped—the decisions that left the virgin boys dead in sands and warm waters all across the Pacific.

"It makes sense," said Swagger. "You need a guy who has the authority, can cut across service lines and bring people together who normally would never find each other in the swamp of a capital at war. He was the go-to guy. He had the power. He could make things happen. But his presence makes this thing all screwy."

"How do you mean?"

"They didn't operate that way."

For all their espionage experience and all their espionage success, the Russians didn't do special ops in the classic sense of putting trained operators far behind enemy lines. They didn't need to. The war, after all, was fought mostly on their territory through 1944. And in all that conquered territory, there were dozens of partisan units, cells, individual operators, all that, *already there,* so in any given locale, they had people on the ground and solid contact with them. So they never had to put together a crew, even one person, move him, her, it, a thousand miles and insert him, her, or it. But, Swagger reasoned, the only rule is, there are no rules. If they sent Mili to Ukraine, it would have been so far outside of normal operating procedures, so unusual, so much in the way of running into resistance from all the players, that it would have to be a guy with juice to make it happen, and that had to be Stalin's Harry Hopkins.

He summed it up for Reilly, who nodded and moved on to background Krulov for him: Second-generation Soviet official. Born in 1913. His father was a Soviet trade official to Germany in the late '20s and early '30s.

"Spy?" Bob wanted to know.

"Sure. So Krulov actually grew up in Munich, and attended schools there, before Hitler took over. His dad, meanwhile, tried to build up trade relations but was probably really coordinating with the trade unions and the considerably large Communist Party in that part of Germany, until he was kicked out when the Nazis took over and began their purges with the German Communists. Krulov was a genius student with a gift for organizing, helped enormously by his father's connections, joined the Politburo in '36 and by '38 had caught Stalin's eye. During the war he was indispensable. He traveled with the boss's orders to all the generals, to all the fronts, and he had considerable success after the war. He might have even been general secretary after Stalin, since Khrushchev liked him, but he seemed to fade from sight. He lost power, interest, I don't know, and he faded from view. You could say he was disappeared."

"I guess he stepped on some toes when he was Stalin's boy, and once Stalin was gone, whoever owned that foot, he stepped back. So let's stick on Krulov and ride him to the end of the trail."

"So," said Reilly, "have you any idea why Krulov sent Mili to Ukraine?"

"Sure. Someone needed killing in a badass kind of way."

"But Ukraine," Reilly pointed out, "although largely free of Germans by July '44, had been a terrible battleground for three years. The Germans had literally killed millions. So among all these murderers, who could the number one murderer be?"

"Another thought. The Reds had partisans in the Carpathians, in Ukraine, where all this takes place, right? So why fly a gal in from Stalingrad or wherever she was after Stalingrad when they could just order the partisan troops to attack the guy and kill him that way?"

"He was heavily guarded?" asked Reilly.

"Exactly. Any kind of straight-up attack was bound to fail in a heavily militarized zone. But she's a sniper. One of the best. She kills people from a long way out, off in the high grass. She might be able to nail him out to, say, five hundred meters. That might be the only way to get him."

"That would make him a Nazi hotshot, right?"

"That's right."

"Hmmmm." She went to Google and typed in "Nazi Official Ukraine 1944."

Click.

They watched as the screen shimmered and blinked and then reappeared with the first twenty-five of 16,592 hits. The same name came up twenty-one times in the first twenty-five.

"Groedl," said Swagger. "Now who the hell is Groedl?"

CHAPTER 6

Stanislav
Town Hall
JULY 1944

For a god, he was a pudgy little man. His face wore too much flesh and hung too loosely on his skull. His eyes drooped, his cheeks drooped, his lips drooped, his mustache drooped. He wore steel-rimmed glasses so thick they magnified eyes that were otherwise wan and pale, bloodshot from late nights.

In personal tastes, he was diffident, as if in perfect match to that fallen face and the fallen body that supported it. Though by rank an Obergruppenführer-SS—that is, in the weird orthographics of that organization, senior group leader SS—and entitled thereby to wear the glamorous black with the silver double-lightning flashes and so many other of the gewgaws of decoration, insignia, and embroidery of the Armed Guard, he instead wore an undertaker's shapeless dark suit and black shoes in need of polish. He looked like a professor of economics, which he was.

It wasn't reverse elitism; he wasn't saying to the world, "I do not have to play the game of the uniform and so vast is my power that no one dare comment upon it." No, it was the way his mind worked, seeing only essentials. If you asked him whether The Leader, at their last meeting, had been wearing uniform or suit (it changed daily, depending on The Leader's mood), he would not know. If you asked him five seconds after he stepped out of the meeting, he would not know then, either. However, if you asked him what The Leader had said regarding Hungarian troop deployments in support of Army Group North Ukraine in the Belarus region in July, he would be able to tell you to the detail, for he had an extraordinary memory. He forgot no data. Everything figured into his decisions, every last mote of data, every report ever sent him, every file he ever consulted, every word he ever wrote. The universe was recorded on paper, in figures and in estimates. Actual flesh itself, in the form of human beings, was untrustworthy and could usually be ignored, with the exception of his beloved wife, Helga, thankfully returned to Berlin, and his beloved dachshund, Mitzi, who had accompanied Helga.

Thus, his mind was clear to consider the issue of railroads.

It seemed the Russian Jabos weren't blowing them up with the same regularity. They knew that Western Ukraine would be theirs again soon, and everything they blew up would have to be replaced, so they had decided momentarily against machine-gunning and rocketing German troop trains, if they were headed west, full of wounded. In fact, since the front was lost and would crumble any day now, they had ceased machine-gunning and rocketing even German troop trains headed east. The arrival of the new troops would just increase the Reds' bag somewhere along the line.

It wasn't that they felt any mercy for the wounded Germans. It was that they would need the track to propel their own troop trains westward, through the Carpathians and into Hungary as they drove for the prize of Budapest in the next few months.

"It is essential," he dictated to his secretary for Directive No. 559, "that we seize upon this opportunity to accelerate certain goals."

It was a matter of priorities. A sound manager—having examined at length the competition for rail space per Reich element vis-à-vis the ongoing strategic situation and need-based budget requirement, the transportation difficulties, the volume of cargo—understood that not everyone could be accommodated. There weren't enough locomotives, there wasn't enough coal, there wasn't enough track. This small window in the dynamism of the war had to be managed precisely in order to gain the most from it.

He went back to his adding machine and

prowled through the spools of calculation, to once again check his numbers.

"Dr. Groedl?" asked his secretary, a lumpy woman named Bertha.

"I want to check it one more time," he said, not really seeing her or noting her lumpiness. Neither did he see the modern angles of this modern room, which had been built by the Poles in 1936, under Bauhaus influence, as an avatar of the future that they thought they faced. Alas, they found out in 1939 that they did not, when the Soviets took over North Ukraine and again in 1941, when the Germans did. He did not even really notice the aerodynamically sleek art moderne desk at which he worked, another example of misplaced Polish optimism. He did not see the Nazi banners that had been hastily thrown up everywhere, or the piles of files, the loose paper, the bound volumes, the records, the log books, the account books, everywhere. He did not see the mess of temporary relocation. He saw only the numbers.

He calculated. Colonel Haufstrau of Medical needs a train of at least eighteen cars to move a thousand wounded men from the front at Trinokova railhead to Hungary. Eighteen cars requiring one engine and eight tons of coal, clear track from Trinokova to Stanislav by night, then out of the true danger zone, through the Carpathians whose rail tunnels hadn't and wouldn't be blown by Ivan, clear track to Budapest the next day. There would be a rest stop at the Uzhgorod rail yards, so that an ammunition train headed for the front could be routed through, and the medical train would have to recoal there, consuming another six tons. The total fourteen tons of coal would reduce the ready reserve by a factor of about 9 percent, when the average daily reduction was under 6 percent, and the 6 percent vs. 9 percent projected to six more operational days in late July when it was expected by Army Group North Ukraine's Intelligence Staff that the front would collapse and would have to regroup and reestablish lines of resistance—tank pits and minefields were already being built—west of Stanislav, possibly in the lee of the Carpathians. The Carpathian passes must be held to enable most of Army Group North Ukraine and all of SS Reichskommissariat personnel to get out before the Reds took everything over.

On the other hand, the train run by the small yet important niche of the SS security bureaucracy called Department IV-B4 had an equal claim to priority. It had assumed as part of its cargo a last load from Lemberg before it fell, and it had added transport cars at several way stations along the route, the trophy of a final sweep operation. Now it waited for coal here in the Stanislav yards, dispensing a foul miasma of stench demoralizing to men who came in contact with it, not just Ukrainian yard workers but also Reichskommissariat staff.

The data: IV-B4's cargo load was by far lighter than the thousand wounded soldiers, and for obvious reasons no time or resources must be spent on maintaining it as a physical property, whereas the medical train needed a constant influx of medicine, water, and food to sustain the lives of those poor wounded boys who were its passengers. This made everything about it problematic and meant added layers of administrative responsibility and refined organizational input. Regarded purely as a logistical contest, there was no doubt that the IV-B4 train represented a lesser allocation of resources than the medical train, and there were certain intangible spiritual elements involved.

Dr. Groedl loathed such considerations. What was "spiritual," what was "moral," what was "ethical"? These values could not be calculated numerically. It took a certain sensitivity to the greater ethos, which he admitted, if only to Helga, that he somewhat lacked.

"I hate it," he had said. "It is nothing. You can't quantify it, you can't shape it, you can't weigh it. What is it? Why do we care so much about such things?"

"I'm sure you'll work it out, my dear," said Helga, stroking Mitzi's smooth head on her lap. "You always do, my genius."

So now he struggled with the issue before him, yearning for guidance, and yet he understood that seeking advice would be interpreted as weakness, and even at this point, the Reichskommissariat was a cesspool of politics, with strivers and whores of ambition, politicals, plotters, cabalists, all of them waiting, just waiting, for him to make a mistake so they could whisper nasty things about him in the right ears, and ease the skids under him while assisting in their own rise. He had so many enemies! If Heinrich only knew, or The Leader himself, what mischief was perpetrated by the human folly of ambition! He was simply too pure for a political world. He lived only for duty, not foolish medals and empty titles or promotions!

"Dr. Groedl?"

"Yes, yes, Bertha, I simply want to be certain."

"It is difficult, sir, I understand."

"But we must forge ahead," he said. He winced, pinched the bridge of his nose, wished he had a cup of tea, and then proceeded. "Where was I?"

" '. . . to accelerate certain goals.' "

"Yes, yes. Continue, 'Thus priorities are henceforth determined. Train 56, under the auspices of Department IV-B4, will be given the coal authority and the track clearance to proceed at once to its destination. All entities are hereby directed to offer maximum support to this transport and further memos will follow adjudicating logistical responsibilities. Train 118, under the auspices of the Wehrmacht medical service, will wait at least twenty-four hours, dependent on the resupply of coal to the yards at Stanislav, which, when it again reaches a level of nine percent surplus under normal operating procedures, it will be allowed to depart.' Sign it Groedl, and you know the rest, Bertha, get it out to our people as quickly as possible."

"You realize the Colonel-Doctor Haufstrau will go to Wehrmacht command to protest your decision, Dr. Groedl?"

"I do. It can't be helped. Whatever I do, I make enemies. Berlin will back me, I believe. Reichsführer Himmler has his own considerable clout. If it reaches The Leader, he will back me. I have always counted on my special relationship with The Leader. There will be grumbling, but one must do the right thing."

"You are truly an idealist, sir. You are my hero."

He smiled modestly, then immediately pulled his face back into its mode of blurred diffidence, humphing with some embarrassment, as direct compliments and expressions of affection made him quite uncomfortable.

"I shall mark IV-B4 Train 56," she said, "as cleared green and full speed ahead to Auschwitz-Birkenau."

• • •

"Groedl, Hans," said Krulov, after unleashing a cirrocumulus of cigarette smoke to curl and lap in the high corners of the Kremlin office. "One of their nastier beasts. Like so many of the truly vile ones, he's overintelligent and overeducated. Prefers to be known as Dr. Groedl as opposed to Obergruppenführer-SS Groedl."

It was odd. Targets didn't have faces, usually. They were anonymous men in *feldgrau* or camouflage, if SS, who scurried this way and that until a moment came when they went still in the embrace of the PU telescopic reticle, and it was her finger who shot them. It seemed not to involve great pain, of which, she would admit to herself and nobody else, she was glad. Usually they would stiffen or step back. She tried never to take a head shot. This was by doctrinal assertion: the head was a far more difficult target from the technical point of view, smaller, more active, unpredictable. But there was a psychological reason as well: a head shot could be alarming if it shattered and emptied skull, broke the face plate into halves or thirds, removed a jaw, all amid a copious outflow of crimson. Sometimes there was an extravagant splatter pattern, and in the snow, the red galaxies of blasted blood could be disconcerting. No, a torso shot was best.

But here, now: a face. Dumpy, undistinguished save by the looseness of jowls, the sadness of demeanor, the lightlessness of expression. He looked so insignificant, like a janitor or an elderly factory worker. Still, a face. He was not a figure, he was a human being.

"Not a soldier but a professor, like your father," said Krulov. "You'd hardly notice him. Hmmm, let's see, yes, born 1890, Linz, educated University of Linz, taught high school, served in staff position in the first war, never left Germany, renowned early for extraordinary mathematical capacity and organizational talent. Numbers, numbers, numbers with this one. After the war, got his doctorate in economics at University of Heidelberg, married, taught at University of Munich, and there was disgusted with the economic policies of Weimar and thus became an early Nazi, party number 133. Met Hitler and exchanged ideas on several occasions. Now he's a favorite. It's all in the file."

Petrova's eyes ran quickly over the documents, confirming the high points. There was a photo of this Dr. Groedl with a grim woman, a picture of him with older people, parents possibly, and in each he had the stuffy formality, the lightless eyes, the awkwardness, the dowdy wardrobe. Finally she came across one of him in an actual SS uniform, and he looked ridiculous. He was trying to do that salute they do, the stiff arm at a

45-degree angle, when they shout "Heil"—she had seen it only in the cinema, for it never appeared on the battlefield—and the result was quite comical. What a grotesque fool; the physical realm was baffling for this fellow, and when he tried to express himself with something even so primitive as that salute, he had a clownish quality.

"Why must he be killed, Comrade Commissar? I mean, all of them must be killed or driven out, yes, of course, and when they come before our gunsights it happens, but this is different. I've never been assigned a targeted killing before."

"Probably something in the woman in you rebels," said Krulov with oil in his voice. "It's to be expected. What you do is 'fair,' on a battle-field, against armed men who would kill you or, more important to someone of your heroic disposition, your comrades. And you can project the ruinous consequences for the nation if these bastards win. But now we take it a step further: we point out one man who, on the face of it, seems an undistinguished little chap, and we kill him. Why? A fair question. Colonel Dinosovich, you're our Groedl expert. You could explain to the sniper sergeant."

"Yes, sir," said the junior NKVD officer without making eye contact.

"He was assigned to Reichskommissariat, which administers what the Germans call 'colonies' here in the east. His specialty from the start was

Ukraine. He helped organize Einsatzgruppen D, which was the SS mobile killing unit in Ukraine. The ridiculous Ukraines thought the Germans were their liberators, and for their troubles, the Einsatzgruppen rounded them up and shot them en masse. Mostly Jews, also intellectuals, politicians, anyone with military experience, anyone bound to be dissident. Evidently Dr. Groedl put the lists of targeting killings together, with the assistance of SS intelligence operatives. He was very good at his job, and under the enthusiastic support of his mentor, Dr. Ohlendorf, head of D, he was quickly promoted. He became director of the Kiev district in Ukraine, once the Nazis had purified it, where his first priority was always total elimination of Jews and dissidents, as well as restoration of economic order for the benefit of the Wehrmacht supply organization. Those bastards might not have lasted so long at Stalingrad and Kursk and killed so many of us if Dr. Groedl's organizational talents hadn't been put to such good use.

"Now he's what's called a senior group leader–SS, a major general, though he normally avoids the military accouterments of his job, and that ridiculous photo of him in his SS getup from 1942 is the only one we have of him in uniform. Promoted to Reichskommissar after Koch left, he has ruled Ukraine for the past six months. During that spell, he has sent over fifty thousand people to the extermination camp at Auschwitz-Birkenau. He has kept the rails running on schedule despite a heroic bombing and strafing campaign by our aviators. Though he never takes to the field, he has organized anti-partisan campaigns that are among the most effective the Germans have, and via his efforts, over six thousand partisans have been either killed in battle or captured and executed. To frighten the farmers, he has executed over a thousand of them. He's cut quite a path through the motherland for a little fatty in an expensive suit.

"Any further questions, Petrova?" asked Krulov.

"No, Comrade."

"Another excellent lie," said Krulov. "Wonderful job of pretending to be a mindless party automaton, what the Czechs call a robot. Nothing but obedience. Even your eyes hide questions. But of course you have questions. You do not ask them, because among such big shots as us, questions equal doubt, and if you doubt, we doubt, and consequences can be unpleasant."

Silence. Krulov was indulging himself by speaking the truth. It was a perquisite of his rank. Even one of the NKVD fools looked a little uncertain at this unusual tack.

"All right, then," said Krulov. "I will ask the questions you have wisely decided to pass on."

"As you say, Comrade Commissar."

"First of all: Why him? There are so many of

them who we will hunt down and deal with after the war. Why this one little dim cog in their vast killing machine? Excellent question, Petrova. There are two answers, the first of which is all right for you to know, the second of which is not, and if any of these three NKVD monkeys report me, I could end up in the cellar of their fortress with a pistol muzzle behind the ear. Right, gentlemen?"

The three monkeys laughed awkwardly.

"All right, Colonel Dinosovich, control your giggles and explain."

"Yes, Comrade Commissar. The key is accessibility. We have captured their high-ranking military personnel before, including a field marshal, but the civilian administrators, who set the policy and then step back, are difficult to locate and, if located, difficult to target. This Groedl operated out of the Reichskommissariat Ukraine—RKU—at Rivne, which was a large military complex. It was heavily defended, not only by SS ground forces but also by an interceptor squadron. Bombers did not get through, no partisans got close enough to strike. So for three years he did his business like any bureaucrat, living with his wife and puppy in a nice house, adding his numbers, making his decisions, a long way from any actual death or dying. That changed in February, when the Red Army finally liberated Rivne after a furious battle. Like all rats, he escaped and disappeared.

"NKVD has been hunting him for some time. Only recently has it come to us through radio intercepts that he has set up temporary head-quarters in Stanislav, in the Town Hall, and that he continues to administer what is left of his shrinking empire with the same ruthless efficiency. Stanislav is about twenty miles behind the front. The difference is that Rivne was a more dedicated installation, with rings and rings of security. Stanislav is an improvisation. The security is ad hoc. There isn't an SS division between him and us. Thus, we believe, he is vulnerable to a sniper. He resides at the Hotel Berlin. Each morning, as a show of how he has tamed that town, he walks the four blocks from the Berlin to the Town Hall, crossing Hitlerstrasse and passing through a nice little park. He has a complement of four Gestapo bodyguards. We feel it would be quite an easy shot for an accomplished marksman such as yourself, Petrova, from any of a dozen buildings along the way. Moreover, Stanislav is in the foothills of the Ukrainian Carpathians, where we have partisans. They will supply logistical support, including transportation and security for your mission. Without knowing it, Groedl has placed himself where we can reach him. If we can reach him, we must. We owe it to our partisans, to the Red Army soldiers, even to the Jews he's murdered."

"The offensive, Dinosovich. You can tell her

about the offensive. She needs to know. And the Germans almost certainly know themselves."

"Yes, Comrade Commissar. Sniper Sergeant, in ten days the Second Ukrainian Front Army will begin a major offensive aimed to push the Germans from Ukraine and open the advance to Budapest. It will be a time of great chaos and confusion in the area, and when that happens, Groedl will be recalled to Berlin. Our opportunity to eliminate him will be gone. So you see, Sniper Sergeant, there is an imposed urgency, a time limit. This assassination must take place before the prey flees, and the prey will flee as a function of the offensive. So the clock is ticking."

"Excellent summation," said Comrade Krulov. "Irrelevant but excellent. Young lady, I'll tell you a truth the lieutenant colonel would prefer not to acknowledge. In war, the strategic is almost always secondary to the personal. And the real reason here is personal. It seems that this Groedl is a special favorite of Hitler's. They go back to the old days. Groedl was one of Hitler's earliest theoreticians. He's one of those picked out for high promotions. The Boss realizes that the loss of Groedl would be especially painful for Hitler, like the death of a father or uncle. That makes this a very personal mission, one in which you are directly expressing the will of our leader against their leader. That is why we searched for the ideal candidate."

"A woman?"

"*A beautiful* woman. Don't you see, it is the perfect cover. The Germans are not fools, but even at the top of their efficiency, they would never suspect a woman so beautiful. Men will do things for love of beauty that they will never do for fear of pain. They will obey, betray, shirk, avoid, and relent for beauty while they rise heroically to defy strength. We are aware of that, and that is why you were chosen."

"When do I leave?" said Petrova.

The commissar looked at his watch. "In about ten minutes," he said.

CHAPTER 7

Moscow
THE PRESENT

He was dully metallic and about eighteen feet tall. His tommy gun was nine feet long and must have weighed a couple of tons, at least. He had on a worker's hat, size 358, and his handsome face was unlined by doubt or fear, set with heroic stubbornness as he gestured his imaginary squad of giants onward, his hand raised with a three-ton Tokarev pistol in it. THE PARTISAN, proclaimed the stature's brass plaque, and like statues everywhere, it had attracted indifferent birds who left their marks of conquest where the Wehrmacht had failed, and sat utterly unnoticed by the busy millions of Moscow except for Swagger and Reilly, who had placed themselves on a bench before it.

"Okay, I think I have something," she said, summing up her day in the Red Army archives.

"I'm listening."

"Ukraine, 1944. Well, it had to be before July twenty-sixth, because that was the date the Germans pulled out of Stanislav when the Russians started their big offensive. There's no record of Groedl being killed."

"So Groedl gets away. The good die young, the evil just go on and on."

"Sightings in Rio, Athens, São Paulo, Shanghai after the war. The Israelis wanted him bad and put a major effort into it. They caught Eichmann in the same net, but Groedl was a lot smarter. He was an econ professor, remember? He also seems to have more people who believed in him and would want to help him. Eichmann was just a drab little clerk. Banality of evil, all that stuff. Anyway, thoughts on Petrova versus Groedl, West Ukraine, 1944?"

"She clearly failed, and maybe Stalin had her 'eliminated' as punishment. He had two hundred thirty-eight generals executed during the war. He was a guy you didn't want to disappoint." Bob had spent the day familiarizing himself with the military situation in Ukraine in that period of 1944. "By July, the Germans had been squeezed out of most of Ukraine. They're clinging to a little piece that included Stanislav and the Carpathian Mountains. But they know the Reds will get around to them and drive them out. On the twenty-sixth, the Russians open fire and the Germans take off. The Russians actually occupy Stanislav on the twenty-seventh."

"Here's where it gets interesting," Reilly said. "There's a last surge of German atrocities in and around the twenty-sixth as the Germans are pulling out. A mountain village called Yaremche was burned, a hundred-odd people were executed."

"I see what you're saying," Bob said, turning it over in his mind. "The Russians are coming, the Russians are coming, and still, in the middle of it, the Germans are committing atrocities. You'd think they'd be busy enough retreating."

"Yes, you would."

"So what's got 'em pissed off so much?"

"That's the question."

"Well, I'm just remembering that when Heydrich was killed by Czech intelligence in '42, they went all berserk. Lidice, the town where the killers hid, that was wiped out in retaliation. There were a lot of executions, a lot of terrible interrogations. So one of their operating policies is to go all crazy when there's an assassination.

Or an attempt." He tumbled on, seeing something new in the old information. "So maybe she took a crack at him. Maybe she missed. But still they went all nuts. Maybe, like in Prague, someone ratted her out. So she was caught and killed. That would save Stalin the trouble."

"It can't be coincidence that it was in August 1944 that Mili ceased to exist. I spent my time looking up all accounts of female snipers and she disappears after July '44. So if Slusskya's right, you have Mili in Ukraine, an unusual atrocity in Yaremche, and Mili's disappearance, all in July 1944, in exactly the same small area."

"God, I hate to think of that young girl dying. Sure, she's a beauty, a movie star, a princess. But if she looked like a handle of a plow, she's still a goddamned sniper, all out on her lonesome, where beauty don't count a lick, and she maybe comes real close to nailing this bastard, which is all anyone can ask of the sniper, and she catches a German eight-millimeter in the throat and dies hard and alone. As I said, the good die young, and the motherfuckers go on forever, pardon my French."

"It's okay," Reilly said. "It's okay to feel something for a hero."

"We have to go to this Yaremche. To South Ukraine," Swagger said. "If I see the land and read the geometry of it, maybe I can understand what happened."

CHAPTER 8

The Carpathians
Above Yaremche
JULY 1944

It was better not to pay too much attention to the machine or the men flying it. After all, what difference did it make? Knowing the pilot's name and what he called his airplane didn't matter. The airplane would get her there or not, depending on a thousand factors over which she had no control. The Germans would shoot it down or they would not; they would have already taken the landing site or they would not have; the pilot found the right site or he did not. None of it had anything to do with her. She could not let herself invest emotion in the idea of this preposterous little kite being night-navigated to a tiny landing field on a mountain plateau surrounded on all sides by peaks and lit only by torchlight. She could not concentrate on the delicacy of the touch it took to set down, the play of the wind, how far the sound of the motors would carry, the whimsy of German patrols high in these mountains. For now she could only sit and feel the vibrations of the engines beat through the frame of the machine and into her bones.

The pilots were children, cheery teenagers, full of bravado. Her NKVD handler, the lieutenant colonel named Dinosovich, had been her companion, though he was neither loquacious nor warm and gave her no support and sat there like a piece of New Soviet statuary. It was known that he represented the special will of The Boss, so everywhere, doors were opened, men jumped to, the best meals were served, obeisance was paid. That was his only value.

Now the Yak-6 was airborne. It was a two-engined transport plane hurriedly designed under wartime conditions to provide the army with a light utility aircraft. It was not designed for comfort. Mostly linen and wood, it seemed more toylike than the heavy fighter her poor husband, the always witty, never depressed Dimitri, had flown.

Occasionally, finding a downdraft, the plane would fall a few dozen feet, leaving her stomach at the previous altitude. In the plunge from gravity, she felt giddy terror and clutched to the airframe, knowing it was a fool's gesture. The airframe would shatter like a vase if hit. Then there'd be fire, and so she prayed for death by concussion rather than by flame. She'd seen enough men on fire to know it was no way to end. She hated death by fire.

The fall, the fear, the cold of the unheated cabin, all made her stomach roil. She had an urge to vomit but knew it would annoy the annoying Dinosovich, and she didn't want to do that, because the less to do with him, the better. He sat facing her, a ramrod of rectitude without emotion on his flat, plain face, aware that he represented The Boss's full authority and determined to carry that responsibility with dignity. No smile would curl his lips, no warmth would leak from his eyes. It was the way all The Boss's boys were, especially the ones who had arrested her father.

The beating of the engines was too loud for talk, the quarters in the cabin too full of the nauseating stench of fuel, and beyond the smeared Perspex of the window it was too dark to see, except for the occasional illumination of a nearby flash as something blew up, men died, buildings turned into craters, towns into ruins. The war was hungry tonight, and destruction's greed pawed at this part of the world. Meanwhile, the plane's grip on the air was tentative, slippery; the machine seemed to slither and squirt ahead, just barely under control.

The cabin door—more a hatch, actually—opened, and one of the pilots, head capped in leather, leaned in. His human eyes were tiny beneath the gigantic insect-lenses of his goggles, which were held above his eyes by straps.

"Made radio contact, have a visual on the landing field, we're vectored in," he yelled over the engines. "The bump may be a bit hard when we touch down, but we'll be fine. We'll put the crate down, you can join your pals, and the whole thing will be over in minutes."

Petrova nodded.

She had Tata Fyodor with her, as she called her rifle. It was a yard of Mosin-Nagant 91, in the caliber called 7.62mm x 54, with its PU scope held by a steel frame atop the receiver. The tsar's troops had lost to the Japanese with it in '05, and then to the Germans in '17 and basically the Finns in '39. It seemed like it was about to win its first war, but there was a lot of killing left to do. This one, built in 1940, was much blooded, as it had been used by Tatanya Morova and Luda Borov. Both were fine girls, both were dead, but the rifle had been a treasure for its unusual accuracy, particularly with Tula Lot 443-A ammunition, which Petrova hoarded. She'd used it over a hundred times, in snow and summer, in mud and dust, in ruins and mansions, in light or dark, in bright wheat fields amid tanks, in Stalingrad, at Kursk. It never let her down, and when it settled back out of recoil, always what she had held in its heavily etched sighting apparatus—three point-tipped bars, two horizontal, one vertical, defining a kill zone—was still. The rifle was wrapped in cloth and secured against her leg. She herself wore a one-piece issue camouflage sniper suit over a peasant's loose dress over the crude cotton undergarments of the rural proletariat. She wore generic Russian boots.

A memory came to mind.

Her husband used to tease her. "If only people would see beyond all that ridiculous beauty," he would say, "they might understand what a decent person you actually are. I'm so glad I did! It wasn't easy, but somehow I managed."

She thought: If he could see me now, all rigged up like a babushka! What a hoot he'd have!

And then she remembered: Dimitri was gone.

"Brace yourselves," one of the boys yelled back through the door, and she felt the plane begin to skid in the air as it lost altitude fast.

Outside, as the craft dipped beneath a certain altitude, the quality of darkness changed; it became a darkness without depth or texture, and she realized it meant they were not above the mountains but within them, in some twisty valley with the mountaintops above. Across from her, the lieutenant colonel's face had gone from pasty white to deathly white, and his jaw clenched so tightly she feared he'd shatter his molars. Then the plane hit—or crashed horizontally, might be a better description—with such force that lights in her brain fired in the shock of vibration. It bounced, stuck again, and then seemed fully committed to the earth, rolling capriciously along, every shock transferred from the landing gear to the airframe to her body.

The plane ran out of energy and slowed to a halt. The door was pried open, and amid a wash of cold air and the smell of pines, hands reached in to help her out. Only then did the lieutenant colonel seem to come out of his trance. As she was pulled by him, he grabbed her by the arm and whispered fiercely into her ear, "Don't fail, Petrova. Not like at Kursk."

Kursk! They knew.

But then she was out of the plane, into another century. Men with beards, their bulky bodies criss-crossed with ammunition bandoliers, their tommy guns hanging across their chests, swarmed everywhere. Potato-masher grenades were stuck in every belt and boot, and their holsters dragged under the full weight of pistols that ran from ancient revolvers to Mausers and Lugers, to say nothing of Toks, all of them dangling and clanking and glinting in the torchlight. Also: bayonets, daggers, hunting and fighting knives, some almost swords, recumbent on straps, additionally adangle. Every man and every woman—there were several—had at least three weapons. They seemed happy because they lived on the edge of violence, each a part of its culture, a celebrant of its values, a survivor of its whimsy.

As she stood on shaky legs, on earth once again, hands reached to touch her, not sexually but as if in wonder.

"*Die weisse Hexe,*" came the call, the whisper,

and all crowded close to see the famous sniper of Stalingrad, as known for her beauty as for her skill. Her hat came off and her hair tumbled free. She shook it, partly because her head was hot and itchy, partly because it was a gesture copied from the movies. It cascaded and, lit by torchlight, seemed to shiver; so blond, so silken, so dense. Her eyes narrowed and she turned to three-quarters profile to confront them and the weapon of her beauty hit them hard; they stumbled back. A man approached.

"I am Bak," he said. "Welcome, Petrova. We are here to serve you in any way."

Bak was the Ukrainian soldier who'd risen to partisan command by virtue of cunning and organizational ability. He had become totally a creature of forest ambuscade and slow night crawl. He was a general but mistrusted by Moscow, a man to watch, a man to fear.

The issue would always be: After the great victory, would he throw his forces against or to Stalin? Was he Nationalist or Communist? If the former, he could well earn nine lead grams from an NKVD agent's pistol instead of a hero's medal. So he carried himself with a certain doomed grace. The fallen lines of his face, she thought, seemed to say: This will end badly.

"I am honored, General."

"Call me Bak. It's enough. The 'general' is bullshit, that's all." He turned and yelled, "All right, get this crate turned around so it can get out of here and take this NKVD prick back to his bath."

The men crowded to the tail of the light plane and managed to rotate it on its landing gear to face the wind while, at the same time, standing clear of the two whirling props. Petrova could see the white faces of the two young pilots behind their control panel, crouched over their steering mechanism, waiting as the plane was resituated. When that happened, they nodded, and the guerrillas faded back. The pitch of the engine rose to a shriek as one pushed a throttle, spitting flecks of grass and debris in the air as well as the stench of acceleration, and the plane began to move forward. With less cargo by the weight of a woman, it dipped, then rose and soon vanished.

"Petrova, come, we have a wagon."

"I can walk. I am fine."

"No walking here. We ride. Can you ride?"

"God, no," she said. "I am a city girl, I'm terrified of horses."

"The White Witch terrified of *anything?* Now I see you have a sense of humor, and I really like you. The wagon, then."

"It'll have to be."

"Good, and it'll help you save your strength for your job. For now, rest, relax, a long journey, still not complete. Some vodka?"

"Excellent," she said, and took a canteen from him. One shot hit her nicely.

"Now, into the wagon. Sleep if you can. It's four hours through the forest to the camp, and we have to make it before light so the Germans don't spot us. They're patrolling all the time, as per the orders of that bastard Groedl, whose hash I hope you settle."

Gripping her rifle, she said, "Get me a shot, Comrade Bak, and I won't miss."

CHAPTER 9

The Train South
THE PRESENT

The train from Moscow was something out of an old detective novel, an Orient Express without an Orient for a destination or an express as a mode of operation. It was old and filthy, separated into compartments where wooden benches sat beneath wooden bunks, the whole car itself a collection of compartments, all the upholstery and curtaining faded red. It rattled along, never surpassing forty, the track itself somehow rough and improvised. It gave him a headache, as did the inefficient air-conditioning. Vodka, please. Oh wait, no, no vodka. On wagon. On train, on wagon.

He forced himself instead to reread in sobriety the only account of the fighting in West Ukraine in July 1944 in English (barely) as translated from the German, a book of intensely professional history called *To the Bitter End: The Final Battles of Army Groups North Ukraine, A, Centre, Eastern Front 1944–45*. It was hardly a heroic poem, being restricted to the battalion-level maneuver, and somewhat distant and rational for a process as improvisational as war. There was no sense of "What the fuck do we do now?" that Bob knew so well.

Still, it provoked him. Who knew? Who knew anything about the East? He'd spent a few weeks reading every damn book Amazon had on the subject, most of them claiming to have found the real "turning point," when the only turning point had to be June 21, 1941, the day Hitler sent his men off on an insane mission. It was like invading space. There was so much of it, endless, rolling, thousands of miles, millions of people. There was nothing but there there. Who could begin to understand it? Facts, sure: Stalingrad, Leningrad, Karkov, Kursk, each with a nice neat date, each charted on a neat construct called a map that showed arrows moving this way, opposed by arrows moving that way, superimposed on a tapestry decorated in unpronounceable names like Dnipropetrovs'k and Metschubecowka and Saparoshe, yielding now and then to vast

83

emptiness where there were no names but only, by inference, grass or wheat. But there was so much more. Forgotten fights that were as big, really, as Normandy, where fleets of tanks threw themselves against each other and men in the thousands died in flames or were torn to shreds by explosions. Or perhaps even worse, the daily grind, a combat environment where men hunted men every fucking day of the year, 24/7/365, a million firefights fought, a billion shells launched, a trillion rounds fired. Over and over, year after year after year, the death toll incomprehensible. Those fights were too obscure to have names. There was a sadness to it. People should know about this stuff. People should care about the sacrifice, the pain, the death that convulsed the world; yet here was a whole huge piece of it so obscure that no one in the West had even acknowledged it. What place is this, where are we now? I am the grass, I cover all.

These ruminations did Swagger no good at all and, if anything, amplified his need for vodka.

He tried to get away from the big picture. So his new strategy was to concentrate on the small picture. Go to Mili, he told himself. Think only of Mili.

Mili, in the Carpathian Mountains, with an assignment to assassinate a German administrator who had murdered, by strokes of a pen or orders to dictationists, thousands, tens of thousands.

What happened to her? He tried to imagine it. But he had no luck. His best gift was useless in a train, when he hadn't seen the area he needed to understand. That was the gift of looking at land and reading it for truth. If he could see the ebb and flow of movement across a terrain, he could make some sense out of it. He'd know where the shooter would have had to place him- or herself to get the shot, and that determination would come from a confluence of factors: first, clean angle to the target; second, concealment, obviously, cover if possible (she would have to weigh cover against concealment very carefully, if it came to that); third, a sense of the play of the wind, because even at five hundred meters, her longest possible shot with a M-N 91, scope or not, the wind could wreak havoc on the shot so she'd be best to shoot in the early morning, when it tended to be still, and if heat and humidity were to factor, they'd also be at their least influential; and finally, escape route. But he could not begin to imagine this, not without a landscape to search for possibility against.

His mind went numb. Beside him, Reilly dozed quietly. Where was I? Oh, yeah, Mili's escape route. If she had one. It occurred to him that in that war, given the losses, given the immensity of the sacrifice, given all the times the bosses had sent rows and rows of young men marching or driving into machine-gun fire and artillery, possibly the nihilism that was so pervasive had infected Mili, too, and so she passed on escape. Maybe she took the shot, saw that she had missed, watched as the SS troopers ran to her, pulled out her Tok, and shot herself in the head. Since she'd been shielded by the villagers—or the SS assumed she'd been shielded by villagers—they burned the place and the people in it. That was the way they operated.

But why would she have been scrubbed from the Russian record? Why was she disappeared? More likely, since she was famous, they'd have used her sacrifice as a platform on which to build some kind of martyr campaign. Her beauty would help there, too. It was the way propagandists worked, he saw, in that the death of one beautiful girl could be more emotionally powerful than the death of four thousand Russian tankers on a single day at a place called—it was another one nobody had ever heard of—Prokhorovka.

Yet they had refused that possibility.

Why?

Reilly, stirred, shivered, yawned, came awake. She rubbed her eyes. "When do we get to Ocean City?" she asked.

"That's a long way away. Enjoy the nap? Pleasant dreams?"

"Never," she said.

Ding! Or maybe *bong!* Or possibly *bing!* It

came from Reilly's phone, which she fished out of her purse.

"That's an e-mail incoming."

Bob waited patiently.

"Well, well," she said. "Now here's something. It's from Will."

Will? Oh yes, *Will,* Reilly's ever patient, enduring husband, her co-correspondent for the Washington newspaper, a guy of whom she talked now and then and revered as one of those real reporters who was more interested in getting it right and getting it fair than in getting it onto *Meet the Press.* Swagger somehow had never had the pleasure.

"He's in Germany," Reilly was saying. "I asked him to check on the divisional records of the Twelfth SS Panzer around that time. The Germans, as it turns out, and why does this not surprise, kept very precise operational logs. Will just dug something out." She handed the iPhone over.

Hi, sweetie, *Will had written.* Aachen is a drab town. But I did find the 12th SS Panzer records and there are some interesting aspects. No. 1, there's no account of any partisan activity, including assassination attempts, at any time between July 15th and July 26th. As you might imagine, it gets very busy on the 26th, because that's when they had the Russian offensive started and they pulled out of Stanislav without firing a shot. There's also a somewhat ambiguous run of entries from the 20th through the 23rd which are simply called "Security Operations." What that means I don't know, except that I don't think it's against partisans, because they have a special category for that, and they use it frequently. "Anti-bandit" operations, they call them. However, and I think this is new, there is an entry for the 15th. It simply says, if I read my German correctly, "Anti-bandit operation, Carpathian Mountains, Zepplin Force reports inflicting heavy casualties on Ukrainian Bandits presumably affiliated with Bak's 1st Partisan Brigade. 35 enemy killed in action."

They even listed the arms recovered. "37 Model 91 rifles, 1 Model 91 with sniper scope, 5 PPsH machine pistols, 28 grenades, 35 bayonets, 12 Tokarev pistols, 9 Luger pistols, 32 bayonets and assorted knives."

"A Mosin-Nagant with scope. That's Mili's. They jumped Mili. But who the hell is Zeppelin Force?" Bob wondered out loud, and in the next second found the answer.

Zeppelin Force seems to be a unit seconded at Senior Group Leader Groedl's request from 13th SS Mountain Division, in Serbia, which was the only Islamic division in the whole German army. I saw in the log that they had just come over a few days before. But it's not just any guys, it seems to be a special force called Police Battalion.

CHAPTER 10

The Carpathians
JULY 17, 1944

It was a Police Battalion operation all the way, and Captain Salid handled his men extremely well. He had learned much in his years among the Germans.

His men were experienced. They had been seconded from the 13th SS Mountain Division "Scimitar," operating in Serbia, where they had been fighting partisans—"bandits," officially—for the better part of three years, and proudly wore the insignia of the scimitar on the left side of the collars of their camouflaged battle smocks, opposite and yet equal in pride of place as the double flashes of the SS on the right. They had left their fezzes at base and, like their commanding officer, capped their heads only in the camouflaged *Stahlhelm* of the SS.

In the Balkans, Police Battalion especially had borne the brunt of the patrol and assault work. Mostly Serbian Muslims themselves, they were all mountain people, skilled in mountain fighting arcana from a life in the high altitudes. They were silent crawlers, camouflage experts, superb marksmen, and especially keen on blade work, for theirs, after all, was a blade culture. They were at their best in anti-Jewish actions, for that was where the passion burned brightest. They did truly hate and despise bandits, not only an ancient enmity but also a recent one, for they had lost as many to those bandits as they had taken from them. But they were disciplined, high-level military, skilled and patient, used to stillness. They were not Arab pirates, thirsty for blood because they were thirsty for blood; in fact, there were few Arabs among them, after Captain Salid only two unteroffiziers and an odd private or corporal among the platoons.

Salid employed the classic L-shape technique of ambuscade, getting two angles of fire from his unit without endangering either echelon to the other, and much used by his forebears against generations of invaders, from Romans to Jews to Crusaders to other tribes, to the hated English, to Turks, to the later arriving Jews. His family had been in the war business for at least fifteen generations, and although he was only thirty-two, he knew a thing or two.

Yusef el-Almeni bin Abu Salid was the cousin of the grand mufti of Jerusalem. The august persona was, alas, retired from his position among the people by British importunings and now rusticating in Berlin, where his weekly broadcasts to the Arab world had made him even more famous and powerful. The cousin Salid had grown up under the lash of British rule in Jerusalem, aware that the British were surrogates for the true enemy of his people, international Jewry, via the hated Balfour Declaration of 1919, which mandated that Jewish subhumans would be accorded land in Palestine. When the mufti, an admirer of all things German, had evinced an early enthusiasm for the Third Reich, a German diplomat had reached out to the man and offered to take certain gifted Arab boys to Germany for technical training. From the age of eight onward, Yusef Salid was raised in the German method, among Germans, whose language he quickly mastered, first in the rigors of *Realschule*, then in cadet school, then in officers' training at Bad Tölz, then infantry school, and finally in a series of specialized SS training programs. He stood out because of his brown skin and coarse dark hair, but his elegance of manner, his eruditition in German and love of German literature, and his excellence in all matters military soon made him popular no matter the venue. His ability to keep his head in tense situations, his coolness under fire, his knowledge of wine—which, being a Muslim, he never drank, but he made it his business to memorize labels and vintages for exactly the popularity it would earn him—and his twinkly dark eyes made him a hero in the SS officers' mess. His assignment to Einsatzgruppen D in the early days of the July 22 invasion and his intense labors on behalf of that unit's aims earned him accolade after accolade, both official and personal.

When the strategy of shooting and burying the Jews of Ukraine proved unrealistic in the face of their sheer numbers, and the unit was folded into the Waffen SS for general military duties, it was Dr. Groedl himself who made calls and pulled strings on the young officer's behalf. Groedl considered himself to have an eye for talent. His mentees were scattered far and wide in the great crusade. It was he who arranged for Salid to be transferred to the 13th-SS Mountain, the only pure Muslim division in the Waffen-SS, where he knew the young man's talents for locating Jews would be put to good use.

It was inevitable that Groedl would recall Salid. When he needed a group of specialists for the delicate mission before him, it took a great deal of wrangling to get Police Battalion, which was acquiring a spectacular record under Salid in the

Serbian mountains, transferred en masse to the 12th SS Panzer Division, the umbrella unit for all SS operations in the West Ukraine–Stanislav area, although the connection was for paper-pushers only, and SS-13 Police Battalion Scimitar reported directly to and worked completely for Senior Group Leader–SS Groedl.

Salid estimated the bandit column to consist of at least fifty men and women, all heavily armed, all well experienced, most mounted on the sturdy-legged Carpathian ponies that made operations in the mountains feasible. He himself had only twenty-five, the best, from Police Battalion's larger pool of mountain anti-bandit fighters. He knew a larger formation on horseback could not move silently through the forest and mountain; he knew they would leave sign and disturbance; this one had to be done with great precision. He also specified ammunition double loads and made certain each of his fighters was armed not with the slow bolt-action KAR-98k rifle but with the MP-40 submachine gun and a P-38 or a Luger pistol. Each man carried three M24 grenades, "potato mashers," in the parlance. The point was to unleash maximum firepower when the column entered the kill zone. It had to be a single over-powering blast, because the targets were wily, would not panic, would return fire, and would quickly form maneuver elements and locate an egress and engineer some form of escape. Their ponies would give them mobility. But there could be no escapees. All must die: no prisoners, no worries, no regrets.

Hauptsturmführer—that is, Captain—Salid put his first MG-42, settled on a tripod for steadiness, thirty meters off the line of march, giving it a good sweeping angle laterally along the length of the column. He placed his second down the line, the only weapon on the left side of the ambush axis, also on a tripod. It would work the back end of the column, with a fire cutoff point established so that it did not leak bursts onto the Serbs on the other side of the path. His submachine gunners and grenadiers were concentrated in the jag of the L and, after the first magazine expenditure, would move on to targets of opportunity. The key was a group of extremely brave men who would be sequestered along the march line. They would wait two minutes, then emerge, there within the confines of the column, and begin to shoot the wounded. It was important that the phases of the ambush—opening ambuscade, suppressive fire, and individual liquidations—happen promptly, without hesitation. It would go so fast that there would be no time for command direction; the fellows would have to do it as they had been instructed, by second nature.

The unit had been afield for three days. It had moved only on foot, only at night. No cooking fires, no latrine pits, no sleeping positions. The men during the day simply melted into the forest and went supine for the entire daylight hours. They carried meager rations and water and were instructed to leave no traces, an impossibility but an ideal toward which to strive.

After ambush, it would take an hour for the armored Sd Kfz 251 Schützenpanzerwagens to arrive, grinding through thick brush under the power of their tracks, while being steered adroitly by their front tires. Each half-track carried an MG-42, so once they were on site, the firepower would be sufficient to stand off an army. But until then, that would be the tensest time, for who knew what of Bak's units were afoot in the forest tonight? Perhaps another was closer than expected and would come to the sound of the gunfire, to find Police Battalion low on ammunition and exhausted from the rigors of the ordeal. It was a gamble, but it was a gamble that had to be taken.

A cricket chirped. The cricket was a Serbian scout, ahead of the ambush site by one hundred meters. That meant the partisans—excuse, excuse, *bandits!*—were approaching down the path. Salid crouched, drawing his MP toward him. His would be the opening volley. He scanned again, saw nothing but stillness under the weaving of brush in the breeze, heard nothing but silence along the darkened forest path. Perhaps to his left he heard the squirming of the machine-gun team setting itself on the edge, rising behind the heavy gun with its endless belt of 7.92mm ammunition, but there were no clicks as guns were cocked or came off safe, for his good, trained Police Battalion fighters carried their weapons hot and ready to fire, to save tenths of seconds when it counted most.

Was it a dream or a fantasy? It had to be a fantasy. Dreams follow their own mad course, welling from an underneath of surrealism, grotesquery, twisted images, strange colors, weird angles. Her dreams were nightmares, all set in ruined cities of dead children. No, this was a fantasy, an indulgence claimed at the very edge of consciousness but still controlled by a rational mind full of aesthetic distinctions.

The scene always a meadow somewhere in an idealized Russia. The weather always late spring, the breeze always soft, the flowers always bright, their smell always sweet. It was a picnic of Petrova's lost family. All had assembled.

Her father was there. That kind and decent man, with his earnest way, and his steadiness, and his intellectual integrity. He always wore a tweed suit in the English style and had round black glasses, possibly French in origin. He smoked his ever-present pipe. His high cheeks and sincere eyes and gentleness of nature were what she felt, what she remembered, what she missed so terribly.

He was sitting on a linen sheet, sipping tea, and making conversation.

"No, Mili," he said. "I would stay with your court game. You have so much talent, and a girl as intelligent as you needs some kind of healthy outlet. Though you are correct in asserting that there is no direct application of the strength and suppleness you develop, I think that it will eat up your excess energy. Believe me, I have seen too many an intellectually gifted woman ruin herself on men, tobacco, and vodka when she goes to university, simply because all her excess energy demands some kind of release or expression. The tennis will save you."

She laughed. He was so earnest. "Oh, Papa," she said, "maybe I should take up the pipe, like you! All the time you fiddle with that pipe, all the cutting, the trimming, the stuffing, the lighting, the inhaling. Is that how you handle your excess energy?"

"Mili with a pipe!" Her younger brother Gregori laughed. "Oh, that's what would attract the boys. You'd end up married to an engineer or a doctor if you smoked a pipe!"

"Mili, Mili, Mili," shouted the even younger Pavel and did a loose-limbed interpretation of Mili sucking hard on an imaginary Sherlock Holmes meerschaum, all curves, fifteen pounds weight, with an obstruction in the stem so that the effort of inhalation hollowed his cheeks and bulged his eyes.

Dimitri, as always, sprang to her rescue. "You

boys, you go easier on your big sister! You're so lucky to have a beauty like Mili—"

"You're pretty lucky yourself, Dimitri!" shouted Gregori, and all of them fell to the warm earth, laughing at the hilarity of it all, even normally reserved Mama.

Gone, all gone. Her father, into the Soviet gulag, lost forever for disagreeing over Mendelian genetics with a Stalinist toady and bootlicker who called himself a scientist. Gregori, burning in his T-34 somewhere in the Caucasus. Pavel, pneumonia over the hard winter, picked up in the hospital where he'd been sent after a severe leg wound in infantry combat. Her mother, shell, Leningrad, second year of the great siege. And last of all, Dimitri, down in flames somewhere in his Yak, not quite an ace but one of the very best, whose luck had finally run out.

Lost, lost, lost. Why am I spared, she wondered. I must survive for the memories I carry. If I die, who will remember Mama, Papa, Gregori, Pavel, and dear, dear Dimitri?

It had begun so joyously, but now the grief crumpled her and she knew it wasn't a dream, it was too cruel to be a dr—

Suddenly the air filled with a sheet of light, an instant whirlwind of incandescent razor blades amid heat and noise, and the very universe itself shivered as malevolent energies were released into it, the energy from the machine-gun bullets tearing into the wood of the wagon, spraying splinters and dust in supersonic spurts wherever their randomness took them. It was a midsummer night's nightmare of industrialized mid-twentieth-century violence.

Her first coherent image was the horse upright on two hind legs, its two forelegs clawing the air. It had been mortally struck and twisted sideways against its halter as it died and fell. It pulled the world with it as its weight overwhelmed the wagon and that vehicle spilled sideways. Mili rode it down, aware that fire poured in from several directions and the air was filled with the lethal debris of battle. Horses screamed and reared, some lurched off in a panic, others went down lumpily as the bullet went through them. All was chaos and death.

She hit earth, slithered backward off the path into the brush and watched as the machine-gun fire swept up the path and down it, a giant whiskbroom that stirred the dust to fill the air. From somewhere too close to be comfortable and too far to be dangerous, a grenade exploded, and with her experience of such things, she knew it was a Stielgranate 24, the German potato masher. Its abruptness beat her eardrums and lifted her from the earth an inch or two.

Six months in infantry battle in Stalingrad had taught her lessons; she identified the spastic ripping of the German machine guns, the slightly slower-firing rounds of their machine pistols, and the abrupt shear of light, pressure, and concussion from the M24s detonating at the end of their long tumble from hand to target. The Germans were well positioned, heavily armed and had no need to conserve ammunition. This was a total murder ambush, nothing delicate. They were here to kill everyone, kill the horses, kill the dogs.

She had no rifle. She had no weapon. But because she slept in clothes, she was fully dressed in the camouflage sniper tunic, and there was but one direction to go, only out, away, beyond, that was, to ease backward into forest. But she did, and a man was on her.

His legs clamped about her, in not the rapist's rage but the killer's. She saw his alien face, the dapple-camouflage of the SS battle-dress tunic—odd, the details that stick—and pure fury. He was slightly tangled in his machine-pistol sling, which retarded his freedom, but he was so much stronger it didn't matter. He pinned her with a forearm as his other arm disengaged from the weapon and its twisted sling, reached to hip, and withdrew eight inches of steel blade—the torque of his body made his helmet pop off—and then raised the arm to strike, and at that point a bullet ripped through his face, tore his grimace, nose, and left eye from him and turned him to deadweight. He toppled off. Mili would never know where the savior's bullet had come from, one of the surviving partisans or an errant SS shot, possibly a ricochet as ricochets followed no law of justice but only their own insane preference.

Now freed, she slithered backward. As she wiggled, feeling her way with boot toes, she heard the high-pitched spitting of the partisan tommy guns, as some had survived the initial blast of fire and were responding. More horses screamed. A beast, riderless, careened down the road until tracers pumped into its flank and it slithered, writhing, kicking dust, to the ground. Another blast came from along the line as the SS bastards tossed more grenades: the two German heavy guns continued to rip sheets of debris from the earth as their operators worked the column over and, less powerfully but still insistently, the German machine pistols sent fleets of bullets into the melee, unleashing jets of spray and splinter wherever they struck.

A silence louder than gunfire enveloped the ambush zone.

All along the line, she saw men arise from so close it frightened her. It struck her that she'd slid into one such waiting croucher, evicted him from his spot, and gotten him killed for her trouble. But the remainder closed into the ruins of the column with dervish speed and meant to finish the engagement with their machine pistols at close range.

Mili ceased to observe. Instead, sniper quiet

and sniper strong and too intent on survival for fear, she edged her way backward, managed to turn, and making surprising speed, put distance between herself and the kill zone. At a certain point she heard voices—not German but some other language, Slavic, possibly Serbian—and froze. Not far from her, men rose to begin their own approach to the kill zone.

Like the sniper she was, she had the sniper's gift for disappearance, and now she employed it as never before in her months of battle.

Salid was on the Feldfu.b2 to 12th SS Panzer element, hunched next to his signalman, who carried the radio unit on his back. He spoke into the telephone-microphone.

"Hello, hello, this is Zeppelin calling Anton, answer, please."

"Hello, hello, Zeppelin, Anton responding, I have you clearly."

"Anton, request move panzerwagens up here fast. I don't know if there's anybody around, I don't have enough men for security, I have taken casualties and we must load our catch and be gone before more bandits arrive."

"Zeppelin, received. The panzerwagens are on dispatch and should reach you within the hour. Mission results, Zeppelin."

"Received and acknowledged, Anton. Mission report: many kills, numbers to follow."

The Germans! Salid thought. They want numbers on everything. They'd want numbers for the hairs on the devil's ass!

"Will pass along, Zeppelin. End transmit."

"End transmit," acknowledged the captain.

Meanwhile, his men were mopping up. He gave the microphone to his signalman, rose, and joined the soldiers, entering the kill zone as he heard the grunts of his machine gunners breaking down their weapons for transport. He walked the line, gun smoke still rancid in the air. Everywhere partisan bodies twisted or relaxed as death took them. A horse or two still breathed, still thrashed, until the finishing shot stilled them.

He issued a quick order. "Second squad, on security perimeter a hundred meters out. The rest of you, carry on. Where's Ackov? Damn him, he's never around when—"

"Captain," said Sergeant Ackov, "here I am." Ackov was a hard man, a former police sergeant in reality, very good at the soldier's tasks. His face blackened from the soot of the small-arms gases, the sergeant approached at a run from farther down the line. "I have numbers, sir."

"Go ahead, Sergeant," said Salid.

"Thirty-five bandits killed, at least nine of them women, but several too mangled by blast to determine identity. No blood trails. Hard to believe anyone survived the initial fusillade, but who can say. In daylight, we can look for sign."

"In daylight, we must be long gone. Our casualties?"

"Two dead, seven wounded, one of the wounded critical and won't make it until the half-tracks."

Up and down the line, spatters of shots crackled in the heavy summer night air. Police Battalion personnel knew it didn't pay to check the bodies from too close a range. You roll one over, and perhaps he has a pistol or a knife and isn't quite dead and yearns to take you with him. Perhaps as he was bleeding out, he unscrewed the cap on a grenade and wrapped the lanyard about his wrists, so that when disturbed, the grenade drops, the striker ignites, and the grenade detonates. Instead, walking carefully, using torchlight beams to guide them, they kept their distance and fired a short burst into each body. It was safer that way, and worth the expenditure in ammunition; only when the column of corpses had been fully killed a second time did the men set aside their weapons and pull the dead out of their positions and into a more or less orderly formation, if flat and still, for more intense evaluation.

"Can you make an identification?" Ackov asked as the Arab captain walked the line of bodies, attending them carefully.

Salid examined each dead face. He felt little but the responsibility of duty and command and the ambitions passed on to him by the One True Faith. The death masks themselves meant little to him; he'd seen thousands in his time, and learned early on in the days of Einsatzgruppen D that it made little sense to dwell on any one face.

At a certain point, he pulled a file out of his camo tunic to make comparisons. "I can't tell about the women," he said. "We'll have to clean them up to make a more precise identification. As for Bak, I had hoped to nab him tonight. What a nice bonus that would be, and earn me a week in Berlin. But unless he's one of the ones with face blown off, I don't see him. Maybe he wasn't here."

The week in Berlin was purely command theater for the perpetually excited Serbs, who loved to rape as much as kill. Salid's own personal tastes were aesthetic: given a week's leave, he would return to his prayer rituals—a luxury quickly abandoned on the Eastern Front— five times a day, and dream of the severe beauty of his beloved Palestine with its groves of date and olive trees, its sun-bleached sandstone hills, its bounty concealed in its near abstraction, its warmth, its bright sun, its needful people.

"Intelligence predicted Bak would be here," said Ackov.

"'Predict' is too scientific a word, Sergeant. They're just guessing, like the rest of us. Under normal circumstances I would call this a most excellent operation. More bodies than Von Bink's Panzergrenadiers have managed to collect in one place in over a year. But the operation was so special, I am not yet sure if we succeeded, and I am not yet sure what sort of report to make to Senior Group Leader Groedl."

"Captain," came a cry from nearby, and an excited man approached. He held a rifle, which he presented to Ackov, who presented it to Salid.

It was a Mosin-Nagant 91 with a PU scope sight and a complex shooter's sling for mooring it to the body at three points.

"She was here," said Ackov. "No doubt about it."

Sniper's luck: a cave.

Sniper's luck: a cave without a bear, a wolf, a badger, some wild thing already in attendance, ready to fight her for squatter's rights.

Sniper's luck: a stream through which she could run for miles, leaving no tracks. More, when she finally exited it, she exited over rocks and climbed a rocky path to get up to stable, dry ground. Again, no tracks.

She huddled within, watching the sun filter its way through the Carpathian forest as it rose. All was still. The scene was exquisite if you had time to appreciate such things, the verticals of the seventy-foot-tall white pine trunks, the horizontals of the pine boughs, the harmony of green and brown, the falling away of the land, the green cloverlike undergrowth, the slanting rays of sun where it penetrated the forest. There was perfume in the air, the sweetness of the pines. So serene was the view that she had to wrench herself from it; it suggested that peace and security were possibilities when clearly they were not.

No Germans came her way, though her visibility was limited. At the same time, no partisans seemed to be searching for her, either. She had no rifle, she had no map, she had no idea where she was. It had happened so fast in that modern way, one moment you're in one universe, on the edge of sleep, dreaming of your loved ones, and the next in another universe, everyone and everything trying to kill you with very loud violence.

Just about every part of her ached. The longer she lay, the more signals of pain came from various body parts as they realized they were no longer obligated to perform at maximum output but now had the leisure to report their discomfort. She had fallen, bruising and scraping a knee. The pine needles had cut her face and hands as she pushed her way through them. It seemed she'd pulled muscles along one rib, and that pull reported its agonies with some urgency. There was the lesser issue of a sprained ankle, but ankles had a way of loafing through the first day, then crying out loudly the next. A hundred scrapes, bumps, tears, pricks, cuts clamored for attention. Meanwhile, she was desperately hungry. How would she eat?

She was no forest dweller. She was a city girl. Her life before the war had been the cinemas and coffee shops of St. Petersburg; like many St. Petersburgers from old St. Petersburg families, she could never think of the place as Leningrad. It was a white city, beautiful in its pale northern light with its great churches and palaces, its abundant waterways and bridges. It was Dostoyevsky's city, literature's city, the most European city in Russia. Nothing about it had prepared her for this.

She knew she needed a plan. Her father, wise and wily, had already figured it out. She heard his voice. Wait another night here in the cave, then tomorrow at late afternoon begin to ease your way downhill. You will be lucky or not, running into peasants who may help or Germans who will kill. But you cannot simply lie here awaiting death.

Now assess. Use your brain. Papa said you were smart, all the teachers said you were smart. Figure this out.

Analyze, analyze, analyze. You must know the nature of the problem before you can solve it. This is as true in physics as it is in war, politics, medicine, or any advanced, refined human behavior. You must determine that which is true rather than that which you want to be true.

That was Papa's truest belief. That was what killed him.

Her father was an agricultural biologist, and

his task, like all those in his specialty, was to find some way to increase the wheat harvest. The motherland lived on her wheat; from wheat came bread, and from bread, life. Someone once said bread was the staff of life. Her father had laughed at that. No, he'd said, there's no staff involved; bread *is* life.

But his education was founded on a stern belief in Father Mendel's genetics. Alas, in Ukraine, a peasant genius named Trofim Lysenko believed in hybrid genetics. He had Stalin's ear and, soon enough, power. It behooved him to enforce his theories, first with letters to the journals, then lectures of admonition by way of faculty supervisors, and then through visits from secret policemen.

But her father would not be still.

One could not alter a wheat stalk in the lab and expect those alterations to be carried on in subsequent generations. Father Mendel made that clear a hundred years ago. It was a truth that could not be denied, and to base Soviet agricultural policy on fraudulent theories of hybridization was to ensure failure and doom millions to starvation.

It wasn't that Fyodor Petrova was a hero. Far from it. He was a mild, calm man, decent to all, a loving husband and father of three. But he was compelled to speak the truth, and he spoke it until he was disappeared. Over wheat!

Now she had fallen into her other trap: bitterness. She tried to exile from memory the night she learned he had been taken, the long months without hearing a thing, and finally an unofficial but not quite by chance encounter between her mother and one of her father's university colleagues, who reported unofficially. "He said they heard that Papa died of tuberculosis in a prison in Siberia."

And that was that. The ugliness of grief is not for words. Nor the grief to come: for two brothers, a mother, a husband. Even the great Dostoyevsky, with all his haunted, tormented mutterers, could not find the words to express it. Survive. Try to forget.

Papa again: Get your sniper brain back. Focus, concentrate, see, understand. Show nothing, hide your beautiful eyes and body and become the earth, the wind, the trees, become the sniper, and pay them back, pay them all back.

Analyze. Assess. Understand. God gave you a brain, use it.

What do you know?

I know that we were ambushed by Germans. Most of us died. I escaped by—

No, no. Do not waste time on the self. Who cares by what means the sniper escaped. She escaped. On to larger issues. Characterize the German effort.

Extremely skilled. They have the best warcraft

in the world and routinely kill us five to one in any engagement. They have better equipment, smarter officers, more creative soldiers. We only beat them only by sheer force of numbers. If they kill us five to one, we come at them six to one or ten to one and, in the end, shall prevail because, all things being equal, we can outbleed them. We can outsacrifice them. We can outgrieve them. We clear minefields, after all, by marching through them.

But even with those truths, the effort of the night was outstanding. It was beyond anything she had encountered in her six months in Stalingrad, her day of killing at Kursk.

Especially considering there were fewer Germans.

There had to be. A large force could not maneuver and emplace so silently; it would leave sign. Bak's partisans were masters of the forest; how could they have been fooled except by those who were more masterful yet?

A small, silent, elite force. A few men.

How few?

Two heavy guns. She recognized the heavier concussions of the 7.92 rounds spurting from the unmuzzle at unattackable speed. The rest machine pistols, their lighter, crisper burr gnawing away in counterpoint to the heavy guns. The automatic nature of the weapons made it seem as if thousands attacked when it could have been but few. She did not believe that she heard any K-98 Mausers. All were armed with automatic guns. All. That was rare for them. If all these men had machine pistols, special arrangements had been made. This was some kind of team, some kind of special unit, not just a line platoon wandering the Carpathians hoping for kills.

She thought about it more. Twenty, twenty-five men. Four on the 42s, the rest with machine pistols and grenades. First the heavy guns fire. Then the machine pistols and grenades, but no more than four grenades. Then, on signal or as if rehearsed, all those gunners go quiet and the executioners spring from nearby—so nearby!—and are quickly among the wounded, the hiding, the dying, firing at close range.

Think about those men. They lie still, making not a sound, while their comrades fire inches above their heads. Both elements know exactly the cutoff point; the execution squad has total trust in the gunners and leaps into action the very second the gunners cease fire. Not a split second is wasted.

Survivors? A freak of luck, maybe, a few out of fifty, herself among the lucky. But superb execution, perhaps rehearsed, so that each man knew his place and move. It didn't feel like a serendipitous happening. These men *knew*. They had superb intelligence. They moved through partisan-controlled forest without a sound, they knew exactly the pathway, and they planned and executed beautifully. They were clearly of Waffen-SS caliber, maybe better. They represented—if she understood the situation here in the Carpathians, where a bitter kind of stalemate existed—the coming of a new energy via a new and specialized unit to the field.

What could it mean?

At that point, she was yanked from her concentration by a flash of motion. She looked sharply, dividing the visible world into sectors and examining each in its time, top to bottom, as methodically as a typist transcribes an interview.

Until she saw them.

CHAPTER 11

Lviv

THE PRESENT

The Germans knew exactly where Bak's unit would be, what time it'd arrive, they did it *perfect,*" said Swagger. "But the point isn't that it's early. It's what 'early' signifies: betrayal."

"Someone snitched them out. Can we determine who it was?"

They sat in a pleasant twilight in the old town square of Lviv, at a sidewalk café called the Centaur. The city itself had that old Austro-

Hungarian empire style going on; they could have been in Prague or Vienna. Swagger half expected hussars in brass breastplates over red jackets with swords at the half-cock to come trotting along the cobblestones at the head of some emperor's entourage. It was so cheerful, it was hard to think of betrayal. One thought more of fairy princesses.

"Let's look at the possibilities," said Swagger. "First: tactical betrayal. It happened because of a natural consequence of combat operations. Say, a German Storch recon plane saw the Russian plane that had dropped Mili take off. It was able to shadow the movement of the column. The Storch team radios time, location, direction; again by coincidence there's a Police Battalion counterbandit team near enough to get set up, and the bandits just walk into it."

"That's not really betrayal," said Reilly. "That's just 'stuff happens.' "

"Fair enough. Okay, local betrayal. One of the partisans is really a German agent. Or maybe some SS major has his daughter hostage so he's forced to turn on his people. He manages to get the news out before they leave to pick up Mili. That gives the Germans plenty of time to get the Police Battalion into play."

"So it's a coincidence of timing that this happened when Mili arrived? Hard to swallow."

"Try this. Bak himself is the Nazi agent. They're building him up to win a lot of battles so he'll be a hero and be taken back to Moscow, and when he's back in NKVD headquarters, he can really give them the crown jewels."

"But they seem to have killed him. After all, he disappears from the story."

"It was an accident. Night ambushes are terrible things. Nobody knows what's happening. He's trying to blow the deal to give up the Russian sniper to protect Obergruppenführer Groedl, and he zigs that way when the linchpin on the MG42 tripod vibrates free, and the gun rotates another few inches, and bye-bye, Bak."

"But wouldn't his death be recorded in the operational diaries of Twelfth Panzer, regardless? Like the rifles, he was booty."

"It would," said Swagger.

"Okay," she said. "Interesting possibilities. They're all wrong, but they're very interesting. Tomorrow I'll tell you who betrayed them."

CHAPTER 12

Somewhere in the Carpathians
MID-JULY 1944

Two of them. Not Germans, definitely not Germans. But partisans, survivors of the Bak column, as was she? Hard to tell.

A heavy one, a light one. In the heavy one, she

recognized the dignity and stolidity of the eternal peasant. He had no partisan affectations, no babushka hat, no crossed bandoliers of ammunition, no potato mashers stuck in his belt, no Red tommy gun. He wore only a shapeless black peasant smock and equally shapeless trousers over the thick boots peasants had worn for centuries. He moved with deliberation; you knew in a second that patience would never be a problem with this one. He could outwait God or the devil if it came to that and, as a hobby, watch mud bricks dry. He would be the one who knew a lot more than you thought, and if he gave you his loyalty, he was giving you everything. Everything about him was big: feet, legs, arms, hands. He could put in a thousand hours behind a plow. He was the man who would plant and harvest the wheat her father had tried to protect for him. He would feed the masses; he was the masses.

The other was leaner, quicker, a lithe man with goatee and glasses, under a frost of prematurely gray hair, wiry and tight. He looked somehow more refined, and if he moved easily through the woods, it was not out of heritage but out of learning. He, too, was as unwarlike as could be imagined, in a well-worn black leather jacket, some kind of bluish shirt, and a pair of threadbare trousers.

She watched as they picked their way along some fifty feet below her, the peasant leading, the thinner man—she had no insight as how to classify him and so would not make the mistake of conferring an identity upon him too soon—following. At a certain moment, the peasant raised a hand, and each halted, dropped to knees, and looked nervously around. After a bit, satisfied that no SS men were about to nab them, they rose.

"Hello," she cried.

They reacted in terror, scrambling back, edging into panic.

She emerged from the cave, pulled herself upright, and started down the slope to them. "Greetings, comrades."

The peasant babbled in Ukrainian.

"She's the sniper!" said the thinner man, having made an immediate calculation.

"*Belaya Vedma*!" exclaimed the peasant. And added something else.

"He says you should be a princess," said the thin fellow.

"There are no princesses these days," said Petrova.

"He says your beauty is a gift from God."

"I hope God is busy giving out other gifts, like mercy and long life. He shouldn't be wasting time on St. Petersburg girls. Are you pursued?" she asked.

"No, madam. Like you, accidental survivors from the nasty business of last night," said the thin man.

"You are with Bak? Why are you unarmed?"

"I threw my gun away," said the thin fellow. "A practical decision. If I had a rifle, I would be shot on sight. If captured, tortured for information, then executed. Maybe if I didn't have one, they'd just beat me for amusement, then dump me in the bushes. I ran into the big fellow in the dawn. We scared the life out of each other. We are simply trying to evade capture."

"I don't think the Germans are here in force," she said. "Despite all the shooting, that was a small team. That's how they moved so effectively through the forest. They had many machine guns, unusual for a German unit. Did Bak escape?"

"I confess cowardice," said the thin man. "I don't know, and not until you mention it did I even think of it. I have been thinking only of my own miserable skin."

"Do you have food? I am famished."

"Not a bite."

"Ach!" She sat back. "What a pair of sorry dogs."

Introductions were made, names quickly forgotten. The peasant was a Ukrainian farmer who had been a partisan for a year. His stoic face may have concealed tragedies, but he did not volunteer them. The scrawny man—younger than he looked under that gray hair and the goatee—was a former schoolteacher. He had been with the partisans only a few months.

"I am not much of a fighter," he said. "But since

118

I have good reading and writing skills, General Bak used me as a clerk. I kept records, made reports."

"So if the SS tortured you, you would have a lot to reveal."

"Only that food is low, ammunition is low, communication with higher authority uncertain, and nobody's happy. They know all this, but yes, they would enjoy beating me until I told them. Then it would be nine grams of lead for me."

"Nine grams awaits all of us if we don't make a sound decision now."

"Tell us what to do."

"First, tell me some stuff. I don't know a thing about this area. I was flown here and dumped."

The Peasant got the gist of her request. "Beyond us, perhaps eight kilometers, is a village called Yaremche," he said as the Teacher translated. "It is built in ravines on the waterfalls of the River Prut. If a case can be made to the villagers, they might take us in or at least give us food."

"What else?"

"Bak's main camp is a farther march," said the Teacher. "It is at least seventy-five kilometers through forest that is unclearly administered. Perhaps German patrols wander it, perhaps partisan units. It would be our bad luck to run into the former and good to run into the latter."

"Next question: food. How do we feed ourselves?"

"He knows mushrooms," said the Teacher. "These Ukrainians, they live on mushrooms. Mushrooms are the secret wealth of the Carpathians."

"Mushrooms, then. After mushroom paradise, we'll head back to the ambush site," she said. "We can look for weapons, foodstuff, anything the Germans left behind. Is it going to rain?"

"By afternoon, yes. I believe," said the Peasant in translation.

"Then we had better get there first and see what the tracks tell us. When it rains, it will wash away our tracks. Once we have gotten what we can, we will rejoin the war. Our little vacation is over."

CHAPTER 13

Highway E50, Due South
THE PRESENT

To the east, wheat fields, classic Ukraine landscape. You could almost feel the Red Army chorus singing patriotic chants as framed in the eye of a New Soviet Cinema camera. To the west, the Carpathians, Ukraine-style, a formidable bank of mountain that curled across the promontory of Ukraine extending across what once was Poland or Hungary or Romania or all three and now was like a Ukrainian peninsula thrust into the sea of Eastern Europe. They were ancient mountains in the five-thousand-foot range, their foothills and lower altitudes mantled in a fetching green of meadow, giving way to a band of dense forest that could and had concealed armies. It was also famous as a haunt of vampires.

Nice to look at on both sides. But what they experienced more than anything was the roughness of the asphalt. Every two miles or so, it seemed there was a we-interrupt-this-highway-for-250-yards-of-bad-road bulletin. Driving was more like slaloming, as the drivers zoomed this way and that to avoid the many crevices that had gone unrepaired since Sputnik 1 ate up the Ukrainian infrastructure budget. It was quaint and rustic for a bit, then a pain in the ass or, more particularly, the head.

Still Reilly soldiered on. "What we haven't focused on," she said, "is that the whole Operation Mili Petrova isn't just missing from the Russian records. That would be remarkable enough. It's also missing from the German records. You have to ask why, how, by whom? What difference would it make to the Germans what happened to Mili? The whole Mili caper—which we're assuming involved first a night ambush and a miss, then her survival in the mountains and her ability to come up with another rifle, then a climax in her failed attempt on Groedl, then her death or capture and removal for interrogation—isn't there. But why would any of that be remarkable to field officers in the Twelfth SS Panzer charged with keeping a combat log? Why would they fail to record it?"

"Okay," said Swagger, pulling around a gas tanker that placidly belched black exhaust into the air, getting his molars loosened for the efforts as he bounced the car through trenches and gullies cleverly inscribed in the road surface while the dust spat up behind him, "maybe the offensive is an explanation. At ten A.M. on the twenty-sixth, the Russian artillery kicked off and the Germans ran like hell. The Russians walked into Stanislav the next day and had pushed the Germans to the Carpathians and almost out of Ukraine except for the sliver that contained Uzhgorod, on the other side of the mountains. Hard to keep records straight in all the hubbub."

"They had time afterward."

"Okay," said Swagger.

"So what we have here is an unusual circumstance where *both* the Russians and the Germans have wiped information off the record, independently of each other. Someone ordered this. Whoever he was, he had juice. He had power. He had influence. His position was very important. If he's a German mole inside Stalin's circle, he's a man of high power, a commissar, Stalin's boy, whatever, so he could order the eighty-sixing of Petrova from Russian sources, but he hates the idea that her tale still exists in one other place, that being the German records. He knows that after the war, it might be checked and give him up. So he explains to his Abwehr contact or his SS guy or whatever agency was running him, he explains that for his own security, the results of what he has brought off, which infer his existence, cannot be recorded. Again, he's a big guy, get it? He's a bigfoot, and what he doesn't quite get is that erasing his footprints doesn't leave *nothing,* it leaves an erased footprint, which can be read almost as well as the footprint itself."

"Basil Krulov, Stalin's Harry Hopkins. Since he's the only big guy on the board, you're saying it had to be him. That's a giant assumption."

"It's the only thing that makes sense if you look carefully at it."

"Does it? What about motive? This guy is Stalin's right-hand man. He's one of the most powerful men in his country. He's got to expect that once the war is over, he'll be even bigger. He'll have power, love, and a mansion. So why is he risking everything to rat out his own folks to the Nazis?"

"He was in Munich, remember. Maybe the Nazis got a picture of him sucking something he shouldn't have been sucking in a public urinal."

"Possible. But . . . you're forgetting. He's real smart. That's why he gets so high so fast. He ain't a likely candidate for that kind of trap. And if he got into it, he is a likely candidate for getting out of it. So whoever the traitor is, he had to really want to be a traitor. He was in the most screwball paranoid place in the world, the Kremlin under Stalin, where thousands, maybe tens or hundreds of thousands, get wiped out for the merest whisper of a suspicion."

"Motive screws up everything," said Reilly. "Why can't this be a movie? Movies forgot about motives thirty years ago!"

CHAPTER 14

The Carpathians
Site of Ambush
JULY 1944

Yes, there were rifles, almost thirty of them. But all the bolts had been removed. They were worthless. Her sniper rifle, with its beautiful scope, was also gone, a German trophy instead of her head. There were no PPSh's, as the Germans prized that sturdy peasant submachine gun and snatched it up whenever they could. The Germans, in their methodical way, had been very thorough, leaving no grenades, no bayonets or knives, no pistols. The bodies, twenty-four of them, lay in a neat double row alongside the path, where they'd been dragged. Most bore the violence of modern small-arms trauma, some horribly, some not so horribly. They had been covered with lime for some reason, as if to shield the forest from them and not them from the forest, but it had worked, and in the intervening night and day, no scavengers had come to enjoy the meat of the predator's kill.

"Bak is not here," said the Teacher.

"That is one good thing."

"He escaped. I would say it looks like a good ten or so made it away."

"No," said the Peasant through the Teacher. "You miscount, comrade. The number seems so small because there are no women's bodies here."

"The women's bodies have been removed?" asked Petrova.

"It would appear so."

"Why, I wonder?" she asked. "It's not like the Nazis have a well-known respect for females. Usually they rape before they murder."

The glade had a haunted feel to it. Now it was restored to the natural order, the white pines tall and majestic, the ground cover curly with small green leaves, the carpet of needles thick everywhere. But a tang of the fired gunpowder lingered in the air, perhaps to be driven away by the rain that threatened. Spent shells lay everywhere, as the fast-firing German guns ate ammunition voraciously. A small non-coniferous

125

tree, close to an M24 blast, had been sheared down the middle, and already its leaves were beginning to brown. The wagon, on its side, lay riddled, almost comically shredded, as if by termites. A touch and it would disintegrate. The poor horse lay in its halter, its guts ripped open, its head at a grotesque angle. It had died kicking and neighing. Other horse carcasses, many split and spilling tripe, lay haphazardly about.

"Look hard, think, and come back to me, each of you, with a report."

"A report on what?"

"On what happened here. Why, how? Give me interpretations I can use. Now, fast, we don't have too much time before the rain, and I want the Peasant hunting mushrooms before that."

"Yes, comrade."

Each man did as he had been ordered, walking the ground of the kill zone back and forth, putting a great effort into it. In time they rendezvoused where she sat under a tree, not far from the wrecked wagon and the spot where the knifer had almost killed her before someone blew his brains out.

"It was a very good ambush," said the Peasant. "These soldiers knew their business. That's why we didn't hear a thing until it was too late. I noticed a scarf tied to a tree at the halfway point, on the far side of the path, which was the marker for the rear machine gun so that it would not fire into the unit's own men."

"Very good," she said. "Now, Teacher, intellectual, tell me something."

"The tracks. The Germans brought up half-tracks—"

"How do you know they were panzerwagens?"

"I could see the tire tracks crushed in tracks of the treads. The treads broke the tire cuts, not the other way around, which mean the tires preceded the treads. Panzerwagens."

"Sd Kfz 251s," she said. "A huge armored beast of a thing. Very hard to kill, with a forty-two usually mounted up top. I saw them all over Stalingrad. How many?"

"I don't know."

"Three."

"I'm sure you're correct. Anyhow, that is puzzling, is it not? Why bring the huge things, crush them through the forest, to remove a team that is very good already at moving through the forest?"

"The answer would be not for the team. For something else. And what would that be?"

"I don't know."

"The women's bodies."

"Exactly," said the Teacher. "Yes, it has to be."

"They knew there'd be women. In the confusion of the fight, they couldn't possibly take time to discriminate in their targeting. It's hard to discriminate with an MG-42 roaring through a belt at a thousand rounds a minute. So they'd have to collect the women. Why?"

She already knew the answer.

The bodies were damaged by blast and burn and bullet strike. The features were blurred or uncertain. They had to examine them carefully, scientifically.

She understood: They didn't just know. *They were looking for me.*

CHAPTER 15

Yaremche

THE PRESENT

"This isn't right," said Swagger.

It was somehow fraudulent. The buildings were all Ukraine mountain-style homes where wood was the prevailing element, the roofs pitched high to shed snow, the houses themselves of stoutly jointed logs, all of it festooned with expressions of the self and clan in bright ornamentation, fences separating neighbor from neighbors quite sensibly, and the yards well tended. The culture was called Hutsulian, and this was Hutsulianism at its purest. Flowers were abundant, spilling every which way out of boxes at the windows, in beds along the sidewalks, climbing up trellises, but it all looked as if it had been built last week.

"Are we in the Wisconsin Dells?" asked Reilly.

Before them stood another iron man on a marble pedestal, not as big as several others they had seen, but again in ruffled greatcoat, heroic, holding a stylized Red tommy gun above his head and waving his unseen iron men forward. It said simply "Bak," and under that "1905–1944."

"No," said Swagger. "All this is recent-built. But this ain't the Yaremche we came to see."

"How can you tell?" asked Reilly.

"Well, we know the Germans burned the place down. So when they rebuilt it, I guess they rebuilt here much farther down the main road. The people who moved in probably weren't the original people, who were all dead. So the new Yaremche is built for the convenience of everybody who don't remember, not for the convenience of anybody who does. But the old Yaremche was built, what, a thousand years ago? In those days, they built the village near a river— no river here—and near the woods and the foothills, so if attacked, the villagers could get into the woods and escape or hide out, as well as see their enemy coming down the valley beforehand. So the Yaremche we're talking about, it had to be a mile or so farther down the valley, toward the mountains."

He squinted, looking around. "See, it ain't just

that. It's the land itself. The valley is wide here. She had to be within five hundred yards, and the nearest crests are half a mile to a mile away."

It was true. The town was situated on a series of valleys that ran along the River Prut, and at this spot, the valley had opened up.

"We don't know it happened here. We don't even know it happened, period."

"She was a sniper. If it happened, she sniped him. Long shot, take the man down. He's probably guarded, there's no way she gets close enough to use a tommy gun or a grenade if he's here. There was an atrocity here on the twenty-eighth, something set it off, there was a sniper in the area, there was an ambush, it all pretty much adds up. Except this place doesn't add up."

"And the fact that the Germans recovered her sniper rifle so she didn't have one makes it even more difficult to understand."

"I know, I know, but I can only figure out one damn thing at a time. Today I am figuring out where it happened. Maybe tomorrow I figure out where she got the rifle."

"Okay, how about this: I will feed you stupid questions. So stupid they get you even crankier. Maybe that way, you'll stumble on a better idea."

"Go ahead."

"Okay," she said. "If it was your shot, how would you do it?"

"I'd be in trees, overlooking. I could infiltrate

through forest, find a lane through the leaves, look down, read the wind, build a position against a trunk, take the shot, then exfiltrate under the same tree cover. The Krauts couldn't get their vehicles up the slope and through the trees, and I'd be gone by the time they climbed up with dog teams to track me."

"So it's got to be somewhere else. Somewhere with high hills within five hundred yards, lots of forest cover."

"Yeah."

"Okay," she said. "Follow me."

They crossed into a souvenir shop—textiles, ceramic figures, photo albums, socks in bright patterns—and Reilly spoke to the lady behind the desk.

After a while, she said to Swagger, "You were right. It's up the road a bit. By the bridge over the waterfall. That's where the village was until the Germans burned it down."

They stood on the bridge. Fifty yards farther on, the River Prut pounded down a twenty-foot drop, throwing up a mist and creating a pulsing, wet roar. White foam burst from the wet rocks, and tumult ripped across the surface of the Prut where it settled. Ukrainians, in underwear, shorts, and swimsuits, sat on the rocks, enjoying the cooling spray. On either side of this picturesque little spot, at high ground along the banks, entrepreneurs had built more touristy bric-a-brac, a mock village of wooden booths where the usual crap—the same ceramic figures, the same textiles, the same socks, the same photo albums—was hawked at competitive prices. It seemed somewhat blasphemous, as it also marked the site of a massacre, but business was business, and the Ukrainians had a hard head for what was now as opposed to what was then. How much nicer if it had been a fallow field where high ragged grass blew in the breeze, the trees nearby also animated and rustling, their leaves shimmering in the sun, maybe a nice plaque commemorating the spot. But there were plenty of those, and the real estate here was too beautiful for a somber intrusion. Just stalls selling stuff. Stuff, stuff, stuff, the universal stuff. A bluff carpeted in high pines loomed in one direction, but it was really the only elevation within shooting distance, except for, a thousand yards off, a mountainside, itself covered in the pines. It was too far.

He stood, he looked up, down, sideways, front, and back. "She'd shoot from up there," he said, pointing at the bluff. "He was down here, maybe on this bridge. The bridge would isolate him from his bodyguard. The range is no more than four hundred yards."

He stood, he looked at the trees on the bluff for a long time. "Okay," he said, "I'm getting something."

"I just see trees."

"Yeah, just trees, but—but look at the colors. Do you see?"

"Uh, green, followed by green, then more green, and finally some green. Is that it?"

"Different tones of green."

She was silent. After a bit she said, "Yes. It's like . . ."

"Go on," said Swagger.

"What I'm seeing," she said, "is that the green of these pines across the closest half of the bluff is somehow different. It's almost like a line, bright one side, dull the other."

"That's it. What I'm seeing is that the trees on roughly half the bluff are somehow, uh, lighter. They're not the dark forest green, they've got less density to the color, there's more light, they seem almost lit up."

"That's it. It signifies something. Newer, older, I don't know, closer to water, in more sun, in more shade, something like that."

They completed the trek across the bridge, then took some wood-hewn steps down to the water's edge and drew nearer to the Ukrainians in the water, whose children ran about eagerly, lost in games.

"Does it give you the creeps?"

"Thinking about what happened here, what the Nazis did, yes," said Reilly. "Otherwise, no. It's just a place. No signs of anything. Covered, gone, vanished. But your instincts are much better than mine. Maybe you feel something."

"Let's not feel. Let's look. Touch, rub, I don't know, experience it really up close."

Swagger bent down. He stuck his fingers into the loam, probed, came up with nothing.

She followed suit. She found nothing.

They continued for half an hour. Nothing.

"Well, maybe I'm full of crap," said Bob. "Maybe—"

But a child ran by them, trailing a fishtail of shedding water, one hand extended in triumph.

"That kid found something."

They watched him head to a supine mother and father, pinkening in the sun on a blanket. They walked over, and Reilly spoke to them, discovering that the mother spoke enough Russian to get by.

Reilly handed something to Bob. "She says the children find these things all the time."

It was black, half of it rusted or otherwise corroded away. Its remaining walls were paper-thin, the whole thing crumbly. But the rimmed head, where the brass was much thicker, was intact, and he turned it to read in the light. "I see a 5, a 17, an S97, and a D, circling the center, separated by segment lines."

"What does that mean?"

"The water must churn 'em up every so often. German production code. If I knew more, I could

tell you the year and the plant. It's a 7.92-
millimeter cartridge casing. A machine-gun
shell."

He thought a second.

"Somebody did a lot of shooting here."

CHAPTER 16

The Carpathians
Yaremche
JULY 1944

Salid was a moral man. He understood obligation, discipline, obedience to God, cleanli-
ness, hard work, the greater good, the greater
cause of Palestine, of Islam, and he used those
precepts as his guidelines.

But he hid this behind an armor of diffidence
and duty, and what he did appeared undisci-
plined. It was SS theater conceived to convey
the impression of random brutality as a way of
encouraging fear and thus cooperation. So while
he walked among the ranks of assembled
villagers, he pretended arbitrariness while looking
for specificity. He required certain indicators.

The first was nasal structure. Was the nose
long, thickened, wide of nostril? Did it lead the
face? Had it that prowlike profile so familiar
from Hans Schweitzer's chilling invocation on

the movie poster for *Der ewige Jude*? Was the chin also small, behind the point of the nose? Were the lips thick? What about the skin? Was it sallow, yellowish, perhaps even Asiatic? And the hair, greasy, brushed back, contributing to the general verminlike profile so common in these cases?

Since these people of Hutsulian ethnicity lived on mud streets in wooden houses under thatched roofs and worshiped at a crude Orthodox church, it was unlikely that any of them were Jews. But some carried the genetic strain. It could have gotten intermingled at any time since the medieval ages, as the Balkans, Ukraine, and Central Europe were a genetic cesspool, so corrupted by cross-breeding that all purity had been eliminated. Semitic genetic expression could emerge, strident and manipulative, at any time. As the hidden moral principle to all Scimitar actions, Captain Salid made the discriminations off of much experience, having acquired a fine eye for such matters.

"That one," he said to Sergeant Ackov, "and the boy."

"That one" had a bit of nasal bulge. Why take a risk? "The boy" had lively eyes, too lively for a dull nothing of a place such as Yaremche. You could see it in his eyes: defiance, intelligence, shrewdness, the defining Jewish characteristics. They had to be cleansed from the world.

In the end, he settled on ten. Each had at least

one prominent Jewish characteristic. He was well pleased. He had advanced both his causes, the immediate tactical and the longer-term geo-political. It was a good day's work. And it was only beginning.

The ten were isolated at the riverbank, under the old suspension bridge. The waterfall continued its roar and splash. Above, on the plateau where the rude shacks of the village of Yaremche were gathered, peasants looked down. One of the panzerwagens bulled its way to the far bank and halted, overlooking the ragged formation.

Salid felt they should know why this was happening. It was meaningless, for it didn't matter and no one had bothered to explain to the Jews in Einsatzgruppen D's pits why it was happening, but Salid wanted to cling to civil grace in spite of all the slaughter and violence of the war. It kept one's mind clear. Maybe it was of more use to him than to them.

He addressed them, unaware that they spoke Ukrainian, not Russian.

"I know you are innocent, in the narrow meaning of the word 'innocent.' I know that you curse your luck, that you are bitter, that you do not see the larger picture. I know that you are frightened. Further, I do not think you subhuman. You are indeed human, not only in the biological sense of being able to procreate with other humans. That is why you are so dangerous and

137

must be dealt with by the scientific mechanism of the Reich. I know you cannot see this and do not understand it, but it has to be. Your death is a sacrifice for the greater good of humanity."

"I have done nothing, sir, oh God, please spare me," a middle-aged man cried from within the formation. Immediately two of the Police Battalion guards rushed over, clearly intending to smash him to earth for his insolence, but Salid, who understood the meaning though not the words, froze them with a gesture.

"I explain to you. There are extremely dangerous people among the bandits in the mountains above you. They must be exterminated. We made a very good start last night, an excellent start. But it was not perfect. Some escaped. It is quite possible that they will leave their sanctuary and come to you for aid and sustenance. You must not even consider such a thing. To do so would doom your village. This is a fact I must impress upon you, for so many of you are slow and backward and incapable of learning such a simple lesson. I chose to do so with this demonstration. It is not meant to be cruel or humiliating. So your sacrifice may help ensure the survival of all those others who were not selected. When they see a partisan, they will refuse aid and report instantly to the first soldier or policeman they can reach. That way they vouchsafe the survival of Yaremche and all its villagers. You are serving humanity, sir. You are serving your village. You are serving the Reich. You should be proud to contribute."

He stepped back.

In the armored hull of the Sd Kfz 251, Sergeant Ackov pressed the trigger of the MG42, which had already been laid on for the target zone. He fired for twenty seconds, about four hundred rounds of heavy 7.92mm ammunition. A blur of spent shells cascaded from the gun, and the gun itself, though restrained in the brace of its mount, bucked savagely in the drama of recoil and recovery. It was like some kind of hideous but brilliant industrial piston, manufacturing smoke, sparks, flame, and heat as it operated.

Its stream of fire ate through the formation of hostages, seeming almost to swallow them in a melee of dust and noise. There was so much debris because, at that range, the high-velocity, high-energy bullets tore through the bodies completely and continued their downward trajectory into the earth, where each one kicked up a spurt of dirt that looked like a geyser. Taken collectively, the disturbed earth rapidly came to resemble a roaring cyclone.

All the hostages—six men, two women, and two teenage boys—fell to the earth spastically, though since the sergeant was an excellent gunner, he kept the stream of fire below the necks of his targets, so the bullet damage was concealed by the peasants' smocks and the copious blood quickly absorbed by the earth.

"More medicine, Ackov," said the captain.

Ackov fired again. The dust danced in cyclonic disturbance as another 250 rounds pummeled the bodies.

"Very well done," said the captain. He turned. "People of Yaremche, learn from this. You must not assist bandit activities. The penalty is death, not only for you but for your wives and children. You will be wiped off the map if you do not comply. You do not want to be forgotten, like Lidice. For your own good, you must obey."

He gave the signal, and the men of Police Battalion remounted their three panzerwagens to move out. Salid felt he had done an exceptionally good job.

He waited until his men had mounted the vehicles, then clambered aboard the lead panzerwagen. Ackov was there with the map.

"Herr Captain, five kilometers down the road, through the pass called Natasha's Womb, it's called Vorokhta."

"On to Vorokhta, then," said Salid, wincing, for it was beginning to rain.

Four Thousand Feet Above Yaremche

They climbed high, above the rain clouds. Beneath them, the world had vanished in a sea of cottony fog, penetrated only by farther peaks in the chain that stood out like islands of an archipelago. It felt safe, though they had no way of knowing whether it was. They found the mouth of a cave—the mountains were pocked with them—and slipped inside. It had to be several miles distant from the ambush site and several hundred meters above the line of the path.

The cave was bigger than the last one and held enough room to sustain the three without closeness. The two men more or less disposed of fungus and spiderwebs and turned it marginally habitable for emergency duty. They settled in, the two city dwellers exhausted. But the Peasant was hardly able to sit still and soon left on a mushroom hunt.

In a few hours, he returned. He had an armful of the dry dead-white things, clusters of a Ukrainian berry that was small, red, and sweet, even a dead rabbit.

"Very good work," she said.

This pleased the Peasant, who recognized the tone of warmth and reported in Ukrainian, which the Teacher dully translated. "He says he set ten snares," he reported. "Tomorrow, first thing, he'll inspect them. Rabbit tomorrow, he is sure."

"Do the Germans patrol this high?"

"No. Not really, not aggressively," said the Teacher. "Come, look, I'll show you."

He led her out. At the mouth of the cave she

could see the reality of the Carpathians: it looked like an ocean of green, that is, rippled with the ups and downs of capricious elevation, dozens of carpeted peaks in the three- to five-thousand-foot range, as random as waves, seemingly endless. It was all tall white pines, their soft, short needles each catching a speck of light, so that the whole mass seemed somehow alive with illumination as the wind animated them.

"It's a big place," said the Teacher. "You can see why the Germans have no real need to conquer it. Controlling the lowland is enough for them."

He pointed, and indeed, if she followed his angle, she saw what looked like a cut through some of the farther valleys.

"A road?"

"Yes, the only one through from Yaremche to other, smaller villages called Vorokhta, Yasinia, and Rakhiv, ultimately Uzhgorod. It's the only road through the mountains south of Lviv. If the Red Army attacks in force and the front collapses, the Germans in Stanislav may flee down it to get through the mountains to their next line of defense. So they patrol the road constantly, because it will have to be kept open when the day arrives. But they seldom come this deep in unless they're acting on very specific intelligence. So we are safe."

"Enjoy your mushrooms, comrades," she said.

"We have to move before the Red Army attacks, or the prey may scamper. I'm not going to live on fungus and rabbit and sleep in a hole without at least killing the SS bastard for my troubles."

Interlude in Tel Aviv I
Mossad
THE PRESENT

You hunt them in the jungle of stuff. Any stuff. Commodities, derivatives, cash transfers, currency manipulations, oil futures, pork (pork!) futures, blood diamonds, anywhere stuff is exchanged for other stuff.

Gershon Gold knew the game, but you'd never guess him a hunter from the outside. He was in his mid-sixties, tending toward weight, very much commercial class of Israeli, a businessman, a financial planner, a retailer, what have you. He wore slacks and open-necked sport shirts, some of them attractive, most not. He wore square-framed black plastic eyeglasses, a Rolex knock-off (why spend all that money for a watch?), once combed his gone-to-gray hair over to the left, though of late had gone with more of a straight-back Meyer Lansky look that earned him all manner of ribbing from friends and wife. He liked black loafers with both wing-tip perfor-ations *and* tassels. Of glamour, élan, pizzazz, grace, beauty, he had none, unlike the young Mossad high-speed operators who went in with blackened faces in camouflage tunics, suppressed Tavors at the ready. He was no Israeli fighter jock, those keen-eyed, Nomex-clad F-16 predators who prowled the skies, could down any MiG or put a rocket in a bull's-eye from so close to the deck that the engine blasts riled up the dust.

"Gershon, watch your calories," was what his wife yelled to him every morning as he left his snug bungalow in Herzliya, the northern suburb of Tel Aviv, for the four-minute drive to what to him was known as the Institute while the rest of the world called it Mossad, also in Herzliya. It was a complex of buildings dominated by a black glass cube nine stories tall. It was full of cubicles, and Gershon's was on the third floor, with a window that looked out to the sea a few miles away, though the view was better from the upper floors, which he knew he would never see.

The third floor was the Anti-terror Section, and his subdivision was Economic Intelligence. In other words, the theory and practice of stuff.

For eight, sometimes ten, sometimes twenty hours a day, he methodically searched for stuff, and it was why he was as much a hunter as the special-forces op or the fighter jock. He lurked in the fringes of a thousand or so markets that could be monitored from cyberspace. The price of coffee in Jakarta, the fall of the yuan in China, the peach-harvest projections in Azerbaijan, the impact of Schwinn's new "comfo-bot-m" seat on the bicycle market, particularly as it presaged Schwinn's controversial decision to target-market the aging baby-boomer population, the cost of an RPG-7 in open trade in the tribal areas of northern Pakistan. That kind of stuff, all kinds of stuff. Melons, tennis balls, grenades, infrared sighting devices, Frisbees (a comeback? looked so for a bit, but today's reports were depressing), Maytag dishwashers in Kuwait, American varietals in the South of France (taking coals to Newcastle!), Duncan yo-yos in South Korea, black-market Duncan yo-yos in North Korea.

There was nothing arbitrary in his nosiness. International Terror fed on stuff. It needed, no matter the perpetrator, the ideological fervor or bent, a constant influx of money to keep itself on track. Money for training, money for travel, money for bribery, money for expertise, money for food and shelter; everything cost, and like General Motors, the conglomerate that was International Terror—he called it InterTer, Inc.— had been hurt badly by the recession, so it was ever on the hustle for a sugar daddy.

Any time there was an aberration, a seeming random happening outside the parameters of the established, it was an indicator that someone was moving product somewhere in some market that would result in a payoff of stuff that would be translated into currency that would purchase plastic explosive, 5.45x39mm ammo, RPGs, or even more efficient and sophisticated instruments, electronics, missiles, long-range radios, artillery, atomic weapons, anything for the destruction of fellow humans. That aberration had to be looked at, analyzed, parsed, and evaluated. Almost always it was nothing, but nobody could be sure it would always be nothing, and so the game went on, 24/7, the world over.

The intelligence agencies who fought the war had long known this, and Israel's EconIntel unit was no different, really, than those fielded by any country, but for one respect: the Israelis had a secret weapon; and its name was Gershon Gold.

Today, which was like every other day, turned out to be the day of COMEX. He selected his markets randomly, off a simple program he had devised that pulled names out of a big hat. It had to be random. It couldn't be by pattern, because a pattern could be detected, and any savvy programmer counterplaying him could recognize him. Not that there was anywhere on earth an indication that such a counter-programmer existed, but he wanted to be thorough, careful, diligent, patient. In the long haul, that was how you won.

COMEX was the international commodities exchange, run by the New York Mercantile

Exchange. It was a total universe of stuff. Gershon attacked it.

He monitored each commodity's performance over a week, quickly translating the figures into a line graph. In units of twenty he projected those lines in space, with time (the week) as the horizontal variable and percentage change as the vertical variable. In normal operations the twenty lines should look pretty much the same, because each line reflected the wisdom of the market in representing value over the same period of time, in the same play of psychological and external factors. That is, in normal operating process, if gold went up a bit, so would tin, lemons, pork futures, and magnesium. The twenty lines, though at different value sectors, would pretty much reflect one another. That was defined as normality, especially when Gershon incorporated his proprictary algorithms to factor in weather and other variables not under anyone's influence.

You could easily engineer a program to certain parameters, and it could mechanistically make this sort of examination and notify its keepers of something unusual, but it really needed a human eye, a human touch, a human instinct to make the final discriminations. That was Gershon.

Twenty by twenty he went, and nowhere was there any indication of abnormality. On and on until he was done and it all seemed okay, and finally it was time to put COMEX down and come up with another market for similar scrutiny.

Except . . .

He'd noticed a tiny little something, almost, not quite a blip.

It was in a midrange cluster of twenty across the value/time index. He went back and called it up and looked very closely. It seemed fine.

But . . .

There was one line with a peak just a little bit out of scale with the echoing peaks above and below.

Hmmm.

Is this real? Is it anything? Could it be anything?

He moused to that one line, selected it, and made the others go away.

A single line zagged across the graph.

He checked the legend.

PL.

What the hell was PL? The slightly higher value meant that someone had bought more PL than the market average. He went back through iterations, looking at the performance of PL over the past year, week by week, and in no single week had there been as big a leap.

What was going on with PL?

Actually, better start somewhere else.

What was PL?

It was platinum.

CHAPTER 17

The Town Hall
Ivano-Frankivsk
THE PRESENT

Y ou had to hand it to the Poles: they really knew how to design an ugly building.

In 1936 they had somehow come up with the atrocity of the Stanislav Town Hall, grotesquely angled as if in homage to some science-fiction idea of the future, which climbed cube by severe cube to ultimately a spindly if angular five-story tower, like a child's ABC-block construction, but great for flying flags of bright national identification. It was a natural for the bloodred swastika flag that had rippled from its top between 1941 and 1944.

"In '43, they killed twelve thousand Jews in this town. Shot them all. Terrible, terrible," Reilly said.

Swagger had no comment. There was no comment to be made.

"Then in '44, when the Russians were pushing the Nazis out of Ukraine, this is where they came to nest as a last stopping point. Groedl's Reichskommissariat office was here."

It was near nightfall. They'd returned from Yaremche and were now in Ivano, checked in to the Nadia Hotel, and out for a walk, looking and trying to imagine the Nazi banners, the Kübel and the Horch cars, the ranks of black-uniformed SS creeps, the dowdy civilians of the Reichskommissariat who had administered lebensraum for their leader, all of the theater of history.

"Want to go in?" she said.

"Don't see no point."

"I understand. I don't want to go in, either."

"We have to go back to Yaremche. Walk that town site more, get up on the mountain trails. You have hiking boots?"

"Yes, and you still have to tell me where she got herself a new rifle."

"As soon as I know, you're number one on the list. Dinner?"

"Always."

They walked the few blocks to what was now Independence Street, which had been Stalin Boulevard, Hitlerstrasse, Warsaw Avenue, and Budapest Utcanev in its time, and found a sidewalk café among the many that had turned the now-pedestrian boulevard so pleasant.

They ate meat, somewhat silently.

"You know what?" said Swagger. "I ain't got no ideas at all."

"Let's do a game called 'know/assumption,' okay? What we do know against what we think we know."

"Sure. Know Mili disappeared in July 1944. Assumption: She was sent to Ukraine on a special mission, according to other sniper Slusskya. Assumption: Guy who sent her had to be this Krulov, Basil, Stalin's Harry Hopkins, because he had the power. Known: Nothing. All circumstantial. Known: There was a Nazi ambush of partisans in the Carpathians above Yaremche, killing a lot, recovering weapons. Assumption: the partisan unit was betrayed; that's based on my interp of the Twelfth SS war diary, which documents too big a haul for the meet-up to be by chance. Assumption: Krulov betrayed her. Because he was the only guy capable of betraying her, being the biggest guy on board. He was also the only guy capable of erasing her records in Russia, with the clout to have them erased in Germany, independently of each other. No motive yet. Next assumption: She escaped. Next week or so, nothing. Know: July 26, 1944, day big Russian offensive kicks off. Know: There was an atrocity in Yaremche, one hundred and thirty-five people killed. Assumption: That was retaliation for what we think was an assassination attempt, unsuccessful, on Groedl's life. Assume Mili was killed or captured and later killed. Know: Germans hit the road, Groedl and the Police Battalion assholes were—okay, here's something. I got something."

"Let's hear."

"Krulov. Who was he? What happened to him? What would his motive have been? Maybe that's where we ought to go next. Can Will handle that?"

"I see nothing wrong with that, except that if I give him Krulov to investigate, he will divorce me. He does have a real job, you know."

"He's a pro. Won't faze him in the least."

"I'll point that out to him tonight in an e-mail."

They paid and got up and headed down the street toward the Nadia. The town was pleasant, pinkish Georgian buildings, dapples of light overhanging the street of walkers, the cafés abustle. He thought of beer. Not a good idea. He turned elsewhere in his ruminations.

It was a blur, the rush of darkness, maybe a little noise announcing acceleration, but somehow he picked it up in his peripheral, got a hand on her to pull her back and pivoted, all this in some kind of supertime where he hadn't been in years, and then the car hit him.

CHAPTER 18

Town Hall
Stanislav
JULY 1944

As instrumentality," said Dr. Groedl, "I find it uninteresting. Guns have never particularly inflamed my imagination. I suppose the meaning is that she is now unarmed, she will need to seek another rifle, and this might be used against her, is that so?"

"Yes sir," said Captain Salid.

The senior group leader–SS was holding the Model 91 rifle with the PU sight affixed by means of a solid steel frame that held the optic tube to the axis of the bore.

"I would imagine ours are more graceful, more modern. It is my understanding that this weapon is over fifty years beyond its design, is that true?"

"Yes sir. It was adopted by them in 1891."

"So it was already fourteen years old at the time of the Russo-Japanese war," said Groedl. "Please explain to me why we are losing to people as technologically inferior as these."

"There are so many more of them, sir. That's all."

"All right, good point. We have the best

machine guns in the world, and we can't kill them fast enough even then."

As happened so frequently, Salid was not sure if a response was required; he didn't know the etiquette here, another function of his exoticism among the rigorously rational, cold-blooded Aryans.

"All right," said the doctor, having lost all interest in the rifle, "data. Numbers. Please, precision in all, as I have said to you before."

"Yes, Dr. Groedl. In the ambush, twenty-four male and eleven female bandits. Then in six villages, ten hostages apiece. The villages were those along the Yaremche road through the mountains that have trails leading up to our ambush zone. We believe there were several survivors who would naturally turn to the villages for some kind of shelter. We further believe that we arrived before any survivor and established by example a serious argument against assisting them."

Captain Salid was nervous. He was positive his ambush had been a success, but he was afraid the escape of *Die weisse Hexe* would count against him, when clearly it was not his fault. It wasn't even certain the woman was in the column, and no witnesses were alive to testify. Alas, none of the female corpses suggested unusual beauty.

The doctor of economics wrote down Salid's figures in a little book, his concentration complete. After a bit, he turned from his desk and slid his roller-borne chair a bit to the right, turned to a calculating machine on a worktable. He bent over it, punching the keys, and finally cranked the lever, unspooling, accompanied by a drama of clackity-clacking, a long strip of paper, covered with blue figures. He tore it off and examined it closely. Data, data.

"You are like a lion who feeds off the fringes of the herd," he said. "As long as he doesn't take above a certain replaceable level, his attacks are fundamentally meaningless and the herd hardly notices him. At some level, instinctual I am sure, every social unit, man or animal, fears its own extinction. That is, it fears reaching a level where there are not enough surplus females to renew at a certain predictable rate that year; at that point, the tribe, the pride, the swarm, the herd, the platoon, ceases to exist conceptually. Thus it cannot cohere, thus anarchy, dissipation, abandonment, and abrogation of the natural impulse. Anomaly."

Salid nodded.

"The smaller village, Yasinia, is of no concern," continued Dr. Groedl. "But the other five, especially Yaremche, are of concern because they are large enough, theoretically, to harbor secret sympathizers for the bandits. Are you following me, Captain Salid?"

"Yes sir. But what I do not understand is whether you are pleased with my first operation or if you believe I have failed. I have to know what attitude to convey to my men, and I need to have a feel for what satisfies you."

"What is 'pleased'? Who is to say what is pleasing and what is not? How does one distinguish the threshold between that which is pleasing and that which is not? I have no idea. I prefer to deal in data. It's pure and clean."

"Yes," said the captain.

"It's all science, math. That is the scientific basis of our race purification philosophy and it is moral, therefore, because it is mathematically— that is, scientifically—based. We do what the data commands. Do you see?"

Salid did not, even if he smiled contritely, trying to make some sort of human contact with the little adding machine in a fat man's body that sat across from him in his office at the Town Hall, beneath some rather gaudy Reich banners.

"Now," Groedl said, "I want you to go back to your quarters and have a nice rest."

"Sir, our quarters are not—"

"I know, I know. But that will be changed. You and your men need more space, more comfort, as an indication of your importance to the overall aims of our policy. For you, the Andrewski Palace."

This was an aristocratic manse dating from half a dozen or so centuries ago, a vast, crenellated, walled castle built not to withstand war but to withstand envy, in its way as destructive as war. A line of Polish dukes had lived there, controlling all of South Ukraine. Some may have lived there as penniless and pathetic wards of the state after the revolution, until The Boss hauled them off to the camps during his occupation of 1939 to 1941, ending the six-hundred-year-old Andrewski line in the form of a ninety-three-pound zek. But the Russians hadn't controlled the palace long enough to destroy its grandeur, and it remained the showplace of Stanislav.

"I know, I know," continued Dr. Groedl, "the Andrewski Palace is currently occupied by parachutists, a specialist unit once a part of the 2nd Parachute Infantry Division, now in Normandy, called Regiment 21. It no longer exists. Its survivors are called Battlegroup Von Drehle. They have uniforms and helmets like no others. Not Waffen-SS, not even army. Rather, Luftwaffe. A thorn in my side. They're much favored by that damned Von Bink. These fellows are out on some sort of job now, but when they return, I will order Von Bink to requarter them in a field adjacent to Fourteenth Panzergrenadier. Digging their own latrines and pitching their own tents and unspooling their own K-wire will do them some good, I think. Meanwhile, Police Battalion goes into Duke Andrewski's house and is to enjoy the comfort it offers. They will need the rest for the days ahead."

"That is very good news, Dr. Groedl."

There was, it could not be denied, something rather impressive about Dr. Groedl. Max Weber called it charisma, a certain aura that all who came in contact with him felt and responded to. It was his utter seriousness, his utter belief, his uncanny gift for memorizing vast amounts of data. When he spoke, it was as if he were inviting you into an elite circle who knew vastly more than others. It was said that when he taught economics in Munich in the twenties, a young artist named Schicklgruber used to hear his lectures and leave, inspired. Later, that young man was able to reward the professor with a position of power in the government and crusade he had begun.

"Tomorrow, I am giving a dinner party in my suite at the hotel. Seven P.M. You have dress uniform?" he said to Salid.

"Of course."

"Seven P.M., bathed, shaved, dress uniform. Meet the generals and the department heads who control what is left of German Ukraine. Impress them, they will give you everything, put you at the head of every line. Tomorrow night I will introduce you to an officer, and if you charm him, those three panzerwagens will be permanently assigned to Police Battalion, no waiting, no explanation, no competing interests in the dispatch pool. They are simply yours, with endless fuel and ammunition, so that you may operate with impunity."

"Excellent, sir."

"And the day after, it is time to expand the base line. I want you back to those five villages along the Yaremche Road, and this time I want twenty hostages shot in each. That should get their attention and their obedience. I want you to make them look extinction in the eye. Their genes will discipline them. It is bred into them to fear and obey. We merely confirm the natural principles."

Altitude four thousand feet above Yaremche

She made him repeat it, and the Teacher translated from the Ukrainian.

"I am to move down the mountainside and, in the dark, enter the village of Yaremche. I will make my recon at dark. Three nights, no rush. I will avoid any contact. I will move silently. I will attempt to recover a rifle."

"What kind of rifle?" Petrova demanded.

"One with a telescope."

"Finally, information. Do the Germans occupy the village? Or do they patrol through it and, if so, how often, in what strength? What is their demeanor? Are they combat-ready, as we might say, or is it a joke to them and they slack off and never get out of their heavy vehicles?"

The Teacher translated.

"I know you'll succeed," she said.

The Peasant seemed pleased, and he ducked out through the entrance of the cave and slipped away.

"The chances of him obtaining a rifle with a telescope are almost negligible," said the Teacher. "You know that."

"He needs an ideal, that's all."

"Only the German army has them, and I'm betting within it, only specialized units. They're not apt to leave any about. They don't forget to put their toys away."

"If he can just get a half-decent, not-too-beaten-up Mosin or even a German Mauser, I believe I could make that shot from a hundred yards with open sights. It is much the same, finding the position, achieving the concentration, controlling the breathing, willing the trigger finger."

"The telescope gives you two hundred yards more distance, maybe two-fifty. It gives you a chance to escape. Believe me, you do not want to be caught by the SS after killing one of their leaders."

"And so I die. It's a war. It happens all the time."

"I believe an executioner's shot behind the ear would be the most you could hope for. That would be a happy ending. I doubt you'd find a German so inclined. The reality is likely far more unpleasant."

"No point of thinking so negatively," she said. "At Kursk, even as we closed with the Tigers, we had no negative thoughts. We thought only of duty."

"I envy you such purity. Anyhow, it's time to rest."

"Thank you, I will," she said.

The Teacher took her by the arm, to help her to move, and the next thing he knew, he was blinking stars from his head while feeling the press of something hard and keen-edged against the precise part of his throat where, less than a quarter inch away behind a thin screen of flesh, his jugular throbbed.

She had turned his weight against him, dumped him swiftly to the ground, and pounced, pinning him there by force of knee jammed into his back and arm wrapped around his forehead that now held a small knife with a sharp blade against the soft, vulnerable part of his neck.

"You know much too much for a teacher, sir," she whispered. "You found me too damned easily for a teacher. Now, sir, tell me who you really are, or I'll cut the big one and watch you spurt dry, kicking, in seven seconds."

CHAPTER 19

Ivano-Frankivsk
The Street

They wanted to take him to the hospital, but it seemed pointless.

"Tell him," he said to Reilly for the policeman, "he didn't hit me. Not really. He brushed against me, I spun, I lost my balance, I fell."

An ambulance had arrived and several witnesses had gathered.

Reilly explained laboriously in Russian that, thankfully, the Ivano policeman understood.

"He wants you to tell him again."

"It was just a sloppy driver. He thought he could beat me to the space and accelerated." Swagger waited for her to catch up. "I caught him coming out of the corner of my eye and stepped back. The car didn't hit me. Its side sort of pushed against me, I felt the pressure, spun, and lost my balance. He probably didn't even know it happened."

It went on for a few minutes. No, they couldn't identify the make or color of the car, no, they didn't get a plate number. None of the witnesses cared to contribute, either, though they were curious to see how the policeman ended it with the two Americans.

As it happened, he ended it by handing Bob a carbon of a report in Ukrainian off his tablet. It appeared to be some kind of incident record, which Bob took and thanked him for, then watched him walk away. The small crowd also melted off into the night, looking, presumably, for other dramas to distract it.

They walked to the hotel, a multicolored slab of building from "Communism: The Perky Years," across the street.

"You sure you're okay? He hit you harder than you told the cop."

"Really, it's nothing," said Swagger. "I expect I'll be stiff tomorrow."

"No mountain climbing for you."

"I guess not."

"So? Did someone just try to kill us?"

"It's just on the line between murder and accident."

"But why would anyone care about something that happened in Ukraine seventy years ago with all its survivors and witnesses gone?"

"How would they even know we're looking?"

"It's not like I've been discreet. It never occurred to me. I've just done what I always do: I call sources, I check on the various Web archives of the various Russian ministries, I talk to people, I go places."

Bob pondered. "Well," he finally said, "we may have spilled somebody's vodka. Let's call Stronski."

Stronski was a former Spetsnaz sniper, a brother of the high grass and the long stalk. He'd done a lot of messy things in Afghanistan and Chechyna. The last time Swagger had been to Moscow, he and Stronski, put together by an American firearms journalist, had bonded immediately. Stronski made his living in highly questionable activities, but as Swagger now said, "Sometimes it was better to have a gangster on our side."

They sat down at a table in the hotel's outdoor bar, and Reilly fished out her notebook, found the number, and dialed it, then handed it to Swagger.

"*Da*?"

"Swagger for Stronski. He knows me."

The phone went dead.

Two minutes later it rang.

"Son of a bitch! Swagger, what you doing? You old bastard, last time I see you, the Izzys were shooting at us in the garden of Stalins."

"That was a fun day," said Swagger. He went on to tell as quickly as he could why he was where he was and why he was calling now.

"I'll be there tomorrow," said Stronski. "Stay in, don't go anywhere. Don't give the bastards another chance."

"Nah, not worth your time. We're not even sure it's a game. Here's what I need. Ask around. If someone's trying to whack me way down here in Ukraine, he'd have left tracks. Calls, associates pushed through via connections, that sort of thing. Someone hiring a freelancer. If there's any real business going on, let me know."

"This number if I get anything?"

"Affirmative."

"Also, allow me, I make some arrangements. Nice to have some way of getting out of there fast."

"We're just asking questions about stuff that happened seventy years ago."

"Pal, look at the cemeteries. The flowers are fresh. Every day, they remember. In this part of the forest, the past never goes away. It's forever."

CHAPTER 20

The Cave
Above Yaremche
JULY 1944

"Please don't cut me," said the trapped man.

"Explain or bleed," demanded Petrova.

"Look, I'll show you how cooperative I can be." He squirmed, and his arm emerged from underneath him and tossed something a few inches away. It was a small automatic pistol. "Loaded and ready, I could have shot you. I give you the gun."

Holding the knife harder against the pulsing blue line in his throat, she reached for and seized the pistol, some Hungarian miniaturized thing, managed to secure it against her leg and one-handedly pry back the slide just enough to make sure the brass of a shell glinted from the chamber.

"Try it. Shoot it off. You'll see."

She backed off, let him up. "Hands on head. Hands come off head, I shoot. Legs crossed. Legs uncross, I shoot."

"Understood. Now I—"

"Cut the shit, Teacher. Too much of it already. You found me where the Germans couldn't. You read the imprint of the tracks and concluded correctly that a panzerwagen left them. That's advanced scouting, unlikely in a schoolteacher. Who are you? Or better, who do you work for?"

"Myself," he said. "I am no agent. I have no affiliation. That is not to say I don't have a secret. I have a very deadly secret. It would kill me in days anywhere I was."

"And what is the secret? Tell me or die now, not in days. I cannot afford to make a mistake. Too much is at stake."

"In the middle of the biggest pogrom in history, I am a Jew."

"A Jew?"

"Yes, absolutely. My papers do not say it because they are not mine. My name does not reflect it because it is false. No one alive knows except you. Bak himself did not know."

"Go on."

"I am from Lviv, where the Germans did their big killing. My family, my relatives, my mother, my father, all gone. I was able to evade. I knew a man in town, a teacher of the Russian orthodox religion. It happened that we somehow resembled each other, being scrawny types with bad eyesight and no particular physical distinctions or assets and the beard further blurring the issue. While all the slaughter was going on, I made it to his house by scampering like a rat through the sewers, after cutting off my yellow star. He and his family had gone somewhere so as not to hear the gunshots of the action, and so I broke in, rummaged through his bureaus, and found an identity document. With that prize, I escaped. I lived by my wits, gradually moving west to the Carpathians, where I heard of Bak and his army. I managed, after several adventures and several near-misses, to join them, under the name on the document. There was no mechanism for him to check on the authenticity of the document. The war, you know."

"Yet in safety, you continued with your deception."

"Nowhere on earth, it seems, are Jews welcomed anymore. These Ukraines, particularly of the rural proletariat who form the bulk of Bak's group, are no friend of the Jews. Many have joined Nazi legions and become the Jews' worst persecutors, at Nazi bidding but based on their

167

own brutal nature. I did not care to make myself known to them. Brave men, yes, as you can see in our friend the Peasant, who does not know or even suspect. He has no idea I am circumcised. Not an easy deception to bring off, I might add."

She considered, then said, "I need more convincing. You still know too much, are too keen, quick, observant, like a trained intelligence operator. I can tell, I've been around them."

"You note that which is my greatest gift and my greatest curse. Yes, it turns out, I am gifted. Because I was smart, weak, not obviously a warrior type, Bak assigned me as his own intelligence officer's aide. He was NKVD, highly professional, and I learned much from him. At the same time, I had what might be called a 'feel' for the work. I come from a fur-trading family. We didn't trap, we didn't sell, we were the middlemen playing both ends against each other while keeping both in the dark. Believe me, it's a business of bluff and feint, fast reactions, quick recognition of the real, timing, timing, and oh yes, timing. Perfect training for intelligence, and I learned quickly. It happened that this officer was killed in a bridge raid, and Bak trusted me in his service, and so I became his new intelligence officer. And that is what you encounter when you see through me, not an NKVD agenda or a GRU loyalty. You're just seeing a frightened Jew."

"I suppose I could believe that story," she said. "It's crazy enough to sound real. No one would dare make up such nonsense."

"I'm trying to serve, that's all. To do my little bit."

She threw the pistol down, but he did not take it up.

"All right," she said, "employ this 'gift' you claim to possess. Impress me with an insight."

"I know through late radio reports from Red Army intelligence that the unit that ambushed us was the Police Battalion of Thirteenth SS Mountain, known as Scimitar. Specialists in anti-partisan warfare, especially in forest and mountain climes. Run by a monster named Salid, an Arab, no less, who learned his trade killing naked Jews in pits for an outfit called Einsatzgruppen D. We puzzled over the significance, and now I see it. They weren't here by coincidence. They were brought in a week ago. Specifically to catch you. What that means is the Germans knew before Bak did that you were coming."

"They knew before I did."

"Yes. And how could they know if no one here, including Bak and myself, knew you were coming? They also knew that a specialist unit with advanced skills was appropriate to the ambush. They didn't trust the local lunks."

She knew the answer. She just couldn't say it.

He did. "You were betrayed from Moscow."

"I understand that."

"Yes, and it means, very simply, at the highest of levels, one of us works for them. Whoever, this person, or so I infer, knew that the monster Groedl was a favorite of Hitler and that Hitler's irrationality would demand that Groedl be protected at all costs. Which led to special efforts to ambush not Bak, who is of little consequence, but you."

"I think I have suspected all of this," she said.

"Perhaps so. But have you considered that your escape is now a major threat to whomever the traitor is? You are the living proof that he exists, and he is trapped in a very small pond. That means the Germans will make a concentrated, labor-intensive effort to capture you. They need you alive to take you to Berlin and work on you and see what you know and to whom you have communicated your suspicions. You are enemy of the Reich number one. But it gets much worse. You are also the traitor's enemy number one. He will use his power to destroy from his end, via Russian means, to crush you. He will use NKVD, GRU, and SMERSH."

"Dear God," she said.

"You see now, as both sides conspire to kill you, that you have already in your young life managed an impressive accomplishment."

"What are you talking about?"

"You are the most hunted woman on the face of the earth. You have managed to get the two most violent governments in human history obsessed and totally committed, out of state necessity, to your destruction. That takes talent."

CHAPTER 21

Ivano-Frankivsk
THE PRESENT

The leg never bruised. But the next morning it announced that it preferred to take a day off. It ached dully from ankle to knee to steel ball in hip, which might have annoyed the steel ball, so it started hurting, too. Bob took six ibus and felt a little sick. But today was not going to be a day of running up hills. He met Reilly in the lobby with his first, most urgent question.

"You're sure you don't want me to drop you at the station and you can go back to Moscow?" he asked her. "We may be in danger."

"No, not at all. It's my story. I'm on it, I will follow it. Now it's even more interesting. What could it possibly be linked to, seventy years later, that would matter?"

They slipped into the restaurant, where a breakfast buffet was set up, and went heavily into yogurt, fruit, juice, and coffee. Then they slipped out to the secluded open-air dining section and sat in leafy splendor.

Swagger had seated himself to watch the entrance; he noted the exits, he examined the waitstaff to make sure each was familiar and dressed identically to the others, he checked everything that moved. He also secretly wished he had a gun and felt very vulnerable without one.

"No climbing today," said Reilly. "All right, there's a city not far away called Kolomiya, about thirty kilometers to the south. They have a famous Easter-egg museum."

"Great idea," Swagger said.

"What's interesting about it is that it's also got something called the Museum of the Great Patriotic War. A great collection, the guidebook says, of stuff from the war—they never forget, it never goes away, it's Ukraine, Stronski told you the flowers on the graves are always fresh, remember? Maybe there's something there that's worth seeing."

"Yeah, that's good, I like that. Plus, on the highway we get to see what's coming, what isn't. Nobody sneaks up on us."

The museum was another melancholy hall of sacrifice and valor. The partisan movement against the German invasion had been relatively successful but monstrously expensive. It was a war without prisoners, mercy, or hesitation, with atrocity common on each side. The Germans wouldn't dignify their opponents with the term "partisans" and officially called them bandits. They specifically determined that the rules of war were not to be obeyed in the matter of bandits, which let the leash off their counterterror troops for ad hoc massacres.

Walking the halls was looking into a tunnel in time, the end of which was a sepia rendition of the gallows, where the Germans hanged so many, or the pits, where they shot so many more.

"It's pretty awful," she said after another exhibit on the subject of a razed village, a community slaughtered. "It's Yaremche times a thousand, so big that there's nothing of Yaremche here. Eight hundred, six hundred, five hundred, gone in an afternoon. Yaremche's puny hundred and thirty-five don't get a mention."

One of the halls turned to the Germans and exhibited uniforms, weapons, communication gear, boots, all of it safely behind glass. Swagger stared at a dummy SS man in the spotty-leopard dapple of the late-war camouflage-pattern smock, heavy jackboots, with an MP-40 in his hands and all the right equipment in place, the bread bag, the entrenching tool, a holstered Luger, a foot of wicked bayonet, the haversack, that instantly recognizable helmet with the medieval steel flare that covered the ears and back of the neck and made every *Landser* somehow look like a Teutonic knight out to slaughter the inferior. Next to the double lightning flashes on the collar of his tunic, the emblem of a curved sword was displayed.

Bob looked at the explanation, which was in three languages. He read the English one.

> Counter-partisan soldier of SS-13th Mountain Division, Police Battalion, which was active in trans-Carpathian area in summer 1944. These men committed many atrocities and were especially feared and loathed by Ukraine citizenry.

"He's our boy," said Swagger. "He's the guy who burned Yaremche and hunted Mili."

"He's scary," she said.

"Mili knew how to deal with 'em. She did the hard work enough times. Great damn gal. Sniper-work, alone, taking fire. Still she'd put one center mass, and then he wouldn't scare nobody no more. I'd put one right between his eyes," Swagger said.

"It's still a mystery, all these years later. These people, their adventure in death. What drove them? How did so many go insane?"

It was true. It wasn't just partisan war, which can drive good men to do evil things. He knew that, had seen it. He thought: I've been on the wrong end of a partisan war. Unless you have, there's no way you can feel the rage, the frustration, the fury that the straight-ahead soldier feels for an enemy who strikes at night, melts into the trees, and smiles at you and sells you a Coke the next day. When your buddies start showing up with their noses and dicks cut off, you tend toward peevishness. It's a goddamn cesspool of bugs and leeches and rats and maggots, and it breeds atrocity, sure as hell.

This was something more. It wasn't just frustration at taking casualties from the partisans. It was something darker, more troubling, a mass descent into the conviction of superiority along some bogus grounds that led them to believe they had the moral right to the slaughter. They had a butcher's mandate. They had become death itself. After seeing so much blood, blood lost all meaning, and some limit had been broken and now there were no limits and one could kill and kill and kill. From the pits to the crushed villages to the camps, it was a melody in one dark tone.

Finally he said, "I'd like to pretend some of them didn't fall for it. They didn't all line 'em up and shoot 'em down, did they?"

"There may have been some good ones," she said.

"We could use a good guy in this story. This poor girl lost in the land of the monsters. When does the hero show up?"

CHAPTER 22

Chortkiv
Behind Russian Lines
JULY 1944

The Auntie Ju took off from the Luftwaffe airfield at Uzhgorod, flew low to the north, and banked east through a gap in the Carpathians at Tarnopol. She stayed low over the Ukraine flatlands as her pilots put her on course for Chortkiv, ten kilometers behind Red lines so that, when she reached the drop zone, she could climb to five hundred meters and let the boys out to do their jobs. She should make it fine, since there was no Soviet radar this far south of Moscow, the Red Air Force rarely flew at night, and even the anti-aircraft gunners, in this lull before the offensive everyone knew was coming, got some extra shut-eye.

What was left of Battlegroup Von Drehle fit into the one plane, though it was tight within the corrugated tin fuselage, all the boys knee to knee, facing each other in the cramped space. All wore the clipped Fallschirmjäger helmet, its flaring Teutonic rim removed so that it looked something like the leather hat the ridiculous Americans clapped to their heads when they played a game they insisted on calling football. All wore the faded "splinter" forest-pattern camo smocks, which the fellows sportingly called "bone bags," knee pads, and lace-up boots, the latter mandatory if you didn't want your shoes falling off while you floated down. All had combat harnesses and their FG-42s or STG-44s strapped across their bodies. All wore a collection of magazine pouches suspended horizontally on either side of their chests, on a kind of horse-collar shoulder harness, and in each pouch nested a box of twenty 7.92s or thirty 7.92 Kurzs. All wore RZ-20 parachutes, which made all uncomfortable, though if you were going to jump out of an airplane, you could put up with a little discomfort. All wore their parachute infantry emblems, a stylized plunging eagle in gold upon a silver wreath. All wore their seventy-five-engagement badges. All wore bread bags on slings, though loaded with M-24 grenades. All weighed a ton with all the junk on.

Some smoked, some just looked out disconsolately into the distance. Hard to read expressions, as all had smeared their faces with burnt cork, so they looked like a very bad minstrel show about to break into a lackadaisical "Old Man River." It wasn't really a group anymore, in the grand military meaning of that term, which conjured divisions and regiments and battalions, and was called one these days only as an administrative convenience. It was more of a squad, one officer, one noncommissioned officer, and thirteen men. But you couldn't say "battlesquad," as that sounded ridiculous, and these parachutists cared entirely too much about their damned dignity.

They were lean young men with the severe faces of mummies. Most had jumped into Crete with Von Drehle four years earlier. Most had served with him in Italy for a year. Most had been with him in Russia now for two. Most had been hit and come back, most had killed dozens if not hundreds of enemy soldiers, blown up every kind of structure imaginable, destroyed tanks and other armored vehicles, most could field-strip their FG-42s blindfolded in seven seconds, or throw an M24 through the door of a racing railway car forty yards away, or cut a man's throat with a yank from the blade of a gravity knife, or rescue a dictator from mountaintop imprisonment. They were very, very good; they were the best, in fact, and they were all that was left of the 21st Parachute Battalion of 2-Fallschirmjäger, one of the storied airborne divisions of the Reich.

They were also sick to death of all this shit. Really, three and a half hard years of war, who wouldn't be? One had been wounded six times, most between four and five. Von Drehle himself had been to the hospital four times, once on Crete, once in Italy, and twice in Russia.

He was not sure if he was a captain or a major, as the promotion had been promised but the paperwork possibly lost, though it was not that important. People usually called each other by first name in the Green Devils, and everybody knew who the bosses were. He also had a great many medals, although he couldn't tell you what they were. He'd once been somebody's idea of the ideal and had his pix in all the rags and was the closest thing the Germans came to an Errol Flynn, with appallingly handsome features, a ginger smudge of mustache, and wavy blond hair. The nose and the cheekbones seemed to have been designed by slide rule, and you could not take a bad picture of him. He was very pretty, but he could fight.

He was used to being famous, loved, and admired. Before the war he'd been a racing driver for Mercedes and had finished third in the Monaco Grand Prix in 1938, at the age of twenty-one, in his W154 "Silver Arrow," a ballistically shaped high-velocity screamer of an automobile. He liked the thrill of speed, a perfect outlet for his excessive hand-eye coordination, his overbusy intellect, his quick-as-death reflexes, his extraordinary vision, and his insane bravery. He liked battle for exactly the same reasons, at least the first three years of it.

"Karl, how long you figure?" asked his oberfeldwebel, or staff sergeant, Wili Bober.

Von Drehle flipped his wrist to look at the Italian frogman watch he wore, on the theory that if it operated underwater, it would probably operate in battle.

"I have 0115," he said. "Didn't Von Bink say the jump estimate was around 0130?"

"I can't remember," said Wili. "I wasn't paying attention."

"I wasn't paying attention, either. Is this one a bridge or a railhead?"

"Hmmm," said Wili Bober, "maybe I'd better ask one of the fellows."

They laughed. It was a game between them to see who could affect the sloppiest nonchalance about the mission. Sometimes senior officers overheard and misunderstood; Von Drehle once had to go to a general to get Bober off charges.

Of course they knew. At Chortkiv, a three-arch stone bridge over the River Seret had served to funnel Soviet elements up to the line for the offensive for a week now, though at a typical niggardly Russian pace. There was no Luftwaffe except beat-to-shit transport buggies like this Auntie Ju here, so it couldn't be bombed, and it was out of artillery range. Now the 2nd Ukraine Guards Army had been ordered into the area, and it was known to have six armored divisions, about six hundred T34s and tank destroyers, all ready to go. The four hundred tanks on this side of the river could be turned back by Von Bink's

14th Panzergrenadiers and Muntz's 12th SS Panzer, but not a thousand. Ergo, someone had to blow up the bridge.

Bober removed his water bottle, unscrewed the cap. "Schnapps. Very good. From some girl, last leave, a thousand years ago. Somehow it got through," he said, offering it to Von Drehle.

"Ah. The blur. Most helpful. What a superb soldier you are, Wili." He took the jug and sent a fiery splash down the throat. Yes, the mallet hit him hard, easing his nerves, slightly defracting the low lights of the aircraft interior, softening the vibrations of Auntie Ju's three engines.

"When we finish this one, we'll kill the whole bottle."

The cabin door opened and the copilot leaned out and shouted over the roar of the engines, "Karl, we're on our final run and will be climbing to altitude in about three minutes."

"Got it," said Karl. He turned to Wili. "It's time."

Wili nodded. "I'll tell the fellows," he said.

Wili was the wise elder of Battlegroup Von Drehle. He'd been there from the start, done all, seen all, survived all. He was the one with six wound stripes. He was twenty-four.

He stood against the sway and vibe of the plane, oriented himself, and grabbed the rail that ran down the top center of the fuselage.

It was enough signal. The young men tossed

out cigarettes; a few crossed themselves or at least looked skyward under the impression that the Almighty still had a rooting interest in the fate of the last Fallschirmjäger in South Russia; all clambered heavily to feet, bearing their load of clanking equipment. All secured themselves by grip to the ceiling rail and hooked up.

There was too much noise and vibration for Von Drehle to give any kind of speech, even if he'd had the pep, but as he slid down to the front of the line, he tapped each of the fellows on the shoulder and gave him a wink or a nudge. They seemed to like that, though how could anyone really tell with the darkened, greasy faces?

He arrived at the jump hatch far down the fuselage, where a crewmember had already placed himself to pull it open on the green light. This boy looked about thirteen. God, were they raiding kindergartens these days? At least this one had gotten a fairly cushy job in the Luftwaffe and wasn't perched on some penal battalion PAK 8.8 waiting for the arrival of several hundred 34s, plus an entire army of drunken peasants with bayonets.

Cinching his static line to the rail, Von Drehle looked back and saw fourteen pairs of eyes, no features, fourteen helmet silhouettes, fourteen fists locked around the rail, fourteen plumes of breath. He also saw the tube of a Panzerschreck, the German version of the American bazooka, useful to open Red sardine cans but a pain in the ass to carry. It weighed a ton, and some poor bastard had to jump with it. Who was on it this time? It seemed like it was Hubner's turn.

"Green Devils, one-eyed Wotan himself salutes you!" he shouted, putting a fist to his plunging eagle badge and saluting, a tradition, and though nobody could hear him, they shouted back, in unison, the same imprecation; he couldn't hear them, either.

The plane suddenly seemed to lift, the pilots got it to altitude in just a few seconds, the light went green, the young man pulled mightily and got the hatch open against the suction of the wind.

Von Drehle stepped into the cold air, went into the spread-eagle as the wind hit him, felt the rush of the fall as gravity claimed him and he had a giddy second of weightlessness—it still thrilled him—and the battering of the propwash against his face. The tail boom sailed by and his static line snatched the RZ-20 canopy from its packing and another second later he was jerked heavily as the canopy took on a full load of suspending atmosphere. Below him, dark and quiet, was Russia.

One of the boys got lost. He just never joined up with the main group in the target zone, a pasture seven kilometers of rural landscape from the bridge itself. Von Drehle hated to lose men. He had lost so many! He hated it! A certain part of him wanted to abort the job right there, send out search parties, find the soldier, and head straight back to his own lines. But he couldn't do that.

"Maybe he'll catch up to us," Wili Bober said.

Everyone knew this to be unlikely. Dieter Schenker, lance corporal, veteran of Italy and Russia, three wounds, two Iron Crosses, was almost certainly hanging upside down in a tree with his neck or his back broken. If conscious, he would have taken out his gravity knife and cut his own wrists, to bleed out in quiet comfort. If the Russians found him, they might take some bayonet sport with him before killing him. That's the kind of war it was.

The second thing that went wrong was the map. It took them on detours around two villages that brought them hard against infantry campgrounds, where Ivan had put some of his six billion or so soldiers to rest for the night before moving closer to the front lines for the big show upcoming.

Battlegroup Von Drehle had to detour from two detours, and that cost time. The point was to get to the bridge well before dawn, eliminate any sentries, rig the explosives and leave a timed fuse, and be some kilometers away when the fireworks went off. This fantasy disappeared almost instantly—old racing adage: no plan survives the first lap—and they didn't get there until the sun began to flare over the edge of the world. So it would be a daylight job.

Fortunately there was foliage along the riverbank, and Ivan hadn't seriously considered a bridge-blowing raid this far behind the lines. He was getting overconfident with his billions of men, millions of tanks, and thousands of shiny new American trucks to spare him bootleather. Well, that was his big mistake. The parachutists, moving stealthily through the heavy underbrush along the bank, were able to get themselves to the bridge. Now they gathered in its lee, could see the sandbags and K-wire Ivan had dumped and strung nonchalantly, more as ceremony than as tactical necessity.

Karl took a quick look and saw what he expected; across the river, the town of Chortkiv, mostly shabby buildings and muddy streets, deserted in the early morning, though Red Army trucks had been parked here and there and presumably their inhabitants had taken shelter in the buildings. Nothing stirred. On this side of the river would be more but less of Chortkiv, its "outskirts," if you will, a couple of buildings of whatever agricultural purpose, maybe some of those typical Ukraine steep-pitched, thatch-roofed huts. Again quiet, a few Red trucks parked here and there.

And up above, on the bridge itself? Couldn't be much in the sandbag nest Ivan had built as a sentry post, more a place for the guards to sit and doze a quiet night well out of the combat zone. So it would be just a few seconds of helter-skelter to reach the sentries and, at least in theory, dispatch them silently.

At this point, communication was mostly by hand gesture. No chatter, and all the boys knew the language.

Four men, Karl signaled, sentry elimination. He and—he pointed to three really good boys, but all were really good when you got down to it—as the designated throat cutters. Then he indicated that two of those four would cross underneath the bridge and come up on the other side for whatever was there. All four would push across the bridge, which didn't appear to have a sentry post at the other end, and set up with their FG-42s or STG-44s. If assaulted from that direction, they would serve as the first line of defense.

He designated four more as demolition party, with the explosives genius Deneker calling the shots. Nothing fancy here, nobody was going over the side by rope and pulley to wire Cyclonite under the arches. Instead, the four would gouge into the bridge surface with their entrenching tools and excavate as deep a cavity as possible. They would pound the Cyclonite—which in demolition form was a kind of gloppy dough carried in two five-pound canvas sacks—into the cavity and leave a No. 8 blasting cap shoved into it, wired with det cord. The package would be wrapped in det cord, the cord then run back across the bridge to safety, where it was crimped into another No. 8. At go time, Deneker would light the safety fuse into the No. 8, which would go off like a firecracker, ignite the det cord— PETN explosive packed around a wire, going kaboom at twenty-one thousand feet per second—the det cord would burn to the main charge in a microsecond and light off that No. 8, which would make the big wad of Cyclonite vaporize the bridge. It had worked all over Russia and Italy, there was no reason why it wouldn't work today. The ten pounds should do the job nicely.

But the next part was a little dicey. The fourteen parachutists—Schenker still missing—couldn't fall straight back along the road on foot, as they'd be intercepted by infantry closing from the flanks. Even as stupid as the Russians were, they'd figure the way out would be to exfiltrate along the riverbank, but they could also run an intercept on that plan and bring fire from the opposite side of the river. The only feasible escape method was to commandeer one of the trucks, disable the others, drive like hell in the aftermath of the blast, ditch it somewhere unseen, and slip back by night across German lines. Some plan. Von Drehle knew it stank, but there wasn't much he could do except refuse to do it, which would get him shot. Even Von Bink would have to shoot him.

Hmmm, too much sun already, though it was still unseen at the rim of the wheat fields in the distance, announcing its presence only by its penumbra.

He nodded. He and his three co-killers slipped off their rifles and put their helmets on the ground. Each removed a gravity knife from a pocket, and with the push of a lever and a flick of the wrist, each popped four inches of the best Sollingen steel—*Rostfrei*, it said on the blade— into the cool air of morning.

Each, as a matter of fact, hated knifework. It was awful. It was always intimate and messy and left regret and depression and self-loathing. It wasn't worth going through for any nutcase paperhanger from Austria, that was for sure, but only out of duty to some other thing, variously defined as the Fatherland or Greater Germany but really just the other guys in the unit, whom you didn't want to let down.

Karl gave a last-second nod to each man, then turned to the two headed under the bridge. He held up two hands, six fingers, made an O with one, meaning sixty seconds, and then nodded a final time, and off they scooted.

One-one-thousand, two-one-thousand, and on and on he went, just waiting in the cool morning air, in the soft breeze, in the gray light, licking his lips a little. It was always like this before the flag dropped, a dry swallow, a feeling of dread and excitement, too and then—

—fifty-nine-one-thousand, sixty-one-thousand, and he was pulling himself up the slope, his limbs filling with energy and purpose, around the bridge wall, and into the sandbag construction, where his noise and energy alerted a man at least enough to turn to face the death approaching him. An older fellow with a pipe and an innocent farmer's look, even if he had a rifle; he wore a bandolier and a khaki side cap with black infantry piping and a red star and the pullover khaki shirt. His mouth came open as this wild apparition, blond of hair but black of face, with a knife gleaming in the light, closed down on him, his pipe bobbled, and Karl stabbed him in the throat.

It was horrible. Karl heard the gurgle as the blood filled the larynx, drowning any outcry, and then was on him totally, forcing him into the sandbags, stabbing him again and again in the throat and neck while at the same time having jammed his other hand into the mouth, just in case. In and out, in and out, in a killing frenzy, shutting him down, *die! die! die! damn you!*, feeling the blade sink in, occasionally glance off fibrous internal structures, occasionally slice something gelid and viscous, until the struggle beneath became tremors and the tremors became shivers and the shivers became nothing. Too close, close enough to see the poor bastard's face, feeling the hot blood pour out, sometimes a sundered artery forcing a little bit of squirt. You couldn't do it without Russian blood getting everywhere. And the poor bastard always squealed, wept, pissed, and shat as he died. Karl pulled back, let the man fall, and turned exactly as his partner in the pit finished sentry number one, having made exactly the same kind of mess, having besmeared himself with blood across arms and wrist and hands. There was a Degtyaryov light machine gun resting on the sandbag wall and a few Russian pineapple grenades, mostly, Karl guessed, for show. The gun might come in useful.

By this time the other fellows were up next to him, and someone handed him his FG-42 and helmet. No words were spoken, and he made some sort of follow-me gesture, nothing dramatic, and began to sprint across the bridge, feeling his three companions behind him.

It was utterly still. From the top of the bridge's arch he could see fog still clinging to the river and some reeds in the river ruffling, and down the way some crude Ivan river craft were moored— they looked prehistoric, hewn from logs by stone tools—drifting on their tethers. He felt his Fallschirmjäger helmet slop around on its straps, his grenades and rucksack jostle, his shoulder harness of magazine pouches vibrate, his Belgian

Browning 9mm pistol jiggle in the holster, his heavy boots dig into the softness of the roadway. Then he reached the bridge end, slid behind a nest of sandbags buttressing the stone wall, found a shooting position, and hoisted the FG to his shoulder.

No targets. Nothing. All quiet in Chortkiv. Now, if the guys would get the hole dug, the shit planted, they could trip the fuse, snatch a truck, and get the hell out of—

Where did the first shot come from? It was unclear and would never be known. It hit in the roadway, lifted a geyser of debris. The next thing, it seemed the air filled with light. The Reds were firing tracers, mostly, from the sound, out of their tommy guns, and a latticework of incandescence seemed to replace the weather, or rather, became the weather, and everywhere bullets struck they stirred a pulse of disturbance, blurring the air with their grit and whirl.

"Fuck," Karl said. "Fire when you have targets," he yelled, although pointlessly.

At the far end of the street, a brave Ivan tried to run to a truck and two Green Devils fired simultaneously, knocking him down. The return fire became general. By protocol, the FGs and STGs were only fired semi-auto unless in close-up assault or street battle. But that didn't mean they couldn't be fired fast and accurately, a parachutist specialty.

Indeed, the little fight became an argument of ballistics. Shooting the main battle rifle cartridge, the 7.92mm Mauser, the parachutists had the advantage of range and power, plus speed. If they could see it, they could hit it. The newer STG-44s, brought in because the FGs were getting harder to find, fired a shortened 7.92 round from an immense curved magazine and, if need be, could become real hosepipes; but at semi-auto they retained accuracy and a great deal of power. Too bad they were so goddamn big and heavy. The Ivans, on the other hand, had many of their tommy guns, and were able to put out enormous volume, but that was a pistol bullet, shaky on both range and accuracy. They could make a lot of noise, raise a lot of dust, crisscross the known world with strings of dust-puffs, but probably not hit unless lucky. So it was simple. Karl and his pals had to stay calm and cool and shoot well. No bursts, just well-aimed rifle fire, shooting at flashes and shadows and bringing people down. But mainly making it bad math on a cost-risk analysis basis to venture any closer.

Both the FG and the STG were a hundred years ahead of their time. For the FG, it took great discipline to master the fierce recoil of such a powerful cartridge in such a light-framed weapon, but its straight-line construction, ingenious spring-buffered stock unit, and muzzle brake helped enormously. Its signature was the weirdly radical angle of its handgrip, almost 60 degrees to the receiver, a cosmetic trope that made it an instant classic, but it was said to be engineered that way for shooting while descending. It looked cool as hell, out of Buck Rogers by way of art deco. It had pop-up sights, fiendishly clever in design, folding bayonet spike, a built-in bipod, and a horizontal magazine feed system located for perfect balance right above the grip. Someone once called it a seven-pound MG-42. Fired at full rip it was a brutal beast to control, but the para-chutists mostly operated it on semi-automatic, where its rifle round could be used for maximum accuracy and high rate of fire. The Green Devils had been using it for nearly a year and loved it dearly.

The poor fellows with the STGs were always trying to trade up to FGs, but their owners would not let them go, and kept them going with tender care and lots of Blu-Oil. The STGs were still very fine weapons, if hideous to look at by purists' standards, with stamped metal and crude finish and aggressively ergonomic design principles turning them into the sort of ugly/beautiful construction that was entirely mystifying. Their issue was the difficulty one had firing from prone with that immense magazine, as well as the temptation of the selective fire, which could turn them into ammo-gobbling beasts and leave the poor parachutist empty of rounds in a minute if he didn't exercise fire discipline.

Meanwhile, across the river all the other parachutists joined in, again the game being sustained by accurate singles, not magazine-eating bursts. Then someone had the intelligence to gather up the Degtyaryov and swing it into action. Whoever he was, he arched pan after pan of 7.62 x 54 over the advance guard and along the buildings and through the windows. He could afford to burn ammo because he had no plans to carry the damned thing out with him.

"Hurry up, goddammit!" Karl yelled, but he couldn't really complain, for the guys digging the hole were wide open to fire, whacking away with shovels at a desperate pace, while all around them bullets struck and screamed off the bridge's stone walls or off its roadway, unleashing gallons of energized dust. They had better things to do than listen to him.

He ran dry, carefully made the effort to return a used magazine to its pouch—also protocol, since the mags were increasingly hard to come by—and was inserting a new twenty when he saw it coming around the corner.

It was a T-34, Soviet main battle tank.

"What the fuck is that guy doing here?" Karl said.

CHAPTER 23

The Museum
Kolomiya
THE PRESENT

The last hall was lighter than the others, as a skylight let the sun's illumination pour in through the roof. Swagger quickly saw why. It was an exhibition of paintings, grandly realistic things that seemed from afar compositions depicting various highlights in partisan battles against the Germans. He went to the first, called *Our Fellows at the Bridge over the Ravokokov*, and examined it.

It looked like a scene from an extremely expensive movie, everything in perfect focus whether it was ten feet from the painter or a thousand. In the center, a bridge split in two as a fiery blot of explosive took its center and it deposited into midair a German locomotive and several armored cars. Screaming German soldiers fell off of it, sure to die when they hit the rocks below. In the foreground a partisan dynamiter exulted as he looked at what he had wrought, having just plunged the handle on a detonating mechanism; around him, handsome men with Red tommy guns leaped and smiled in celebration at the defeat and destruction of the train.

"They call it socialist realism," said Reilly. "Very big under Stalin. Art was for the purpose of celebrating and advancing the state. Many of the big moments are commemorated in artworks."

"The guy sure was careful," said Bob. "There's four cooling slots in the sleeve of a PPSh-41, and damned if he hasn't got all four of 'em. Also, he's got the bolt back, which is how they'd carry it for fast shooting, and that opens the ejection port on the top for the empties to fly out, and dammit, he's got the bolt back and the port open. He may have been a tommy gunner himself."

"I'm sure the Ministry of Culture and Moral Improvement provided him with one to copy. They may have even blown up a bridge and crashed a locomotive so he could get it right."

Swagger walked on, encountering dozens of perfect little war scenarios as depicted by state-sponsored artists of the day. Each one boasted the same immaculate research, the absolute perfection in equipment—T34Rs, not T34Cs, when appropriate—and the same crew of happy, handsome partisans celebrating this or that triumph over the German beast. The artists—it all looked like it was painted by the same very busy guy, but indeed there were at least a dozen in this hall—had the same range of attributes: a good mechanical draftsman's sense of machinery, weapon, aircraft, structure, and vehicle, and a good feel for weather. Skies were mottled with storm clouds, snow scythed down horizontally so that you could feel the ice pellets stinging your face, the wind was cruel and cutting. The illusion broke down slightly at the humans, who seemed to share pretty much the same face and posture. Hands good, particularly when gripping weapons, torsos a bit awkward, as if he didn't quite under-stand the underlying struts of the body, legs seeming to get in the way.

There was no fear, no squalor, no fatigue, no filth, no sweat, no despair, all common to Swagger's experience of war. Also the snow was pristine where depicted, and since Russia was a wintry sort of hell, there was a lot of it depicted. No dogs or men had pissed in it, there wasn't a sense of the eternal stench of war, which was a miasma of burned powder, blood, shit, sweat, and various kinds of rot and decomposition. No blood was seen anyplace, nor were any blasted bodies, nor grievous wounds to face or head or limb or gut.

"It's all kind of phony to you, I suppose," she said.

"Yeah, but I get it. You don't want to tell people how it was but how they wanted it to be. Maybe the kid got a bayonet in the guts and it pulled his entrails out and he died three hours later. You don't want to tell his folks that. So you tell them

197

he got it clean between the eyes as he led the squad up the hill. The kid don't care. It's for the parents, to ease their pain, so I think it's okay in the long run."

"Too bad there's not one for Mili," she said. "*The White Witch Slays Obersturmbannführer Von Totenkopf in the Town Square at Stalingrad,* something like that."

"No snipers," he said, "it ain't that popular." He was thinking, The truth is, after the war is over, people get sort of nervous about snipers. Unlike taking the hill or blowing up the tank, the sniper works in cold blood. It's murder. Yeah, I wouldn't have said that twenty years ago, and I never allowed myself to think of it that way, because it's just the kind of doubt that'll get you killed in war, but still and all, I know, I face it, it's real, it's just cold-blooded killing.

She nodded somewhat glumly.

"Okay," he said, "that was a downer, wasn't it? Let's get out of here and get back to the hometown. Have a nice dinner. Then tomorrow we can go mountain climbing."

"You got it."

They turned and walked out, and then Reilly said, "You know what? That sort of sniper queasiness you just mentioned, that's late, isn't it?"

"What do you mean?"

"I mean nobody felt that way after World War II. That was a Vietnam thing."

"I suppose. After Vietnam, I got drunk for fifteen years or so, so I don't exactly recall."

"Maybe the same thing happened here after Afghanistan. Before, 'partisan sniper' was a popular subgenre, but as a new generation came along, the authorities or whoever decided to downplay it."

"What are you thinking?"

"Maybe there's a room in this very museum full of sniper art."

"Well," said Bob, "let's find somebody to ask."

CHAPTER 24

Chortkiv
The Bridge
JULY 1944

The tank lumbered closer, impervious to the clangs and prangs and dings of the parachutist bullets, which glanced off, harming only the dull green paint job. The T-34 was a monster, a thirty-six-ton concoction of steel domes resting on immense treads, capable of crushing anything it chose to roll itself over. Yet it, too, was vulnerable, with a tendency to burst into flame if appropriately pricked. But nobody had told this tank sergeant.

His vehicle ground onward, devouring the earth beneath it, setting it to shiver. Its hull machine gun mounted to the left of the center of the frontal armor plate fired spastically, sending out a fan of high-velocity destruction, though without much accuracy. Another flaw: the gunner didn't have a lot of visibility when the tank was all buttoned up. Though a huge battle beast capable of massive destruction, it was hampered by poor visibility in close-quarters combat; it could destroy enemy panzers but a few scampering rats like the Green Devils, not so much. It felt its way toward the bridge, making corrections in angle every few yards. It was like the blinded Cyclops trying to kill Odysseus's men by feel. But still, it was getting closer; it would crush them or machine-gun them to death if they ran.

"PANZERSCHRECK!" yelled Von Drehle.

Poor Hubner. He had to dislodge himself from whichever safe borough he had dipped into, lug the heavy tube of anti-tank rocket launcher to the bridge, as well as his STG-44—which bounced painfully against his body, to which it was roped by sling—then sprint the whole way over the triple arches to the sandbag fortification, which contained Von Drehle and a boy named Neuhausen, all under fire.

Yet good Green Devil that he was, that was exactly what he did, amid a storm of enemy ordnance that raised dust in clouds through which he raced. He arrived out of breath, not so much halting at destination as falling wretchedly. Ouch, that must have hurt. He lay there on his back, gulping at oxygen, oblivious to the ruckus, trying to regain dignity, clarity, and composure.

"Too bad we're out of medals, Paul," said Karl. "That deserves two or three."

"I'll take a three-day pass instead of another Iron Cross," gulped Hubner.

"Me, too," said Neuhausen. "Who needs medals?"

"Are you able to shoot?" said Karl. "Hit any-place?"

"I think I'm okay. But I don't want to shoot it. I don't know how. I was never trained. I thought my job was just to carry it."

"Can you shoot it, Neuhausen?"

"Sure, I can shoot it. But I've never shot one, either, so God knows what I'll hit. Have you shot it, sir?"

"Officers don't shoot in the German army," said Karl.

"But aren't we in the air force?" said Neuhausen.

"Excellent point," said Karl. "All right, I guess I'm nominated. Is it loaded?"

"Sort of."

"What do you mean, 'sort of'? I don't like 'sort of.'"

"The rocket is in, but the leads haven't been

connected. I'll connect them when you get it on your shoulder."

"I am full of confidence."

Von Drehle somehow got the thing off the wheezing Hubner's shoulder and transferred it to his own, settling in under it. It was not light, at twenty pounds, with a rocket inserted holding seven pounds of Cyclonite contained in an armor-piercing warhead. Its weight threw him off a bit, and he almost stumbled out of the protective lee of the sandbags. But then he had it.

He sensed Hubner behind him.

"All right, I think I did it," said the man. "I think I got the right ones connected to the right things, whatever you call them."

"Watch out. You don't want to be behind this stovepipe when I light it off."

"No sir."

"Ready?"

"All set."

"Quick, quick, quick," universal German army speak (*Hoppe, hoppe, hoppe*) for do it now, and the two men rose, FG and STG on full auto, and barked off twenty and thirty rounds apiece of suppressive. As they completed their magazines, Karl rose behind them, peering through the small opening in the blast shield appended to the muzzle of the Panzerschreck to keep the rocketeers from frying their faces off in the drama of the launch, put the crude sight on the front armor plate of the tank, which had gotten too fucking close, and squeezed the firing gap, a trigger-like device on the rear grip, which did something to a magneto—no one was sure what—with the result that an electrical current zipped through the wires to the rocket engine and set it off.

The engine was still burning as it drove the 88mm rocket from the tube, trailing a noxious spray of exhaust and flame that dilated roaringly—hence the blast shield—obscuring clarity, but the rocket hit the tank dead-on, detonated, and in a split second something inside the tank co-detonated. The explosion was tremendous, and the tank shivered as it went all Mickey Mouse on them. That is, the interior blast was so percussive that it blew the twin oval hatches of the 34 into the open position, where they stuck, giving the turret the profile of the famous cartoon rodent's circular ears. Smoke and tornadoes of flame gushed from the open orifices that Mickey's ears had revealed. It was best not to consider what was happening to the Ivans in the guts of what had become a crematorium.

"Set to blow!" came a scream from behind them.

Karl dumped the Panzerschreck, not caring whether Hubner bothered to save it, and yelled, "Fall back, fall back!"

By commander's obligation, he felt the need to

be the last across, so as his men peeled back, headed over the arches of the bridge and past the primed and set chunks of explosive buried in the roadway, he stood and fired three round bursts at the clumps of Ivans he could see moving toward the bridge through the city streets. Some he dropped, some he persuaded to think up another solution. When he ran dry, he quickly switched magazines, pulling a fresh one from the shoulder-harnessed line of pouches, even as he was moving backward step by step, aware that death whistled by and around at jet speed, protected only by the belief that God favors pretty boys. He almost made it. In fact, he had made it when something hit his water bottle hard and the shock transferred through his body, corkscrewing him down. His head hit hard against the bridge stone, and steel football helmet or not, the shock reached his brain, too. Instant headache, brief moment of where-the-fuck-am-I? confusion, the sensation of hot, thick syrup pouring through his system, making him stupid and slow. He groped, found his FG-42, meant to pull it toward him, and saw that three Ivans had made it to the bridge, seen their opportunity, and now dashed to finish him with their tommy guns.

He struggled to arm himself for the close-up gunfight, but his dull fingers couldn't find enough purchase on the FG, so he diverted to the thirteen-round Browning Grand Puissance he carried in his holster. Again the sluggish fingers wouldn't get the hasp off the holster flap.

Then suddenly the three Ivans went down, knocked asprawl from behind by a burst of fast pistol fire, and who should come hustling out of the smoke of battle, face smeared with sweat and blood, Luger with toggle locked back signifying empty magazine, but long-lost orphan of the storm Dieter Schenker, who raced to him and pulled him to his feet.

"Dieter, what are you doing on that side of the bridge?"

"I couldn't remember which side we were attacking from. I guess I got it wrong."

"Remind me to get you two or three more medals."

"Come on, Karl, we'll discuss it later. Aren't they going to blow this thing?"

"I believe so."

The two men hobbled across the bridge, sheathed by smoke from the burning T-34 and the heavy suppressive fire from the parachutists on the far side, who hammered every living thing they could see and by simple luck, which seemed always to favor the brave in war, except when it did not. At the same time, it was quite a long thirty seconds, proving the relativity of time, because to Karl it seemed like thirty years, and he was only twenty-six.

At last, more or less unscathed but for the

ringing in his ears and a variety of soon-to-sting scrapes, bruises, and contusions, he made it to the bridge's end and rolled clumsily to the left with Schenker all twisted up against him, both of them screaming, "Blow it! Blow it!"

Explosive genius Deneker lit the one-second fuse to pop the No. 8 cap, which in turn set off the det cord, which exploded its way to the ten pounds of Cyclonite wadded into the center arch of the bridge, and the world yielded to a grand clap of chaos and energy. The charisma of the explosion once again asserted itself as all fell back before the titanic rupture in the atmosphere, since when energy changes form, it's not a good thing to be too close.

The geyser speared 250 feet into the air, at the same time sending a hard surf roaring along the surface of the River Seret to shake the boats moored in oily serenity. There was a bridge at Chortkiv, and in the next nanosecond there was no bridge at all, only a sheer gap of thirty feet in the center stone arch, while all around clumps of rock and timber floated down out of the cloud that had been raised and was itself, after having reached apogee, beginning to collapse.

"Karl, Karl, are you all right?" someone was yelling into his ear. It was Wili Bober.

"Who are you?" Karl asked.

"He's concussed," somebody said.

"Well, drag him along to the truck," said Wili,

"and the rest of you, disable the ones we don't take. We've got to get out of here before Ivan figures out what's happening."

Two men more or less pulled the daffy Karl along, though in his brain fog, he had a tendency to wander off. He started noticing things of no consequence, like some placid chickens in some peasant yards, unperturbed by the human drama ongoing before them, with no comment on life, death, honor, courage, whatever; a deserted tractor, actually red, a half-hoed garden plot, a barn. Most of the grass and shrubbery needed trimming, though in summer, growth went wild. All of this was of no use to the parachutists, who ran to the four trucks parked haphazardly along the roadside, their crews having disappeared somewhere out of the free-fire zone. With no one really telling them to do so, a couple of the Green Devils ran to three of the trucks and fired a three-round burst into the engine blocks, then put a single shot through the rear tires on such an angle that it would proceed under power of its high velocity to the other tire and puncture it as well.

Someone shoved Karl into the cab of the remaining truck while talented Wili Bober cracked the plastic dashboard with his rifle butt, pulled out a wad of wires, did some diddling, and the truck shivered to life.

"Everybody aboard?" he hollered, and the truck bounced on its springs as the boys climbed on.

"Wave good-bye to the nice Russian fellows," said Wili, and cranked through the gears as the vehicle accelerated down the dust road out of Chortkiv and hurtled along through wheat fields at forty-five miles an hour. They were miles behind enemy lines, but the truth of military operations was that no land is ever completely suffused with troops. Instead, units are like amoebas sprawled across the landscape, taking up positions, intensifying in density as they get closer to the battle zone and the importance of logistics becomes paramount, with all the auxiliary units clustered close to the combat troops, but for huge amounts of area, there's really no military presence at all. The truck roared through quiet rural zones and copses of trees, once passing a Soviet truck whose driver merrily waved, causing Wili to wave back. Two things were immediately clear: Ivan wasn't quick enough to get airplanes into the air, and the Russian communications efficiency left much to be desired.

The Germans, for their part, had no idea the name of the road they were on and no idea specifically where they were headed, other than to some mythic west, defined by a line descending from around Tarnopol down to Kolomiya and even farther to Romania, that demarked the place where the two vast armies faced each other, known as a front. It might have looked coherent on the maps, but the maps were always delusionary: it was more like a random assortment of those amoebas slopped everywhere, and on any given day within the framework of operations the general east-to-west course of the war was not observed. No matter your affiliation, you might find yourself in the local theater fighting and withdrawing in any direction. In this vast zone of chaos, the parachutists were relatively unnoticed, though they knew at a certain point they'd have to get off the road, hide the truck, and find a soft place in the lines to get over to their own side. They'd done it enough times to know it could be done, even if it was never fun, because a bullet fired mistakenly by one of your own would kill you just as dead.

The key navigational instrument was the compass, which indicated the road traveled westward. That was good enough. It rolled down empty farm roads; always turning to the west and the mountains when faced with a decision, they'd be all right.

Around about now, an hour into the journey, Karl began to come out of his brain fog. "Ach," he said with a little jerk. "Where are we?"

"Who knows," said Wili. "No Ivans about, so wherever we are, it feels all right. How do you feel?"

"Like the hangover I had after the party in '38," he said. "I've got someone else's head where mine used to be, and it's stuffed with concrete."

"I've always wanted to ask," said Wili. "Did you actually sleep with Ginger Rogers?"

"A gentleman never tells," Karl said. "I will say, though, I had a drink with her at a Monaco club and she was delightful, like all of them I suppose, somewhat more human in the flesh than on the screen. Got any Bayer?"

"In my kit. You'll have to twist and dig to get it out. Wash it down with schnapps."

"Excellent, Wili."

Karl did exactly that as the truck gobbled up kilometers of emptiness in a universe largely of summer wheat under an immense Ukraine sky, though now and then they'd pass a farm or, more likely, some kind of Stalinist agricultural collective, and now and then a sullen peasant woman would watch them go, waving mildly to cheer them up. It was unclear if these poor souls thought they were German or Russian; more likely they didn't care and just waved on the sound principle that, in a time of war, it was best to wave at any truckload of men with guns.

"We're more or less on course," said Wili. "I mean, we hold the mountains, and those are mountains, right?"

Karl looked and indeed they were. Somehow the Battlegroup Von Drehle had crept to the horizon dead ahead, a blue blur turning green as the sun rose, revealing a frozen sea of rolling landform, random and clotted, hill on hill, all carpeted in high pine.

This meant they were approaching their own zone of operations, where they knew the land and where the lines were soft and they could negotiate the front and get back to their comfortable palace in Stanislav for a few days of drunken recreation after this mission and before the next one.

"We're pressing our luck in the truck," said Wili. "Another few kilometers and we should dump it and get out on foot by night. We can rest tomorrow and cross between the lines tomorrow night."

"An excellent plan," said Karl. "I'm glad I thought it up."

"It's my plan," said Wili. "I'm the clever one, remember? But go ahead, take credit for it. You always do."

Interlude in Tel Aviv II

Platinum was mined mostly—but not entirely—in South Africa, where it was controlled by a corporation called AngloAmerican Platinum, AMPLATS. It was a dense precious metal, the metal of kings and conquerors, even if it lacked the sexy glow of gold and no one ever made a movie in which its dust drove Humphrey Bogart insane. It was mined north of Johannesburg in the

Bushveld Igneous complex, then shipped to AMPLATS headquarters in Jo'burg for refinement, processing, and further distribution. The jewelry it yielded was, like so many things rich people adore, exquisite and dull. It had other uses, which was primarily why it was so aggressively traded. It was a staple of the catalytic converters used in American automobiles, where most of its production went; it was used in electronics, in turbine engines, in oxygen sensors, and in cancer treatment. It also had certain catalytic functions useful in production of certain widely applied compounds that were useful in the manufacture of other compounds, and on and on. Its advantage, also a disadvantage, on the world market was that it was highly liquid (and thus highly volatile), which made it a compact form of wealth to exchange for goods and services; second, being ubiquitous, it was considered banal and uninteresting so that it was not much tracked by various market monitors, including intelligence agencies, as were gold and blood diamonds and cash.

Gershon quickly made himself an expert on its mining, marketing, and usefulness, as well as its history, culture, and reputation. He saw that, like the world as a whole, recession had bitten deeply into the industry, with the giant AMPLATS in the process of cutting jobs, against the wishes of certain powerful South African labor unions, and much trouble was ahead, lowering the value even more. On the plus side, the Russians (the second largest producers) and the South Africans were looking into the possibility of starting a kind of regulation board and exchange, to bring discipline and steady pricing to the unruly business, which was swell but didn't help the current downward trend.

Gershon saw that the peak he had detected was indeed anomalous, given the economic climate. In other weeks, maybe not. But in this week, unusual. So he ran his finding against market averages in other markets and confirmed his thesis: an unusually large amount of industrial-grade platinum had been purchased on a certain day in the last month, that was what the market was telling him. Demand drove up cost, the law of the universe. For one day, someone went a little platinum-crazy, gobble gobble hungry bird, and on that day the COMEX market showed gains of a little over half a percent, not much . . . but enough to demand scrutiny.

Within a few days Gershon had learned from something called the Precious Metals Industry Reporter, an expensive, exclusive wire service he was able to penetrate, that an entity called Nordync GmbH, new to the precious-metals market and headquartered in Switzerland, had indeed bought over ten thousand troy ounces of platinum from AMPLATS. What was Nordyne, and what did it need all that platinum for?

It turned out that Nordyne didn't exist before it bought and paid (promptly) for its platinum. It had a website of exquisite beauty and zero information, fronted by one of those logos that are high on style and brilliantly devoid of content. Looking carefully at it, Gershon noted two graceful lines running parallel to each other in the right half of an oval, the other half filled with the company's motto, which was:

Nordyne:
Facing
The Future

He examined the lines more closely. They resolved themselves in left profiles of generic humans, earnestly (and, he had to admit, brilliantly) scrubbed of distinguishing tribal or ethnic features. Two humans facing the future, what could be more harmless?

Then there was the name. Disambiguated, it meant "northern power," another meaningless post-industrial trope. Typically corporate, typically opaque, designed not to express but to enable, in the way of letting any potential client project onto the image of a bright future faced squarely behind considerable power.

It also contained links, "Our Philosophy," "Our

Staff," "Our History," and "FAQs"; none of them worked. No business publication had covered its founding, which was, for the record, in Lausanne as opposed to Genève, where most of the big, swaggering, sharkish multinational corporations were headquartered. It boasted no staff; there was no preening CEO to pose for business-style photography of plump rich men in suits with smiles showing yellowed teeth. It was registered only as a trademark but not as a corporation, and its stock, if it existed, was privately held. It seemed to have no assets except the money it paid via a Swiss bank. Gershon sniffed the air, as he always did when his hunting instinct was aroused, and he leaned forward to the screen before him and focused his entire thought process on the mystery of Nordyne's platinum.

He thought, he thought, he thought. If the bad boys of Hezbollah were trying to pick up a small tac nuke, they'd need a great deal of up-front dough, but assembling it out of gold, diamonds, bearer's bonds, and other forms of wealth might set off alarms all through the intelligence community, and sooner rather than later they'd have a drone-fired Hellfire up their asses. Platinum's utility, liquidity, and lack of glamour might do the trick, for many reasons. Move the physical stuff to a holding vault and deliver ownership certificates, easily carried, to a middleman, and somehow whoever was selling—

Chechen rebels, big players in the game, corrupt or ideological Chinese military, money-hungry Pakis, demented Hindus from the overpopulated subcontinent, maybe even a money-grubbing rump group of ex–South African military—might be able to put a big egg in their basket for scrambling Tel Aviv into fissionable ruin. That was one thesis, but only the most obvious. It had too many flaws. Everybody watched nukes, and it would be hard to move one without every satellite in the heavens sending a flash-coded message to home base. The movement of the weapon—delivery, security, transpo, storage, deployment, tactical initiation—would be intensely fraught, interception-accessible any place along the route, and after all, that was what drones were for. You went anywhere with a tac nuke and you got Hellfire and it was a bad day with temperatures ranging in the ten thousands at blast epicenter. It might not even be American or a Hellfire, as all the players in the nuke game had a vested interest in keeping newbies away from the table.

Ten thousand troy ounces at current market value was about $15.9 million, call it $16 million. That was easily within the budgetary reach of most big InterTer, Inc. operations, from Hezbollah to Al Qaeda to Taliban, but it also X'd out the myriad of smaller wannabe local actors, the MILFs (Moro Islamic Liberation Front), for example.

Again, the big guys were watched very carefully by so many players that a $16 million transaction would be noted and acted upon.

Gershon concluded that this was somebody new, not a longtime gamer, somebody with very deep pockets. The attributes—big money, great security, ubiquitous but banal wealth methodology, low profile—suggested something like a onetime high-pub-value hit, a giant stroke that would astound the world. That would mean: first-class operators suddenly disappearing, falling off the grid, as they were absorbed into the new operation. If you had a minimum of $16 mil in play, you probably had more, and that would mean you could get very good guys on your team. Talent, as always, was expensive.

So: Who was missing? Who had disappeared?

The institute had a database of the world's leading operators, indexed by niche, constantly updated. Spy novelists had gotten some things right! So he demanded of the mother lode before him:

List A (operation executive and administrative experts): Missing agents 01-01-13 to present.

There weren't many. Anwar El-Waki, a veteran commando leader blooded heavily in Afghanistan, Iraq, and back in Afghanistan, had apparently quit the game and retired to a village in the northern Pakistan tribal area from which he had disappeared. But he was an AK-74 and RPG guy, not the sort to be involved in an international operation based on subtle financial manipulations. He threw grenades, he didn't buy atom bombs. Dr. Jasmin Wafi, University of Saudi Arabia physicist who had been educated at King's College, Oxford, was briefly missing, though later discovered on sex holiday in Bangkok, where his penchant for small boys attracted little attention.

Gershon sifted through the other categories.

Nuclear scientists?
Chemical-biological engineers?
EMP experts?
Missile technicians?
High-tech assassins?
Explosives professionals?

That yielded nothing except a few more names of small-potatoes guys like El-Waki and Dr. Wafi, of no particular potential for the kind of operation Gershon suspected might be building.

His next move was to go by area rather than specialty and to ask the institute's database if, on a country-by-country or region-by-region basis, there were any missing men, units, whatever.

Again not much.

But . . .

But . . .

Yes, there was a little "but . . ." In Grozny, capital of Chechnya, a former sergeant in the Chechen army turned up as disappeared, though his vanishing was resolved when it was learned he had been in prison. However, on his release, whoever had been watching him stayed with him long enough to learn that he had formed a security group he called Intrusion Prevention Associates; he had hired fifteen members of his clan. The training, according to satellite blow-ups acquired routinely from either the Americans or the French or maybe even one of the seven Israeli birds, showed primarily drills on what would be called "area security." That is, protecting something from somebody: where you set up outposts, how you run patrols, where your observation points are, how quickly can you get your people deployed to a point of attack. The idea, Gershon supposed, was to build a reliable cadre of security professionals in hopes of luring international corporations into establishing plants, factories, laboratories, what have you, in the Chechen postwar economy, which was going to take off any day now. Question from Gershon: Where'd he get the start-up dough? The training facility, while not up to Israeli or Western standards, looked surprisingly sophisticated. Where'd he get the moolah? Who paid?

It didn't take long by routine network penetration maneuvers against the Chechen company for him to track down and view the accounting records. A check for $250,000 had cleared through a bank in Lausanne and was from a firm called Nordyne.

CHAPTER 25

Kolomiya
The Museum Annex

A certain donation had been made, and by and large the curator was quite helpful. He was young, fluent in Russian, eager to talk to Westerners, and took them to an outbuilding behind the museum proper.

"Times change," he said. "Tastes change. We try to keep it interesting. Now we have the best of the big battle pictures on display, but it was a cottage industry in the old Soviet empire, particularly after the war. If you could paint a tank, you had a job for life under Stalin."

"Do you think of it as art or history?" Reilly asked.

"It's really politics," he said honestly. "You see what the Russians valued and how they found those who could give them that and excluded those who could not. The paintings are technically correct, but that is the only kind of truth they tell. That's not art, is it?"

He unlocked the door and took them in. It was like a library of paintings, most of them shelved edge-out in bins in the three or four rooms of the secondary building.

"I wish I could help you. No index, alas. I was not here when the restoration came and an earlier curator made the winnowing decision, picking the best by his lights. The museum draws well enough to keep going, so I am not going to second-guess him. Someday I'll go through and see what's here. I do think there is some sniper imagery here, it certainly seems logical, but I cannot address you to any particular bin or room."

"We'll be fine," said Swagger.

"It's two; the museum closes at six. If you need to come back tomorrow, that's okay. And as I say, madam, any coverage that can appear in *The Washington Post* will be appreciated. Publicity: the new treasure."

"I won't let you down," Kathy said.

After he'd left, they agreed to start at opposite ends and work to the middle.

The time passed, and images of battle, highly stylized by the dictates of Soviet socialist realism, fled under their sorting. The Russians were big on machines, with the T-34 the most prized of them all. That meant a lot of Panzers,

Panthers, and Tigers were depicted, most of them burning or spilling burning men. After a while Bob grew bored with the German beasts catching the raw end of every exchange, especially since the casualty lists said otherwise, but the tank battle was the undeniable king of postwar combat art, with the air fight the second. The Russians, like all who had suffered terror on their behalf, hated the Stuka almost as much as the King Tiger tank, so any perusal of socialist-realist war art yielded fleets of burning, smoking Stukas, their dome canopies shredded by spiderwebbed galaxies of machine-gun fire, their gulled wing joints leaking flame and smoke, their unfoldable landing gear turned to scrap, as they augured in for a last rendezvous with Planet Earth while just behind them a triumphant Yak-3 or some other Red war prince was already into its victory roll. The aviation artists seemed to have a special gift for cloud work; these storied dogfights always took place against a vivid panoply of tumbling, backlit vapor architecture that could have supported Valhalla, either knifed by lighting or rouged to a healthy sun glow.

Of land warfare, much less, perhaps because the figure work was a little shaky. Only a few of the artists called upon to serve had much luck coming up with men hunching behind cover or running through fire, and even less with the ragged sprawl of combat trousseau worn by such men in such

222

circumstances. In this view of war, the tunics and shirts were always immaculate, pressed, precise, because nobody wants to deal with rips, folds, drapes, weathered stains, salt crust, all that hard stuff of fabric under stress as worn on a body under stress. As well, unfolded, the uniforms were a proper platform for display of rank and medal, which seemed to be a fetish on both the Russian heroes and the German villains, many of whom—in fact, nearly all of whom—were members of the SS. From the paintings, you'd think the SS had invaded Russia with just a few trucks and autos from the larger German army in the background. That was the one war the Waffen-SS had won—the war for art direction. They had the coolest uniforms, no doubt about it.

Of partisans, more bridge and rail blasts, a few vehicle convoy ambushes, a few martyrs' executions and/or heroic passings. Bak died two or three times by two or three different techniques, once shot, once hanged, once bleeding out in the arms of his men.

Other images of sacrifice enjoyed some popularity. Heroic doctors and nurses were a tradition, some operating even as the fighting raged outside the medical tent or the shells detonated not too far away. Our Fearless Leaders was a theme that pretended the Russian general staff wasn't drunk for four solid years and were all men of such physical prowess that they could have played interior linemen in the NFL, including, always paramount, the big boy himself. Leading Charges appeared to be a close second to Our Fearless Leaders in the human-interest category, and it seemed the primary requisite of leading a charge between 1941 and 1945 on the Ostfront was the strength to lift a handgun high, whether it was a nice Tokarev automatic or an antiquated Nagant revolver. Swagger had done three tours in Vietnam and didn't believe he'd ever unholstered a pistol, much less led a charge with one, much less seen it or heard about it, but it seemed to ignite the Russian imagination.

Even defeats were occasionally chronicled. *The 113th Transportation Brigade Defends the Bridge at Chortkiv* was one, featuring truckers shooting it out with German paratroopers at some long-forgotten medieval bridge the airborne people had dropped in to demolish. Bob could tell they were airborne because of the distinctive helmets and camo battle smocks they wore and the odd weapons they carried, all unique to Fallschirmjäger, as the socialist-realist artist had clearly researched his stuff. And Bob saw the argument that painter was making: the truckers were noncombat guys miles behind the lines, but when the commandos appeared from nowhere, they gunned up and did their best, though outclassed by the presumably more proficient special operators who, in the picture, commanded the bridge and the far slope of the river and pretty much martyred the transpo amateurs. It must have been a good day to be a German paratrooper and a bad day to be a Russian trucker.

And yes, now and then, some sniper imagery. The best was a partisan in a tree, in full camouflage, barely visible in the foliage that surrounded him, giving his all to his M91 and PU scope. It had all the nuances of the sniper's craft right and proper, though Bob had never been in a tree in his life, but the tension in the body, the tightness of the musculature, the lightness of trigger on finger, all that was right. *Sniper Viktorvich Brings Death to the Enemy*, a brass title plate announced, after Reilly translated it; he had no doubt that Sniper Viktorvich had indeed brought death that day. Bob would have proudly bought that one had it been for sale.

But at the end, it was a wash. They unearthed a total of three sniper paintings beside the one of Viktorvich bringing death, one of them even a woman sniper, in a snowy setting somewhere, moving into position to pick off some hun.

The young curator arrived exactly as they were returning the last of the paintings to their bins. "You know, I had a thought," he said.

"Wonderful," said Reilly. "We're fresh out of them."

"As I say, I took over in '07, but the man I

225

replaced had been here for over thirty years. And he was the mentee of the man before him, who founded the museum in '46 and had been in Bak's partisan army. It occurred to me that the founder might have taken or hidden these 'suppressed' paintings you're looking for—that is, instead of burning them, as NKVD demanded. He was a Ukraine patriot, after all, and not a fan of the Russians. Besides, the Russians had condemned Bak's army and declared all in it enemies of the state. That was before Bak was officially reformed, when Ukraine became an independent state. At any rate, I called, and yes, he does have some paintings from the founder, though he has not looked at them. I will give you driving instructions."

"You are so helpful," Reilly said. "Maybe we'll get lucky."

Just as a precaution, Swagger did not take the directions that the curator had provided, but charted another course. They got there to discover a feisty white-haired old lion who had nothing but contempt for his successor—"Young idiot, not even Ukraine!"—but he did have some paintings, which had been rolled into tubes, wrapped and forgotten. He told a long story that Bob pretended to listen to, as the old guy seemed under the impression that Bob understood him. But after a bit, it was time.

On his dining room table, he unwrapped an old, old package as dust rose and the senior curator's wife clucked and twitched at the defilement of her home, to her husband's utter indifference. One roll, five oils on canvas were unveiled; he delicately unscrolled them and peeled them free, one at a time. It was clear why the Stalinists thought they'd be better off destroyed; they told too much truth for totalitarian minds. They were far from socialist-realist glory. The first was a somewhat crude evocation of the SS shooting the Jews outside of either Kolomiya or what used to be called Stanislav, though it made no difference, as actions had occurred at both places. The second was a starved farm woman, her face crushed in grief, warding off nurses who'd come to feed and rescue her. She was clearly too weak to care and would die soon. The third was a burning village, bodies all over the ground. Yaremche? Probably not, as no mountains were visible. It could have been any place in Ukraine in any year from 1941 to 1944. The fourth was five partisans hanging at a gallows, no other details. And the fifth was the mass execution of some German prisoners of war, by partisans. It was squalid, for the men begged even as the gunners sprayed them.

"Nothing," said Swagger. "And that's it?"

The old man answered. "Paintings, you said. Yes, that's it for paintings. However, there are some items with pictorial representations on them. Folk art, they would be called, certainly not a part of the formal socialist-realism tradition. You know, peasants or soldiers who scribbled something on something. A textile, a piece of pottery, a gunstock. I have a few. It's not much."

"We'd like to see them."

He brought out an old leather suitcase, much battered, sealed off by straps. It took a second or two for him to unlock and uncinch the thing and open it. He brought out the objects one by one and placed them on the table. It was a collection of the shabby and the forlorn, most crude and earnest, by amateurs. They even had an American Indian feel to them, like those images of the Little Big Horn from the Sioux point of view, both childish and gory.

Two pictorial weavings, musty of smell, which appeared to show pictographs of partisans and Germans shooting at each other. A ceramic pot with a German tank burning on it. A heroic triumvirate of Ilyushin Sturmoviks flying in tight formation, on a plate, poorly drafted. And finally, another plate.

Bob looked at it, struggling to make sense of the lines, which were messy, and the jumble of the composition, which was uninformed by any sense of perspective, but ultimately he found the right angle from which to view it and saw that it depicted a rifleman hunched in trees, bent over, concentrating on, giving himself to a generic rifle; far off, some kind of netting bore three figures while fluffy clouds rose around it. Loki shoots at Thor in Valhalla? William Tell updated to gun guy taking out Geisler in Switzerland? What could it be?

"Somebody's shooting something," Bob said to nobody in particular, noting that the scale was all off, that the artist had no convincing sense of human structure, that if you worked it out, the rifle was nowhere near aligned with the target, which he now saw was a kind of pedestrian bridge.

Familiar somehow. Why did he get a buzz? His deep brain was aligning points, drawing associations, making connections. "Does this—" he started to ask, but then it leaped into his mind. The netting was a rope-and-spar bridge over the River Prut at the waterfall, producing the clouds of mist, in old Yaremche. The three figures were the targets on the bridge. Bob shifted his eyes back to the sniper, saw what looked to be a cascade of brightness at the head, and realized in that second it was her blond hair.

"It's Mili," he said. "Jesus Christ, she got her shot."

CHAPTER 26

The Hotel Berlin
Stanislav
JULY 1944

A nd do I understand, young Captain, that although you are renowned for your discriminating knowledge of wine, you yourself have never tasted it?"

"Yes, Herr General," Salid said to 12th SS Lieutenant General Muntz, "it is so. In my faith, one does not drink alcohol. It interferes with one's absolute fealty to the will of Allah. But it is also true that to an Arab, there is no more profound responsibility than to be a fine host. How does one reconcile these seeming contradictions? My father, who was a man of power and prominence in Palestine, had a brilliant idea: he assigned a son to learn all that could be learned of wine and thus be able to welcome sophisticated Europeans to our household in a style to which they were accustomed and in which they would feel the warmth of Palestinian hospitality. It was a responsibility I cherished. And when I came to Germany in my teens for training and to further cement the bonds between our two peoples, I was able to find enough time to continue my passion."

The young officer was quite the hit. Even Nazis were drawn to stars, and he was fully a star. Slim, handsome, elegant in his jet-black uniform, his epaulets and flashing SS runes on his tunic collar opposite his 13th SS Mountain Division scimitar insignia, his shiny boots under his sharply pressed riding breeches, his gloves immaculately white, his ceremonial dagger glittering in the candlelight of the garden of the Hotel Berlin, Stanislav's finest, he was a picture of masculine beauty and exoticism; but it was his fez that made him seem so special. Bloodred, with the national emblem of the art moderne eagle grasping the twisted cross over the chill explicitness of the SS death's head in bone white on the forehead, it had a red tassel hanging raffishly off it, and it made him seem like an exotic exemplar of Eastern royalty, a warrior prince from the land of the great white desert. The fact that he'd killed a lot of Jews was a definite social plus.

"And so you chose the wines tonight? And this was after or before you destroyed the Bak bandit group in the mountains?"

"It was actually after. We returned from that mission, and I came to the hotel and discovered a wine cellar as yet undisturbed by the fortunes of war. I would not say it was an extraordinary accumulation, strong on the French reds, a little weaker on the German whites, but not without a few items of interest. I think you will find the sensations to your palates quite amusing."

"Hans, Hans," the lieutenant general squealed at Dr. Groedl, "where did you find this lad? He is such a delight!"

All the glitterati of the Kommissariat were present, dressed to the nines in the latest Nazi high style. These were the men of power, drawn from the administrative and military lords of what remained of the Reich's Ukraine empire. Besides the slashing black of the SS dress uniform, the others wore immaculately tailored evening attire, white-jacketed, as it was broad summer.

"The man has the most educated nose in Europe," someone said, and Sturmbannführer Salid modestly accepted the compliment.

"Especially for sniffing out Jews!" someone else said, to much laughter and a little melancholy, for all understood that the days when the Reich's most sacralized mission could be talked about openly were coming to an end.

"More so than you realize," boasted Senior Group Leader–SS Groedl, now sporting a monocle, as well as an elegant ivory cigarette holder for his Effekt. "He was one of the most enthusiastic and aggressive advocates of our policies in Einsatzgruppe D. His work was tireless and self-sacrificial. Onward and onward he pressed. It was truly the spirit of his Allah that moved him to such energies."

Applause, which the young man demurely accepted.

It was like the last night on the *Titanic*. All knew the cold black ocean was their destiny. In a day or a week, the 2nd Ukrainian Guards Army would unleash a million Katyusha rockets—they sounded like banshees under the torturer's whip and were called by the Germans "Stalin's Organ"—followed up by the grinding inevitability of a thousand thirty-six-ton T-34s, against which poor Muntz and his operational commander Generalleutnant Von Bink of 14th Panzergrenadier had but four hundred Panzer IVs and a few StuG III anti- tank hunters. The Russians could not be stopped, denied, distracted. They were inevitable. And all this gloomy sense of predestination hung like a cloud over the dark balmy garden lit by candlelight and assuaged by four violinists playing Rachmaninoff with extraordinary sensitivity. Those gathered knew that in a very short time, they would scramble desperately to get across the Carpathians and into Hungary, to live to fight another day. Or to die at their posts, as circumstance decreed.

"So, Captain," proclaimed the unusually expansive Groedl, "tell us what you have planned."

"Of course, Dr. Groedl. Gentleman, I begin you with a palate-pleasing Laphroaig 1899, bottled by Mackie and Company. One of the finest of our English enemies' malt Scotch whiskeys. How it ended up here, I have no idea. Sip it, perhaps over ice. Note the peat-bog intensity, the sense of smoke and fog, the somehow 'brown' sense of flavor. Use it only to sharpen the palate and to absorb the tiniest of blurs from the vividness of its impact. When we win the war, it is my dream to violate my religious discipline for one night and drown myself in its glories, preferably in my new castle in Glasgow, but until then it must be savored at the micro level."

"I don't know what he's talking about," said Panzer Muntz, "but by God, I like his spirit."

"Next, with the Ukraine wheat-fed filet de boeuf, I offer a superb 1929 Château-Chalon. That was a wonderful year, with a cold winter and a beautiful spring and summer. It is by far the queen of the evening's selections, and I hate to spend it so early in the ritual, but the chef informs me that beef must precede fowl and fish, by ancient tradition."

"It is so *wrong*," said Panzer Muntz, "when fowl precedes beef!" It was meant as jest, so everybody laughed, including Salid, including the Ukrainian mistresses.

"Then with the fowl," said Salid, "I am delighted to announce a Gustav Adolf Schmitt Niersteiner Heiligenbaum 1937. It does not stand up to the other two, but if you regard it, chilled, as mild comic relief, you will find it acceptable. I mean this as no comment on the great tradition of German wine making, only as a comment on what was available."

"At least he's not trying to stick us with any Ivan pisswater," said Group Leader Schultz, perhaps enabled by too much Laphroaig. There was some laughter but not much.

"The birds, by the way," said Salid, "are Hungarian chukker, flown in fresh. Dr. Groedl found room on the plane, God bless him."

Applause, and in the flickering candlelight, Dr. Groedl took his bows.

"Then, for the fish course," said Salid, "which would be cold Latvian sturgeon, again fresh, supplied courtesy of General Muntz from 3rd SS Panzer attached to Army Group North," to more sincere rounds of applause, "a Château d'Yquem 1921, the amber vintage so storied in wine legend. I regret I could not find a Loire, since 1937 is widely heralded as the greatest year for that superb vintage. But alas, as we have all found, one must work with what one has."

"And he hasn't even told you about the dessert," crooned Dr. Groedl.

"The dessert! The dessert!" went the cry through the small throng of guests, in thrall to the young Arab aristocrat.

"I suppose I shall go ahead and unveil the surprise," said Salid. "I thank whoever was the sommelier in the Hotel Berlin here before the war, as he had one bold stroke that I think you will enjoy. Perhaps it was meant as an exhibition or something to attract a sporty European ski crowd to the Carpathians as part of Poland's own five-year plan. The fellow managed not only to acquire a Veuve Clicquot Dry 1927—not the best, but still a fine year—he acquired it in a quantity that I think will impress you and that I guarantee will ensure this to be a memorable night for all of us lucky enough to be in attendance. Gentlemen, I give you . . . Balthazar."

Balthazar was not the biggest champagne bottle, but up near the top of the list, and at the captain's command, four husky Serbs of Police Battalion, in their own dress 13th SS Mountain uniforms and red fezzes, appeared from the shadows with the huge green bottle. It contained twelve liters of M. Veuve and M. Clicquot's superlatively refined and delightful bubblejuice and resembled one of the mighty siege mortars that Von Manstein had used to level Sebastopol a few years earlier, in the Reich's headier days.

"I assure you, *le déluge* will be to your liking," said Salid.

"Gentlemen, to our table *hoppe, hoppe, hoppe*," said Groedl.

The food was gone. The candles had burned low. The monocles and pince-nez had fallen to the ends of their tethers. Ties were loosened or removed. Cigar smoke filled the air. Some of the more adventurous of the men had slid off into the shadows and glades of the garden with their mistresses or companions, and occasionally an orgasmic grunt would signify another German victory over the Reds. Those who remained at the table had gathered at its head, where Dr. Groedl presided benevolently. He had just finished a fascinating story of the mystery illness that had plagued his beloved dachshund, Mitzi, throughout most of 1943, and her miraculous cure at the hands of a Jewish veterinarian whom Groedl had made certain to provide with authentic Kommissariat citizenship papers so that he would not be carted off to—well, no need to specify.

It was at this moment that the question on everyone's lips was finally broached.

"Dr. Groedl, your immensely talented protégé has been silent on his most significant victory. It is spoken of everywhere, high and low. Perhaps now, so late, among those of us who remain and are discreet by nature, he could be encouraged to tell."

"Yes, tell us."

"We must know. It is so fabulous."

"I presume, gentlemen," said Dr. Groedl, "you are not referring to his victory in the mountains, when he brought off the most successful anti-bandit operation in the history of the Kommissariat."

"No, no, that is mere soldiers' duty. The other one."

"All right. Yusef, I officially unlock your lips. Tell us how you defeated Battlegroup Von Drehle and its Green Devil assassins in the campaign of the Andrewski Palace."

The laughter was intense. All loathed and hated the parachutists for their élan, their disdainful attitude, their contempt, quite openly expressed, for the goals of the Kommissariat, and for their very cool boots and helmets, which no one but they were authorized to wear.

"I fear I disappoint you," said Salid modestly. "Like many legendary actions, its reality was far more prosaic. As Dr. Groedl authorized, we of Police Battalion had taken over the Andrewski Palace as our quarters and base of operations. Dr. Groedl understood that we needed security, comfort, and containment to foster unit cohesiveness. We needed privacy for our prayer rituals, which sometimes create enmity among the unenlightened.

"Laborers had already removed all personal gear and storage, as well as communications equipment and ammunition, left by the Green Devils. I supervised the removal, and I was diligent. It was not done harshly or punitively, and nothing was lost or damaged. There was no cause for complaint. I could not be responsible for Army Group North Ukraine's baffling refusal to inform Battlegroup Von Drehle of the move to new quarters, or rather, to a set of tents adjacent

to shop platoon of Fourteenth Panzer's maintenance section. That was not my responsibility! I
owe no apologies for that. I cannot interfere in
army business any more than I would accept the
army interfering in mine.

"So there I am at 0100, going over intelligence
reports, when I hear screaming and yelling at
the gate. I immediately go out to investigate, and
there is a phenomenal scene. These men—
soldiers I could not call them, they were more
like Indians or, I don't know, scouts, cowboys,
Natty Bumppos, I don't know what, certainly not
military—were demanding admittance. They all
had beards and unkempt hair, and their faces
were smeared with black dirt like war paint, and
they were dressed in these tattered ragamuffin
camouflage smocks, and they had these comical
conelike helmets. Eventually I located their
commanding officer, this Von Drehle—"

"That one! The race car driver! Oh, possibly he
slept with an American movie actress five years
ago and thinks he's a god or something!"
somebody said bitterly.

"I explained that we were fresh in from the field,
and a very successful foray it had been, and Dr.
Groedl himself had approved our occupation of
the Andrewski Palace. It was a military necessity.
Well, it came down to rank, and it turned out the
fellow wasn't even sure if he was a captain or a
major! Imagine. That's how indifferent he is to

military protocol. I managed to hide my shock and keep things at an even keel and explain that while I hated to flaunt connections, so unnecessary between officers, I did have the ear of Dr. Groedl and I would not hesitate to use my connections and it would be in his interests to relent on this one. I told him I had no choice. I was obeying the will of the party, the Kommissariat, Dr. Groedl, and I could not be held responsible for quartering decisions. Then the feldgendarmerie arrived, and after a bit more yelling, the fifteen parachutists were finally led off to their new bivouac area."

At that point, a young officer in the uniform of a Wehrmacht Hauptmann entered the room stiffly, his eyes locked unerringly straight ahead. He came to the senior group leader–SS and bent to present a message.

"Hmm, what's this?" said Dr. Groedl as he took it. He opened it. In a few seconds, his eyes lit up, and then a smile blossomed on his blubbery little face. "Well, well, good news from the front for the first time in quite a while. It seems some of our fellows blew up a bridge somewhere, and all the Ivan tanks will be stuck on the wrong side of the river for a few days as they lash together some pontoons. Our little outpost here in Ukraine lasts just that much longer!"

The gentlemen raised their glasses.

"Long live our leader, our brave boys, and our crusade of purification," said Dr. Groedl.

CHAPTER 27

Outskirts of Kolomiya
THE PRESENT

The old curator allowed them to keep the plate. If it brought glory to a partisan and refocused attention on Bak's brigade, he was all for it. He wrapped it in tissue, then in brown paper, taped and tied.

They shook hands and hugged, and it was all very nice, and Bob and Kathy made to leave, but the old man's wife pulled him aside and spoke rapidly in Ukrainian. He turned back to them, his mood more somber. "Do you have enemies?" he asked in Russian.

"It's a long story," Reilly said. "But yes, it seems someone doesn't wish us to look into this matter."

"My wife says that a car came along the road recently, but once past the house, it pulled to the side of the road and turned its lights off. No one got out. It is still there. Puzzling, if not unprecedented. We see very little traffic here, especially after dark."

"Ask him if he has a gun," Swagger said.

The old woman knew the word in English and was shaking her head before she even got the sentence out.

241

"They want to know if they should call the police."

Bob thought.

"I think that'll just confuse matters. Okay, thank him, we'll go to the car, let me think this one through."

They walked to the car nonchalantly through the quiet Russian night. Lots of stars filled the dark sky in pinwheels and tendrils, a gentle breeze pushed the leaves this way and that, not much illumination around, humidity in the summer air, bird sounds of no specific place or species.

"I'm scared," she said. "Maybe we *should* just call the cops."

"Here's how it will work. We'll pull out, see if they follow. If they do, I'll gun the engine, break contact, and let you off somewhere downtown. You take the plate. You head to the train station, catch the first train to Ivano, then check in to another hotel. Don't go back to the Nadia. Meanwhile, I'll cruise and see if I can pick them up. It shouldn't be too hard. I'll see what their intentions are. I'll lead them way out of town. Then somehow I'll dump them. I'll give you a call and we'll figure out what to do next based on where I end up. These games take patience, so if I don't call right away, don't worry."

"Bob, I can't let you do that," she said. "It's not right. This is my story."

"Kathy, these games are tough enough to run if you're only looking out for yourself. I can't be worried about you under those circumstances and operate, too. This is best. Trust me. I know this part of the forest."

They got in, started the engine, and backed out.

"If anything happens, you go to the floor in a little ball. Not sure how this is going to play out, but you're probably safest there. Get your legs crumpled up facing outward. I think you'd rather get shot there than your head."

"You've done this before?"

"In a gunfight, every time is the first time."

"That's reassuring."

They drove at a moderate pace from pool of light to pool of light under the occasional street-lamp, slaloming around the more vivid potholes, missing a few for some hard riding.

"He's back there, all right. Lights off, but he's just a little too close, so I can see him in the edge of the overhead lamps. Like I said, sloppy."

They rounded a corner, came to a stoplight. It was another two miles into downtown Kolomiya.

"If he's coming, he's coming now," said Bob.

The light changed. Another few blocks passed, and ahead, the more intense illumination of the center city blocked out the sky.

"His lights just went on," said Swagger.

"Oh, great," she said. "Tell me this isn't happening."

"Unfortunately it is. Now, please. Get down. It's going to guns."

She squirmed to the floor just as the Mercedes behind them closed the gap and then spurted around them, pedal to the metal, to pass and maybe shoot from the left. His shocks squealed as he accelerated, and the Mercedes rocked back on its tires under the speed-up and roared by the Chevy and, from the passenger side, the muzzle of an AK-74 emerged.

Moscow
The Krulov Investigation
Will French, Reporter

Arkhiv Prezidiuma Rossiyyskoy Federatsii—Nope.
Gosudarsrtvennyy Arkhiv Rossisvkoy Federatsii—Nada.
Rossiyskiy Gosudarsstvennyy Arkhiv Literaturi i Iskusstva—Nothing.
Rossiyskiv Gosudarstvennyy Voennyy Arkhiv—*Zilch*.
Tsentr Khraneniya i Izucheniya Dokumentalnikh Kollektsiy—Whiff.
Tsenstralnyy Muzey Vooruzhyonnykh Sil—*Nyet.*

Not a damn thing. Where had he gone? Where was Basil Krulov?

He had been erased, that was clear. Will French of *The Washington Post* knew that it happened in the Russian records all the time, often for the most banal of reasons. Lots of people to keep track of, budget cuts playing hob with the staffing of the archives, the haphazard nature of the Soviet and later Russian federation bureaucracy, the terrible chaos of both the purges and the war and finally the postwar Stalinist era, the struggles for power. So it was quite possible that Basil Krulov was an innocent disappearance, one of many thousands, maybe tens or hundreds of thousands.

But Will couldn't let it go. Like his wife, Reilly, he was driven not by vanity or agenda or hope of a talking-head spot on D.C. TV but by curiosity. Who, what, when, where, why? Those five W's were the key questions of his business, if now mostly forgotten: What does it mean? Or: Who does it help? Call him old-school or whatever, but his plodding earnestness had earned him a superb reputation and a Pulitzer Prize for documenting the hideous conditions under which ships were "broken" on a certain shore of the Indian Ocean, by hundreds of men, most of whom died in their late twenties for all the asbestos they breathed while hacking the giant beached vessels to pieces for the salvage money.

Now, not for the *Post* but for a force more implacable than any in journalism—that is, his wife (also a legend, but that's for another time)—

he was determined to get the who, what, when, where, and why on Comrade Krulov, who was featured in many war histories, always heroic but never in hard focus, was glimpsed occasionally in the postwar histories, and then seemed to fade out, as if broken down like a ship to tiny untraceable parts by sweaty men in loincloths.

He'd tried the archives, he'd called all the older folks—both old American correspondents and retired Soviet-era politicians—and had gotten nothing, or nothing real.

"Oh, that one. He was a force to be reckoned with. Whatever happened to him? Do you know?"

He'd worked the Internet, finding his way into certain largely unknown databases. He'd tried American, British, French, and Australian intelligence services, all of whom had distinguished themselves with penetrations during the Cold War. But no, it was too long ago, it had faded, so much other stuff had happened.

And so he was down to his last play.

It would cost.

He needed a chunk of dough.

Will, he told himself. You've done enough. Don't go there. You don't even know what you're going to find out. How will you tell her if it doesn't work out?

He couldn't face that reality. The music of the five W's, those Circes of a journalist's honor, kept sliding through his brain, rapturous, seductive, alluring, undeniable.

He went to his laptop, keyed in "Bank of America," and transferred ten thousand dollars from his—their—savings account to his Moscow bank.

In for a penny, in for his youngest daughter's college education.

Who knew, maybe she'd *like* community college.

CHAPTER 28

The Carpathians
Above Yaremche
MID-JULY 1944

The patrols came closer and closer. Sometimes they went high, sometimes low. Sometimes they were very aggressive, moving loudly, making a big important-mission show; sometimes they were secretive, employing great woods skill, moving and hunting quietly. Sometimes they traveled circularly, sometimes vertically. Suppose they left trailers, listeners in the night? Suppose they left silent ambush teams? Suppose they left their own sly traps that could drive a stake through you or drop a boulder on you? Worst of all, suppose they left snipers?

With the fear of constant discovery, they could not get out to hunt for mushrooms without great anxiety, which had its psychological and nutritional effects. They were surviving at subsistence level. Days had passed.

"The Peasant will return," she insisted. "He will have a rifle. You and he will escape deeper into the mountains, where it's safe for now. The Red Army will liberate Ukraine. You will survive."

"What happens to Petrova?"

"If he gets a rifle, then I will head down the mountain and into Ivano and find a place to shoot. If I can't kill Groedl, I'll just kill Germans until they kill me. I'll die a sniper's death, as so many have before me."

"You are delusional, Sergeant Petrova. The Peasant is dead, obviously. We are lucky he didn't rat us out under torture. He won't be back. There is no rifle. The Serbs will find us, and that Arab will torture us, you more than me."

"The Peasant is too sly."

"I only wish. Here's the reality. He's gone."

It was true. Where was he? Had he been caught in Yaremche on his rifle-hunting expedition? No sign of him. Maybe he had simply lit out, used his skills to survive and evade, and abandoned them. But he would not do that. The Peasant was a strong man and would never yield to craven temptation. She could not believe he was gone.

Yaremche
The Inn Cellar

Which wine went with which dish was far from Captain Salid's mind. He yearned to return, if not to that very interesting wine cellar and whatever treasures it might still contain, then to a treasured volume in the original French, *Varietals of the Loire River Valley*, compiled in 1833. To know the present and expect the future, you had to know the past. But there was other business to attend to.

"Look, friend," he said in good Russian to the man on the table, "this is getting us nowhere. We both know how it must end. It's only a question of the journey to that spot. You would do the same to me were our positions reversed, so there's no morality here, really. It's war, that's all, and duty. So why not make it easy on yourself?"

And me, he thought.

He finished his cigarette and stubbed it. The cellar of the inn made a rather poor torture chamber, but one did what one must. One adapted. It was the soldier's way. As he saw it, he was not cruel, he was practical. Certain goals had to be achieved.

"Don't bore me with the lost-peasant routine. Peasants don't wander about, not in time of war. They understand the danger. You'd only be out and about on a mission, a job, and I think I know what that is. So please, tell me, and it'll go so much easier on you."

The man was spread-eagled, secured by ropes. He was largely naked, except for a crude wrap that provided modesty. How much longer would it last? His nose was crushed, his teeth smashed in, both eyes swamped in puffed-out, blood-filled tissue and crusted scab. Blood ran from a dozen or so slashes and contusions randomly placed on his limbs. His body was a festival of bruising, hemorrhaging, cuts and, worst of all, the angry red blossoms where they'd laid the torch against him. Fire was man's most primitive fear, his most painful prosecutor, his cruelest adversary, and Salid had no compunctions about using it against his enemies.

"Let's go over this one more time. We picked you up scurrying uphill, into the mountains, with three loaves of bread, a bunch of carrots, three potatoes, and a large piece of salted beef. Someone here in the village gave you the food. That we know. I'll tell you what, I don't even care. That's fine. Petty heroism by some other peasant fool, no need to get all indignant about it. I don't care, Himmler doesn't care, nobody cares. That's your victory, all right? You protected your allies, you gave no one to the hated Police Battalion torturer in the silly red hat, you are heroic and a tribute to the ideal of the new

Stalinist Man. I'd kiss you for your bravery if I had the time.

"But you're a bandit. Of course, what else can you be? You were getting food for other bandits hidden in the mountains, survivors of the gun battle some days ago. Possibly one of these survivors is a woman bandit known to be a sharpshooter. One of your missions surely was to abscond with a rifle so she can complete her mission. Now you mean to return, which means you know where they are. So this is all I ask. Tell us. Lead us. Turn them over to us. Do that, and I'll let you survive. We'll cut you free, get you medical aid, your people will be here in a few weeks, days maybe, you'll go into a refugee center hospital and all the villagers will say, He did not give us up. He was a hero, that one. You'll get some kind of red banner and, when all this is over, go back to your village with a chestful of medals and scars, a hero in the Great Patriotic War. Every June twenty-second, you'll wear your medals to remind people of your bravery in the partisan war against Hitler."

The man said nothing. He stared grimly at the low ceiling in the room. His consciousness fluttered in and out and waves of pain came and went, each seemingly more intense than the one before. He was not a heroic man, and his horizons had been limited by his education, of which he had none; his culture, which demanded total

251

obedience; and his workplace, which was the earth and demanded only sixteen hours a day in toil to nurse a living from, assuming the Stalinists did not take too much grain that year. There was only one metric by which he could be considered "free": he would not talk.

"I think it's the fire that gets you the most," Salid said. "Peasants fear fire. It can wipe out a crop, burn down a hut, scatter the cattle, alert the Cossacks, and in a single night everything is lost. So the fear of fire is deep in you. I wish I hadn't wasted so much time having you beaten. That was foolish on my part. You can beat a Jew, he has no resistance to pain, a little of it lights off his imagination, and soon enough he's selling out his family, his parents, his rabbi, his children. Believe me, I've seen a lot of it. But your life is so harsh that pain means nothing. We could beat on you until we were exhausted and then you'd ask, What's for dessert? Foolishly, I wasted time and effort from my fine Serbian colleagues here."

There were two of them, in boots and trousers, their muscular chests and thick arms glinting in the torchlight. Not a lot of pity and even less interest showed on their faces. They were professional torturers and had seen a lot of things themselves, so nothing this fellow underwent had much meaning to them.

"So again. Please. Speak. Water, food, comfort, morphine, schnapps, or that awful vodka shit you people like. Then you take us for a nice walk in the forest and point out where these bandits are hiding or your rendezvous, whatever is your next step. Then for you: more of everything, more than you've ever had in your whole life."

The man stared at the ceiling through his swollen eyes. He said nothing.

Salid turned. "The torch. Again, in burnt and unburnt areas."

He went upstairs and outside to sit in the sun and have another cigarette. He could see clouds of mist floating up from the waters of the River Prut. The roar of the water tumbling drowned out the screams.

He sat, smoking, thinking.

The man would break. Soon. No one could stand up to determined torture; that was an operational value shared by both SS and Arab nationalists actively plotting war against the British, whose ranks Salid would lead after the war was over and at last bring purity to Palestine. The Arab revolt of '36 to '39 was nothing! Why, the next time—

He glanced about. Today's stroke was masterful. Instead of rolling into the village in his three panzerwagens, he halted a kilometer outside and sent fast-moving lightly armed flanking patrols around to see what they could flush. Indeed, they'd flushed this peasant. Now it was a matter of time. He would lead them, they would net the girl, and it would be another triumph for the great Salid. More important, it would get him sent out of this hellhole, with a huge Ukrainian Guards Army about to jump on him, and back to the Balkans, from whence, when the time came, escape was not only simpler but set up under the auspices of a certain section of the SS. He would get out, get back, and reemerge in his own world, though now a legend; he would be a great weapon in that war, the next one, and he would win the peace on the terms he thirsted for so voraciously.

He just needed this bastard to break *now!* Time was growing short. The offensive could break at any time, and who knew what that would unleash? That was why having permanent possession of the three panzerwagens was so important. With them, he could get his men up the mountains and over the Yaremche road to Uzhgorod. Without them, he might be another fool in a six-mile parade of hapless victims headed north to Lviv for the Red Air Force to strafe and bomb at will.

And this other thing: now Groedl had decided on a risky plan to catch the sniper. He would submit himself to her marksmanship, albeit from a good distance out. He would bet his life that she could not hit him, just as he would bet his life that she would have to try. Groedl had decided to make a visit to the delightful village of Yaremche. The White Witch would be lured into a trap, which he, Salid, would spring. But what if he failed? That thought petrified him. Allah would not let him fail. But it would be *so much better* if this bastard would crack and lead them to her—

"Captain, come quickly. He has—"

It was one of the torturers, and from the look of alarm on the face of the man, Salid understood the news could not be good. He rose and followed the man into the inn and down the cellar steps.

The peasant was still alive on the table. But . . . both of his eyes had been gouged out. They bled profusely. He shivered in pain, writhing against the binds of the rope.

"Why on earth would you do such a thing?" Salid demanded of his torturers. "For God's sake, what use is he to us now?"

"We didn't do it, Captain. He got his right hand loose, I don't know how. And in a second when I had turned away to acquire a new torch, he used his thumb on each eye."

The man said through his pain, "Be quite happy to guide you now, sir." Then he laughed.

"Cut his fucking throat," said Salid.

CHAPTER 29

Kolomiya
THE PRESENT

The Mercedes came hard, pulled almost even to the Chevy, and at that point, Bob gunned his own engine and lurched ahead slightly. The Mercedes responded as the heavy-footed driver put more into the pedal and his vehicle jumped ahead. Precisely as he pulled near even, Bob hit the brakes hard, and the satiny black German vehicle shot by on the left.

Swagger saw the open window, the muzzle come out, but then he dipped behind the Benz and gunned his own car and hit the bigger vehicle hard in the left taillight. The crunch of metal on metal sent a shock through the Chevy, his wheel fought him, but he gained control and rammed again. The big car wavered as its own driver fought for control, then lost it, went to brake, panic-skid, and, raising a howl of dust as it slid over road, shoulder, and grass, slewed to the left and came to a halt.

But Swagger had pedal to metal and the Chevy, surprisingly fast, jetted ahead. He turned right at the first big road, left at the next one. Then he pulled to the side of the road, across from what appeared to be a restaurant with a couple of cabs outside. "Okay," he said. "Out. There's a cab. Maybe he'll take you all the way to Ivano. Do you need cash?"

She seemed dazed but shook her head to clear it. "I'm fine."

He reached into the money belt under his polo shirt, pulled out a wad of American hundreds. "Here. Okay, wait for my call. Stay low, don't go out. Tomorrow, maybe longer, don't know."

"I think I should stay with you."

"I saw rifle muzzle. AK-74, very powerful. If he gets one burst into this car, we're both dead. This is very real and very tough. I can't lose you to something stupid like this, and I can't worry about you. Get out, get out of town, hole up, and wait for my call."

He left her on the road, churned ahead, driving into the strange city. Ha ha, there was the Easter-egg musuem with the giant Ukrainian egg in front of it. At least he got to see that.

He came to a large road, seemingly leading out of town, and without the faintest idea, pushed on, sailing along, as fast as he could—traffic was thin—but he tried to find the maximum speed at which he could avoid the various excavations in the road surface, the continual presence of repair zones, the occasional big truck hustling along.

He drove, he drove, he drove. He thought, he thought, he thought.

But not about who was trying to kill him. He wanted to, but his mind kept returning to something troubling about shooting at Groedl on the bridge. He had to face it: she missed.

The issue was range. If she was on that bridge, the best vantage point—seemingly the only vantage point—was that high bluff to the southwest, the one with the somehow "lighter" tone to half its leaves. That put her between one and, say, five hundred yards out. Now, if she had all day, with any rifle she could estimate, fire, record her hit, and walk the rounds into the target. She'd eventually get it. But not in the middle of a war. She must have made what's called a cold-bore first shot. The only rifles available, and he didn't even know for sure she got one of them, would have been a Mauser K98k and a Mosin 91, without scope, and a five-hundred-yard shot, say, with one of those without a scope—cold-bore first shot hit—is pretty damned hard.

He realized what had happened. They'd lured her, knowing she'd take a long, impossible shot, knowing she'd give up her life for just a chance, a one-in-a-million long shot, of bringing it off. That was Groedl's plan, that was his game.

They used the sniper's honor against the sniper.

No sense getting upset about it now, was there? What the hell, it was seventy years ago. Then why did he feel so much old Bob at this moment? He had the killing fever.

· · ·

Reilly sat alone in the backseat of the cab that was hauling her to Ivano. She, too, thought and thought and only came up with more questions. But then the phone in her purse rang. She snatched it up and answered. "Swagger?"

"Swagger? Who the hell is Swagger?" asked Marty, the foreign editor of *The Washington Post*, from his office at Fifteenth and K.

"Sorry, Marty, I was expecting a call from a friend."

"What time is it there?"

"Near three A.M."

"You keep long hours. It's eight here. But I'm glad I didn't wake you. We need a backgrounder for the website, maybe tomorrow's late editions."

"What?" said Reilly, thinking what every reporter thinks in such a situation, which is: Oh, shit.

"Remember Strelnikov? You interviewed him, remember? He's just been appointed minister of trade by Putin."

She knew that was big because this Strelnikov was hard right, very nationalist, much feared and hated by so-called liberal factions in Moscow. He was one of those billionaires who decided to get into politics, maybe the Michael Bloomberg of Russia. But this was a surprisingly meaningless position for him to take, so nobody was getting it.

"Can you give us a thousand off the top on

Strelnikov? Who he is, where he comes from, what he does, all that suff you already know?"

"Absolutely," she said. "I'm in transit right now, but I'll be in shortly, and I'll file in a couple of hours."

She was secretly pleased. The best anodyne to anxiety, she knew, was work. She could bury herself in the arcana of the hopelessly preposterous Strelnikov, billionaire, poseur, fraud, and phony, one of those bizarre rich guys all reporters hated because they were allowed to turn narcissism into reality by virtue of their bucks. It took her mind off of Bob on the run.

Swagger pulled over in the dark—sun starting to creep up against the horizon, advancing itself with a trace of glow—and dialed.

"Da?"

"Swagger for Stronski."

The phone went dead. Five minutes later it rang.

"What's up?" asked Stronski.

Bob explained his situation.

Stronski said, "Dump the car. They have the numbers on the car, they're looking for the car. Dump it in a village, take the next out-of-town bus that arrives. The car is death, but you may be all right if you separate from it now."

"You think these guys are wired in to the police and all the cops are looking for the car?"

"It's Ukraine, pal. Anything's possible."

"Okay, I got it."

"I'm going to set up an escape for you. You need to get the hell out of town, and I mean it, Swagger. Like the last time."

"But like the last time, I still have shit to do. Have to get back to Yaremche and look it over. Can you have me picked up there?"

"I'll work on it. But don't doodle around. Serious boys are after you."

"So who?" said Bob, thinking, The gangs, the cops, some oligarch's henchmen?

"I hear a certain fellow picked up five or six freelance tough guys on an out-of-town job. I was checking on it with police sources, and it just came through that the group went to Ukraine with big suitcases."

"Who?" said Swagger.

"You're going to love this. I know who the certain fellow works for. I know who's behind this, who's bankrolling it."

"Who?"

"The Americans."

CHAPTER 30

New Quarters, Battlegroup Von Drehle
Outside Stanislav
MID-JULY 1944

I t's not war per se," said Wili Bober. "Nor is it the prospect of death or maiming. Or a life spent in a Russian prisoner-of-war camp on the far side of the Arctic Circle. No, none of that bothers me. It's the latrines."

"War would definitely be more fun without latrines," said Von Drehle.

The two sat over rude holes in a rude bench over a rude ditch not a hundred meters from their new empire, itself quite rude. It consisted of six tents in a muddy field, each with room for four men. In the squalid heat of July in Ukraine, the tents were unendurable, even with the flaps pinned up. Many of the jägers preferred to sleep outside during the hot nights.

They ate at the mess of the 14th Panzergrenadier, whose vast tank maintenance facility they abutted. Such was the reward for the heroes of the Bridge at Chortkiv. At every minute of every day, the roar of Panzers and Panthers could be heard while Division Workshop struggled to keep as many of the machines in play as possible, which meant the beasts turned over their engines once every few hours to keep the hot-weather-thinned oil in circulation. All well and good for the war effort, but the practical consequence was the constant torrent of exhaust fumes at the 21 Para village.

"I thought we were heroes," said Wili. "You have at least, what, fifteen or twenty Iron Crosses? You may even be a major."

"Have to look into the major issue," said Karl. "I do miss the glorious bathrooms of the Andrewski Palace. I miss the sheets, the decor, the sense of order. This is like a Hitler Youth camp in 1936. Next they'll have us singing 'Horst Wessel.' "

"You should have shot that little Arabian bugger," said Wili.

"Think of the paperwork," said Karl.

"Speaking of paperwork, I think I'm done with today's operation. I mention it because I seem to lack paperwork."

Without looking, Karl handed over the latest *Signal*. Wili paged through it quickly and came up with an article called "National Socialism: Its Spiritual Essence."

"This will do the trick," he said, and ripped the pages out. He got through the engagement quite nicely, then enjoyed applying a heroic photo of The Leader to his posterior. He reassembled kit and stepped down from his throne and pushed beyond a sheet hung for privacy. Ouch, bad news. A Kübelwagen had just entered the compound bearing an earnest 14th Panzergrenadier lieutenant. The young man had stopped for directions, and a couple of lounging Green Devils pointed him to Karl, who was emerging from the latrines.

"Major," said the young man, stepping from the vehicle that had just delivered him. He threw up a completely unenthusiastic "Heil Hitler" salute that looked like a broken-winged sparrow fluttering its bad feathers at a predator, and Karl responded with his normal impression of a drunken clown waving at a lady in the stands whom he wanted to boff. So much for Nazi ceremony in the regular military.

"So you *are* a major," said Wili.

"Apparently," said Karl. "Yes, Lieutenant, what can I do for you?"

"Sir, the general requires your presence. Tomorrow at 1400."

"Say," said Wili to the youngster, "you don't happen to have any copies of *Signal* lying about? We need it for the inspiration."

CHAPTER 31

His spleen hurt, his head hurt, his lips were dry, he was out of breath. That was bus travel in Ukraine. The ancient vehicle, finding a last few potholes to further test its shocks against, turned in to the well, "station" wasn't quite the right word. "Station" connotes order, discipline, coherence, a system. Here, the boarding and deboarding process appeared to take place in some kind of Darwinian sink where the buses just butted and bluffed and brazened their way close to the building until they could go no farther. Consequently, the yard was a riot of buses as they jammed this way and that at odd angles, the whole thing mad and fraught. It looked like a bus station after the end of civilization.

The driver nosed his way in, honking and cursing and maneuvering heroically until at last there was no farther to go. End of ride. He turned the thing off—the last dying breath of low-wattage air-conditioning died without a whisper—and cranked open the doors to let his passengers out into the melee.

Late last night, Bob had dumped the car in a copse of trees outside of a town whose name he could not remember, much less spell. He'd hidden in the same trees until full light, then moseyed into town, trying to look inconspicuous in his jeans and gray polo shirt. He'd seen a batch of people waiting in the square and joined them. When a bus came, he got aboard. The driver demanded payment, as this was no longer socialism, and Bob, ever the ugly American, shoved a wad of bills at him, watched him harvest them, and had no idea one way or the other if he'd been robbed blind or given a generous discount. Then the three hours of torture began.

He was pleased, at least, that Lviv turned out to be the bus destination, remembering the pleasant old-town evening of a few days before. Plan: find a hotel room, pay cash, call Reilly, set up a meet in Yaremche, call Stronski, arrange that quick exit, get to Yaremche, and then get out of town. It seemed simple enough. He waited as the pile-up to exit cleared, then eventually stepped free and enjoyed a breath of fresh air, however laced with exhaust fumes. Meanwhile, honking and shouting, shoving, rushing, dodging, broken-field running, various funny walks, and lots of old ladies prevailed in the labyrinth between the buses as passengers from his own and all other buses attempted to negotiate a way out without getting crushed by entering or exiting vehicles.

Bob took his time, not shoving, not shouting, trusting that any direction was as good as another and basically going the way of least resistance, and that was when he got shot.

It felt like someone whacked him hard in the side with a near-molten fireplace poker. But there was no sound, even if, ahead of him, he saw a pop of debris as a bullet hole erupted into the skin of bus.

He knew in a speed that has no place in time that someone behind him had taken a bad shot with a suppressed pistol and missed center mass. He jigged right, then left, speeding up, turned hard left at the next bus, chose another path, jigged left and then right, moving too quickly for a one-handed shooter to stay with him. He tried to lose himself in the chaos of the labyrinth and its crowd.

Someone was trying to kill him. He realized the guy had been off on his first shot because he'd fired from the hip. Presumably he carried the pistol against his leg, hidden under a coat, had seen the target clear, and rushed a shot.

Swagger had no idea who. He turned back as people filtered this way and that, none of them suspicious at all, just the usual glut of Ukraine working folk, scraggly students with backpacks, a few survivors of the tsarist epoch, and some febrile young kids who couldn't keep their hands out of each other's pants. His side burned but did not bleed a lot, and though it hurt, he knew that until it bruised, it wouldn't impinge his movement. Getting shot wasn't the biggest of deals to him; it had happened before.

He turned, turned again, simply trying to stay afoot. Ahead the bus riot seemed to be thinning, and he thought he could get a cab and get far away. But it occurred to him: I cannot escape. If I escape, he, whoever, finds me as he found me here, and this time prepares better for his shot, and I am down and he is gone.

I have to find him and drop his ass.

Old Bob, maybe real Bob, maybe even the only Bob, took over the brain. He felt his vision clarify and deepen, his muscles fill with killing strength, his will focus to one point and one point alone. He liked it when the world vanished, there was no civilization, no bullshit about rank or caste or what was expected and how you had to act. It was just him, the other guy, and a jungle that happened to be constructed of buses. He liked it that way just fine.

He turned and headed back into the crowd and began to work his way more or less randomly through the corridors between the vehicles. One pulled out suddenly. A horn blasted. A mother pushing a carriage squawked at a driver who cursed back. Swagger thought he might die beneath bus tires, never mind the efforts of his assassin.

He forged ahead, trying desperately to read each passerby for sign: hands hidden, or someone walking at a kind of oblique angle to conceal the pistol from witnesses, or a heavy coat on a hot day. At the same time he had to do this with Zenlike chill, without seeming effort, because if he eyeballed too noticeably, it would alert the shooter, who would take him from afar.

Come on, buster, he thought. Come on, go for me. We'll see how good you are.

He felt his eyes dilate even wider, his breath come in cool spurts, his muscles go to tense. He walked on the balls of his feet, knowing it gave him a little advantage on first power step. He was in full warrior brain, total Condition Green, ready to go at any second.

This way, that way, that way, this way.

Was the guy looking under buses, looking for Bob's New Balances as the tell? Was the guy behind him, slowly closing in? Swagger cranked around, but nobody seemed to be moving fast with any purpose, nobody had a white face and tense lips, all giveaways for a hunter on a job.

He turned again, roaming more or less randomly, waited as a little knot of people cleared, then edged through and found himself between two buses as, up ahead, three old ladies picked their way along, one on a walker.

He kept his head down, moving slowly, ready to yield when he reached them.

The babushkas had dark faces under scarves and broad black peasant dresses. Each wore a shawl bunched around her shoulders, held tight by a fist, and they were—

He hit the one in the middle with an open hand, palm-up strike to the nose, enjoying the crunch beneath the thrust even as the shock traveled up his arm to tell his head the blow had been well placed. Felt so good.

The lady reeled back and the pistol came out, a Makarov with six inches of suppressor at the muzzle, but Swagger nabbed the wrist with his left hand and twisted it away and took another hard-palm, right-handed shot into the nose, which issued blood outflow in torrential quantities. He heard screams, shouts, had the peripheral impression of people fleeing. He kicked his opponent's feet out from under and she went down hard, though he held the gun hand tight enough to snap the wrist, and he pivoted, stepped viciously, driving heel first into her face while controlling the gun. Then he reversed on the arm, finding leverage against the elbow, and felt it bend as it sent high-voltage pain into the fallen body. He twisted the loosened pistol out of the woman's hand. He deftly shifted it and placed muzzle against the throat, feeling the opponent go to surrender against the pressure of the lethal instrument,

The trigger was such a temptation. It would sound like a refrigerator door closing, and then this one would be with the angels. But he didn't yield. He didn't pull the trigger. He leaned over and whispered in meaningless English, "Hairy knuckles, dumb motherfucker," then elbowed the bloody, damaged face again, feeling teeth break at the point of contact.

He rose, turned to find people at each end of the corridor staring at him, while from one of the buses a whole load of passengers had come to the windows.

He leaned over, grabbed the top of the woman's blouse, and pulled it open, yanking free a brassiere stuffed with tissue to reveal a heavy, hairy male chest wearing a galaxy of tattoos. He twisted the body so that the spectators could see it. The false woman groaned in pain and put the other hand to his tormented biceps.

"Mafia," Swagger said, knowing the word to be universal.

"Ahhh," came the roar of the crowd, and he dumped the damaged shooter back to the ground and turned, and the people parted to let him past. Now they understood. Someone pointed the way, and he followed a couple of turns, saw a cab, and went to it.

Moscow
The Krulov Investigation
A Not So Respectable Location

"All right," said Mikhail Likov of SVR, "you want something. Fine, you got money, lots of it?

I'm no traitor, but for a certain amount, ha ha, anything is possible. Capitalism, you know."

"No money," said Will. "But I know you'll get me what I want in trade for what I have to offer."

"What you want?"

Mikhail downed another vodka shot. It was okay. Nothing special, but at least potato-based, unlike some of this new age shit.

"A file. So old that it was started back when they called the outfit NKVD. So old I don't think it's that valuable. That's why I'm an idiot for giving you what I'm going to give you for it."

They sat in a rude Moscow strip club called the Animal, so rude that a woman onstage was in a further state of undress. There were many women there trolling for business in the dark enclaves of the joint, all to the beat-beat-beat of loud, bad Russian syntho-rock. Naturally, it was Likov's favorite place, and many SVR guys came here. They were known to the girls, who liked them so much they never gave a discount.

Mikhail had helped Will on a few tough-to-get stories in the past, usually for a modest tip—it was for his kids, he said, but at least three of those kids, Eva the blond one, Jun the Asian, and Magda the Czech—were here tonight.

"What's so important about this file?"

"That's the funny thing. I don't know. Maybe nothing. But I've been hunting in archives for three days and come up with nothing, as if it's been erased. But whoever's doing the erasing, I'm guessing he couldn't erase it out of the collective memory of the KGB."

"They had standards, those boys," said Mikhail. More vodka. Eye contact, Jun. She seemed to be available. He winked. She came by and sat on his lap. She licked his ear and whispered something he found quite interesting, then she stood up and undulated away, trailing come-hither glances, perfume, and jiggly ripeness everywhere.

"Pretty girl," said Will. "I see why you like her."

"Now and then I contribute to her college fund," Mikhail said, finding his own joke hilarious. Will did not, because he had looted his own daughter's college fund for tonight's fun, but he pretended like he did.

"This file, anyone I know?"

"Doubtful."

"If he's a big man, he should be in the archives of the other places," said Mikhail.

"See, that's the deal. Someone erased him, I think."

"Lots of erasing goes on in Russia," said Mikhail. "People make some money, then they erase themselves and start a new life. Happens all the time. Some stories I could tell you."

"I'm only interested in one man's story," said Will.

"So what's the offer?"

Will held his hand up. Jun came over. She smiled at Mikhail. Mikhail smiled back, then noted that Will's hand was still in the air. Magda, the Czech, came over. She smiled at Mikhail. Then she licked the inside of Jun's ear, and Jun ground her pelvis once or twice into Magda's hip. But wait. The hand was *still* up. Eva inserted herself between Magda and Jun. She put a tongue in each gal's ear, one and then the other. All three of them smiled at Mikhail.

"You've made an arrangement, I see," said Mikhail. "Will you be joining me?"

"Ah, I think you can find your way without my guidance," said Will, thinking, God, I hope I can get this party past the *Post*'s expense account mavens, or daughter number two is going to Prince George's Community College next year.

"What file?" said Mikhail, rising.

Will already had it written down: "Basil Krulov, Stalin's assistant, 1942 to 1954, disappeared sometime in mid '50s."

Mikhail didn't even look at it. "I'll have it for you day after tomorrow."

The girls led him away.

"Better make that day after the day after tomorrow," he called back.

CHAPTER 32

Headquarters,
14th Panzergrenadier Division
Outside Stanislav
MID-JULY 1944

For their command appearance, Karl and Wili brushed out their bonebags, scraped the mud off their boots, shaved, and bathed, even fished out the white summer cap they, as Luftwaffers, were entitled to wear. If they said so themselves, they managed to look pretty spiffy. You could never predict who you'd run into, so spiffy was always the wise move.

Not being assigned a Kübel themselves, they were driven to the HQ building, a mansion under some trees from an earlier century. If there was a mansion, the staff found it; 14th Panzer had found a beautiful old house set in some trees on the far side of the tank park. Actually they'd found the house first and established the tank park next to it. The dwelling, of Georgian grace and with an aristocratic background until the Reds had turned it into some kind of potato collective in '39, was festooned with gaudy National Emblem banners and 14th Panzer flags, surrounded by security behind spools of K-wire

275

and MG-42 posts, the lawns and shrubbery all cut and smashed by the treads of the armored beasts.

Inside, it was all business, as about all the division's needs were serviced by a Panzer cadre who scurried about, administering a twelve-thousand-man/four-hundred-tank military entity, in the field, in constant contact with the enemy. Communications rooms, a huge study where a topographic map was being examined by officers while enlisted men pushed little painted blocks around it, and other rooms turned into offices where ammunition was ordered, tracked, and stocked, fuel levels monitored, supplies listed, living quarters assigned, mess supplies provided. There was hardly ever time for tea.

But today General Von Bink made time for tea. Von Bink, his white shirtsleeves rolled up, his Knight's Cross with oak leaves displayed not at his neck but in a drawer somewhere, his riding breeches with their red stripe for general officer disappearing neatly into his highly polished riding boots, his gray hair bristly, was one of the old guys. He was Panzer Aristocracy: he'd fought in the Great War, then Spain, and rolled his machines across the flat countries of both Europe and Ukraine. He'd been shot at a million times, wounded half a dozen, and was still full of pep and vigor. He really did enjoy the hell out of war.

"Nice of you fellows to come by," he said, as if an issue of free will had been involved.

"Sergeant, you're the one with six wound stripes, is that so?"

"Yes sir. Almost as many as you," said Wili Bober.

"Sir," said Karl, "I'd like to get him sent back to Germany. He'd make a superb training NCO. The new boys could use his wisdom."

"An excellent idea. If we were winning the war, I would say yes, yes, immediately. But as you know, we are losing, and the situation is somewhat different. Oh, and Sergeant, I have six, too, but I was sitting down when I got most of mine!"

That brought a laugh. Yes, sitting down in a burning Panzer IV with Ivan 76s whizzing through the air! Anyway, he poured each parachutist a little more tea. He was nothing if not a stickler for ceremony.

The office was huge, with a wall map of the immediate operational area obscuring one whole side. Otherwise, it was the kind of room where piano recitals may have taken place, and coming-out parties and all the social niceties that filled the work of Tolstoy but not Dostoyevsky. Compared to the frenzied activity on all other floors, this room was serene. The outward wall was given to broad sheets of window, out of which could be seen a terrace, cherry orchards, Panther tanks, and mountains.

"Well, you know you're here for a job."

"Yes sir."

He led them through the glass doors to the patio beyond. It was a cooler day than normal, and for once the oppressive humidity wasn't melting everything. A breeze kept the exhaust miasma in circulation, so the air seemed fit to breathe. It was a good day to be alive, even if too many like it weren't left, both the "good day" part and the "alive" part.

"Come, over here," the general said. He pointed. "The mountains." Not so far away, the bulk of the green Carpathians humped up against the western horizon.

"We used them to navigate our way back to the lines after the bridge job."

"Good, then you're familiar with them. A road runs through them, called the Yaremche Road, for the biggest village along the way. It's too steep and too unstable, the engineers say, for tanks. At most it could support a Panzerwagen, but no more."

"Yes sir," said Karl.

"The road takes you through them, and then to Uzhgorod. At a certain point, four-point-six kilometers beyond Yaremche, it rises and passes through a gap, high stone cliffs on each side for about a hundred meters, which is called Natasha's Womb. No one knows who Natasha was, but the point is, we need to hold her private parts."

"Yes sir."

"Ivan has a partisan army in those mountains.

He may order them to the Womb. He can land several platoons of paratroopers not far away. He might infiltrate a special group, commandos like yourself, overland, through the forests. If he closes it off, he cuts down what I think many see as a last-minute escape, the shortcut to the next operating area behind our newly established lines. I cannot move a tank army or an infantry division through it. But there are many who could make use of it, men who want a quick, sure way out, our staff, the other divisional and regimental staff, the intelligence people, the signal people, anyone too valuable to join the long, slow-moving escape north of Lemberg and link up with what's left of Army Group Center, subject to strafing, bombing, artillery, do you see?"

"And of course the SS?"

"Yes, yes, the SS, correct."

"It's sort of a secret escape route for the SS, then?" said Karl.

"I sense sourness in your voice. Why can't SS invest its own troops in protecting its way out? The answer is, the Waffen-SS units are very badly mauled, almost nonoperational. We do have a new group from Thirteenth SS-Mountain, called Scimitar, a police battalion I'm told, but they're specialists in anti-bandit operations, not in static warfare. This would seem perfect for them, but they're on their own special security assignment for Dr. Groedl. They work directly for him. Not available. So it's fallen to us. That means I need a bunch of extremely professional boys to hold Natasha's Womb until the very last second, then blow it so that no Russian vehicles can pursue, and get out the best way possible. Obviously, Battlegroup Von Drehle is best suited for a special-needs job like this."

"Yes sir."

"Now, not so down, Major Von Drehle. It's quite possible Ivan won't be interested in it, won't consider it worth sending troops. He can't get tanks up there, and it's quite likely, given his lack of attention to details, that he'll just ignore it. It may be like a summer vacation for your fellows, and when you get the signal, you can blow it, come out of the Carpathians, having had a nice rest."

"On the other hand, we could get hit by a battalion-sized unit, isn't that right, sir? All fifteen of us?"

"Major, if that happens, I know you will inflict massive casualties on the enemy before withdrawing. And if it's close, between you and me, I don't give a damn if you engage the enemy or not. Just blow the goddamn thing and come through to Uzhgorod."

"So we just wait until the signal and blow it?"

"Well, there's another thing. While you're up there, you'll have to assist Police Battalion."

"Rounding up Jews?"

"I think most of them have been rounded up," said the general. "It's one of the things the SS is reasonably good at. No, it's not that. Evidently at some high level, one of our intelligence agencies has learned that Comrade Stalin himself has sent a sniper in to liquidate the senior group leader."

"I'll happily hold the rifle for—"

"Sergeant Bober, you flirt with destruction both in and out of battle. There are people in the very next room who would have you shot for uttering such a thing. Von Drehle, if you can't control him, I'll have a couple of large sergeants tape his mouth shut."

"I understand, sir," said Von Drehle.

"I can watch my tongue, but not my brain," said Bober.

"A fair compromise. Anyhow, the word is that this sniper isn't a him, it's a her. It's a woman who has operated in battle against us in Stalingrad and at Kursk. Her name is Petrova, she's got over a hundred kills, she's very skilled. In the east, they have a name for her. They call her the White Witch."

Von Bink narrated the adventures of the White Witch in evading the ambush and probably preparing to assassinate Groedl.

"Police Battalion has been conducting sweep operations and intelligence gathering in the villages beneath Natasha's Womb. I believe hostages have been shot and interrogations are vigorous. Typical SS operating procedures."

"Aren't they run by some kind of Arabian pimp, sir?" said Von Drehle.

"As I understand it, he's not a pimp but the cousin of an important Reich supporter who broadcasts to the Middle East from Berlin these days. This cousin is a very determined young man. Do you know him?"

"We've had words."

"So he has developed some information that suggests one area as a likely hiding spot for this White Witch. He means to run a sweep with dogs up that way. If she's there, she will head for Natasha's Womb and escape into uncontested country."

"What is the Russian army going to be doing this time, sir?"

"Almost certainly attacking. Yes, it will be quite busy around here. The First Ukrainian Front has over one-point-two million men, twenty-two hundred tanks, and twenty-eight-hundred planes. Sometime soon they will launch all of them in our direction. We have only Army Group North Ukraine spread through these parts, about half as many men and machines, and the men are, many of them, Hungarian, perhaps not that inclined to give their all. So when Ivan comes, he will come in deadly earnest. And in the middle of that will be poor little Battlegroup Von Drehle, hunting for a single girl. Your job is to catch her, if indeed she makes for the Womb, and hold her for Police Battalion. Please pay no attention to the one-point-two million Red soldiers."

"Yes sir."

"I've made arrangements for you to draw ammunition and other supplies. You'll also have a radio transmitter, and you know how hard to get they are. Division intelligence has already put a map package together for you. I want you to check with them for detailed briefing; they're expecting you. Your transportation will get you through Yaremche tomorrow at 0630, and I want you in place by 1200. I'll want a daily report, as will Police Battalion. SS must be kept in the communications network or they'll make trouble, and this Police Battalion officer has Groedl's ear."

"Understood, sir. One question, if I may."

"Go ahead," said Von Bink.

"If I'm in the shit and I have to hold on against a large attack, I'd dearly love to have a Flammenwerfer in my bunker. Ivan hates the bite of the Flammenwerfer. A few squirts of burning fuel and he loses his taste for the charge."

The Flammenwerfer-41 was the flamethrower, which spat out bolts of pure fire for twenty-five meters in half-second units. Everybody hated to go against it; that was the primal power of flame.

"Yes, but not right away. It seems Police Battalion has requested them, and with their high Kommissariat authority, they've got them all, for some damned reason or other. I'll put through an order so that when they're done with the things, they'll radio you. I'll give you a Kübel so that you can run back to Yaremche and pick up your Flammenwerfer."

"Very good, sir."

"Look, I know you don't like this, but we are all going to be in the shit in the next few days as we fight our way through another retreat. Be glad you're not on some lone 8.8 battery facing Ivan's thousand T-34s."

"Yes sir."

"And Bober, watch that mouth. It could get you killed."

Interlude in Tel Aviv III

It hit him in the middle of the night.

"Gershon, where are you going?"

"To the office."

"Gershon, it can wait until morning. Come back to bed."

"I can't sleep."

"There is some yogurt in the fridge, but I am *not* going to get up to make you coffee. You can make your own coffee, you madman."

He drove through the quiet streets of Herzliya, a suburb not unlike any in the civilized world.

Now and then a light was on in a house, but mostly it was dark, people asleep and secure in their beds. No one would come to arrest them and send them off to a bitter destiny of night and fog, he thought, recalling that his grandparents had not made it out of the night and fog of Poland to disappear in the Shoah, as had most of his wife's family. His children, a photographer and a gym teacher, had no idea about any of this beyond perfunctory acknowledgment, unrooted in emotion, of family history. He himself rarely thought of it, as his mind was mechanical in its genius, based on mathematics, memory, the ability to see patterns or factors where no one else did, as opposed to empathetic, a conjurer of emotions. But for some reason, tonight the Shoah seemed alive to him as he drove through neighborhoods of sleeping Jews. Nobody protected them then. Who protects them now? Well, the best air force, army, and navy in the world. Also Gershon Gold.

He arrived at the Black Cube, where a sign of stability in the world was that no upper floor lights blazed away; he got through a surprised security without issue and went to his cubicle after a stop in the cafeteria for bad machine coffee, black, then got to work.

His insight: Platinum not as wealth, not as finance, not as operational lubrication. But platinum as stuff. As physical property, of weight and size, requiring transportation, security, delivery to—? Well, to where?

Today's working thesis: The newly purchased $16 mils worth of stuff had to be delivered to a shipping location. They couldn't just FedEx it. It weighed—he calculated—about 685 pounds, but, because of its density, was about the size of a shoe box, although typically packaged in a container designed to be loaded on a pallet. Where would it have been picked up, where would it have been shipped? It didn't take long for him to ascertain that the vast majority of AMPLATS platinum was railroaded to Port Elizabeth from its refinement in the Johannesburg complex, then shipped to its destination by freighter, because in most instances the amount was too unwieldy to ship by air. But this platinum was a different issue. Six hundred eighty-five pounds was easily transportable by air, and air traffic being more crowded than sea lane traffic by a factor of about twenty to one, it would be more difficult to track.

However . . . Gershon knew this game . . . and he knew that all exporters in South Africa, including AMPLATS, are required to register with the South African Revenue Services, called SARS. They used a single administration document to make the clearance of goods easier and more convenient for importers, exporters, and cross-border traders. One purpose of this document was to ensure that exported goods were properly declared to SARS. The form required the exporter or his agent to indicate the foreign consignee, the place of export, the form of transportation, and the estimated date of departure. The document was submitted to the commissioner of customs, a division of SARS.

So: how to crack SARS firewalls and read the AMPLATS export documents for a $16 million shipment of platinum?

The answer: Cain & Abel, a program obtained from the Darknet, the under or illegal side of the Net known to most professionals but unreachable by outsiders. Cain & Abel was a password discovery tool that allowed easy recovery by first sniffing out the network, and then cracking encrypted and scrambled passwords using dictionaries, brute force, and cryptanalysis methods if needed. Not only that, Gershon had used it to record voice and video transmissions over the Internet and grab cached passwords and trace routing protocols.

Gershon activated his copy of Cain & Abel, pointed it at the authentification server for the South African Revenue Service, and waited. It wasn't a long wait. In South Africa, a data entry clerk signed on, and Gershon walked into the system in his shadow; all the data that existed became visible to him.

He called up the enormous file on AMPLATS, reduced his frame set to transactions of a few days—on the assumption that Nordyne had bought fast and paid fast and therefore wanted shipment fast—and discovered that among the tonnes dispatched to car makers, the grams to jewelers and the pounds to oncological units, one shipment, AM43367, was dispatched to Nordyne Ceramics, located in Astrakhan, on the Volga River at the northeastern tip of the Caspian Sea, in Russia.

So who in Russia wanted $16 million in platinum, particularly when Russia was the world's second largest producer of . . . platinum? It was the classic coals-to-Newcastle scenario, which made sense only if the point of the transaction was the secrecy of the transaction.

Suddenly there was another indicator pointing exactly to that one place: Astrakhan, which turned out to be a grimy seaport supported by petroleum sucked from under the Caspian, as well as sturgeon—the eggs were called caviar. It was a dreary Russian town of about a half a million luckless souls. But it turned out that he was able to intercept—another Cain & Abel transaction—an e-mailed request from a member of Intrusion Prevention Associates' team to the home office in Grozny for an upgrade in per diem, because presumably the price of whores in Russia was higher than that in Chechnya.

So he had a security team, $16 million in platinum in a city in Russia. But where in that city?

One option: get beyond the firewall of Narimanovo Airport, see what cargo flights had arrived in Astrakhan from Johannesburg, what imports had been cleared, and where they had been routed to. Yes, but it was too far for the plane of choice—a Boeing 737 chartered to a Panamanian company called Hurricane Cargo—to fly straight from SA to RUS nonstop, so the plane would have had to stop for refueling, likely at the halfway point in Eritrea. Possibly Eritrea was listed as the point of origin on the Narimanovo documents. Sorting that would involve another level of search, which would involve time, time, and more time.

Instead, he decided to run recent industrial real estate transactions in Astrakhan and found them to be on the public record, so no clandestine penetration was involved. He guessed that if you were going to do something, anything, with 685 pounds of platinum, and if you had a security team standing by to protect the investment, you probably needed an old factory, and you needed to upgrade the joint with new fencing, TV surveillance cameras, sirens, location indicators, pressure-sensitive intrusion detectors and so forth. You needed electricity and water, some kind of fire prevention system. Most likely you needed equipment, and the equipment would pretty much reveal what it was that Nordyne was manufacturing.

You naughty boys, trying so hard to keep your games hidden. But Tata Gershon will find you in the end.

He got back to work.

CHAPTER 33

Yaremche
The Carpathians
THE PRESENT

The grazing wound in the side never bled. But the elbow did, presumably cut on the gunman's breaking teeth. Swagger had washed and bandaged it but was surprised by the stiffness and bruising that seized his whole left arm and made the lengthy ride by bumper car to the mountain village the next day quite uncomfortable.

He didn't tell Reilly about it, not wanting to alarm her. Nor did he mention Stronski's claim about "The Americans." It was another screwball, which threw everything out of whack, adding a new dimension of conspiracy that could lead anywhere or nowhere. But it weighed on him over the distance of the drive. He turned it over and over in his head, trying to define an American interest or angle in obscure events in a sliver of Ukraine in the middle of another nation's war seventy years ago, about which most Americans knew nothing.

Now they had met at and checked in to a hotel, rested, and were standing on the walking bridge over the River Prut, just beyond where the water tumbled off the rocks and hit below with a roar and a splash, filling the air with mist. This clearly was not the exact bridge as crudely etched into the plate, since it was buttressed, sunk in concrete, and of strong metal itself, heavily engineered. But a bridge had stood here, and if the drawing was right, it was about here that Groedl was when Mili took her hopeless, doomed shot at him.

"Trying to figure out where the shot came from," he said, looking around, trying to read the data of the place.

He saw the falls before him, the low bluffs of the river, and to the right, way off, a mountain slope. In the crude drawing on the plate, the officers next to the man were pointing more or less in that direction. But Bob didn't buy it. Clearly the artist hadn't seen the event but was re-creating it from an oral tale. The shot couldn't have come from way out there.

"See, that's way too far. A thousand yards. Not with any rifle she had could she have hit him from there. It has to be pretty close."

He looked at the closer landforms. Surely the Germans controlled the banks of the river. They would have possibly crowded the villagers down there, on a little shelf of land just under the bridge, where Swagger had found the machine-gun shell.

He rotated 180 degrees, passing over the faux Ukraine village of souvenir booths where the old village itself had stood, and continued to examine the lay of the land. More riverbank, controlled by the Germans, and above it, on the left, a vast two-hundred-yard-tall slope of white pines that extended for another half mile from the bridge, perhaps half of it the chunk of land where the pines were somehow lighter, as they'd noticed before.

"She had to be there," he said. "But I don't see how they controlled it. She could get close enough over there to hit with any rifle. Wouldn't need no scope. How'd they bluff her into shooting from so far out she had to miss?"

They stared at the slope rising above them.

"She had to be up there," he said. "Notice anything?"

"Just a lot of mountain."

"Look at the trees. The color, remember?"

In the sun, the demarcation between the lighter timber and the darker was clear.

"I'm getting something, I've got a feeling. Damn, nothing. But maybe—" He paused, thinking it over, and yes, it made solid sense.

"What is it?"

"The lighter green?"

"Yep."

"It's green because it's new growth," he said. "It's been grown since 1944."

"All right, new growth."

"I think I know what they tried to do."

CHAPTER 34

Above Yaremche
The Carpathians
MID-JULY 1944

It happened rarely enough, but sometimes there was good, deep sleep, dreamless. It exiled her fear, her fatigue, her predicament. It was pure bliss. Deep in the cave, buried in leaves, she finally found nourishment in sleep. It seemed to last forever, velvety and seamless, the utter pleasure of deep sleep and—

"What? What?"

"You must see this. Come, really, you must look at this."

It was the Teacher. His voice was so strained that she did not bother to argue. Whatever it was, she had to see it.

It was the hour before the dawn. The night sky was like her sleep, velvety, dark, without depth or luster. But to the east, there was a strange glare.

"What is that? What is going on?"

"Come, see, it's amazing."

She followed him down the dark path through the forest, feeling the trees swaying in some kind of breeze, hearing the rush of the pine needles moving against each other, hearing the creaking and groaning as the heavy limbs moved reluctantly.

"Is it the offensive? Has the Red Army arrived?"

"No, something else. I don't know what to make of it."

He brought her to a promontory looking down through a notch between two mountains, and she recognized the landforms from the maps she'd studied, and knew she was looking into Yaremche. But the back slope of one of the mountains that obscured the village issued a glow above its crest that filled the sky, and even this high, this far, the acrid residue of smoke reached them. More strangely still, every now and then a tongue of flame could be seen in the darkness, though where it landed was behind the back slope.

"They're burning it," said the Teacher.

"Flammenwerfer-41s," she said. "I've seen them before. They used them against us in Stalingrad. They're systematically burning the slope of that mountain over the village, clearing it. But why?"

"That is what I meant to ask you. To do that much work that fast, they must have had to bring in every flamethrower in the area. Why? What on earth can it mean to them? And why do they do it now, when they know our troops are about to jump off and those weapons can halt or slow advances all up and down the line? Yet they gather them here for this madness. It makes no sense, does it, Sergeant Petrova?"

"You're the intelligence assistant, Teacher. You tell me."

"I have no idea. Well, except—"

"Go on."

"They fear you."

"What?"

"They have not yet caught you, and it drives them mad with fear. They do not know if you have a new rifle. Thus, to be safe, they denude the mountain of its forest cover surrounding a town. The point is to deny the White Witch cover from which to fire. But why would she come to this town, in this zone?"

"I can think of only one reason."

"And that is?"

"Groedl himself, for some reason, will soon be in this town."

"How close do you need to be?"

"With an infantry rifle, I'd need to be within two hundred yards, and there's no way I'm going to walk down a barren slope of burned hillside with a nice long rifle to within two hundred yards."

"No, they'll massacre you."

She tried to think of herself making a long shot without telescopic sights. It was—impossible. At over three hundred yards, he'd be a speck, a tiny dot. Worse, she'd have to hold over him, and he'd be gone, hidden behind the wedge of the front sight, and she'd have nothing to index to, unable to read the distance. The wind would play, the humidity would play, every tremble in every fiber in her body would play.

You have to do it anyway.

It's madness. It's death. It's folly.

But she was caught. She felt the only way to prove to an NKVD that concealed a traitor that she was not herself a traitor was to make the kill. But the range was too far, the rifle not precise enough now that the Germans had scorched the earth.

"I have to shoot from the edge of the burned zone," she said.

"It's too far. I see, it's a trap. That's where they *want* you to shoot from. Men will be there."

"It doesn't matter."

"You don't even have a rifle."

"I will get a rifle. Tomorrow that is our mission."

"No, tomorrow we scrounge for food, because if we don't find it, the day after, we will be too weak to find a rifle."

· · ·

The next day they took a chance. They had to eat. She was a mile or so away from the cave, in a nondescript glade of trees given not so much to the high white pines but more to spruce and juniper and the groundcover called snowball. It was in precincts such as these where the fungus thrived, though it took a good eye to spot it nestled in shade in the undergrowth or at the base of trees away from sun. She looked for a brown thing with black edging and fins along its stalk called a honey mushroom, which the Peasant had told her was edible. She had a sample and rooted like a pig, probing and sniffing for the dead white flesh of the things. But in one second, the world changed.

She melted. She slid down and, on the ground, squirmed as gently as possible deeper in the tangles and the tendrils of the snowball. She felt her heart begin to hammer. It was . . . what? An odd sound, a wisp of odor, a peripheral clue that flew straight to her subconscious. She lay, still as death.

Slowly they emerged. No, they had not seen her. A roaming patrol, their own woodcraft exceedingly high, they were slipping through the white pines, hunting.

She had not seen SS men since Kursk. She lay motionless in the brush as the hunched, tense soldiers moved through. They were bent double, ready for action, camouflaged in the dapples of the summer forest, their weapons black and held easily in hand, unslung for fast action. She heard them shout to each other, though in Serbian, not German, and it was clear they were highly professional, good at quiet movement, men well experienced in the stealth of war.

A trickle of sweat came down her neck, then another and another. She could not move to squelch the discomfort, but instead tried to focus on it, reduce it to components, the wetness, the subversive irritation, the irrationality of her need to rub it hard and make it stop annoying her. Then a hundred other tiny infractions of order began to tickle her supine body, the pain of abrasions, the dry twitch of an itch, the further tracking of sweat, the nasal dryness of her reduced breathing, the agony of a finger trapped at an odd angle under her hand, which was in its place trapped under her body, the hum of small insects fluttering at her ears, drawn to her by the odor of that sweat, the brush of their landing, the miniature sting of their bites, not in themselves annoying but, as they multiplied in time, truly uncomfortable. To move would be to die.

Loud crushing. Boots trampled brush so close at hand. They raised dust, which drifted, floated to her dry nostrils, and settled their veil of grit within. More kicking; suddenly they were before her, black hobnailed things, well used, well worn, extremely comfortable to their wearer. He stopped, and though blurry through the slitted vision of her eyelids—she was afraid to close them, too much noise!—she recognized repose as the fellow stopped to pluck something from his pouch, diddle with it, adjust it, make preparations. A zip came from above, followed by the stench of sulfur in the wind, followed by the sound of a hard suck, followed by the odor of pipe tobacco as it took full ignition.

His right boot was less than a foot from her. He sucked hard on his pipe, enjoyed the mellow blast of the burning tobacco, and exhaled a cloud of smoke, which drifted over her like the raiments of sackcloth. The SS man was taking a nice little break from his hunt, presumably using the quiet to give his eyes full freedom to roam, to search for telltale sign, a track, a fractured bough, a scrape, whatever, that would lead him to his quarry.

His boot was so close. She remembered the SS boots at Kursk, as she had seen so many. Involuntarily the memories, which she had pressed so hard to forget, came over her as if in a sudden tide from her subconscious, where she had tried to lock them away.

It was called the Special Purpose Detachment, an ad hoc emergency assemblage of sharpshooters from all over the southern front, not just vets of Stalingrad but of Rostov, Sebastopol,

Kharkov, Kiev, wherever the sniper had practiced his trade. Though most, like Mili, were army, this was strictly an NKVD operation. It was something only NKVD would think up.

"Tomorrow," said the commissar, "July twelfth, two great tank armies will clash. Look at the map, comrades, and see that it is ordained. The Second SS Panzer Corps will send eight hundred Panzer IVs and Tiger Is and we will greet them with fifteen hundred T-34s from the Fifth Guards Tank Army. It will be the greatest tank battle in history, and you are privileged to fight in it."

They were in a village called Prokhorovka, in the southern aspect of a salient that the German armored forces were trying to pinch off, then destroy, from two directions. Though a terrible melee on the ground, the battle was simple: the Germans would meet up, cutting off and surrounding the salient and turning it into an encirclement, then destroy the trapped hundreds of thousands; or they would not. It was up to the tankers of the 5th Guards to prevent that.

"At 0400 you will be distributed among the tanks as they rally and begin to move to the fields outside the village. There will be five of you per tank. You will ride them into battle, as our tank riders have done so heroically throughout the war. At a certain moment after daybreak, you will engage the German panzers. Those of you who survive the transit through the German artillery barrage will wait until the two tank armies are fully involved and then peel off and find some sort of shooting position, behind a ruined vehicle, in a copse of trees, in a scruff of vegetation, at the lip of a shell crater.

"You will see before you a field of ruin as the tanks begin to destroy each other on a massive scale. You have a specific job. You will note that when a German tank is hit and brought to a stop, it may or may not burn. That depends on the hit and a thousand other factors. If it does not burn, its crew will scamper out the hatch and head on foot back to German lines to acquire another tank and continue the fight. Your job, snipers, is to kill these men before they make it back. Shoot them down without mercy! Punish them for their cruelties, their atrocities, the evil of their invasion of the motherland, their destruction of our villages and towns. That is your holy mission.

"I have a warning as well. As I said, the German tanks will burn or not burn, depending on the placement of the shell. If the tanks burn, oftentimes their crew or some of their crew will make it out. These men will be aflame. Perhaps you have seen as much in your experience, and you know that watching a man burn to death is no easy thing.

"But your heart must be steel. You would not be human if you didn't feel the impulse to put a mercy shot into that screaming, dancing apparition and end his agony. You are not permitted, under pain of execution, to shoot the flamers. You must concentrate on unwounded Germans. You are not permitted to waste time and ammunition on our own flamers. Order 270 will apply tomorrow on the killing ground. Remember: waste not one bullet on mercy."

Order 270 was Stalin's decree that the families of deserters or shirkers would be arrested as a consequence of their criminality. Mili snorted privately; her family was dead.

Within hours, she found herself clinging by a handhold to the hull of a T-34 (the commander was twenty and blond, reminding her a little of her dead brother Gregori) as it roared, amid a legion of its brethren, out of the village, deployed into a large wedge formation in the dawn light as far as the eye could see, and began its passage through the fields and the German artillery toward combat with another tank formation. The tanks scuttled and adjusted as they squirmed into the formation, cranking this way and that to find the right line and distance with regard to the others until all, more or less, had formed up. Like some kind of dinosaur army, they lurched forward, grinding across hill, dale, creek, tree, gully without regard, spewing smoke and grit, their long cannon barrels slightly upraised. They looked like beetles with a knight's lance tucked into their mandibles.

They were on a plain under a dome of sky. All was flatness. It was an infinity of flatness under the towering clouds of the Ukrainian sky. It was a battle reduced to its essential elements with no distractions, almost an abstraction: the existential flatness of the plain to the horizon, the vaulting blue arch of cloud-filled sky, the sense of tininess of men and machines on this construction that only a mad god could have invented. The tanks lurched ahead.

The sensations attacked her nervous system: the overwhelming smell of engine smoke and gasoline, the cruel bouncing as the tank's suspension absorbed and then passed along the shocks of its encounters with the rough ground, the shriek of the incoming artillery, the percussion of its detonation. Nearby, a tank was hit and, in a second, vanished into a shearing blade of light as its destruction issued vibration and shrapnel through the air, to beat and cut at what lay in its route. She clung desperately, trying to stay with the beast beneath her, but it was not easy. Another sniper, clinging to another handhold on the other side of the tank, slipped off, as if into a gritty sea, and was never seen again.

The tanks rolled through the storm and through an ocean of noise as each engine, each shell, each crack of a tree limb crushed beneath treads seemed to hang in the air, like a whole climate of noise, all of it beating at her senses until so powerful was the experience that it seemed to numb her out.

Then she saw them, a mile off, small and seemingly inconsequential. The machines of the 2nd Panzer Corps, three divisions' worth, Das Reich, Totenkopf, and Leibstandarte Adolf Hitler. From the distance, they were black shapes on the horizon, which rose and fell in accordance to their own tank's course through the dips in the landform.

At a mile, the Germans opened up. It was simple strategy; any child could figure it out. The German armor was thicker, the German guns bigger and more powerful. Distance was the German ally. If it was only about shooting, the Germans—superb tank marksmen, superb battle-field maneuverers—would triumph. The tanks of the 5th Guards had to close the gap, get inside the German formation, find angles into the enemy that would let their lighter 76mm shells penetrate and kill. The cost of this adventure was paid in life. Sixty percent of the Soviet tanks would make it to the target; the other 40 percent would die in flame and high-explosive energy at the end of the 88mm trajectories. So it had to be. So it would be. The price would be paid. Who would pay it?

Around her, tanks began to light up. Some, hit squarely by the 88s, vaporized and, when the smoke abated, seemed not to have existed at all. But there were so many variations on death in that charging wave of vehicle and bravado. Hit, a 34 might be tilted askew, flames licking at it, until it suddenly blossomed, went to total fire. Or it might not burn at all, merely throwing a track and thrashing in roaring frustration as its treadless wheels ground away, spitting earth and buzzsawing itself more deeply into the ground.

So powerful was the vibration of her vehicle, Petrova could see none of this clearly. Her eyes were teared up from the dust that had settled in them, her purchase on survival was focused entirely on the strength in her hands that clung to the steel rung preventing her from slipping off and away, her head pounded in pain from all the vibrations that shuddered against it, the fumes of engine exhaust, explosive residue, and the smell of cooking meat. Images seemed to fly before her and vanish, as if she were in a cinema where the projector was mounted to the back of a crazed horse and pitched its visions on the walls and ceiling. Burning men. The shear of light from a blast. The recoil when her own tank fired. The pressure from others. The far-off blisters of illumination from the Tiger 88mm muzzles, the rain of dust, the smack and sting of debris, it was all a kind of Dostoyevskian vision of hell.

Then it went away as her tank slid into a dip in the land and, with dozens of its co-attackers, was momentarily out of the view of German gun-sights. It felt like an abrupt passage to heaven as the ground beneath became smooth, almost reasonable. The tanks were grinding through a wheat field; she looked back to see the long scars each vehicle inscribed into the undulating sheaves of wheat, that staple in which her father had invested his life and even, it could be said, died to protect.

I will not let you down, Tata, she thought. I will be as brave as you. I will protect the wheat.

At that moment they crested the slope, their momentary disengagement finished, and plunged into a storm of violence. The German tanks were close. She'd seen them before, crawling tentatively through Stalingrad's wrecked streets, but not like this, columns and columns of the things, with their remorseless angularity, their pitiless precision, the somehow Teutonic-knight definition of their profiles. The Germans were beyond panic; they were beyond anything but pure, calm, relentless battle skill. The gunners chose and worked targets as the Soviet force closed, and even when it became obvious that there were enough survivors of the charge to breach the German formation and turn the battle into a melee, the German gunners simply lowered their trajectories, tracked their targets, and continued to fire.

The two forces closed.

Now it was tank on tank, almost like a naval battle as the vessels of each side maneuvered at speed for positional leverage, angle to unarmored vitals, accuracy, and firing speed, kicking up dust, spraying debris and mud as they adjusted. It had Trafalgar or Jutland or the Armada entwined through it. The smaller Russian vehicles juked, switched attack angles radically, feinted, and jitterbugged, looking for that elusive sideways angle into the slower, bigger vehicles, which, though not as maneuverable, had more able gunners and seldom missed a shot.

She was in a cauldron of blast heat and concussion, wondering how on earth she could get a clean shot off. At that point her own vehicle came to a halt, almost spilling her, and she heard a mechanical buzz and whirr as the twenty-year-old in the turret rotated. One hundred meters ahead, seen through the squalls of smoke that dominated the battlefield, a Tiger emerged from behind the burning wreckage of another Tiger, and her boy fired. She felt the rock as the tank discharged its shell, saw it hit the flank on the squared profile and detonate, casting a galaxy of sparks pinwheeling into the air. The German was not fazed; his own turret ground another few degrees and he fired, the shock of the blast ripping up the earth beneath the muzzle, and in the next nanosecond the impact tossed Petrova, light as a feather and frail as a sparrow, into the sky. She landed with a bone-jarring, concussion-inducing thud, her mind fragmenting into slivers as stars danced and planets crashed. In a second, alone and feeling naked on a battlefield full of raging monsters, she picked up enough sense to seek shelter behind the burned-out wreck of a tank, so melted and charred that its alliance could not be discerned. She crouched, looking back to the vehicle that had ferried her to this place, and saw it listed over, smoke issuing from its hatch, until it was engulfed in flame. Nobody got out, and of its other snipers aboard, none could be seen.

She disengaged her rifle from its sling, cinched up, and found a shooting position. She looked for targets. In time, her peripheral vision oriented her toward a blur of movement, and she saw a Tiger grinding through a glade of higher vegetation. It was hit, and a massive geyser of dust engulfed it. Then the cloud cleared and she saw that the thing had taken a shell in the tread, the tread snaked free, driven by the power axle, though the tank was immobile. Its turret hatch opened and she found her position, waited for a man to emerge at the tip of the post reticule in her scope. As he came, her finger killed him. His head jerked at the shot, and his body seemed to turn to liquid as he slipped back into the vehicle. Then a smear of incandescence erupted at the juncture of turret and hull, and in seconds the thing was leaking smoke like blood, then flames, and it was gone to inferno. The dead man had blocked the others from escape.

She looked over her sight, preferring to immediately abandon that image and let her eyes adjust after the brightness of the flame, and scanned the battlefield, seeing vehicle after vehicle conflagrated, all the smoke rising, drifting skyward to form a pall over the battlefield, a low, dark sky that portended the world's end. Noises—screams, detonations, the rip of metal tearing—filled the air, and waves of heat and grit rode blast zephyrs into her face and eyes. Ashes floated, blotting skin where they landed.

Another tank emerged from the haze, already leaking a tendril of smoke. Who knew what hell it concealed. She planted the rifle against her shoulder, steadied on the turret—not a long shot, less by far than two hundred yards—and felt her trigger stack. He came out—aflame. He rolled back across the hull, over the engine cooling grate, kicking, his arms flailing, nothing left but his agony. Her finger killed him with one shot. Another flamer crawled out and she killed him before he could roll off the turret.

Once she'd committed the unpardonable sin, she could not stop. The plan was ill conceived because the visibility on the battlefield was so limited that scampering panzer crew could not be seen at all, but the dancing flamers, their garish ignition fluttering brilliantly through the drift of smoke and ash, were easy to spot. She shot them all. It didn't matter.

She made a shot at five hundred yards, holding

half a man high; she made one at fifty yards, drilling him as he leaped out of the half-track that already had turned into a bonfire. She shot not at men but at flames, for the men were largely indistinct in their cloaks of flaring brilliance. Russian, German, peasant, aristocrat, who knew? Their insane jerkiness contained their suffering; she could not abide it and she put them down into stillness.

It was almost ritual. When the rifle fired dry, she slid another stripper into the breach and thumbed five more cartridges into the magazine well, then tossed away the empty stripper and rammed the bolt home, and remounted the rifle against the tension of the strap. Through the circle of the optic, she saw it all, death at the apex of industrial application, but by now her ears were numb, so it was silent cinema, the same thirty feet of film over and over in an endless loop, the flamer clawing at the pulses of energy that consumed his flesh in agony and then the arrival of the message of mercy as his blazing body went slack and he tumbled down. Cock and look anew for a target. In the end, she killed more than fifty unrecorded men that day, only the first one without the flames.

It abated around five. The few surviving tanks limped back to their own lines. It was clear that while the Russians had lost far more, they had stopped the Germans. In fact, it was clear that the war was now technically over. Only a thousand miles of mopping up remained, and though that would be a hideous task and claim millions or more lives, the shattering of the 2nd SS Panzer Corps ended Hitler's invasion. He would, he could, never be on the offense again.

If she knew this, it didn't matter. She was exhausted and somehow ashamed. She felt no glory. Around her there lay a wilderness of dead machines, half of them burning, amid a stench of gas and blood, the occasional loud blast as a shell was lit off by flames, but nobody was shooting anymore. Everybody was too tired to shoot. The setting sun burned through the haze of smoke and ash in the air, and it went all red on the world, on this hunk of field outside Prokhorovka, as if to signify the shedding of so much blood. All was red in the light, the gray German tanks, the green Russian tanks, the dun-colored wheat, the green trees, the white flesh: all suffused in the red of blood.

She disengaged her water bottle, unscrewed the cap, and put it to her mouth. A warm swish of water cut through the phlegm of ash that encased her lips. She took off her hood, felt her hair cascade free. She looked around again.

Remember it, Petrova, she instructed herself. Infinite destruction. Ruin to the horizon and death everywhere. Stalingrad in the wheat fields without a ruined city to hide the ripe slaughter.

• • •

A whistle, loud and urgent, came from close by, jerking her from the field of ruin and death at Kursk to the German boot a few inches from her face. She heard him grunt as if cursing. He tamped his pipe against the receiver of his machine pistol. Burning tobacco from the emptied pipe fell to the ground a few inches ahead of her. His boots finally lurched forward. She heard a few shouts, the exchange of Serbian curse words, and some crude laughter. The boots vanished.

She raised her head just an inch or two and opened her eyes fully.

The German patrol had vanished in the woods.

Someone had recalled them—urgently.

She waited another half an hour, then picked herself up.

The boots. She remembered the boots. A thousand burned corpses lay about the flatness of Kursk, some licked by flame, some just blurred chars. Yet almost all had their boots still on, because for some reason, while the flesh burned, the leather didn't. Everywhere she saw nothing but the boots of the dead.

CHAPTER 35

The Carpathians
New Village of Yaremche
THE PRESENT

There's not much to do in the Carpathians after the sun goes down.

"Get a good night's rest," Swagger said. "Tomorrow we'll go up into the hills and I'll see if I can find where she shot from. I want to see her angle from the edge of the burned zone and get a read on distance."

He knew she had to shoot from beyond five hundred yards. She had to. She couldn't be in the burned zone because she'd be wide open. But at the five-hundred-yard mark, where the trees offered cover, that's where they'd put people. They'd have camouflaged guys there. They'd have dog teams nearby. That's the trap, and they know they've got her, just as they know she has to go for it, because here he is, her target, this is the only opportunity she'll get.

Swagger knew how a sniper's mind worked. She'd shoot high to low, especially if she's already high. How would she even get to low, the place is crawling with Germans? They built a real good trap. Groedl's a smart piece of shit.

But it was the rifle that had him buffaloed. Not where she got it but why she did what she did. She could not have hit him with a Mosin, even with a scope. There was no record of a one-shot cold-bore kill at five hundred yards with a Mosin. If she fired, she was doomed. She was throwing away her life on a zero chance of probability. It was effectively a suicide, a sacrifice for the good of a tribe that denied it. But she had to do it. She had no choice.

He thought hard about the site. The bridge, the mist from the waterfall, the image of the shoot on the plate by some anonymous artist who probably hadn't been there. The burned zone on the slope to the northwest, the only high space to shoot from. The slope barren to a five-hundred-yard line, and poor Petrova up there, as close as possible, taking the shot that would let the dogs out on her. Maybe she shot twice, took the one at the far-off Nazi, and then put the muzzle in her mouth and hit the trigger. No torture, no interrogation, just a case of the sniper giving all to duty. But then an image came into his head.

He first saw it as a golden wall. What the hell? It floated just beyond his knowing but close enough to tantalize him: a gold wall.

Then it came into focus. He recalled that beyond the hill whose slope overlooked the waterfall and whose foliage had been half burned away, to the southwest, there was the golden wall of another slope, so far off it was hazy in the distance.

It had to be a thousand yards out.

You could not hit a man at a thousand yards with a Mosin-Nagant.

You could only do it with a—

Bob had to laugh. Now, *there* was a funny idea. Somehow Petrova manages to get her hands on—

It was impossible.

Wasn't it?

He thought a second and went to his e-mail on his iPhone. "You up? Need talk urgent. Can you call me at—" and he listed Reilly's satellite number. A few seconds later, her phone rang. He took it. "Swagger."

"Well, hello, chum. How's the Yank?" It was his friend J. T. "Jimmy" Guthrie, the sniper historian from the UK.

"Hi, Jimmy, how're you doing?"

"I'm swell. I assume you're calling because you're going to come to our Sniper Match at Bisley. The fellows will be so excited."

"No, no, it's something else. I need to rent your brain."

"It's yours for a penny. If you haven't got a penny, then a ha'penny will do."

"Last we talked, you were working on a book on the World War II British sniper rifle."

"My favorite, the Enfield No. 4 (T) with the No. 32 scope. A classic."

"Still working at it?"

"Chop chop, tap tap, got to keep churning them out, it's what I do."

"Can you verify any one-shot cold-bore hits with it at over a thousand yards?"

"Several times. In Italy, in northern France, and in Twelveland itself, near war's end. The No. 4 (T) was the ace of sniper rifles."

"Any other shots that long that you know of by other rifles?"

"Haven't come across anything on record in Europe. The No. 4 (T) had a most helpful ballistic eccentricity. Out to 250 yards, it was quite ordinary. But British and Canadian snipers soon learned that there was something about the .303 Radford Arsenal 176-grain bullet, the No. 4 (T) as bedded and with scope mounted by the geniuses at Holland and Holland, and maybe the superb optics of the No. 32 telescopic sight, which, although it was only 3.5-power, had lenses that offered unusual clarity out to long distances. Somehow if the .303 deviated from trajectory, by a property to this day not understood, the in-flight bullets somehow adjusted, trimmed, I don't know, 'fixed' themselves. So if they came back to the original trajectory and stayed spot-on, the result was unusually proficient long-range accuracy."

"Is there any way one of those rifles could have showed up in the Carpathian Ukraine in July '44?

It don't make no sense because we're five hundred miles or so from the nearest British troops, which would probably be in Italy. Does it make any sense at all?"

"Not a lick," said Jimmy. "Not a whisper. Which doesn't mean it didn't happen. I have the Holland and Holland records, I have the British army records, I even have some still-classified stuff from clandestine hugger-mugger done by something called the Special Operations Executive, whose charge was to set Europe ablaze. Possibly they could have set Ukraine ablaze while they were at it."

"Can you check? Sooner would be better than later."

"Yes, well, I've got the stuff here and I'll get on it straight away. By the way, I'm doing a chum a favor, I'm hoping he'll do one in response."

"You got it. I'll be at the match, when, October, was that it?"

"Swell! Yes, it would mean a lot to the boys. Okay, I'll get cracking."

Moscow
The Aquarium
The Krulov Investigation

Will sat on the floor of the KGB file depository on the ninth floor of the Lubyanka. The ordeal before him at least got his mind off the mysterious adventures his wife was having in Ukraine and his sense of longing for a nice quiet night in the apartment. Wearing a surgical mask and tight rubber gloves, plus a sweater because the room was kept so cold, he paged through the lengthy mass of Krulov papers, reading by flashlight because the light in the vast green room packed with files was so poor. He had to hurry, as Likov could guarantee him only six hours. Anything else and there could be trouble.

He paged through, scanning the well-typed onionskin, reading the Russian swiftly, and thanking his torturers at the Monterey Language School, who had beaten Russian into him and Kathy fifteen years ago. He confirmed much that he already knew about Basil Krulov: four years in Munich, '29–'33, in Munich with references to NKVD file Archangel 78-B11256 (Arkady Krulov), presumably documentation on his father, who was the supposed trade representative of the Russian Export Ministry but was really coordinating with the German communists and trade unions as they were jockeying for power with the boys in the twisted-cross hats. The boy attended German *Realschule*, as they call it, vigorous German high school, very fine education. Learned German quickly, which is commensurate with a high IQ. Then he enrolled at University of Munich and was there for two years before Hitler came to power and kicked all the Reds out, even the diplomatic ones. God, NKVD was thorough: they even had his syllabus and grades at that university. Will guessed it was part of German pedantry; they never throw anything out, the syllabuses, the report cards, the notes to Mom about dunking Peggy Sue's pigtails in the inkwell, the Dueling Society scars. Yes, the boy was brilliant, all 1's, meaning A's, and Will's eyes ran quickly over the ancient information dredged out of a dead world. Then he noticed something that made him blink twice.

Jesus Christ!, he said to himself.

It was the first of what turned into a night of Jesus Christ! moments.

Yaremche
The River Prut

They awoke, took a hearty breakfast—the hotel's specialty—and then drove to the waterfall site. They parked and moved quickly to the halfway point of the bridge.

He pointed over the faux village to a wooded slope golden in the sun. Its details were murky at the distance, at least a thousand yards, but he stared hard at it, finding it so provocative.

If she had fired from there, he thought, with a decent rifle

"So what's the plan?" Kathy asked.

"It would be better if I had a range finder, if I

had a compass, if I had a pair of binocs, but I don't. So I'll just sort of mark some potential firing sites from here, and we'll see if we can find them up there. Then I can satisfy myself as to what kind of rifle she had to have."

"Oh, look," she said. "Another American."

She pointed. At the far end of the bridge, a young man stood, smiling at them, posing as if in a hip commercial for a soft drink. He was wearing a yellow Baltimore Ravens cap, a polo shirt, a pair of jeans, and some trendy hikers. He looked like any young dad in a mall. He wore wrap-around tear-shaped sunglasses and a big smile. He walked over to them.

"Hi," he said. "Jerry Renn. It's a pleasure to meet Bob Lee Swagger, Bob the Nailer. You've been a hero of mine for a long time. I've been looking forward to meeting you."

CHAPTER 36

The Carpathians
Yaremche
LATE JULY 1944

The fire defied him. It would not burn fast enough, even in the drought of late July. He willed it to consume its tinder, to race down the slope, to despoil the forest and reveal the raw flanks of earth to the world, so that no sniper could hide and have the pleasure of a slow and easy preparation on the shot.

Even with ten of the Flammenwerfer-41s spurting out their Flammoil-19 in arcs of bright flame, igniting all that they touched, the natural world would not consume itself quickly enough for Captain Salid.

Like all his men, he wore a gas mask, for the acrid smoke hung low and dense and no wind came to push it away. He watched the blackness that followed the wall of flame as it spread slowly down the slope, devouring the greenery; he heard the crackle and pop of the spruces and junipers snapping as they were oxidized into a new form of matter; he watched the low black fog scuttle this way and that.

So much to worry about. The big Russian offensive would jump off any day. Katyusha rockets, a blizzard of artillery, then tanks and tank riders with tommy guns in the thousands, maybe hundreds of thousands. How quickly would they slice through Von Bink's shorthanded Panzer army and get here?

Another worry: when would the parachutists get into position? It meant nothing to run a sweep up through the mountains if there was no blocking force. It also meant nothing if the Russians attacked by air and the parachutists were wiped out and escape to Hungary was cut off. With his three panzerwagens, more valuable than their weight in gold, he could possibly get his men around the mountains to the wider road to the south and out that way. But without the woman, it was a failure; without the woman, he would not win his Iron Cross, he would not return home a hero. Without the fucking woman, he was nothing. Aggghhh. Frustration clotted his vision and assaulted his brow, and the air, though purified by the filters of the mask, tasted foul and rancid. He almost threw it off, and took a cigarette, and dreamed of a cool, shadowy oasis far from all this madness and—

It was his signalman.

Both pulled up their masks.

"Sir, the Kommissarat. The senior group leader himself."

"Oh, damn," said the captain.

He turned, signaled for his Kübel to approach, jumped in, and directed the driver to the signals hut. He entered, and a lance corporal leaped up in front of the radio unit.

"Captain, urgent signal from the Kommissariat. I believe the senior group leader himsel—"

"Yes, yes, make contact immediately."

The man sat down, worked the dials and radio protocols, then turned the telephone receiver over to Salid. "Hello, hello, this is Zeppelin Leader," he said.

"One second, Captain," came the voice at the other end.

A second later, "Salid, Groedl here."

"Yes sir."

"I want your men assembled in full combat uniform for assignment in one hour."

"Sir, they are on details spread around Yaremche and—"

"One hour. Get them here quickly, Salid. I require your utmost in a very dangerous situation, do you understand?"

"I—But sir, the White Witch may escape without the pressure of the patrolling, and I thought—"

"Priorities. That is why it is hard to command. Show me that you deserve to command, Salid. Trust that I understand all ramifications, have calculated them against the situation of the war, and have made the proper judgment."

"I will comply, sir," he said.

"That is all. Salid, I'm *counting* on you."

"I won't let you down, sir. End transmit."

He turned, as two NCOs had noticed his sudden arrival to the signals hut and come to see what was going on.

"Get me runners to the patrols and send people to the flame operators. We are recalling all troops, and I want at least two of the panzer-wagens on the road within half an hour. The third can remain for stragglers, but we are needed in the city for emergency duties. *Hoppe, hoppe, hoppe!*"

323

• • •

It was not an easy trek. Von Drehle did not believe any of Bak's people had wandered this far south; it was far more likely that, aware the Red Army was about to drive the Germans out of the Carpathians, they would hunker down and prepare to celebrate their survival. Thus, the chances of ambush were slight. But he could not be sure, so he determined that the ascent should be made on full combat alert. The radio, the treasure, was secured in the Kübelwagen that Wili Bober drove; it was also loaded with cans of belted 7.92 for the MG-42s, as well as unbelted 7.92 for the FG-42s, 7.92 Kurz for the STG-44s, a supply of M24s, and two Panzerschrecks with rockets. The buglike little Volkswagen also pulled a small cart loaded with rations and large water cans. The whole graceless, unlikely contrivance, dappled with smeary camouflage paint in the tones of the summer forest, muddled along the edge of the road on the way to Natasha's Womb, after having been dropped at Yaremche, which was covered with smoke and the smell of burning wood, though there was no sign of the SS group. Maybe they were off on a picnic somewhere.

At the halfway point, Von Drehle called a break, and the boys flopped to the earth but knew enough not to gorge on the water. Instead, they took small, measured sips, enjoying the liquid as it cut through the slime on lips and tongues. He himself looked urgently through binoculars for sign and picked up nothing save more densely packed trees, more treacherous undergrowth.

"Karl, do you think we should make a radio check?" asked Wili Bober.

"No, it would take too long to set the goddamn thing up and then take it down. I do not like being on this open road. The sooner we get up and get a perimeter established, the better. Besides, whatever is happening down there, we can do nothing about, and it can do nothing about us, so what difference does it make?"

"Got it," Wili said.

"Okay, let's get moving. Teatime is finished. Green Devils, off your asses and back into the war."

There was grumbling, but there was always grumbling; only its absence would have been remarkable.

They reached the gap at around seven P.M. He could see the cliffs narrowing in to the road, forming a natural choke point. Natasha's Womb, in its narrow glory.

"Ginger's Womb!" somebody cried, and everybody laughed.

Karl blushed. "Enough of that," he said, but knew it was too late. A nickname, once given and accepted, was never rescinded.

He looked at the narrow walls, chalky in limestone, a soft rock, easily cracked or blasted.

Blockading it, then blowing it, wouldn't be difficult. But not now, after the long, tense trek. Looking around, he could tell they were surrounded on all sides by the Carpathians and, in the fading light, saw an ocean of waves in the earth's surface, ancient mountains beaten smooth by the passage of eons and now shrouded and softened in pines. He ordered a quick setup of a night defensive position, arranged the guys along the road on either side. Finally he ordered his signalman to set up and make contact with base, for any reports and to make his own.

But in a few minutes, Signals called him over.

"Karl, I can't get through. Everyone's on the net, I can't make contact with Zeppelin, I can't reach Panzer headquarters or the Kommissariat."

"Has the offensive gone off?"

"It's not combat traffic, it's—well, political."

"Political?"

"I hear—arrests, worries about loyalty, protestations of innocence, intense allegiance swearing, all a mess. Here, listen."

He peeled off the earphones and Karl squatted down to dip in to them. He heard a crazed staccato of chatter, no protocols at all, signals coming in and out, basically confusion. It wasn't like a German army to lose control of procedure so radically. What the hell could be happening?

"Damned strange," he said. "Is there another channel?"

"I've tried them all, sir. Everywhere it's crazy."

"Damned strange," he said again. But the radio buzzed, meaning incoming transmission. Von Drehle took up the telephone mike with the send button. "Hello, hello," he said. "Oskar Leader here, I repeat, this is Oskar Leader."

"Yes, dammit, Von Drehle, Zeppelin Leader here, where the hell have you been?"

"Advancing five kilometers into the mountains, Captain."

"Are you in place?"

"Yes, we have arrived. We'll wire the cliff for demo tomorrow and set up defensive lines. I do need to pick up that Flammenwerfer, old man."

"Haven't you heard? My God, man, get your head out of your ass!"

"I don't—"

"Someone tried to assassinate the führer. Early reports were that he is dead. But he survived a bomb attempt."

Von Drehle thought: It was bound to happen. The man is a maniac, without concern for his troops. But he could only say, "I receive."

"Police Battalion has been dispatched on security duty. We are making arrests from an SA list of probable suspects. I need you to hold secure in your area, be very alert for partisan movement, make certain—"

"Arrests? Who are you arresting, goddammit?

There's no one to arrest in Fourteenth Panzergrenadier, for Christ's sake, these men have been fighting for two years out here."

"I am not at liberty to discuss direct orders from Berlin with some parachutist captain on a mountaintop. You will hold your position, build defensive breastworks, patrol for bandit activity."

"Zeppelin Leader, I am in receipt of message. End transmit."

"End transmit," said Salid from wherever he was.

Von Drehle sat back, confounded. What the hell was going on? Arresting suspects? What did that mean? Who was in charge, how would things change, what was his duty now? You had to watch yourself in these crazy times; anyone could end up in front of a firing squad.

He decided he'd best double-check with 14th Panzergrenadier to make certain his orders remained as the Arab had said. He told Signals to reach division headquarters. Certainly there'd be no way he could get to Von Bink, but one of Von Bink's able assistants would at least know what the policy was.

It took a while, but he got through, at least to a low-level command.

"Hello, hello, this is Oskar calling for anyone at kingdom headquarters."

"Oskar, Oskar, we can't raise headquarters,

either. This is Lieutenant Colonel Rungen, Fifth Battalion, Third Regiment, Fourteenth Panzergrenadiers."

"Sir, Major Von Drehle, Twenty-one Para, Battlegroup Von Drehle."

"Yes, Major."

"Colonel, what is going on?"

"It's a confused situation, and I have to say, it doesn't look good. But be careful who you talk to. They're going around arresting people and hauling them off. Just before a Red offensive, too. Excellent timing."

"Sir, I'm up at Natasha's Womb with orders to hold until relieved. I just wanted to make sure that was still in accordance with General Von Bink's orders."

"I would have no way of knowing. SS has sealed off division headquarters. Now SS Panzer Muntz, that moron, is in command of all armored units. I regret to inform you—General Von Bink has been arrested."

CHAPTER 37

Yaremche
The Bridge
THE PRESENT

"And you, Ms. Reilly," Jerry Renn continued, "I have to say, ma'am, ever since I've been in Moscow, I've read your *Post* stuff and I don't think anyone gets this place better than you. Incredible job."

Swagger and Reilly looked at each other. Then Swagger said, "Cut the shit, sonny. Who are you, what do you want? Who do you work for?"

"People who like you."

"You like me so much, you tried to nail me in Lviv."

"Let's say we've abandoned that policy. It was a mistake."

"Yeah, sure."

"We could have taken you standing here on the bridge if we'd wanted to. No, we want to try something else. Cooler heads have prevailed. I'm sure we can get it squared away. Just so you know, I'm unarmed. Except for this."

He pulled out a pistol. It was the suppressed Makarov that Bob had taken from his would-be assassin in Lviv, which he'd left in his room.

Jerry tossed it over the bridge and it disappeared with a splash.

"Make your pitch, junior. What's this all about? What's it to anybody what happened in Ukraine seventy years ago? Where's an American interest?"

"What you've discovered just so happens to shine a light where we don't want light to shine. It could begin a process of unraveling. I know, it's such a little thing, one event in a war over seventy years ago, who on earth could give a damn? But it leads somewhere."

"What is he talking about?" said Reilly.

"Spy shit. There's a secret here these jokers need to keep quiet. I haven't figured it yet, but I'm working real hard on it."

"We're the good guys, we're the last great hope, but if you publish, Ms. Reilly, you do a lot of harm. A lot of harm. We're very uncomfortable with that."

"See, in the old days, they just said, 'We'll kill you,'" said Swagger. "Now they say, 'We're uncomfortable with that.'"

"There's no need to talk of killing," said Renn. "Look, I'm not just asking for favors, I understand the quid pro quo that underlies every political transaction. I'm authorized to tell you that if you cooperate with us on this, all sorts of good stuff can happen. We can make selected deliveries of very hot intel for Reilly. When you get back to D.C., you can have the phone numbers of some very important folks who, at our request, will always call you back. Not saying you're a failure now, no, not at all, but we can move you into the big leagues. You'd be stunned how many of D.C.'s leading journalists have been helped along by us."

"What're you going to get me," said Swagger, "a new rocker?"

"Any one you want, even the deluxe version. But how about if we get your pal Nick Memphis off the Bureau shit list and back on the A team? Deputy director? That's what he wants, right? What about if some real nice scoops fall Nikki's way at FOX 5? That can happen. Does Miko want to go to Harvard, then Harvard Law? We hear she's smart enough, but it isn't just about being smart. We can make it happen. Yale, Princeton, Virginia. Where does she want to go? Be a shame for her to have to end up as a Boise State commuter student. What I'm saying is, if you're good to us, we'll be good to you. That's all. If you say yes, you can drive out of here—that is, when I give you your distributor cap back. You go on back to your lives, and the good stuff starts happening. No monitoring, no observing, nothing like that. The whole thing runs on the honor system, because we know you're honorable."

"What if we say no?" said Reilly.

"Ouch," said Renn. "I'd hoped that wouldn't

come up. You asked, so I guess I'll answer. I've got five guys. Heavy-metal guys from some Moscow gangs. Dumber than stumps but packing a ton of heat. Boy, they love that 74, don't they? To me it doesn't hold a candle to the AR, but don't tell them that. Anyhow, Jesus, don't make me do this. It would be so tragic. These boys, you know, they *like* this shit. I'd have to let them loose. I have a secret to protect. It *has* to be protected. Here you are, standing on a pedestrian bridge in a Carpathian tourist trap, unarmed, and suddenly you've got six real bad operators on your case. I guess by the time I got them back here, you'd have at least an hour head start. I suppose you'd try and hide in the mountains, but an old guy with a stainless-steel ball where his hip used to be and a grandmother, over rough country, in what is basically complete wilderness, I don't like your chances. Plus, we have a dog. I'd hate to see it happen. Guys, it's up to you."

Swagger looked at Reilly, who nodded.

"Tell him good," said Reilly. "So he understands."

That was it. He turned back to the younger man.

"We ain't here for God, country, and baseball, and excuse me, I don't think you are neither. We're here for Mili Petrova, who was betrayed by everyone and everything. Nobody stood for Mili. She was all alone. Still she found a way to get her job done. But then the big boys got to her and crushed her and her memory. Now, seventy years later, you fucking birds come along, and you're the same action. Crush Mili. Destroy Mili. She's so goddamned inconvenient. Mili's nothing. Mili's disposable. Nobody cares, nobody knows, nobody gives a damn. Not this time. This time she's got some pals. That's us, the old man and the old lady. So if you want to go all black ops on us, we'll go black ops. You better be good, sonny, because I may be old, but I'm still who I always was. I'm the sniper."

CHAPTER 38

The Cave
The Carpathians
JULY 1944

A bird tweeted from the trees nearby, except it wasn't a bird at all, and with a crash and a stumble, a large body broke free in the clearing. It was the Peasant.

"Sergeant Mili," he called in Ukrainian, "I have returned."

Mili felt a surge of pure bliss. He wasn't dead at all. Nobody could kill him. He smiled as he shambled closer. From inside the cave, she heard the Teacher stir, as the mild clamor had awakened him. The Teacher came out.

"He says the Germans are gone," he translated. "The Germans are gone?"

The Peasant began unpacking his sack, explaining in Ukrainian what he'd brought, though Mili could see for herself: bread, salted beef, vegetables.

Then he said something about the Germans—Mili understood the word—and the Teacher grabbed him, yelling in Russian, "How do you know the Germans have left?"

The Teacher translated the Peasant's story: "I have been lying in brush for days. It was horrible. I made it to the outskirts of the village and took my chances with a man, and he'd lost sons to the Nazis. He volunteered to help. But he was bringing me food, and they nabbed him not a hundred meters from where I hid. They beat him and dragged him off, but I was too close to move. I had to wait that long day for them to come for me. They never did. I don't know why."

He went on with his story. He had lain there all night, and the next morning the Germans had sent out more patrols but also started their burning operation. They burned for days, and the Peasant watched as the flames came nearer and nearer to his hiding place. He had no idea why this burning was happening, though he knew that at night-fall he'd have to make a run for it. But at midafternoon yesterday, the German officer was called to his communications hut, and several minutes later the Germans commenced an emergency evacuation. They'd waited until two panzerwagens were loaded with troops, which headed out immediately. The stragglers all arrived, and the third panzerwagen left.

"Yes, we noted the same thing. I was almost discovered when the signal to withdraw came. I don't know what it means," said Mili. "Were you able to get a weapon, any weapon?"

"This, only this. No rifles about, but I'm told this fell off a German truck two years ago, early in the war, and an old lady recovered it." He pulled his treasure from his bag.

It was an M24 hand grenade, the famous potato masher, a gray metal can affixed to a wooden shaft with a screwcap at the end, which, removed, allowed access to the twine pull-fuse inside.

"It's no sniper rifle," she said. "But it's a weapon."

The Teacher said, "Sergeant Petrova, it's not enough. It's just—"

"Here's the plan," she said. "You have a pistol. It's small but lethal at close range. With that I'll get close enough."

"You have to be very close."

"I will shoot him or one of their officers. I will shoot Germans until I run out of ammunition, then I will pull the cord on the grenade and join Dimitri and my father and brothers."

"It seems folly to me," said the Teacher. "You

will not kill Groedl. At best, you kill a few Germans. In a war where millions have died, what's a few more or less Germans in exchange for someone like you, with all you have to contribute?"

"I don't have a choice."

If she waited until the Russian offensive and turned herself in to the army, her failure at her mission might doom her. Her failure at Kursk might catch up with her. Her traitor-antagonist in Moscow might destroy her. There was no going back.

"I have to finish my job," she said. "Survival is not the concern here."

"All right, then," he said, sighing. "Try this for a plan. You kill Groedl. We all escape. We are all glorious heroes. We meet every year on your dacha outside Moscow and eat caviar and drink very fine champagne and laugh ourselves sick because life with a full belly is the best revenge."

"That's a fairy tale," she said.

"No, it's not," said the Teacher. "It can happen. It's only a matter of guns."

They looked at him.

"I know where there are guns," said the Teacher. "Lots of them."

Interlude in Tel Aviv IV

The four P.M. Mossad meeting on EconIntel was before the director himself, as well as the section chief and several other department heads. It was organizational theater, full of balding late-middle-aged men in open collars, smoking like fiends, arguing and sniping at each other with the brio that office warfare brings out.

Finally it was Gershon's turn.

"Brother Gold, you've been so quiet. You didn't even try to devastate Cohen's suggestion that the Japanese Red army has booked a week at a Sea of Galilee spa."

"I've been to that spa," said Gershon. "Believe me, an attack by the Japanese Red army would improve the food."

Cohen was quick on the defense: "How would Gershon know? Linda would never let him go to the buffet. It's nothing but yogurt and raisins for Gershon."

"People, people," said the director, to quell the laughter and keep Gershon and Cohen from chewing each other alive with zingers for the next twenty minutes.

"All right," said Gershon. "I do have a situation. Not a crisis, not an emergency, not a catastrophe, but a situation."

"Enlighten us while I eat my knishes," said Cohen.

"Item one: an unheard-of firm buys a great deal of platinum in South Africa, surreptitiously flies it to Astrakhan on the Caspian. Item two: it turns out that this same firm, called Nordyne GmbH, out of Lausanne, Switzerland, has also quite recently acquired a defunct ceramics factory in Astrakhan, spent several million refurbishing the place, spent several hundred thousand fencing it, and has hired a Chechen security team for twenty-four-hour surveillance and protection. Bad boys, shooters, heavily armed. Ready to repel commandos."

"Why would commandos be interested in ceramics in Astrakhan?" asked Cohen.

"Why would Jews be interested in ceramics in Astrakhan?" asked the assistant director.

"Because," said Gershon, "that same firm has just spent yet more money, all of it, by the way, nearly untraceable so far, acquiring the following equipment from various surplus industrial manufacturing suppliers. From the Poles, a fractional distillater; from the Turks the Turks!—a crystallization reactor; from the British, a filtration system; from the Swedes, a ten-thousand-cubic centimeter drying tunnel; and from the Germans, metal bending equipment. As well as belts, electric motors, bins, the bric-a-brac of manufacture. However, a quick check of

339

local job-shop printing manifests turns up no links to Nordyne Ceramics, meaning no quote sheets, no catalog, no printed packaging, no advertising, and by inference, no sales force."

"A world without salesmen," said Cohen. "Perhaps they should get the Nobel Peace Prize!"

Laughter, and Gershon almost responded with "A salesman named Herzl put us here," but he knew that would set off a crazed war of quips and cracks and instead took a breath.

"Another development," said Gershon. "It seems whoever is running this plant hasn't hired Russians but has brought in a Chechen work-force, about twenty women, related to the same bunch that handles the security. I learn this from the indefatigable Precious Metals Industry Reporter, which is worth every penny of the $4,775 yearly subscription fee I don't pay. Consider: the Chechen women will be isolated, keep to themselves, may even live on-site, under the watch of the gunmen-boyfriends. They won't be circulating in Astrakhan proper, and they won't be part of familial and clan networks, so the yakkity-yak factor is eliminated. More security, cleverly thought out, but not so high-profile as to capture attention."

"What does platinum have to do with all this?"

"If I knew, I'd tell you," said Gershon.

"There's not enough data to blow it up," said the director, again to laughter. "Maybe tomorrow."

"Platinum, I do know, is remarkable for its catalytic abilities," said Gershon. "I have to call a chemist for more details, but it has an odd capacity, with its very presence, to change something into something else. By magic rays or something, I wish I knew. Are there any geniuses here?"

"I flunked high school chemistry in Passaic," said Cohen. "Does that help?"

"Gershon," said the director, "take a day off tomorrow and come back the next day with all the possibilities of platinum as a catalyst. You need to get out more, anyway."

"I will, I will. I merely call your attention to the fact that a chemical manufacturing concern of unknown sponsorship and product involving a great deal of tradecraft and security expertise has been set up not far, by sea, from the Iranian port of Bandar-e Anzali. I consider that suspicious. Whatever product they are manufacturing could be of some threat to the state of Israel, and once in Iran, by either official or unofficial action, it could be deployed against us by any number of means. Moreover, as we know, our intelligence assets in that country are focused on Tehran, their nuclear facility, and certain military installations. As for the huge land of the interior, we have no feel on the ground, and if anyone in that vast region wants to cook up a nasty surprise, we might be the worse for it. As I say, a situation, not an emergency. But I would like to have a satellite flyby authorized for a closer look at this plant; I would like to assign consular personnel in Switzerland to investigate Nordyne GmbH; I would like to suggest that intelligence concerning Nordyne GmbH be sought in our barter sessions with cooperating agencies; and I would like to suggest that we all brush up on our high school chemistry, especially Cohen."

CHAPTER 39

The Carpathians
Above Yaremche
THE PRESENT

Though it wasn't easy going, at a certain point they found a hiker's channel, not quite a path but a kind of groove in the forest where others had traveled below, and in a shorter time than he expected, they hit a path that headed south by iPhone compass at about the three-thousand-foot mark. His hip began to throb, his elbow was already sore.

"Make the call," he said.

She fished the satellite phone out of her bag, dialed. "Stronksi," she said.

She handed the phone to Swagger, who waited a second for the callback.

"Yeah?"

"Okay," Swagger said, "we have done got ourselves in it, bad. I do need a way out."

"Where are you?"

"I am about three thousand feet up the east face of a mountain that more or less faces Yaremche. We're at a path, we have to know which way to head."

"Call you back. Stay put."

"Let me emphasize we are in a kind of hurry. Guys with guns after us. We are unarmed."

"I copy," said Stronski.

The time ticked by.

Swagger said to Reilly, "I have to have a talk with you."

"Go ahead."

"The whole point of Jerry Asshole's deal wasn't to buy us off but to bluff us into coming up here. If they kill us down there, it's a flap and a half. What story was she working on, what's going on, what did they find out, who's murdering reporters and old snipers? That's the last thing they need, that's why they didn't do it down there, and believe me, we were easy.

"He wants us up here, he wants to whack us up here. We go into a hole in the ground or a cave, we are never seen again. It's at least days, maybe weeks, before they come looking for us, months before they give up. The whole thing is defused. It's a mystery. I'm thinking time is important to them, they have to stop you now, at this time, and whatever comes out in five years doesn't matter."

"I get it."

"So you have to get your war mind on. You can't be a reporter, not and survive. It ain't fair, is it? Well, pardon my français, but fuck fair. Fair don't exist no more."

The phone rang. Bob answered, listened. Then broke contact. "Stronski's got a chopper on hire. There's no way he can pick us up out of the forest or on the slope of the mountain; he can't get his rotors close enough to the incline and he doesn't have a winch. He'll hit it and go down. So what we have to do is make it toward something called Natasha's Womb, a narrow canyon through a gap, but just in front of it there's a nice clearing where the bird can set down. He thinks it's about four or five miles, due south, but he says the path is pretty good and there's no rough climbing or anything. He'll move there in a few hours and look for us."

"Can we outpace those guys? I don't see how."

"They've still got to come up, they've still got to decide which way to go, they're city boys, probably in eight-thousand-dollar silk suits and Gucci loafers."

"I can't believe you know what a Gucci loafer is."

"If it turns out they're closing on us, I will try

and figure out some way to hold them back and let you get to the clearing."

The path was not treacherous, but neither was it a sidewalk. Gnarly roots protruded, rocks bulged upward demanding detours, the earth itself was not only uneven but uneven randomly, so a sudden misstep could put a hurtful strain on already stressed ankles.

Reilly's satellite phone rang again.

"It's for you," she said, handing it over, and Swagger looked at the number and saw that it was Jimmy Guthrie.

CHAPTER 40

The Carpathians
Ginger's Womb
JULY 1944

Deneker the explosives genius plotted it out very carefully. He would place three 10-pound units of Cyclonite at one-third intervals about the base of the northern cliff. He would run det cords of equal length from each No. 8 detonating cap, so that when ignited, the det cord would ignite each chunk of explosive simultaneously. The cliff would topple and block the passage of any vehicle, at least until the Russians managed to get heavy construction equipment to the canyon, which he doubted they'd bother with.

"And I'll plant Tellers beyond the fallen-rock zone. So if men come over the rocks, one will trip off a Teller, and kaboom, his legs are on the way to Moscow."

"The Russians don't care about mines," said Wili Bober.

"Think of the psychology," said Deneker, also the unit intellectual. "You have to consider psychology in all things. Russian peasants who are being driven by NKVD troops don't care about mines, on the theory that the mines are uncertain death, depending only on random footfall, while defying the NKVD is certain death, of the Mosin-Nagant 7.62-millimeter kind. If boys get up here, they'll be elite troops, parachutists, some sort of commando or special group of Ivan prima donnas. They're already heroes, they value themselves highly, they have many tales to tell if they survive, as well as a happy postwar experience to look forward to. They do not want to get blown up crossing a mountain gap when they've already won the battle as well as the war. They'll hold back and go round up some peasants to frog-march through the minefield. That'll take hours."

"I think he has a point," said Karl.

"All right, then. Mines here but not in front of our positions," said Wili.

"Hmm," said Karl. "And *he* has a point."

"Karl, you're the boss. You have to decide."

"I hate to decide," said Karl. "That's why I joined the parachutists. So I wouldn't have to decide things."

"Split the mines?" said Deneker.

"Sounds fine to me," said Wili.

"There, see, you didn't need me at all," said Karl.

There weren't many other decisions to be made. Sandbags were filled, mines planted, trenches with firing notches dug and connected by crawl alleys so the men could fall back out of sight, trees that interfered with the lanes of fire felled, water collected, the radio monitored. Log frames were built and strung with K-wire. The machine gunners found the best natural points to put the two MG-42s on tripods, then broke down the ammunition for quick use, being sure to set up several shorter belts for the drum-shaped belt carriers, lighter and easier to manipulate, so that if the gunners fell back, they could take the guns off the tripod, grab the drums, and use them in fire and movement situations, say, covering the other men as they retreated beyond the site of Deneker's big explosion. Other men broke down the typically overengineered cardboard crates that each contained twenty boxes of twenty 7.92mm cartridges, and inserted each cartridge into the FG-42 mags, until all were filled; the surplus went into a pile contained in the emptied crate, so that men could dip in and help themselves to handfuls if the fight went on too long. The Panzerschrecks were loaded and spare rockets placed next to them. Grenades also were laid out, their screwcaps half unscrewed, all oriented uniformly so the man grabbing one could flick off the cap, pull the fuse cord, ignite the fuse, and toss the thing with no wasted motion. Bandages, splints, wound wrappings, sulfa, morphine needles, miles of gauze and tape, anything to save a man from bleeding out, it was all there in easy reach. Karl didn't have to say a word. Someone even erected a sign in exquisite Gothic calligraphy: *"Die Gebärmutter des Gingers"*—Ginger's Womb.

As far as the scouting duties, they, too, took care of themselves. Wili had drawn up a master rotation way back in Italy, and though much reduced of manpower, it still governed turns by which, at any given moment, six men were on sentry duty. They moved to places beyond the northern outskirts of the position, on the assumption that if this mythical Red-White Witch were to come, she would come from that direction. If she cut lower, good for her and too bad for her stalkers, as she'd evade. But the betting was that she'd head to the Womb if on the run, for the simple reason that beyond it would be safety, since any Germans would be interested only in fleeing to Uzhgorod far below that side of the Carpathians and wouldn't be looking about for snipers. She could go to ground for a few days, wait till the situation had calmed, then sneak over the crest and link up with Red Army units.

Pipes were smoked, as were Effekt, Ring, and Select cigarettes; uniform regs were ignored; some genius really put in a hard day's labor making the latrine as pleasant as possible and built a shower out of a six-gallon water can; schnapps was drunk; candy and cookies and Ukrainian bread were eaten; and generally it was not a bad little excursion. Jokes were told, card games with penny-ante stakes were played, memories were recalled, masturbation ignored, there was a whole pile of *Der Signal* magazines to use for clean-up duties.

All preparations done, all duties fulfilled, there was not much left to do but the eternal ordeal, waiting for action that might or might not come. However, the next morning, after an eventless evening, the odor of burning trees drifted up, carrying the information that the SS Police Brigade was back.

"Wili," said Karl, "they must be close to done with those damned things. Take the Kübel down with Deneker and see if you can pry our Flammenwerfer loose. Get two if you can. They'll buy us extra time if it comes to that."

"Be back in a couple of hours."

"Bring some Ukraine gals and beer back, too, Wili, if you can," one of the parachute infantrymen hollered, to the delight of all.

The run to Yaremche was easy enough, just a few kilometers, especially now that the cart had been detached from the Kübel. Wili and Deneker arrived in an hour and a half, sighting nothing on the long crank down the road. They found the village shielded in smoke, though not as densely as before, and could see crews deploying Flammenwerfers on a last stand of trees, which blazed almost colorlessly in the hot sun, sending out waves of heat. But where there had been ten or so, now only two of the fire-spurting units were in play. In fact, six of them lay in the shade of the hut that Wili saw was Salid's command location on the Yaremche road, for he noted that a hole had been punched in the roof and the triangular wire unit that formed the aerial of a radio transmitter extended through it. A panzerwagen and a truck also denoted the spot as important.

A couple of SS fellows came out, including a sergeant like himself, swarthy fellows, familiar in their battle tunics, though foreign in the silhouette of some kind of curving Arabian sword on their tunic collar. It was a festival of camouflage, with the spattered mud pattern the SS favored competing in busyness with the

Parachutists' bonebag splinter pattern, splashes versus slashes. In Wili's opinion, the splinter was far more amusing than the splatter.

"Good morning, Sergeant," said Wili. "I'm Bober, Twenty-one Para, Battlegroup Von Drehle, from up at the canyon position. I'm here for one of those Flammenwerfers. General Von Bink set it up for us to relieve you of one. I'd take two if I could get 'em. Ivan does not like flamethrowers."

It developed that none of the SS men spoke German, only Serbian. But in a few minutes—the SS guys meanwhile offered the parachutists some water and cigarettes—a man with both languages arrived.

Wili repeated his request, the German speaker translated it to Serbian, and the answer, in time, came back through the same conduit.

"Do you know Von Bink is no longer in command of anything? I can't let you have the equipment without my commanding officer's okay. And he's currently occupied."

"Please," said Wili, "I don't have time for any runaround. Think of the order as coming from Command, not Von Bink, but we can't wait here for your guy to show up. What is he, shitting in the woods or screwing a whore?"

The humor did not translate well, even if Dencker thought it was funny. And the Serbian NCO started to make some kind of excuse, so Wili cut him off airily with, "Look, let's make this easy. Hop in, we'll drive around and find your CO, he can give you the okay, and we'll be out of here before nightfall. No one knows when Ivan's coming, and no one knows how fast he'll get here. We need those weapons on our line."

The Serbs looked at each other, and Wili picked up some kind of odd signal between them, as if they weren't sure whether to comply, were uncomfortable with the idea of compliance, but at the same time didn't want to get in some kind of dispute with the two parachutists, which might have its own ramifications.

In time, the senior NCO agreed, if reluctantly, and Deneker climbed into the tiny backseat while the Serbian sergeant—Ackov seemed to be his name—climbed in front.

"Point the way," said Wili, and Ackov pointed into Yaremche proper. It was the usual Ukraine shit, a lot of shoddily constructed wooden houses with hay roofs, each with a chicken yard, the grid more approximate than precise, though the waterfall and the pedestrian bridge over the river that cut the village in two was an interesting touch. No one had trimmed grass or pulled weeds this century, which the precision-oriented Bober found offensive. No one had planted flowers, no one had raked plots or swept the wooden side-walks. Such peasants! What could you do with them? Before they reached the bridge, they reached the village's only substantial structure, a church, also wooden and not constructed of stone; it looked like a strong wind would blow it down. Parked in front stood another camouflaged panzerwagen with a tall radio antenna, clearly the command vehicle of Police Battalion.

"Hmm," Wili said to Deneker, "I guess our fellow is a pilgrim to the holy land," and Deneker laughed, because both knew Salid was a Muslim.

Outside, a couple of 13th Mountain SS thugs stood guard with MP-40s, but under Ackov's nod, they cleared the door, and Wili and Deneker stepped in behind the Serbian sergeant.

Wili expected religious darkness lit only by stained glass, but that was not what he got. He got illumination. At the far end of the church, where the altar once was the centerpiece, a bright beam—dazzlingly bright—defined a rectangle, and it was so bright that its harshness bled the image of color. Laboring in the pitiless glare, three husky Serb SS men, stripped of tunic and smock and down to undershirts, labored sweatily with hammer and nail to erect some sort of wooden gantry, its crossbeam perhaps seven feet off the ground. They were not accomplished carpenters, and the construction looked fragile, supported by a clumsy network of buttressing lumber. But they seemed to be nearing completion.

Then Wili noticed what appeared at first to be some sort of mechanism on a tripod, but since it was outside the zone of illumination, its identity wasn't clear. He stepped closer, and it resolved itself into a moving picture camera.

Next to it stood a cluster of men who turned at the intrusion. They were all SS, but only one was in Mountain Division camouflage, and he came forward as Ackov hailed him, and Wili recognized him as Sturmbannführer Salid, with his dark glossy hair, his penetrating eyes, the delta of mustache against his mouth, under his prominent nose. His skin was coppery, his expression so earnest and duty-driven that Wili doubted he'd ever laughed at anything in his life.

He and the sergeant spoke animatedly in Serbian and then he turned to Wili, who raised his hand for a somewhat desultory "Heil Hitler," which Salid returned smartly.

"So, Sergeant," he said in the same impeccable German that Wili recognized from his argument with Karl at the gate of Andrewski Palace, "you've come for your Flammenwerfer. I take it you are well dug in up at the canyon."

"Yes, Herr Sturmbannführer," Wili replied, not finding it within himself to call an Arab pimp "sir," "we've constructed a superb defensive position and mined the canyon itself, so that when the time comes, we can close it in one second to any Ivan tanks. Thirty pounds of Cyclonite make a very persuasive argument."

"Good, good, I'm pleased. But you understand that is only part of the mission. The other part is to nab any bandits we drive before us when we sweep through."

"Yes, Sturmbannführer, that has been explained. Major Von Drehle has half his complement on patrol in the forest to intercept any bandits on the move to the Womb."

"I will make this point to Von Drehle over the radio, but I state it here for the record so there can be no misunderstanding. In two days or so, we will begin this sweep operation, and it is crucially important that we intercept a certain bandit."

"The woman. The White Witch."

"So they call her. She's up there. We must get her. It is a Reich priority from highest head-quarters. The obergruppenführer-SS is bravely putting himself at risk in order to lure her into the open so that we may take her alive. It is an honor for your unit that it was selected for this job. Clearly your operations have impressed all. No common group of infantry dregs could be trusted. It's vital, because this woman must be interrogated in Berlin by specialists, so that the full breadth of her knowledge of various—"

"Who is that?" said Wili, interrupting.

"Excuse me. Please do not—"

"My God," said Wili. "What the fuck is going on here?"

He had noticed a solitary figure sitting in the front row of pews, motionless. Wili stared, shifting slightly to get a better angle.

"General Von Bink! What on earth are you doing to General Von Bink?"

"This is no concern of yours, Sergeant Bober. I have authorized the transfer of the Flammenwerfer-41. Now please go about your business and leave me to mine."

But Wili pushed past him, past the knot of men, got to the front of the church, and there indeed, ramrod-stiff, sat General Von Bink. His hands were clearly tied behind him. He wore his Knight's Cross tight around his neck, his service cap with the stiffener removed for raffish effect, his black double-breasted *Panzerjackit*, a brown belt, and black boots, highly shined, under riding breeches with the general's red stripe. His holster was empty, its flap open.

"Good afternoon, Sergeant Bober," he said. "How nice to see you. I would rise, but you know, it's difficult under the circumstances."

"Sir, I—What is going on?"

"Evidently these gentlemen have arranged transport to my next duty assignment, which appears to be in hell." He smiled.

"This officer is to be hanged by piano wire," said Salid, who had followed Wili to the spot. "He has been found guilty in absentia in Berlin. We are following orders. His execution is to be filmed and forwarded to Berlin. Now get out of here, Sergeant. You have your duty."

Wili turned. "Are you mad? Or a fool? This

officer has six wound stripes. He's fought in three wars. He's been in the front line of every tank offensive since 1939. He's a survivor of Kursk and Stalingrad, Sebastopol, the entire Ukraine going and coming. He has the Knight's Cross with oak leaves and every other goddamned bit of ribbon and tin there is. He is a great man, a hero of the nation. He is no traitor. You cannot treat him like this."

"Sergeant, you grow wearisome. Don't force me to have my men discipline you."

"You crazy Arab bastard, you have no right to—"

"Sergeant, watch your mouth. You have already committed insubordination and are dangerously close to treason."

Salid was suddenly surrounded by three of his men, including the muscular carpenters and one of the door guards with the MP-40. At the same time, Deneker had gotten around to Wili's shoulder and was whispering quietly, "Wili, Wili, Wili, let's not lose our heads."

"You're the fucking traitor, Arab. If you harm one hair on this man's head, I'll see you burn in hell. Who the fuck—"

"Sergeant," barked Von Bink, "disengage now. Sturmbannführer Salid, the man is simply a blowhard, he meant no harm. Please excuse him."

"You cannot hang this man on piano wire in a

desecrated Ukraine church," said Wili. "It is a sacrilege. It is against all that the German military stands for. It mocks the sacrifices of millions of men who gave their lives here in the East."

"The Reich considers him a traitor, and I have very explicit orders."

"Sergeant Bober," the general said, "I am ordering you as commanding general of the Fourteenth Panzergrenadier Division to cease and desist. You do no one any good this way, and you rob me of what little dignity I have left. Please leave at once and return to your duty post. This is a direct order, and I expect it to be obeyed."

Wili had a mind to draw his P38, shoot Salid, then turn and shoot Von Bink between the eyes. Better that than strangulation at the end of a piano wire loop lifting him six inches off the ground for the pornographic pleasure of Berlin perverts watching the film a week later. If the Serbs shot Wili, so what? He wasn't going to survive the war anyhow, what difference did it make? Best die for something he believed in instead of holding open a pass so that SS motherfuckers like the Arab pimp here and his crew of Serb Jew-killers could make their getaway.

"Wili," whispered Deneker, "think of the mess. You'll get Karl and the fellows all fucked up, the politics will be a nightmare, they'll go off to Dachau. After all the shit we've been through, they'll end up hanging on piano wire."

"Listen to your friend, Bober," said the general. "He speaks wisely."

Wili turned. He snapped to attention. He saluted the general with his right hand snapped sharply to his brow in the classic old style.

"Herr Generalleutnant Von Bink, my compliments and compliments of Second Parachute Infantry, Regiment Twenty-one, Battlegroup Von Drehle. You, sir, are a hero, an inspiration, and a gentleman. We were lucky to serve under you, and we will never forget you."

He turned and stomped out.

CHAPTER 41

The Carpathians
Heading South
THE PRESENT

You sound like you're running," said Jimmy, two thousand miles away, presumably sitting on a sofa before a fire, sipping fine whiskey from a decanter.

"The same long story. Do you have anything?"

"Actually, yes."

"You talk, I'll walk. Pardon the heavy breathing."

"We had very good chaps in radio intelligence and coding," said Jimmy from his sofa, "and it seems we were aware that by 1944, Stalin was cutting off partisan units he didn't trust in their pro-Soviet enthusiasm. He knew he'd won this war; he was trying to win the next one. So our people saw our own opportunity for some mischief-making. SOE sent a 'black' Halifax bomber to Alexandria. The SOE used its genius for code-breaking and was able to talk to a number of partisan groups. We offered the supply on which Stalin was reneging. This bomber went forth every night and flew from Alex into the underbelly of Europe and Russia, dropping C-containers of arms and ammunition to designated groups. I'm sure some were Russian ruses, but I'm also certain many were legit. The C-container load was exactly what one would need to run a guerrilla war, a revolution, a coup d'arms: one No. 4 T for sniper and assassination duty, five Stens, two thousand rounds of 9mm, fifty of .303, twenty-five Mills bombs, and five Webley revolvers. According to the records, the Bak Brigade of the Ukraine People's Front received their loads—three C's—on February 9, 1944. So to answer the question, that is exactly how a No. 4 T could be and in fact should have been available to your sniper in July 1944."

"One last question. Any info or insight on how the T was zeroed?"

"Ah, nothing there, but the normal kit sent to infantry units was a T in a pine chest, some tools and gizmos for maintenance, a guidebook, as it were, and the rifle combat zeroed to a hundred yards. Of course, the individual sniper would alter that to his needs."

"So if she had to make a hit at a thousand, she'd have to zero it?"

"Absolutely."

"Got it," he said. "You're the best, old man."

"See you in October, then?"

"Yep," Swagger said, but his mind was elsewhere, racing through certain possibilities.

"Good news?" asked Reilly.

"Yep," said Swagger. "Mili got her gun." He explained briefly.

"Ah," Reilly said, "well, I suppose that's—"

"You're missing it, Reilly," said Swagger, oddly still and concentrated. "Don't you get it yet?"

"Get what?" she asked.

"If she had that rifle, and it sure looks like she did, the thousand-yard cold-bore shot wasn't impossible. If she could find a way to zero it at a thousand yards, it was makeable."

"So that she . . . you're saying . . . I'm still not quite with you."

"I'm telling you why the American army and the British army and the Russian army and the Israeli intelligence service could never find Groedl after the war."

He paused.

"She killed him. She killed the son of a bitch."

361

CHAPTER 42

Above Yaremche
The Carpathians
JULY 1944

So what are you doing with a British container of guns and bombs?" she asked as they shambled along.

The Teacher told her. He finished with: "We received three C-containers full of weapons and sabotage explosives, dropped nearby from a low-flying bomber during the night. Bak did not want any one man to know where all three were hidden. I took one team, he another, and one of his lieutenants the other."

They'd come to an illuminated section of the path where an unblocked sun shone more brightly, as on either side of the path, no giant pines sealed off the sky, no juniper or snowball clotted the pathways between the trees. On the upward slope, some force had torn down a swath of forest, revealing a strip of barren ground—small trees had begun to reassert themselves but were not tall enough to be counted as trees—littered with boulders and scrub. This gash climbed the severe slope of the mountain until the raw stone broke from the swaddling of green earth a thousand yards or so up, then rose, raw and barren, even higher, to snowcaps.

"It's called a scree field," said the Teacher. "I think this is the place. We came in from above, so it was not so bad. Now we climb."

A thousand rough yards later they achieved a little shelf where they could sit and rest a bit. The Teacher said, "All right, here we are." It took him a few minutes to locate, semi-hidden behind a large juniper brush, the entrance to the cave, not nearly as grand as the one that had shielded them the past few weeks.

They slid in through the small opening, blinked as the light disappeared, coughed as the dust from their slither rose to their noses, then lay still, the three of them, waiting for the dust to settle and their eyes to adjust. It was larger inside than the entryway promised, and in a bit of time, the shaft of light from the entrance permitted their eyes to find details.

"Here," said the Teacher. He pulled and yanked something into the sunlight: a heavy metallic case, about five feet long, two wide, and three deep. A latched lid encapsulated it. He bent, unlatched the three fixtures, and then rotated the lid back on hinges placed along the length. Opened, the case revealed manna from heaven, accompanied by the odor of gun oil: five pipelike objects, dully gray, wedged into the notches of a wooden frame.

She recognized a Sten gun, the cheap, crude, but effective British submachine gun. Steel pipe, a few screws, all the welds messy, stamped-out parts; the whole thing seemed improvised in a cellar workshop.

He pulled another piece of magic from the lid: a crenellated egg, with a lever tracing its oval curve from a central mechanism at the long end, in which a linchpin sporting a steel ring had been inserted to hold the thing together. It was a Mills bomb, the British pineapple grenade.

"The rifle," said Petrova. "You said a rifle."

He reached back in and struggled for a second to pry open another long box within the container, then pulled out, with some effort, a four-foot object wrapped in oilcloth, which he yanked off.

She took it, feeling its density, complexity, solidity, intensity. It was shorter than her Mosin-Nagant, yet weightier. She took it into the light, recognizing the common parts of the rifle, the trigger, the magazine just forward of the trigger, the bolt, the encasement of the long barrel in wood. It featured a kind of face rest, a sculpted form of wood screwed into the top of the stock, where her chin and face could rest when she was locked behind the scope. But it was the scope—or rather, the overengineered mechanism that clamped the scope to the rifle—that seemed so bizarre, even eccentrically English. It looked like something out of the Victorian Age, a railroad trestle over a deep gorge, with struts and turning knobs and screws and rivets enmeshed in a pattern too complex to be believed, to secure the black steel optical tube to the rifle by stout rings clamped tight. The scope was a whimsical gizmo with adjustment turrets indexed to ranges, screws everywhere to keep it from popping apart.

"It looks like it was designed by Lewis Carroll," said the Teacher.

She slithered out the cave's entrance with the rifle and assumed a prone firing position. The two men inside could hear the action working, the bolt closing, and the click of the trigger being pulled as she acquainted herself with it.

She came back in. "Now we have to zero it."

"Zero?" asked the Teacher.

"You don't just mount a telescope on a rifle and shoot a man at a thousand yards. No, I have to test it very carefully at that range and adjust the sight so the sight points exactly to the bullet strike. So when I fire at the real target, I am confident the bullet will go where I aim."

"Excuse me, are you mad? You cannot do a shooting program up here. Yes, the Germans are gone, but for how long, and how many men have they left behind? With every shot you fire, they become more aware of where you are. Perhaps they have men up here, waiting for just that situation. Perhaps they've made arrangements with the Luftwaffe to send Stukas when they think they've isolated the site and dive-bomb it. Perhaps it just riles them up and they execute another two hundred or so hostages on general principle. You get one shot, and that is at the worm Groedl."

"I only tell you the reality. You need a thousand yards, not one less," said Petrova. "Do you see any thousand yards around here?"

They were silent.

The Peasant asked the Teacher to explain, which he did, and the Peasant listened and then responded.

"He says you could shoot from inside the cave here. That would dampen the noise. You could shoot downhill across the scree field at a boulder a thousand yards away."

"As usual," said Mili, "the Peasant is smarter than the intellectual."

CHAPTER 43

The Carpathians
THE PRESENT

The mountains offered beauty in every direction, vistas of lyric perfection that touched primal memories of Eden. Neither cared. For each it was just pure ordeal, bathed in sweat, cinched in pain, driven by thirst.

Finally Swagger said, "Okay, let's take a rest." He sat down against a boulder, breathed heavily.

"You're the expert," she said, "but don't you think if we rest, we get killed?"

"Good point," he said. "But a thought just came to me."

"Go ahead. We've got nothing but time."

"She's got to zero the rifle. Right?"

Reilly couldn't help but issue a dry little spurt of a laugh. "As if I'd know? I don't even know what 'zero' means. It's all secret code to me."

"Zero the rifle. Adjust the scope so that it's indexed to the point of impact at the range you'll be shooting at."

"Is this the right time for a ballistics lecture?"

"Stay with me a sec. See, she's got to zero at a thousand. How do you find a thousand clear yards in a forest? Do you just wander until it's there? But maybe it's never there."

"Look," she said, "it can't be that hard."

She pointed up the steep rock-strewn slope. "There, there's one, right there."

Indeed, a gap in the trees inclined upward from where they had come to rest. Here and there tall trees interrupted it, but basically there was too much stone on the ground to permit complete forest growth. It was like a scar ripped in the mountainside, as obvious as a nose on a face. How could he have missed it? And then she realized he hadn't.

"All right," Reilly said, "what gives? What game are you playing, Swagger?"

"She's got a rifle. She has to zero it. She needs a thousand yards. This is a thousand yards, right?"

"All right."

"This is what's called a scree field. Meaning at some time in the past, a rock slide poured down the side of the mountain and ripped the forest up. Some trees grew back, as you can see, but imagine the place seventy years ago. It's wide open."

"So?"

"I was her, I'd be up there." He pointed. "I'd shoot at a target down here. Maybe there's a cave up there, she could shoot from inside, cutting down on noise. I'd track my shots and walk 'em into the target. A great shot, she wouldn't need that many. I'd smear some color on one of these boulder faces about the size of a man's chest. I'd keep adjusting until I could not only hit the chest at a thousand but put three into it inside ten inches."

"So your idea is that we should stop fleeing men who are trying to kill us and look for a target? And if we find the target, what then?"

Swagger pointed to the boulder against which he was leaning. There was discoloration of some sort, roughly the shape of a man's chest. It was faded and peeled, but it was there, definitely.

"Blood, I'm guessing. She or somebody with her killed a rabbit. They cut it open right here, drained its blood on the rock. Like paint. It dried, it stayed. Here it is. See any holes?"

She looked. Three pockmarks were etched in the stone face in the blood zone, two four inches apart and a third perhaps six inches from them but still in the target.

"She or someone with her knew where there was a British C-container with a No. 4 T, five Sten guns, twenty-five grenades, and two thousand or so rounds of ammunition. My guess is, it's up there. A thousand yards up that scree field in some kind of cave or other."

"So we have to climb—"

"I'm afraid so. But as you say, we ain't going to make it outrunning them. Up there is the one thing that's going to get us out of this jam."

"And that would be?"

"Same thing that got Mili out of her jam. Same ones, in fact. Guns."

CHAPTER 44

Stanislav
The Town Hall
JULY 1944

It's quite humorous, actually," pointed out Senior Group Leader Groedl in his office late that evening with Sturmbannführer Salid, "here I'm the one trying to talk you into it, and you're the one trying to talk me out of it! Don't you see? It should be reversed."

But the humor was theoretical rather than actual, and neither man laughed.

They sat on the leather sofa in Groedl's office. Before them was a Mouton Rothschild from 1927, which the senior group leader was in the process of finishing while the young Sturmbannführer was merely sniffing occasionally. That meant they were equally drunk. Dr. Groedl had even loosened his tie.

"It's just that the senior group leader is so inspirational," said Salid, "has touched so many with his passion and his logic, has reached across generations, it terrifies me that he risks himself in such a way."

"War is risk, Yusef."

"But certain risks are a part of making war, such

370

as attacking a hill or dropping a bomb or being under artillery fire. This one you assume is arbitrary. It has no meaning in the war. It puts you in great danger for no gain at all."

"Immense gain. For reasons I should not divulge to you, the White Witch is enormously important. She may not even understand her value, though perhaps she does. Without realizing it, she has it in her power to reveal the identity of a certain agent within Stalin's inner circle. Oh, I shouldn't be telling you this. My wife watches my drinking, but you come here with a fine bottle, and two glasses into it, I'm talking my head off! Yusef, you must swear to me. I will tell you more on only one condition. That is, if you swear on that desert god of yours that you will not be taken alive. This is too precious a secret to be spent stupidly. Save the last Luger cartridge for yourself, do you understand?"

"By Allah, I swear," said Yusef.

"Then hear me and understand. I owe a particular debt to this man. And his intelligence is very valuable. It wasn't in the manner of brigade movements and timetables. That material is much overrated. No, no, he was with us in our other war, *our* war, Yusef, working not for military intelligence or the high command or anything like that, but working for and reporting directly to IV-B4, RSHA. He was their agent. His reports went directly to Müller and were turned to action by Eichmann. He was their own private intelligence network against the Jews of the Soviet Union. How do you think we knew when we got to a Soviet city where the Jewish quarter was? How do you think we knew who the Jewish leaders in that city were, who the intelligentsia were, who the merchants were? How were we able to round them up on the first night and see that they got what they deserved? Those long lists of names and addresses, Yusef, that guided your actions when you were a part of Einsatzgruppen D in the early years, and all the other Einsatzgruppen actions, A, B, and C as well, and took the thousands to the pits and buried them there. Not only because they were Jews but because they were leaders. We had to cut the head off the Jewish beast, Yusef, that was the key to the whole thing, and that will be our legacy that the world, which holds us in contempt now, will recognize later."

"This man provided all that?"

"Yes, he fought the real war." Groedl laughed giddily. "Not the business of generals and tanks but the far more important business of racial purity, of cleansing the pollutants and the toxins from the human strain. When you look at Russia, you and I both see a vast carnival of German death. The millions! Think of the boys from Heidelberg and Hamburg and Dresden and Munich and little farm towns you never heard of, who came to Russia to find their bitter end under the snow, in the rubble, in the wheat fields. Those millions of German dead must have some meaning, or life is not worth living or clinging to. And that is what has made the sacrifice worthwhile and made our legacy worth building upon."

"I see," said Salid, taking another delicious whiff of the Mouton Rothschild, its subtleties pressing the hairs of his nostrils.

"Yes, yes," said Groedl. "He was able to give IV-B4 invaluable information that informed our operations. It may have been the biggest intelligence operation in history, because this man realized that his obligations to his race transcended his obligations to his country. As he rose and acquired power—helped by gifts of intelligence from our own people—he got us more and more. Under the guise of a 'survey,' he was able to provide us with names and numbers in the thousands. A whole Soviet department actually worked for IV-B4! Can you imagine? And when he learned that this woman had been sent to kill me at the personal order of Josef Stalin, he took action to save my life at great risk to his own. That is why he must be saved and the information of his true loyalty controlled. We must find out if this woman has any suspicions, if she has figured out his identity, and if she has communicated her thoughts to anyone. Do you see now why I risk my life? Not only to protect a hero but to protect our cause!"

The slightly drunk SS captain nodded.

"Not only that, she cannot hit me."

"She cannot hit you?"

"Not with a Soviet rifle, and that is the only rifle she could have. I had the master sniper Repp, Lieutenant Colonel Repp, hero of Demansk—"

Salid was mightily impressed. "Repp! Repp of SS–Death's Head Division! He killed a hundred Russians in one day and lived to laugh about it." Repp had even been on a postcard.

"Yes, that Repp. He is a friend of mine. At my request, he ran tests using a captured Russian rifle with its sights. Even the great Repp could not hit a target beyond five hundred yards with that rifle. Repp, the Reich's greatest marksman!"

"That is very good news."

"So let us go over it one more time."

"Yes sir." Salid took another sniff. Explosions and thunder and lightning. Craziness. Clarity when the noise had ceased.

"You will arrive by military convoy, in a staff Horch car from SS-12 Panzer and two panzer-wagens. It should be obvious to anyone in the mountains who is paying attention that the senior group leader is arriving. Nevertheless, you will halt at our command position outside the village for an hour or so, giving her ample time to move into a position. But she cannot get within five hundred yards, because that burned space is open and being patrolled by Police Battalion personnel. She'll have to shoot from somewhere in the forest at five hundred yards. We have noted all the spots in that cone of territory that yield a vantage point on your activities in the zone. We will infiltrate two-man teams in heavy camouflage to monitor each one. If and when she approaches, they will let her settle in, let her concentrate on her job, then take her alive. Upon the sound of shots, if shots are necessary, the other two-man teams will converge rapidly on the site. In case, a half mile out of the zone, we have two dog teams. If she should evade immediate capture, the dog teams will close on the locality in a matter of a few minutes and pick up her trail. The dogs will run her down. The dogs are very good. At the very worst, the very worst, they will drive her toward Natasha's Womb, where the parachutists of Battlegroup Von Drehle will intercept her."

"The flaw in the plan is the parachutists. I had nasty words with their oberfeldwebel over the issue of the execution of Von Bink."

"They will do their duty, I will see to that. I will have Muntz call and explain things to them very clearly. They will obey or they will be dead. That is the only option they have. And if they hinder you, then it will mean nothing to me or to the Reich if you execute them. I am not ordering you to do so; I am telling you that is your prerogative if circumstances warrant. You have wide latitude."

"Yes sir."

"Then you take the Yaremche road through the mountain to the airbase at Uzhgorod, where that FW 200 awaits you and the White Witch. Then you go straight to Berlin."

"Sir, I'll hold the plane for you if the Soviets have started their offensive."

"No, no. You must leave with her instantly. The woman is everything. She is *everything*."

There was one last thing to do, and Groedl did it the next day. He spoke at length to Muntz, Brigadeführer of SS 12th Panzer and now, upon the death of Von Bink, commander as well of 14th Panzer and all the units under its umbrella. Muntz, later that afternoon, went to his communications unit and had the men reach Oskar, as the Green Devil position was code-named, and ordered the signals NCO to reset to a different, much less used channel. Once that was accomplished, he ordered Oskar Signals to locate Oskar Leader, Von Drehle himself. It took a few minutes, but then Von Drehle took up the microphone.

The general explained that he had great faith in Von Drehle, even if he believed several of his men were subversive. He mentioned a particularly impertinent NCO under Von Drehle's command. He would hate to order executions and would be far less inclined to do so if Von Drehle's men performed their duty at Natasha's Womb, especially in the matter of the woman sniper called the White Witch.

He went on: "If you are successful, once she is turned over to Police Battalion, I will forget all about Bober's intransigence. Moreover, I will personally intercede with the general staff and see you and your men given two weeks of leave, then a transfer to the Western Front, where you can rejoin Second Fallschirmjäger. Then, Von Drehle, find a nice American patrol to surrender to, tell them how you loathe the hated SS, and survive the war. Are you reading this, Major?"

"I am, sir."

"Excellent. Do we have an understanding? You help me, I help you, we both help the Reich, and everything turns out for the better. The bandit woman is to be taken alive."

Interlude in Jerusalem V

Certain things worked, certain things didn't. It turned out that platinum as a catalyst was so widely used in the world that its name alone implied thousands of possibilities, some of them potentially lethal or at least weaponizable, some of them not so much. To plow through them and test them against a potential act-of-terror template would be a colossal waste of time. You needed two points to draw a line, establish a direction, a destination. One point indicated nothing except the universe around it.

Routine low-level exchanges with other friendly intelligence agencies—and even some not so friendly ones, surprisingly cooperative with the institute—yielded nothing, either. That meant Nordyne GmbH was either harmless or so far below the radar that it had been expertly buried by the best pros in the business, but there was no other indication of professional involvement. The mere presence of armed guards, even if some were Islamic extremists who'd been to war against Russia, meant nothing. Whoever owned Nordyne GmbH may have been manufacturing lawn-mower engines with catalytic converters for the American market and wanted to protect his investment.

All right, smart guy, Gershon argued with himself, why would he go to such lengths to camouflage his operation? Why would he locate it in a spot conspicuously close to Israel's greatest enemy, an enemy that hungered for destruction and death, and yet at the same time, why would he seem to have—no independent penetration had yielded it—no connection with Iranian intelligence or Hezbollah, Hamas, or any of the world's too many professional Jew-haters?

On top of that, the report from Lausanne was that the "address" for Nordyne GmbH was a fraud, just a post office box of a franchise operation in a mall. There was no headquarters per se, yet somehow, from a certain Swiss bank, payments were regularly sent by wire to receiving entities.

And—new element in the puzzle of the plant itself—why was there no outflow? If something were being manufactured, why was it not being shipped? Why was it linked to no distribution system, why was it unrepresented by a marketing department, why was it not publicizing its product at trade shows, whatever its trade might be? Why was it completely disconnected, as far as Gershon could tell, and that was pretty damn far, from any government sponsorship or even linkage? Its civic connections consisted of local property taxes paid promptly, water and electricity bills paid promptly, safety inspections passed, probably in the sense that someone "passed" someone else a couple of thousand rubles and the inspector went away happy, never having gotten past the cyclone fence and the gun muzzles of the Chechen thugs.

It just sat there, doing whatever it did, going nowhere, seemingly producing no salable product. It seemed operational only at night, because an American satellite, otherwise picking up zero activity, managed to confirm an operating temperature at a certain sector of the plant of about 1400 degrees centigrade. Why did they need all that heat, or, since he knew nothing much about chemistry, maybe the question should be "Why did they need so little heat?"

"Sorry," said a professor at the university, "fourteen hundred centigrade is nowhere near the limit of industrial possibility in chemical manufacture. It's not so hot, it's not so cool. It's just sort of in the middle."

"Which means it tells me—"

"Nothing, except that somebody's cooking something to make something else."

"I think that's what we already knew."

"Now you know it even more so."

And that was the most satisfactory conversation he had.

It didn't help that Israel had no assets on the ground in South Russia. Moscow, St. Petersburg, yes, Volgograd, even beyond the Urals and in towns of special strategic value, yes. But way down south in the ass-end of Russia, near the Caspian, no way. And since the assets they did have at closest proximity—Odessa, Kiev, Lviv— were so well watched, it made no sense to send someone over from, say, the Odessa consul to check out the plant as a casual tourist. That would be sending SVR a telegram that the institute had something going on, was watching somebody, and who knew how SVR would react and how that reaction would mess things up.

"We know they're making something; we don't know what. We know they haven't shipped it anywhere. We know they're close to Iran, a night's voyage by freighter. We know they have deep pockets and are highly paranoid about security. We don't know who's paying."

"Gershon, what I don't get is: they rushed, they rushed, they rushed. And now . . . nothing?"

"Odd, isn't it? Represents a kind of mind that wants everything under control, overthinks, over-prepares."

"Gershon, you've just described the director of the institute, the prime minister, the entire cabinet and, God rest her soul, Golda Meir."

"I know. Psychology gets you nowhere in this game, because everybody in this game is already crazy, including me and Cohen. But especially Cohen."

So it was odd that Cohen came up with an idea. "Gershon," he said, "considering your platinum mystery."

"Yes."

"If we're monitoring the plant by satellite and secondary intelligence sources and our friends at Precious Metals Industry Reporter, and there have been no large-scale, industrial-appropriate raw materials shipments to the plant, then would it not seem possible that whatever else they're using in their manufacturing process would be available locally? Perhaps that's why they located there, because whatever else they needed was abundant, and anyone ordering large supplies of it would not attract suspicion."

"What a horrible idea," said Gershon. "So stupid, so useless. I wish I'd thought it up."

What was abundant in Astrakhan besides fish eggs? It turned out only gas and oil; the Caspian Sea was a vast body of water sitting on a concentration of unpleasant-smelling substances that were of extraordinary value in the world's energy market. Pipelines already ran from Azerbaijan to Turkey; drilling stations already dotted the coastline. The spindles and turrets of refineries already rose against the sky, and noxious fumes already clung miasmatically to all nine ports that ringed the world's largest lake. How the fish survived to lay strings of the little black eggs that people gobbled on wafers with champagne seemed a minor miracle, one that perhaps did not bear investigating too closely. The caviar still tasted great, and the oil and gas still powered many of the civilizations that flourished in the fertile crescent.

Gershon ended up with a list of raw materials, chemicals, enzymes, compounds, end products, by-products, and waste products that such aggressive siphoning of the planet was known to produce. Natural gas alone was not an industry but a mother of industries: its product list included engine oils, industrial coolants, compressor oils, bearing greases, endless varieties of fuel and energy, fertilizers, fabrics, glass, steel, plastics (endless), and paint. It went on and on. My head, why does it hurt so? My indigestion, why does it burn so? It was too much stuff. It was as if the stuff had won. He, mighty Gershon, defeated by the abundance of stuff!

Since it was late and Cohen wasn't around to provoke him, he tried a last exercise, the dullest form of investigation known to man, requiring no IQ, no education, no sensibility for the game, no experience: the good old random stab.

He went to his good friend Dr. Google.

He entered: "platinum."

Then he entered the name of a substance that the Caspian was known to produce in copious quantities. The result, for minute after minute, clicking drearily into the night, was gibberish, nonsense, pointless.

I must be cracked, he thought.

If I am, it's all right with me.

He tried one more. What the hell?

PLATINUM + METHANE

Tick-tock, tick-tock, tick-tock, more gibberish until . . .

What on earth was ANDRUSSOW OXIDA-TION?

Another question for Dr. Google.

Ultimately, in Gershon's mind, Dr. Google, the world's greatest spy, loafed and dithered, took time for a shit and a nice bicarbonate of soda, and then answered. It must have been quite obscure, because it took Dr. Google .0742 seconds to answer, instead of the average .0181. Reading quickly, Gershon learned that the Andrussow Oxidation seemed to be a process invented by a Leonid Andrussow at IG Farben in the '20s that enabled methane (Caspian-abundant) and ammonia (Caspian-abundant) in the presence of oxygen (world-abundant) at a temperature of about 1400 centigrade over (imported at great cost and under serious security) platinum to oxidize, if he understood it, into something called hydrogen cyanide, sometimes called Prussic acid, which, when combined with a stabilizer and an odorant, became . . .

He gulped, he swallowed, he reached for the phone to call his department head because the situation had just become an emergency and he wondered how soon it would become a catastrophe.

The end result was Zyklon B, the killing gas of Auschwitz.

Someone was making a lot of it.

CHAPTER 45

The Carpathians
Above Yaremche
THE PRESENT

They climbed the scree, picking their way among lumps of rock, twisted juniper bushes, the occasional stunted and unstunted pine, and at about the two-thirds mark, despair set in.

"Suppose we get up there," she said, "and there's no cave. Then what?"

"There'll be a cave there."

"How do you know? Maybe the container is a mile away. She just carried the gun up here to get the thousand yards, shot it, zeroed it, and then walked the mile back."

"This was a good place to hide 'em. If they dug a hole, they had to figure out some way to mark it and register it on a map. This place, easy to ID, being at the top of the scree, and if you're a young partisan, instead of two broken-down old cripples, it's easy to get to."

"I hope you're right," she said.

I do, too, he thought.

She fell twice, cutting her knee badly the second time. She had gone from gray to ashen to something like the color of wax. He helped her over some of the rougher spots, but it disturbed him that her fingers were cold to the touch.

"How's your hip?" she asked.

"It's fine, no problem," he lied. His hip hurt like hell. It hurt more than his lungs did, but it felt better than his throat did; he could feel the gunk of phlegm drying into something like pottery on his lips. Then there was his elbow, which was bleeding again. Goddamn that bastard's sharp teeth! Then he thought, I am too old for this shit, for about the thousandth time.

"Maybe they'll miss us," she said. "Maybe they'll keep going."

"They won't. They have a dog."

"Oh, that's right. That kid said so, didn't he."

"They think of everything," Swagger said.

"Well, do me a favor."

"Sure."

"Please kill the dog," she said.

"Ain't the dog's fault. He's just trying to make a living."

"Kill him anyway. On general principle."

It was rocky and slippery, and the incline decided to get serious at a certain point and jutted more pugnaciously vertical. The new angle slowed them even more, but they never saw any pursuers. If there was a view—and there was—they didn't see it. If there was beauty—and there was—they didn't see it. If there was the same huge blue lake of Ukraine sky that overwhelmed the world out to the horizon anywhere you looked—and there was—they didn't see it.

"Maybe they're not following us?"

"Oh, they are. They won't let us see them. They will have reached the edge of the scree, hung back, and got us marked by binoculars. They'll come up through the trees on the right, out of sight. Tougher climbing because there ain't no handholds and the footing is much less stable, but they're young guys."

They climbed, they climbed, they climbed. It ached, it hurt, it distracted, it disoriented, it robbed vision and imagination. Nearly everything hurt.

"I can't go much farther."

"You don't have to go no farther. We're here."

Reilly lay against the incline, breathing hard, resting on what appeared to be the track of an old stony path, maybe centuries old, maybe trod by the original tribe of Russ a thousand years ago. She breathed, sucking in the air. She was covered in sweat and abraded in a dozen spots, all of which burned fiercely. But she looked and said, "I don't see a cave."

Swagger collapsed next to her.

"If there isn't a cave here," she said, "I'm just going to lie down until they come and shoot me. I can't go another step."

"Your body won't let you give up. You're too tough."

"I feel like a powder puff, I look like a home-less person, I hurt everywhere, and you tell me I'm tough."

"I'll put a gun in your hand. Then you're tough as any man alive. That's why they call it the Equalizer."

"I don't see any guns."

He pointed at the path. "Look over there."

About ten feet along its track, a groove had been cut into it, not more than six inches wide.

"So?"

"If she had to shoot downhill and wanted to do it from the cave, they'd have to do something about the path. See, it's in the way of the line of sight to the boulder they shot at. So they some-how dug, cut, scraped that groove in it so she could get the angle downslope a thousand yards."

"They?"

"Sure. She had friends. I don't know who, I don't know how. But someone had to know these rifles were here, someone had to guide her to them. Maybe another survivor of the ambush. We'll never know, but someone got her up here, someone dug that groove. And I'm guessing someone went back down and called her shots for her as she zeroed. She'd shoot and someone would mark the spot. She'd adjust, shoot again, and he'd mark that spot. Until she was on. It was a team effort."

"Someone who—"

"Someone who knew what he was doing, I'm beginning to feel. Come on, let's see what we done dug up."

He lifted himself, went to the spot where the groove was located, turned to the scrub vegetation clustered behind it, pulled out a scraggly bush, and started to kick at seventy years' worth of dirt and sediment. Dust flew, both coughed, and it did their lungs no favors, but in a little while he had opened a man-sized hole.

"You're a genius," she said.

"Hardly," he said. "I just show up and pay attention."

CHAPTER 46

The Carpathians
Above Yaremche
JULY 1944

Mili and the Teacher moved in by night, their faces darkened, festooned with pine boughs threaded through their clothes. They were dressed as assassins. They *were* assassins. It was a slow crawl, three forward, one back, pause, listen, three forward again. The British compass guiding them took them over rocks, through brush, around trees on a steady course toward an overlook on Yaremche, if one existed.

The Peasant wasn't there to set an ideal of indifference to pain. He was back at the cave, guarding—well, guarding nothing—with his Sten gun. The idea was that if he heard close-by gunfire, he would rush to the spot and intercede with machine carbide and Mills bombs to perhaps rescue the fleeing assassins, if it came to that. It probably wouldn't, as these things never work out so neatly. Meanwhile, the ground was unrelenting in its urge to hurt Mili and the Teacher. It tore knees and scraped elbows. At least twice in the night, they thought they heard Germans close by and froze, but nothing came of it. Finally they were there, halfway down the slope, a thousand yards to the southwest of the bridge.

They appeared to have found a kind of promontory, a rock outcrop a thousand yards above the village, which was partially visible. Through a V-notch between two hills, she could see the river, the waterfall, and the bridge from this position; they were also a thousand yards from the burned slope where the Germans expected her.

"Does it work?" whispered the Teacher.

"Perhaps. In darkness I cannot tell if smaller branches interfere. Even a leaf can knock a bullet off its course, as too many snipers have found out the hard way. In the light, I'll get a better view."

"I hate to move when it's light."

"If we have to make adjustments, we make them in the morning."

"All right, then. Try to get some sleep."

Sleep! Yes, certainly, inside German lines, crouched with rifle, torn and bleeding from a long crawl, heart thumping. Exactly—get some sleep!

But she did. And when the light struck her eyes, she had a moment's confusion, was all mixed up in now and then, who was alive, who wasn't, what lay ahead. She blinked, and the forest registered, as did the flare of sun to the east. A bug hummed at her ear and she came to a fuller clarity. She blinked, feeling her eyes and limbs return to her control.

"You're awake?" asked the Teacher.

"Yes."

"Is this place okay?"

Not quite. Prone was out of the question, as too much undergrowth interfered. Sliding up the tree, she found a good hole in the pine boughs that yielded a tunnel that in turn allowed a good clear view of the bridge, but at that point the trunk was barren and she'd have no support for the rifle. It was too far by far to take the shot without support.

She needed to set herself against a tree, with a branch upon which to rest the rifle. If she was too far into the depth of the tree, she'd have to peel away the boughs and needles that interfered with the course of the bullet.

"Rest here, I will find a spot." He slithered off. In time, he returned. "All right, it's about thirty meters lower, and if I'm not mistaken, there seems to be an old track that should get us back to our path more quickly. Are you ready?"

"Yes. Let's feed this bastard a breakfast of nine grams and get the hell out of here."

Salid checked his watch for the third time in three minutes.

0855. Five minutes until Senior Group Leader Groedl arrived. Well, no, it couldn't be five minutes. They weren't traveling along Berlin streets but driving by Horch field car over back-country roads, accompanied by panzerwagens full of 12th SS Panzergrenadiers. They could be hours late.

"Ackov?"

"Yes, Captain?"

"Check again, please."

"Sir, you just checked a minute ago."

"You are right."

The check had revealed exactly what he knew it would reveal. Everyone in place, men hidden in the foliage, a little farther out, the dog teams. The Vizslas would pick up the scent, and in minutes they'd take the shooter down. Moreover, a good corporal with a telephone to report in and communicate with these deployed troops by whistle. His own Scimitar troopers in panzerwagens

392

hidden in the lee of the church, ready in seconds to grind out to a spot where they could access the action, if it came to that. Finally the damn parachutists at Natasha's Womb, a few kilometers down the Yaremche road, fully alerted and expecting the fleeing fugitives to be driven to them.

At that moment, 0900 precisely, the first 12th SS Panzerwagen pulled into view. In seconds the open Horch car, top down, an immense vehicle that was configured like an automobile but built like a truck, emerged, and then behind it, the second panzerwagen.

Without even being asked, Ackov spun the knob on the field phone to send rings to the men on the line, then handed it to him.

"Hello, hello," said Salid, "all Zeppelin units, this is Zeppelin Leader. On your toes now, the senior group leader is here, you must react quickly and close at high speed on targets when they reveal themselves."

The small convoy closed the range to the command hut and halted. First SS men disembarked from their vehicles, formed a defensive perimeter. The machine gunner in each panzerwagen turned his MG-42 to the mountainside above the scorched-out zone.

A sergeant got out, saluted sharply to Salid, exchanged protocol greetings and salutations. Salid responded, then went with Ackov to the car, where Senior Group Leader Groedl sat smoking a cigar. As usual, he chose to dress in civilian clothes, more professor than general, and in gray suit, spats (spats! the quiet audacity of the man!), his wire-rimmed glasses, a muted tie, and a gray homburg, he waited patiently.

"Good morning, Herr Senior Group Leader, welcome to Yaremche."

"Good morning, Captain. I understand you have a beautiful waterfall here."

"It'll be my pleasure to show it to you."

"I know I don't have to ask you. I know all your men are positioned properly, briefed properly, controlled properly. I know the instant of the shot, they will respond."

"That is all taken care of, sir."

"All right, shall we begin our little tour?"

"Yes sir. May I ask, do you have some sort of body armor beneath your coat, as I recommended? A shop platoon mechanic could hammer such a thing out easily and—"

"Not necessary, as I have told you. The data again. The data informs us that with any weapon she could have, she could not make the shot from over five hundred yards. Physically impossible."

"Yes sir, I know. But perhaps a safeguard."

"I will not have it be said that fat little Groedl was not as brave as any infantryman who goes naked into battle. Now, shall we proceed?" He got out of the car.

Then, accompanied by Salid, he began his bogus tour of Yaremche, full of pigs and farmers who were ordered to be exactly where they were, and who had been searched a hundred times over by SS during the night. Even the pigs obeyed. Who was not terrified by the prospect of incurring SS wrath? Everybody nodded and smiled and took hats off, all in their Sunday best. A little girl in the bright doll-like clothes of Ukraine gave him a bouquet of a dozen roses—for some reason she had plucked out and thrown away a thirteenth rose just before he arrived—and he bent and gave her a kiss and her mother as well. Then the ladies were shoved aside as the procession continued its tour downhill toward the bridge over the River Prut.

It was all security theater, designed to bring the economics professor and mass murderer to the bridge, where he would be most exposed. There he would stand until—well, until she fired or his feet fell asleep and he had to be carried back. But all believed she would shoot. She had to shoot. If she didn't shoot, she would be executed by her own kind. Stalin, after all, had executed more than two hundred of his own generals for failures, some of them actual. He certainly would not hesitate at eliminating a failed sniper and those of her family who could be found.

The grubby buildings held no interest to any German, least of all Groedl. But he pretended politely to be fascinated as Salid pointed out various highlights, or rather, as Salid pretended anything in the dismal place could be considered a highlight by a German intellectual.

"Actually, the whole fucking place should be burned down," said Groedl mildly. "With all the people in it. These benighted undermen and their monkey-children never should have been permitted to occupy a land so beautiful and rich in natural resources. It is ours by right of evolution. The lesser breeds must fall away into extinction. They are Neanderthal, their time is up. A massive correction is needed. We are the correction. We are here to restore natural order by obeying the data. Data, data, data."

He went on and on in his civil, slightly amused informational voice, revealing these sacred truths, as they reached the bridge across the water to the second but equally unimpressive half of the village. They separated, feeling the bridge sway slightly under them, and headed across single-file. At the center, Groedl came to a halt.

"Not too close, Salid." He turned to Sergeant Roffler, the SS NCO in command of the 12th SS Panzer detachment. "Spread your boys out, Sergeant. We want to give the White Witch a nice clear shot at me. It's no good if we don't tempt her."

CHAPTER 47

The Carpathians
THE PRESENT

Y ou talk, I'll load."
They were in a glade off the northern trail up to the cave, just north of the scree field. Swagger had before him ten seventy-year-old Sten magazines which he was busy loading with thirty seventy-year-old His Majesty's 9mm ammunition. Mili's sniper rifle lay to one side, as did ten No. 36 Mills bombs, pineapples full of TNT.

"How do you know it will work?" she asked.

"It should. It was in waterproof containment in a cave that by all indications was dry. No rust, no corrosion anywhere on the guns or on the container. No corrosion on the ammo. It should be okay."

"Swagger, I'm scared."

"To be expected. Get your mind off it. Make phone calls. Check your e-mail. Give me your latest. Do you have any long shots? You only scare yourself into ineffectiveness if your mind goes empty or numb. So just fill it with little shit, and you'll be all right."

Threading the cartridges through the lips—

rather sharp, actually—so that they nested against the follower or the round against a spring pressure that grew only as the amount of rounds pushing it down grew, too, increasing the compression rate, was not fun. It put a hurt in the fingers and wrists. But it was also easy to fuck up, as in putting a round in backward or at the wrong angle, and he didn't want to take a chance on that happening, so he pushed on.

"Okay, I'm done here. I'm giving you one Sten gun and three magazines. I want you to stay here. I will run the ambush. I will throw the grenades. I will do the killing. You stay here and shoot anything that doesn't look like a Swagger, got that?"

"I got it," she said. "Except I'm not doing it. I will fight and shoot and do what's necessary."

"Reilly, this ain't your kind of work."

"That premise is no longer operative. You're fighting for your reasons. You're in love with Mili, you old coot, don't say you're not, and it's the best fight you ever had. Well, I'm fighting for mine, which is that no asshole comes along and says, 'Sweetie, do us a favor and don't write the story.' I will write the story, if I have to be Mili Petrova to do it. Nobody tells me to go away like a good little girl. I was never a good little girl. Good little girls don't become reporters. Besides, the story's already on the budget."

CHAPTER 48

The Carpathians
Above Yaremche
JULY 1944

S he built her position carefully. It's all about solidity of structure, so that at the instant of firing, bone supports bone, buttressed by the earth, unhampered by the flutter of breath. To shoot like a machine, you must become a machine.

She chose sitting, at a slight cant that rested her body against the trunk of the tree. The rifle was before her, its weight borne not by her muscles but by the thickness of the branch on which it rested. Actually it didn't rest on the branch, but on a carefully folded wad of glove, so that it nestled in, and the possibility of it slipping as she torqued through the trigger pull was eliminated. The cheek rest was helpful in supporting her face, as it rested in precisely the correct position to place her eye four inches behind and directly centered on what the British designated a No. 32 telescopic sighting device. At this point she breathed easily, naturally.

Beside her crouched the Teacher, a spotter without a scope who was of no use except psychological support. "I see them," he said. "Do you see them?"

Of course she saw them. The optics were superb, far better than her own PU scope. To her, through the glass, Herr Obergruppenführer Groedl was but 333 yards away. She saw a pudgy man, by looks one of the meek who would never inherit the earth. A faintly comical quality to him, expressed in the vividness of his spats, the formality of his suit, the daintiness of his walk. He had stepped out of an operetta. He seemed in earnest conversation with Salid, the other monster, as they moved in a phalanx of SS troopers down the central street of Yaremche. Salid pointed out interesting sights, as if there could be an interesting sight in such a degraded place where nobody had ever gotten beyond hay as a roofing material, and while Salid was quite animated, the face of her target remained dull and uninterested.

"Unless he has an interest in medieval Russian agronomy, this is all fraudulent. No doubt they mean to trap us."

"They think they're so clever," said the Teacher.

She broke eye contact with the scope, as she didn't want to develop any strain; her muscles relaxed, no need to apply them forcefully to the rifle yet, as it would wear her out, and the more fatigued she was, the more the chance of a tremble or a rogue yip arriving perfectly to destroy the shot.

She closed her eyes, gathering strength. She had clicked the trigger a thousand times in the cave after the zeroing, to learn the nuances of its release. It could have been better, but it could have been worse. A slight grit as she pushed straight back, maybe two rough bits of metal grinding against each other inside; but then it stacked up nicely at the penultimate location, and it took just the slightest effort, almost magical in its responsiveness, to slide the sear from its engaging restraint and set the whole thing in motion in micro time as hammer lunged forward, drove firing pin forward with exactly the right energy to detonate the primer, which led to . . .

She knew what it led to.

The issue was, to some degree, the scope. Though clear and robust, it was also quite crude. It had zeroing capabilities out to a thousand yards, though they'd proved difficult to achieve, and the Teacher had to help her with the mechanical manipulations to scope. But it was zeroed now. One last problem: the aiming point was the tip of a blunt, conical projection thrusting up from six o'clock, which at this range covered too much of the tiny target. She would settle the tip of the cone on the man's head, then slowly press—

"All right, he's still."

She went back to the scope. There he was, at the magnified range of 333 yards, standing in the center of the bridge, isolated with no man within three feet of him on either side. His face was dull, his body posture unimposing, and it seemed his companions had drifted off as if to grant him solitude for his contemplations. If he had any. He looked bored.

She took a breath, then willed half of it out, and waited for a space between her heartbeats as her finger brought the trigger back to its staging point and she thought of shooter's imprecations that, by rote memory and instinct, she always recited at this moment: Press straight back. Do not rush but do not loaf. Master the rifle. Be strong, confident. Follow through, keeping eye to scope, pinning the trigger.

The rifle obeyed her unstated directives and, by itself, surprised her as it broke the shot.

Data. Data. Data.

The 174-grain spitzer bullet, lead-cored but streamlined behind a thin gilding of copper, exited the muzzle at approximately 2,400 feet per second, in a parabolic arc that was calculated to drop 120 inches at 1,000 yards and had thus been aimed via scope adjustment at a point exactly 120 inches above the target. At 500 yards, the velocity had dropped to 1,578 feet per second, the muzzle energy 962 foot-pounds. It had fallen 31 inches, as determined by both gravity and air resistance, equally stern masters whose mandates could not be ignored, and continued tracing a rainbow across the sky with no deviations left or right because this early (0922 hours Soviet war time) there was no wind, and no tremor or hesitation had marred the trigger pull, thus deflecting the muzzle. If it wandered off course, by the nuance of its design and construction and the harmonics of the barrel that guided it on its track, it came back to exact trajectory beyond 600 yards and continued its descending flight. It struck squarely. When that occurred, after approximately 2.2 seconds time in flight, its velocity had degraded to 955 feet per second, its energy to 412 foot-pounds. And it had dropped the full 120 inches. Still, the combination retained enough surplus efficiency, particularly as Senior Group Leader Groedl had turned his neck slightly to the right, as if something had caught his attention. Perhaps it was the fluttering of death's wings.

The bullet struck him on a lateral transective angle approximately six inches below his left ear, that is, a bit lower than the root of his neck on the torso, a little in front of the medial line of the shoulder, issuing a sound that reminded those nearby of a crowbar slamming into a side of beef. It entered the corpus at an angle of 80 degrees as it was falling, not approaching on a flat line. The full impact of the energy caused him to shudder violently and his exquisitely cut but nevertheless rather fully draped suit to inflate with disturbed air from the bullet's wake under the shock, while a puff of atomized blood, skin, and wool fiber rose in a spurt of pink mist.

As the bullet penetrated dermis and subcutaneous matter, it slowed somewhat but not radically; it plowed through gelid tissue below the laryngopharynx, it ruptured the vestibular fold, the vocal fold, atomized all thyroid and cricoid cartilage in its path, and deformed slightly at the resistance of the flesh that defiled the integrity of its swim, causing it to yaw. It lacerated a length of both carotid and subclavian arteries, exactly where the sternoclavicular articulation passes upward to the medial margin of the scalenus anterior. Yawing fully now, it more or less staggered drunkenly—it had become a random event by this time—along a line that included the left lung, heart, aorta, right lung, diaphragm, liver, and colon, opening a massive swath. It came to rest, spent, bent, part of its copper gilding lost somewhere in its odyssey through the body, in the man's colon, having brutalized the liver into pâté. Liver wounds are inevitably fatal, but by the time that organ was pulverized, so many other causes of death had been inflicted, it hardly mattered.

The senior group leader did not fall instantly. Instead, as his hydrostatic pressure decreased in the order of several magnitudes and his knees became the final destination of all 412-foot pounds of energy, he stepped laterally on his right foot. Some internal gyro, unaware that the body around it was already dead, performed its stabilization duty, and as he lurched, it corrected by pulling the remaining leg forward to reacquire balance. This had the effect of causing him to twist even more, so that he came to face Salid as he commenced to topple. He hit the rail of the bridge, which broke his fall, and slid sideways to the slats of the construction, and it shuddered slightly on its rope moorings.

His body was dead, his brain not quite. As he fell, his eyes communicated thought: perhaps disbelief, perhaps disappointment, perhaps even curiosity (how had she made that shot?) before, at the half-topple mark, they went all eight ball and lost the spark of life. He hit the slats hard, as no inhibitors were left electrical enough to issue corrections during the fall. There was a weird after-death reflex by which his legs and arms curled up.

Captain Salid was horrified to discover that an atomization of blood and skin and other cellular material adhered to his own clothes and face.

He looked at the dead man in shock, just as, finally, the far-off sound of a rifle shot reached his ears.

CHAPTER 49

The Carpathians
Scree Field
THE PRESENT

I t should work. He had set her up with the gun, shown her how to use it, more or less, warned her about the safety notch, how to shift mags. Bullets facing OUT. Really, that's it. Bullets facing out, into the housing till it snaps, pull the bolt back, and start shooting again. OUT. OUT. She didn't have to learn the difference between "bullet" and "cartridge," which was beyond the scope of all journalists, especially the ones who'd been to Harvard. Fortunately she had good education for this kind of work: she hadn't been to Harvard.

Her job: when she heard him scream, "Go!," she was to lean around a rock with the weapon locked under her arm at hip height, point the gun at the men as best as possible, and squeeze the trigger. It would fire thirty times in about four seconds. She should try and hold it low, fighting its need to rise, but not worry about targets. The point was to send a fusillade down the pathway so their trackers would leap off it into the brush, seeking cover, and consider their next move.

At that point, from behind them, Bob would pull five pins on five No. 36 Mills bombs and toss them exactly where the bad guys had gone to rest. Those whom five blasts and one thousand pieces of supersonic steel filling the air didn't kill would be quite dazed. Moreover, a turmoil of dust and smoke would blur everything. Bob would step into it with his Sten and shoot anything that still moved.

"Get the dog," she said.

"I can't make no guarantees about the dog. But he will probably die."

He thought the dog would probably be turned to Alpo by the blasts, but who knew? You can't never outthink a dog.

So now he sat with his Sten and his No. 36s behind a rock a few yards farther down and a few yards off the path. It was just waiting.

"A lot of war is waiting," he'd told her. "You go crazy waiting. Don't go crazy. Think of something else."

Swagger himself thought of weapons, those he wished he had and the lesser quality of those he did have. Each grenade was a classic olive-drab egg, cross-checked by grooves meant to facilitate fragmentation. It had a mechanism at one end that sustained a pin, and the pin locked down what some called a spoon and others a lever, just a junk prang of metal that would pop off under spring tension when the pin was removed and the thing thrown, as the hammer pivoted under spring power to smack a detonator that lit a fuse that, 4.5 seconds later, turned the thing to noise and death. Grenades were tricky. You did not take grenades for granted. Drop it at the wrong time and it killed you, not them. Another grenade problem: you tossed it, it hit an overhanging branch or limb and bounced back. Not pretty. Thus he had checked and made sure his throws would have free passage. He also made sure all pins were loose in their holes, easy to yank. Too many guys had died from grenade mistakes in Vietnam. Grenades were heavier than they looked, and although some men got quite good with them, it took practice, and Bob had not thrown one since 1966, first tour in 'Nam. He got through two more tours without any grenade work and counted himself lucky.

But these were seventy years old. Boom or no boom, that was the question. That was why he would throw five, because if only two went boom, he still ought to win the war. Or at least get to the Sten part.

No uglier gun existed. You could not love it unless it saved your life countless times, and even then it would take some willpower. It was just a variety of steel tubes welded together at 4:57 P.M. Friday, British summer war time, three minutes before the end of the shift. Blobs and smears of liquid weld, now hardened into little disfigurements, littered its ostensibly smooth surface. They looked like lumps of butter hardened and spray-painted. It was beyond nuance, as if designed at the kitchen table, and in fact, that was where it had been designed. It rattled, nothing in it fit well, all angles were sharp and punishing to the hand or body. It was just a tube with stuff sticking off it at weird angles. The magazine inserted horizontally so that it was infernally out of balance; its trigger guard appeared to have been engineered before anyone thought up the curve. It lacked elegance, streamline, grace, ergonomic concession, or solidity. It lacked a front sight; its rear sight was a small nubby projection with a hole in it, which was why nobody ever used them. It even had a stupid nomenclature; machine carbine. The only thing it did well was kill people.

If he had to fight for his life, this was not quite what he would have come up with. However, the British won their part of World War II with this stuff, so in for a penny, in for a pound. Mili Petrova was worth it. He would have fought with a can opener for her.

Now he heard them. At last. It was almost a relief. By canting a little and staying low, he was able to get an eyeball on them.

There were six, seven if you counted the dog, who came first, sniffing bravely for pheromones that weren't there. It pulled Thug One on a leash and was followed by Thugs Two through Five, in sweatsuits or jeans, really heavy, strong, tough-looking guys. Gangster meat, each carrying a short-barreled AK-74 with the long forty-round plum-colored magazine. Jerry Renn hadn't flown in an A-Team from Dubai or anything like that. He'd hired off the Moscow street, probably Mob soldiers, cheap and expendable, complete with heavy brows, jawlines stark with testosterone, necks like diesel tires, huge hands, an aura of instant, thoughtless brutality so necessary to instill terror in potential resistants and keep others in the outfit in line, as well as to guarantee the boss's comfort. Drug couriers or security, rule enforcement, lords of snitch discipline, collection experts, takedown crew, gunfighters, whatever was called for, these men provided it without a lot of thought before or guilt afterward. They were the universal soldiers of the Mob, any Mob. They did it for the blow, the chicks and the gold necklaces. On a good day they got all three, on a bad, nothing but lead at twelve hundred feet per second.

Then came Jerry, last in line, but with a shorty AK as well. That made him one of the boys, that made him killable. Bob tried not to personalize this stuff, but he thought it would be kind of cool to kill Jerry. You could tell he was convinced he was pretty hot stuff, and that Swagger was years beyond effectiveness, an old goat with a bad case of crankiness and a steel ball for a hip. Be nice to blow the smug off his face with eighteen or twenty Sten-gun rounds.

Jerry had added a baseball hat, khaki, and one of those shoot-me-first tactical vests the contractors all wore. All his shit was sand-colored, so he'd spent a lot of time in the sand. He also wore Oakley killer shades, what looked to be a SiG 226 strapped to his thigh in a Tommy Tactical rig, and a nice pair of too-expensive tactical boots. He looked like a model for the iTactical.com site.

At least the six weren't talking, bullshitting, smoking, joshing, or laughing. They weren't quite that cocksure, though their postures were far from the kind of Condition Four readiness that kept you alive on combat patrols. It was clear they thought they had this one whipped. An old man with a bad hip, a not quite so old woman, an actual grandma, no weapons, no water, in wilderness about which they knew nothing, mostly moving uphill as fast as possible, but grinding down every step of the way. What was there to worry about?

Reilly couldn't think of Paris. She couldn't even think of Ocean City. It wasn't fear, not as some experience it: weight, dread, air painful to skin, breath raw and raspy and somehow not satisfying. It was more like: Do I really have to do this? And: I can think of a lot of reasons why this is not a good idea. What would Marty say? "You *what?* You killed gangsters? Don't tell Legal."

411

So she tried to think of something else, something that she really loved, something that had sustained her over the years. She didn't want to think of Will or her two daughters or her grandchild, because she feared that would make her shaky and full of remorse.

So she thought of newsrooms.

She knew she had been so lucky to live her life in newsrooms, among funny, ironic, not terribly serious people, some geniuses, some hacks, some fools, some crazy. You got the weirdest memories from a newsroom. There was a reporter who went out on a story and managed to lose a company car. That took some doing, although alcohol was involved. There was a strange old lady, who every day wore a pilot's leather cap and a dress made from the Maryland flag. There was a failed priest who spent his lunchtime feeding quarters into peep machines in a nearby porn strip. There was a man who slipped off to massage parlors. There were several toupees wearing men beneath them, several princesses of WASP, Jewish, and Asian persuasion, a managing editor whose pants were too high, followed by one whose pants were too low. She'd weathered a storm when one new regime brought in anyone they could hire from Philadelphia, including, she supposed, the delivery drivers. There was a guy who went on to become a TV producer, another who wrote some novels, but most just drifted out of the business into something with regular hours when their wives or husbands wore them down. Then there were the pros who were really good at it and just loved the hell out it, working sixty-hour weeks whether it was necessary or not. They did about 70 percent of the work but never held it against the others who disappeared at the crack of five.

Of course it changed. The corporation took over, the model mutated from pay-the-most-for-the-best to pay-the-least-for-the-worst, and she'd watched it change from loon show to midsize insurance company, with mediocrities typing at monitors all day, so that the dull clackity-clunk of finger on plastic took over for the staccato spatters of fingers on typewriters, with the occasional slam-bang of a bell dinging when Johnny Ace hit the end of a line. She even remembered the hot-metal days, being just old enough to have caught a few years of that particular ancient tech and to work with the surly roustabout printers who actually knew what they were doing, even if most of the actual makeup people who supervised them had no idea, had been its own special kind of initiation. She remembered her first makeup editor, who'd saved her career a dozen times in the composing room, and could play the printers like a violin, knew them all and their kids by first name. Man, he was a newspaperman! She remembered rewrite desks, copy paper pasted together, rolled up, and fired to composing in a pneumatic tube that made a plumph sound that you never forgot if you ever heard it. She remembered a new copyreader saying, "Oh, I see. You put a headline on *every* story!" She remembered editors with the imagination of hamsters, hamsters who should have been editors, and the odd drunk and the odd suicide (it seemed the coming of computers had wiped out a whole generation of old men with gin-gray skin and shaky fingers who could turn any screamer's phone call into prose in a minute's time but were lost in cyberspace). She remembered the affairs, the hatreds, the vendettas, and the passion, the loyalty of people who loved and respected each other helping each other up rung by rung. She'd helped; she'd been helped.

It's been a wonderful life, she thought. If I have to leave it, at least I had the golden age. The only thing is, none of us had any idea it was a golden age.

"Go!" came the call from Swagger.

She stepped out, assumed the position, and was amazed by how close they were. She pulled the trigger, and the metal machine in her hands became some kind of twitching, energetic pneumatic hammer as it turned the physical world to a storm of disturbed grit, while the noise was terrific. There seemed to be lots of cracking and shattering as the bullets struck whatever they struck and did whatever they did next. The gun's stock beat sharply into the arms and ribs that locked it into place. A blur of brass refuse spurted from a slot in its side, and at its muzzle, blurring her vision, a rippling pulse of incandescent flash danced crazily. She closed her eyes as the gun rattled itself empty and opened them to get a glimpse of the mayhem she had loosed on the world at the last shot. She saw two men down and crawling and the others rolling or having already disappeared. Best of all, she didn't see the dog. She hoped it was dead.

Swagger had placed a grenade at each three-yard mark and the Sten at the end of them, thirty yards down. He threw the first as he yelled, "Go!," then ran down the line to lift, pull pin, and toss over the screen of boulders that separated himself from his hunters. One short toss, one long toss.

The God of Grenade was good that day. He let each of his children achieve its destiny. Five for five. Each lever popped off, each grenade began to hiss and spit, and it was away. Four-point-five seconds later, it became a chaos event, releasing energy and pressure totally out of scale with its size and weight, turning its shielding into bullets and its doughy center into pure killing force. To be near it was to be unlucky. It was very unkind to living things. Only the dog escaped unhurt, turning at the machine-gun burst to flee like its own kind of hell on wheels and sprint at warp speed out of the kill zone, those good dog reflexes giving it advantages at survival that the men around it never had. It darted off and clear to become feral, to acquire a new master, who knew?

Swagger snatched up the Sten and found its one advantage was its easy pointability, its hunger to find and destroy targets. A shape staggered by him and he put a burst into it and it went down. He got around a rock and faced the alleyway of carnage. Visibility nonexistent, just a seething sea of dust and gas, silent because all ears had shut down among killer and killed alike. Another figure appeared before Swagger, severely injured by the look of the walk. But mercy was not on the menu, and he shot it till it went down—this guy took a lot of killing—and as he finished him, still another figure flashed by him, running like hell. Bob pivoted to fire and saw that it was Jerry Renn, absent I-am-cool baseball hat, running like a halfback. Too bad for Jerry. Swagger fired only two shots, both liberating geysers of raw debris at the target's feet, and the gun had run dry. He raced through a mag change, but by the time he was hot to go, Jerry had vanished. He hunkered down, waited a while as the dust settled, and beheld what he had wrought.

Four dead, opened up badly by the blasts or the Swagger stitches, one barely moving. Swagger put a burst into him before Reilly got into the picture, he didn't want to argue the moral complexity of the coup de grâce, he just wanted the guy out of the situation.

"Clear, all down," he yelled, then retraced his way to his entrance point into the alley, where he'd set the Enfield No. 4 (T). He snatched it up and ran to a spot he'd reconnoitered earlier, a kind of promontory where an arm of rock stood out right at the margin of the scree field and gave him best vantage on what lay below.

Arm snaked through sling, rifle to shoulder. Position built from bones outward. Both eyes open but the dominant one, at the precise point of maximum accessibility to the scope, in charge. He nestled for support, feeling his bones line up, feeling his joints lock. He was against the rock, leaning over a shelf, looking down the descending line of trees, and he caught a flash of movement, vectored to it, identified Jerry by his loping stride and because he was the only living human male in the immediate world, and tracked.

Tracked.

Tracked.

Range about six hundred, so gauging that she had zeroed at a thousand, he held low, at foot level, pivoted to stay with Jerry until he led him by a good six feet, and then his finger, on direct-command line from his deep brain, P-R-E-S-S-E-D the trigger. He came back on target to see the bullet hit Jerry somewhere low and toss him, as it had a thousand or so pounds of energy left. He went down hard and lay still.

"Did you get him?"

"I did, yes."

"Yay for the man from Texas!" she shouted.

He said, "Say, weren't you G.I. Jane?"

"I just pulled the trigger and hid."

"That's how wars are won. Sorry, didn't kill the dog. Maybe next time. Got all your stuff? We ain't coming back."

"Got it all." She had remembered her bag, all her phones, even the carefully wrapped plate.

"Good. Let's see what we bagged."

Interlude in Tel Aviv VI

There are better killers in the world today," said the director. "The best that science, government, and unlimited budgets can devise. Why would anyone go to so much trouble to manufacture this old garbage?"

"Indeed, there are more efficient chemical and biological weapons," responded Gershon. "Nerve agents, anthrax, sarin, Ebola, all sorts of vapors, dusts, unguents, and gizmos for murder. Moreover, the methods of deploying the Zyklon are awkward and prone to difficulty. It works best in a locked chamber disguised as a shower room. That is, in controlled circumstances. It is heavy for its effect, difficult to transport, and lacking, outside the extermination camp, sophisticated dispersal technologies. It's old-fashioned.

"But that's not a mistake, that's the very point. I see this as what might be called a 'tribute atrocity.' That is to say, a sentimental act of murder, a gesture in which the murderer's true motive is not merely to kill but, by killing, to pay homage to an earlier generation of murderers. In other words, someone wants to replicate and sacralize the Shoah and to inform the world with his method that the ancient Nazi genocidalists are still out there, waiting, watching. It has nothing to do with Allah, not really, and is uninterested in Islam, other than as a means to an end. No, this fellow kills in the name of Hitler, and to him, it doesn't matter if he kills five, fifty, five hundred, or five thousand, though the more, the better."

The faces at the table stared at him. He had their attention. It was well past midnight, the lights of the black cube burned brightly, and in the conference room not only the director and several department heads stared at Gershon, but so did IDF representatives and an emissary from the prime minister. In the background of the room, a silent TV carried a newsfeed from CNN, and the screen bled blue light into the dim space.

"How could they deliver it?" Cohen said. "I don't think the shower-room trick will work twice on us."

"No, indeed. The 'crystals' are actually placed under pressure and become embedded in porous stone or wooden disks and locked in airtight containers for transport and deployment. Air releases the vapor; water releases it more quickly. The Nazis packed them in pellet form in sealed cans, opened them, and dropped them into water to release the gas. So, bulk would be a problem. To kill a lot of people, you need a lot of stuff. On the other hand, he has a lot of stuff. Given what we know about his manufacturing process, he could have churned out ten thousand pounds of the stuff. Consider a low-flying plane that crashes into Tel Aviv in the night without warning, loaded with the pellets, releasing their gas into the air when their fragile containers break open. The gas—without the odorant to tip us off to its presence, and being heavier than air—would drift at low level through the city air, smothering people in their beds. Thousands could die. That would be the mega-disaster. In smaller applications, a shopping mall might contain people and gas long enough for hundreds of deaths, a school, any building would do. It could be added to water supplies, its deadly vapors drifting this way and that off the breeze. It could be packed in rockets and fired from Gaza. Fifteen rockets and people come out after the all-clear, unaware they're walking into a poison-gas cloud. Dozens, hundreds could die.

"Then, too, when the dying is over and the investigation begins, think of the furor after it is discovered that the death gas was our old Nazi enemy Zyklon, the cyclone. The world press would go nuts, as they love to run pictures of Nazis, which are sure magazine and newspaper sellers. All the old footage is rerun. Someone digs out *Triumph of the Will*, and the parades are run over and over on the news channels. Everyone loves to hate the Nazis, bad boys of a hundred thousand silly plots. Why, it would be like National Nazi Month. It would be the best month the Third Reich has had in seventy years. That in itself would be a major victory for the author of this event."

"Which brings us to the point of this meeting, Gershon. Who is he? Who is Nordyne? How do we find him? How do we kill him? How much time have we got?"

"Well," said Gershon, "I'd be trying to answer those questions myself if I weren't at this damned meeting."

Where are you, mister? You must have left a trace, a clue. You have to be somebody. You're not just a spirit of malevolence that seeped out of a grave, you're corporeal, of flesh, and mind, and hair, and stench, and somewhere, somehow, you've left a trail. I will find it.

All around was activity, but Gershon was calm.

He was where he wanted to be. He was hunting.

I cannot hunt you in your Swiss bank, you putz, because those institutions are notoriously secretive, and I cannot get to your accounts without the validating algorithms. It could be done but would take far too much valuable time. Running your little ploy out of Switzerland was a master stroke.

So what have you left? Only the logo.

Yes, the logo. Two stylized faces staring off, "facing the future."

He stared, he stared, he stared. Was there a significance in the image? What could something so simple, so banal, conceal? Just another corporate bromide; who would look twice at it? A trademark, amusing to eye but devoid of content, as designed. It had no signature, no house style or indication of what graphic artist had confabulated it. It seemed offhand, yet the artist had captured in those two light lines a true glint of human intelligence, individuality, and flesh. Maybe it was steganography, a method of encoding information in graphic presentations. In some cases, not here, microdots. But Gershon thought that somewhere in the images, or in the imagination that conceived and selected and refined the images, there was a code of sorts, perhaps unconscious.

Besides: he had nothing else.

So: Two faces, facing left. Two profiles.

Shapes. Though they're technically lines, they're really shapes. Your imagination attaches them to a head and completes the image in the eye of you, beholding.

He knew of a Darknet site called Imagechase .com, which hunted for selected images, just as other search engines found words, names, anything in the universe of print. He called it up, activated it, and fiddled and faddled, defining the original image from the Nordyne website, cutting it and then pasting it to the software screen "target" area of Imagechase. Maybe in the posture, in the alignment, there was something, and Imagechase could hunt it down. It might lead to something that had inspired the actual artist in his studio, wherever he was.

He pressed SEARCH.

A magic animated disk appeared, the universal symbol that the elves inside were at work. The seconds dragged by. But then the screen changed and produced a chain of mini-images, each of which could be full-screened by a click.

Mostly the click wasn't necessary. It was a selection of left-facing profiles, many banal, many of no use whatsoever. Easter Island seemed to predominate, those odd busts from time unimaginable, two stories tall, as viewed in profile, endless fodder for speculation and photography. It seemed unlikely, however, that Easter Islanders were behind Nordyne GmbH.

American presidential editorial cartoons, on the theme of the president posing for a sculpture, were the second most common, the joke always being the sculptor's idealization or contra, truth-telling, about the stentorian great man posing before him in the required profile. Hand in breast of jacket strictly optional.

Then an odd run of middle-tier European talent expressing itself in hagiographical portraits of powerful nobles. It seemed that the pose was favored by those with a strong sense of self-importance, while others preferred to face the instrument of record straight on.

And finally . . .

What have we here?

He clicked.

The image jumped out at him. Two strong faces, lean of jaw, forceful of nose, taut cheeks over bed-knob bones, foreheads caparisoned in helmets or hats, and the future they so dutifully faced made possible by the three words immediately before them, *Garanten Deutscher Wehrkraft*, or "Guarantors of German military strength."

It struck him how similar the two stylized faces in the logo were to this piece of Nazi poster kitsch. Gershon quickly diverted to another software program called Abonsoft Image Compare, which let him run more exact comparisons between the poster and the logo and enabled a fast pixel-to-pixel comparison. He loaded the two images and zoomed in on the lines of profile, bold in the logo, less strident in the poster, isolated them, aligned them, and clicked. Abonsoft found that the profiles of each were almost an exact match in pitch of forehead, angle of nose, cast of mouth, shape of chin. Whoever had designed the logo must have known about, studied, perhaps even idolized the image from the poster, which was ascribed to an artist called only "Mjölnir."

Mjölnir was quickly revealed by Dr. Google to be Hans Schweitzer, house artist of the Ministry of Propaganda, pet of Dr. Goebbels, the Nazi Norman Rockwell. The Internet quickly revealed the scope of his work. It seemed that he was a specialist in heroic profiles staring off to the left, as all manner of SS men, SA men, and Waffen-SS *Soldats* were captured in that pose, even a couple of rather horsey German women, though once in a while he'd turn them to face the other direction. He was also responsible for the poster for a Nazi movie called *Der ewige Jude*, with an image of the eternal jew as a kind of Fu Manchu facing the world in sinister yellow skin behind two squinting, malicious eyes and an enormous massif of nose.

Gershon felt a little sick, as did most people when they saw this shit laid out before them.

But he continued, becoming an expert in two minutes on Hans Schweitzer, who, after the glory days of the war, settled back into obscurity as a commercial illustrator and didn't die until 1980. But it was all right. Justice was served. He was made to pay a fine.

So: who would allow himself to be influenced by Hans Schweitzer?

Who found the imagery so powerful and raw that he'd commissioned its replication seventy years after the last real Nazi was gunned down in the rubble of Berlin by Red Shock Army troops?

Begin with family. He went to an Institute database, found nothing, then sent an e-mail to a friend at the Holocaust Research Center and in very few minutes heard back.

Gershon, I don't approve of holding a son guilty for a father's deeds. It's even more questionable here, as Schweitzer was really only guilty of what can be called Artcrime. Yes, he specialized in the world's most hateful imagery, and prospered from it, and enabled the killers in some extralegal philosophic sense, but he himself did nothing except draw.

You assure me this is necessary for some national defense issue. Then I will dutifully comply and tell you that Schweitzer had a son with some graphic talent who worked in advertising for many years. The son's son has the same talent and now is a

426

senior partner in a graphics firm in Berlin called Imagetorrent. The man's name is Lukas Schweitzer, and it saddens me to report that he did in fact change his name back to Schweitzer to capitalize on his grandfather's "fame." It seems to have worked. Do what you will with this information, but remember, these people are guilty only of translating into imagery the sick fantasies of the truly evil. What does the world become if you are guilty of "drawing bad things" and can be punished for it?

Gershon had no plan to punish Lukas Schweitzer for his grandfather's intellectual crimes, but he did plan to do some actual spying.

That didn't take much effort, as the firewalls around Imagetorrent's internal affairs were quite fragile, easily penetrated, and it took only a few minutes to crank into the e-mail of Lukas Schweitzer and call up its "trash" file, where that which had been erased lay in perpetuity, and pore through it until he came on a file of e-mails labeled "Nordyne."

It was a back-and-forth between artist and patron.

Artist: I'm sorry you are disappointed in the submission. I find myself reluctant to pursue your ideas any further. Yes, I profit by my family associations, call me a hypocrite, but it is still a painful area for me.

Patron: Bourgeois sniveling. You have accepted a generous payment. You have agreed to follow my ideas. Your opinions of them are not interesting to me. Use your talent as I have directed and as I demand, or there will be ruinous legal problems for you and your firm. I want the same purity of line that marked the great Mjölnir's work; that talent is in your veins. Embrace who you really are.

Artist: Let me know if this works for you. I have tried to eliminate any supremacist content and utilize only the core of my grandfather's imagery. You don't WANT associations with him, do you? You can't. You just want some essence of his "spirit," right? I hope so.

Patron: At last. Yes, it is acceptable, and the final fee will be paid, with a bonus. All these e-mails must be destroyed, incidentally. But you knew that.

The patron's e-mail address was Anton1 @Toryavesky.net. It didn't take long for Gershon to learn that Toryavesky was the holding company at the center of a certain Russian oligarch's empire. That man was Vassily Strelnikov, about to become the new minister of trade of Russia.

CHAPTER 50

The Carpathians
Yaremche
LATE JULY 1944

Inna lillahi wa inna ilaihi rajioon.
To him we belong, to him return.

Having spoken directly to Allah by means of a dua, as such direct declarations were called, Salid came out of his religious trance. It was still the same, only it was five seconds later.

The senior group leader SS lay on his side on the narrow width of the bridge, in a gigantic puddle of blood that soaked his clothes and gleamed in the dull light of the occluded sun; some of it slid through the slats and drained down to the swirling waters below. There was so much blood you could smell it. The corpse's eyes were open, as was his mouth. Blood ran from his nose and welled into his mouth from his throat but had not overspilled its boundaries yet.

Where could the shot have come from?

It had to have come from a long, long way out,

so far out that its noise largely dissipated before it so tragically arrived.

Salid blinked, hoping for the arrival of a clarification. Men looked at him in stupefied horror, waiting for orders. He himself wished someone were there to give crisp, concise, well-thought-out orders. But in the absence of Dr. Groedl, he was the senior officer.

He could think only of himself.

The man I was sent to protect is dead despite my best efforts. I will be blamed. I am, after all, the outsider, the one who does not belong. My greatest sponsor was Dr. Groedl, and now he is gone, the sniper has escaped, I have shamed my father, my grandfather, my cousin the Mufti, my family, my faith, my destiny. The Germans will shoot me for gross incompetence.

Allah, send me wisdom, I pray to Thee help your son Salid at his hour of maximum terror among the infidels, to whom he is nothing really but a nigger of no account who, given responsibility, has failed it utterly.

"Sir, what—"

It was Ackov.

Salid tried to think.

What? What? What?

The dogs.

"The dogs will find her. Nothing has changed. She is up there, somewhere above the burned-out line. No, no, the bullet hit him frontally. The shot

430

had to come from there!" He pointed to a much farther flank of pine-carpeted mountain a full thousand yards distant. "Where's the field telephone?"

Ackov waved over a man, who had a box containing the Model 33 field phone and the long cord. The field telephone, in its hard-shell Bakelite container, was the primary communications device of German ground forces, as it was far less fragile than the radio, far less temperamental, and wire could be laid quickly to put units at a great distance in contact. Its batteries were more reliable, it wasn't as heavy, and it never blew a tube. Salid opened it, took out the phone, and turned the little crank to send a signal to the other end.

"Graufeldt here." Graufeldt was a steady lance corporal, one of the few ethnic Germans in Police Battalion.

"Did you hear the shot?"

"Yes sir. It wasn't from our area."

"The dogs, Graufeldt."

"Sir, I've already released the dog teams, and they're headed in the direction of the shot. They will pick up any scent. Since the shot was so far away, I directed the men to dump their machine pistols and packs and proceed under armament of pistols. I thought they'd have to move quickly and stamina would be the determining factor and—"

"Yes, yes, good. How much wire have you got?"

"Two spools. Another half kilometer. Should I move with them?"

"Yes, stay as close as you can."

"Yes sir."

"Keep me informed. I will be moving soon and beyond the reach of the field phones. You will communicate by flare pistol if you catch her, and you will proceed along the high path to the choke point. If nothing else, your presence will drive her into the parachutists."

"Yes sir."

"Good man, Graufeldt."

"Sir, how did—"

"I don't know, and it doesn't matter. What matters now is only that we apprehend the woman."

"Yes sir. End transmit here, as I move to new position."

Now Salid was thinking more clearly. He handed the phone back.

"Sir, should we mount up for the trip to the Gap?"

"Not yet, Ackov. Have the men roust all the villagers and lock them in the church."

"Yes sir."

"Then have a crew use the Flammenwerfer to burn all the buildings. I want the place razed. I want there to be no record of the place where

Senior Group Leader Groedl was murdered. There will be no monuments here."

"Yes sir. And the church, sir? With the villagers."

"Burn it, Ackov."

Mili would not abandon the rifle; she had it slung across her back. The Teacher had a Sten gun and kept checking back, looking to see if the Serbs had closed the trail.

"Look," she said suddenly, pointing. "He's burning the village."

"Had to happen. It's the way his mind works. Here or at Lidice, anywhere the partisans strike, the people pay."

No details were available through the trees. Instead, columns of heavy smoke drifted upward and over the crest of the mountains, then mingled into a single miasma by the thrust of the winds. It didn't take long for the odors to reach them, a mesh of crispy burned wood, the bloody tang of burned animal meat, a slight petroleum bite from the stench of the flamethrower's Flammoil-19. No screams were heard, but how could they be from such a distance?

"Enough smoke," said the Teacher through gasps of air as the oxygen debt put pain into his lungs. "He burned it down, the whole thing."

Then came the sound of the dogs. The sound rose and ebbed, depending on whether the waves caught some freakish echo effect. But it was clear that the animals were howling with the excitement of the hunt.

For the longest time, as they headed along the path, the dogs seemed distant. At one point they even seemed to disappear. But the dogs were strong and the young men running them were strong. When Mili heard the barking again, it seemed much closer.

Then, somehow, it got closer still.

"We're not going to make it," she said. "We can't outrun the dogs."

Another few minutes passed. The barking grew louder. They broke into a trot, and then Petrova fell, chopping up her knee.

"All right," she said, "closer. Give me the machine pistol. I'll stay and kill as many as I can. Then I'll spend the last bullet on myself."

"Sorry, not possible," said the Teacher. "I will be the one who stays behind. I hate dogs. To kill as many as possible will be a pleasure. Go, go."

Then they saw them. Six muscular, tawny beasts, unleashed at last, coming like rockets, all muscle and speed, dashed into view, driven forward on that bounding hound run, a coil and uncoil action, as of a powerful spring or piston. On they came.

He shoved her. "Run," he said. "Damn you, run!" and turned with his Sten gun to face the horde.

The smoke from the village obscured everything, so Salid moved his position about a half mile down the Yaremche road. From there he only saw a wall of smoke, drifting columns in the sky and the flames eating the odd building. It was better for his men, too, for they could not hear the screams of the villagers locked in the flaming church as the fire dissolved their bodies, although Salid himself did not really notice.

"Anything?" he barked in Serbian to Ackov.

"Nothing," said the sergeant, who stood guard at the field telephone.

The captain shivered. He had to capture the woman. She meant more than anything. With her, he could turn his life into a triumph and his return to the sun and the sand of the desert into a mythic passage. It wasn't ambition.

He did this all for Allah. At his core he believed in the primacy of Allah over all nations and men and that those who had not given themselves to Allah were infidels, unworthy of life and doomed to an afterlife in the fires of hell. As much suffering as they would endure in the forever, what difference did it make to them now?

O Allah, he prayed, humbly I beseech Thee to look with favor upon the enterprise of Your servant Yusef Salid, who seeks only to please and obey in his hope to earn the right to come to heaven in the afterlife. Please, please, can You give me this one gift, it is all I ask, it is all—

"Sir," said Ackov. "It's Graufeldt."

Salid took the phone.

"Graufeldt reporting."

"What is happening, man?"

"I believe they've made contact. It's the dogs, sir. They yowl and yelp when chained, fighting and feeling frustrated by the chain, but when they're released, their voices achieve the full throaty barking and are more widely spaced because they are running flat out. They wouldn't have released them unless they'd made visual contact. The dogs, sir. The dogs are on her."

On came the dogs, by now their white canines gleaming like SS parade daggers in the sunlight, foam flying from open jaws, throats undulating with the working of their larynxes as they growled, on to the kill.

The Teacher checked his as yet unfired Sten gun, positive that it was cocked, the bolt free and not engaged in the safety notch, sure that in one burst he could kill at least a few of the beasts, maybe get rounds into all six before they were on him. Then maybe he could pull the 6.35mm Frommer that had been his only protection until recently and kill or wound the others. But he knew he would be so slashed and bitten, and there was no way he could—

A screaming came across the sky.

It was a chorus of banshees or other dead creatures or ghastly apparitions: high-pitched, full of vibration, a howl, the yell of death, the fall of civilization, the hungry screaming of the harpies as they tore something into shreds. Then the high pitch went away, buried in a lower, more sibilant roar that spoke of fire and death.

The Teacher recognized it. It was the sound of a battery of seventy-two Katyusha rockets blasting from their truck-borne carriers to obliterate whatever resided in their scatter of random hits. The shriek was so intense it traveled for miles, a pronunciamento for the Red Army, a signifier of battle for the German. To the dogs, with their more refined hearing, it would be hideously loud.

The Red offensive had begun.

If the Teacher knew, the dogs did not. To them it signaled the approach of another predator, a mythic predator; it meant they were to be swept up in dinosaur jaws, crushed, ripped, gobbled. Their brains could not handle the fear.

Thirty meters shy of the quarry, they hit a wall. It seemed to be made of glass, but it was made of terror. They lost their grace and focus, they slid, slithered, slipped, rolled, each pounding into the other, each in the abyss of pure animal panic. And just that fast, they were gone, seeking survival in the cover of the deep woods.

Meanwhile the artillery, a thousand guns at

least, maybe two thousand, commenced, a rush of noise swallowed in detonation, a whistle of shells obeying the laws of gravity and descending from their rainbow arcs to vaporize all that lay within their blast zones. It was so loud that the dust fell from the trees, the ground shivered, and the world seemed on the tippy-tippy edge of destruction.

But the Teacher understood it was still miles away to the south, as far as Kosiv, which had been the closest Russian strong point and clearly would be the offensive step-off site; it simply proved an old point—destruction is loud. He turned, hoping to see something through the screen of trees that stood between him and the valley four thousand feet beneath, but he could see nothing.

He turned and headed up the path. Without dogs, the Germans would be helpless. He would catch up with the woman, and the two of them would diverge from this path to the brush, where tracking them by eye would be impossible. Maybe in time the Germans would round up the dogs, get them calmed down, but it would be hours before they found the scent again.

He rounded a slight turn and saw the sniper walking ahead. She turned, feeling his eyes on her, and waved. He raced to her, breathing hard in the thinner air.

"You're alive!" she said.

"Scoundrel's luck once again. The noise of the Katyushas. It terrified the dogs."

"It scared the hell out of me," she said.

"Come on, this is our golden opportunity. We must get off the path, we must progress overland, through the brush and trees. It'll take hours to find our trail."

"Yes."

"But dump that rifle. It slows us."

"No, no. You can never tell. Come on, we're wasting time."

It took another two hours, but in all that time, they heard no sign of their pursuers. The journey quickly resolved itself into pure ordeal, the two fighting through thorns and bracken and the needles of the pines, some very sharp, all at an uphill angle, going primarily on faith. They were washed in sweat, which drained into their eyes, as the branches whipped backward to catch them in the faces, or roots tugged and twisted their ankles.

"I think it's just ahead," said the Teacher.

They reached a familiar glade.

"COMING IN!" yelled the Teacher, and he and Petrova cased ahead.

"Why can we not stay here?" asked the Peasant in Ukrainian. "Our army will arrive soon, a day or two. We can just wait and—"

"No, no," said the Teacher in the same language.

"The Germans will gather their dogs in a while. They'll come after us. Eventually they'll pick up the scent. They'll find this cave. We must be long gone when they get here."

That was true. But there was more. What the Teacher didn't say was that he wasn't eager to simply walk to the Red Army with hands upraised. He had no idea how good these troops would be and if they were of poor quality—many were—they might shoot anything that moved. Then there was the issue of Mili Petrova, quite possibly hunted by her own people. He had to get that settled.

"We have a long journey, at least three miles to the canyon they call Natasha's Womb. It's a choke point holding us in this sector. We'll get through it and find a cave or a glade on the other side. Once the Red Army has driven the Germans out of the mountains, we'll figure a safe way to return to our side."

They walked, they walked, they walked. It took close to two hours to make it to the site of the cave at the head of the scree field where the canister was hidden. It was not far from the Womb.

"Here, rest," said Mili, "but only for a moment." She gave the Teacher her rifle. "Replace it now. Your weapon, too. I will strip off my camouflage, and from now on, we are peasants fleeing the battle."

The Teacher took her weapon and his own and ducked into the cave, replacing the two guns and all the ammunition, then latched the container tightly.

He emerged, finding them both ready for what lay beyond. They were so close.

"Just a little farther," she said. "Another few miles. When we get close to Natasha's Womb, we'll go to ground, and I'll squirm forward and make certain we're all right."

"Petrova, that should be my job," the Teacher said. "Who knows what lies ahead, better I go than you, who've already accomplished so much."

"You're an idiot," she said.

"Certainly," he said, "but we should take just that little precaution."

With faith and vigor renewed, they set out along a higher trail, which seemed to take a downward track as it worked its way to the gap in the mountains at a significantly lower altitude. Still they bent against the incline and felt their thighs fight for strength as the walk became difficult with the need to defy gravity. They went down in silence, except for the sound of their labored breathing, the far-off detonation, the hum of insects attracted to the salty sweat that lubricated their skin and dampened their clothes.

As yet unseen, Natasha's Womb came closer. So did the sense of other, larger mountains abutting them, which was why the formation afforded a gap, while the others demanded mountaineering.

At one point, Mili called a halt. "All right," she said, "here's where you'll lay up. I'm going to work my way ahead and get a glimpse, just to make sure there's no mischief up here. And—"

"Sergeant, please," said the Teacher. "This should be my duty, and I—"

"*HALTEN SIE!*" came a sudden cry.

Two men stepped out of the brush ten yards away, weapons leveled.

CHAPTER 51

The Carpathians
Above Yaremche
THE PRESENT

O kay," said Reilly as they advanced toward Jerry Renn, "you should see this. I think it explains something."

She handed Swagger her iPhone, which displayed a message from Will. After worrying why he hadn't heard from her, he got to the gist: *Got Krulov KGB file. Longer memo to follow, but here's the key stuff.*

Bob read it.

It laid out the life and times of one Basil

Krulov, his education, his wartime experience. His upward climb in the '40s, his domestic situation, his fate.

"There's the motive we were looking for," said Bob. "I think I get it now. He thought he was doing the right thing. They all say they're doing the right thing, the motherfuckers."

Jerry lay against a rock, having pulled himself to it from the path. He was in agony, and the bone sprouting from his thigh meant he wasn't going anywhere soon. His Sig, originally pulled as a show of bravado, lay next to him.

"You move for that gun," yelled Bob, "and I'll cut you in half. Offhand, pick it up by the barrel and toss it my way."

Jerry did it.

"Now the knife. You cowboys all have them folders you think is so cool. You dump it now."

Out came the knife, and it was tossed.

Bob came out of cover, the Sten gun leveled, and approached.

"Jesus Christ," said the agent, "where'd you get the fucking World War II shit? What is this, *Bridge on the River Kwai?*"

"Shut up," said Bob. "And listen hard. I'm going to lay out two possible futures for you. You get to pick what happens next."

"I'm bleeding out, man."

"Nah, you just got a busted leg. You won't be

dead for at least a day, though it'll be a long day."

"Christ, it hurts," Jerry said.

"Cry me a fucking river. My friend Reilly and I are going to walk another couple of hours, and a helicopter is going to pick us up. It will fly us to Uzhgorod, and there a private jet will fly us to Moscow. In Moscow, she's going to write the story of Mili Petrova, and her newspaper is going to publish it. All the dirty wash gets hung out to dry. Now, you can help us, that's one possibility, and if you do that, we'll make a phone call to a number you give us. Too bad you dropped your phone as you ran, too bad I found it, but that's how it goes. Okay, I make that phone call, and I'll give your people a GPS position, and they'll get here fast enough to get some plasma into you. Maybe the Carpathian wolves get here first, I don't know, but I can't make no guarantee about that. The other way is just the same, except I don't call nobody, and you become the den chew toy. Or you dehydrate out. Or you bleed out. I don't know, I don't care. But you ain't going home on this op, that I will guarantee you."

"Swagger, I'm just an action guy. Low-level. An operator. They just give me targets, that's all."

"Then you're dead."

"But I know enough to warn you that you are betraying your country if you go that way. It's not too late. You're the macho man still, if that's what

444

this is all about. I don't care. I'll be beta, it's fine. Just don't fuck this up for your country."

"You ain't my country. Not with a shoot-on-sight license for Reilly and me."

"Oh, Christ," said Jerry.

"I'll lay it out for you, and you pitch in. I think I got it figured."

"I tell you, I don't know stuff. I just run a rifle."

"Bullshit. First, you wouldn't go on an op like this without a convincing reason. Second, if you get this info back to them, they can take steps to be ahead of the shit storm, not behind it."

Grudgingly, Jerry nodded. "I fill you in, you make that call?"

"If I tell you I will, I will."

"All right, I'm down with it."

"Near as I can figure, in '31 or '32, a kid named Basil Krulov, son of a Soviet trade delegate in Munich, went to some classes at the university under a professor named Groedl, a kind of guru on genocide, racial hygiene, all that crazy Nazi shit, right?"

"I don't know any of that stuff."

"Take it from Ms. Reilly here, he did. She has the records."

"My husband dug them out of the KGB archives," she said.

"It changed Krulov's life. He bought in a hundred and fifty percent. He went back to his country in '33, graduated University of Moscow in '35, and began his climb in Stalin's outfit. But his heart belonged to Adolf, at least in the war-on-Jews department. Somewhere in there he contacted Groedl and volunteered to do what he could to help the Nazis whack the Jews. He reasoned that he wasn't betraying Russia, since it wasn't military info he was giving but Jewish intelligence. So that's what he did. He became the Nazi Race Department's own personal mole in the Kremlin. He must have shit a brick when the nonaggression pact came, but he kept playing. Deep in the war, his mentor, Stalin, gives him orders to kill his hero Groedl, but he can't, so he snitches out that mission. Groedl gets wasted anyway, because Mili's so damn good, but Krulov knows that if anyone looks too carefully at it, they'll see for sure Mili Petrova was betrayed, and it had to be Krulov. So he uses his power to erase her from history. Right so far?"

"I told you, this is news to me. I didn't know anything about it. Maybe if I'd have known, I'd have played it differently."

"He gets through the war, everything's fine. No news or suspicion of his treason ever comes out. He's the aces. But I'm guessing sometime in '46 or '47, some American intel team is going through recovered Nazi records, and they get proof that Krulov was a Nazi spy. So now they own him. He has to dance their jig or they burn him and he catches one behind the ear."

"I just know they recruited him in '47. They said he was a walk-in. That's where the story begins for me."

"So for the next nine years, he's our number one guy in Russ. I'm guessing it was so top-top they didn't even run him out, because they thought the Agency had security problems."

"It's something rinky-dink in the Pentagon. Office of Defense Procurement Review. The dope they got from Krulov was slipstreamed into Agency product, that's how they got it into policy play. It still works that way."

"Then in '56, someone separates Krulov from his head. Right? It's all over. But is it?"

"He had a son," said Jerry. "Guy named Strelnikov, mother's remarried name, still the son of Krulov. Who got high in the government, became a billionare when Communism fell, and is now getting back into government."

"And he's your guy."

"I don't know when Strelnikov went active for us. Mid-'60s, early '70s, maybe. But I see why now. If it comes out his dad was a Nazi spy, they will look at him hard, and he's finished. He never gets anywhere. He's a bus conductor for life. I didn't get that part. I thought it was idealism."

"It was leverage. So this whole thing is about protect your asset. Here's what you geniuses never got. Strelnikov, like his father before him, *because* of his father before him, still wants to

447

destroy the Jews. He was never a Communist, he was never a Nazi. He was *only* a genocide guy. He wants to live up to his dad's heroism, be the man at the tip of the spear in the war against the Jews. He was really still working for RHSA fifty years after RHSA was dust and burned steel. You didn't care, you even helped him, because the stuff he was giving you was so good. You made a deal with a guy, but you never looked at him carefully enough to realize he was the devil. And now he's about to become trade minister. Now he's even more vulnerable to the revelation that Daddy was a spy, which will lead to the fact that he's a spy, and it all goes back to Basil's need to bury Mili's heroism to protect his own ass. She won the war, and yet she's the one you birds are betraying."

"Why does he want to be trade minister?" Reilly asked.

"They don't know. It has them worried," said Jerry. "It's not in the main target area. The econ stuff he'll get us is great, but they think it's a loss of opportunity. They don't want econ, they want strategic. But nobody could talk him out of it, and that's what he's going to do. Maybe it'll pay off long-term. I can tell you, nobody's going to get off the Strelnikov train yet."

"Oh yeah. Well, I'll tell you what you don't know yet," said Swagger. "Wake up, Agent Jerry, and see how the game is played. When she blows his cover in the *Post*, their intel people are going to pull Strelnikov's ass in hard and fast. And they are going to take him apart. Every deal, every communication, every meeting, they'll pull it out of him. You haven't just lost an asset, you've turned a gold mine over to SRV. I'll bet he's got a package all set against this possibility, to keep him out of prison. He's got tons of stuff on you guys, and all the good he's done you goes away, and everything he's figured out about your other sources, he gives that up. That's the mess that's about to land on you feet-first."

Jerry said nothing.

"Too bad your leg's all busted up," said Bob. "Otherwise, you might have gotten the hit on Strelnikov. Sounds like fun to me."

CHAPTER 52

The Carpathians
The Yaremche Road
JULY 1944

It was another soggy morning at Ginger's Womb. It looked like rain, with low clouds sealing in humidity, sweat rising quickly to the skin and just as quickly dampening the combat smocks of the parachutists. Fortunately there wasn't much to do. Karl had his sentry rotation running efficiently; all the guns were cleaned, Blu-Oiled, locked, and loaded; Wili had gone over the Flammenwerfer-41 and made sure that a trigger pull sent a lick of hungry flame dancing forty meters through the air; all the Teller mines were laid, all the wire strung and camouflaged in greenery; both the machine guns were locked into their tripods for defensive fire in the heavy mode, but all the pins lubricated, so when the time came, they could be yanked free and turned into something more flexible in a second; all the ammo belts were rolled and stored, all the ammo to reload the FG-42 mags if necessary torn from boxes and collected in crates; all the grenades were out, all the pins examined so they wouldn't hang up on some burr of metal when needed; all the canteens were filled; and all the latrine duties were taken care of.

"All right," Karl yelled, "bayonet practice."

The announcement was greeted with laughter, not only because the FG-42s had a spike bayonet that was stored under and pivoted outward from beneath the barrel and was largely considered useless by everyone, but also because nobody had practiced bayonet skills since 1939. No one in living memory had killed an Ivan with a bayonet, though if he thought about it, Karl could recall an episode in Italy when the spear of the blade was used to prong open a can of American tomatoes. "I'll teach this tomato the meaning of German steel!" he remembered Wili Bober saying sternly as he pierced the thing.

At 0930, when Karl had his first pipeful going well and had settled in for the tonic of more melancholy over the death of Ziemssen in Mann's great novel, a shadow interrupted what dim light fell from the cloudy sky, and he looked up to see his signalman.

"Zeppelin Leader on the radio. Wants you and you alone. Sounds all fucked up, even for an Arab."

"He *waited* until I got my pipe going nicely, I know it," Karl said, raising, stretching, willing his way through all the scrapes, abrasions, pulled muscles, strained muscles, tired muscles that always visited after a combat engagement, and went to the Commo Tent, where he took up earphones and spoke into the microphone. "Hello, hello, Oskar Leader here, go ahead."

Over the earphone, he heard disturbance—chaos, screams, noises, hard to say exactly what. At the same time, just by chance, he saw a column of smoke rising from behind the foothills in a valley approximately where the village of Yaremche should be.

"Are your people in position, Herr Major?" Salid, the junior officer, hadn't even bothered to go through the officer-officer-brotherhood bullshit of radio protocol.

"Yes, Captain, though I wasn't aware I reported to you."

"Von Drehle, she did it. She got him. The damned bitch made the shot."

"I'm sorry, I don't—"

"The White Witch shot Senior Group Leader Groedl through the throat ten minutes ago."

"Is he dead?"

"She practically blew his head off. Half his neck is gone."

"Good Christ. Is that why the town is burning? I can see the smoke."

"These fucking Russians must be taught. Never mind that, I have my dog teams out—"

"I thought you had burned out all the cover so that she couldn't hit—"

"I don't know how. She must have shot from a thousand yards. I don't know, it doesn't matter, we have the dog teams out, and I have the rest of my men in panzerwagens, and we will now travel to the road up to your position. Please put all your men on interception duty. This woman must be caught."

"Wasn't your explicit responsibility to protect—"

"I don't report to you, either, Von Drehle. Now, I know the SS lieutenant general has had a chat with you, so if you value your men and dream of a postwar future, you will give this assignment your total commitment. I would put all my men out there in the net; this woman is obviously a tricky bitch, and I hope you are up to handling her."

"I will do my duty, yes, as I am a soldier until peace is declared, Captain."

"You radio me this channel the second you learn something or there has been a development."

"Is that an order?"

"Goddammit, Von Drehle, don't play games with me. I speak for the lieutenant general, the entire SS, the SA, so when I tell you to do something, that is the authority I bring to the conversation, and if you doubt that, you radio Muntz yourself for a clarification. End transmit."

"End transmit, Ali Baba," said Karl to a dead microphone.

He rose. By now a few men had gathered outside.

"Well," he said, "the Russian woman sniper they call the White Witch has cast a magic spell on Dr. Groedl. She magically turned him into a corpse. That means I want you in the woods on picket duty, all of you, because I have been informed that she has been flushed by dogs and may be in transit to our picnic area. She has to be taken alive."

"In the meantime, suppose the Russians attack and we are out there looking for a girl?" Deneker asked.

"I don't set these priorities, but they have been set. And you can grumble all you want, but you have a stake in the outcome, too. I have been told by Brigadeführer Muntz that if we do capture her, once she is turned over to the SS, we are formally released from the hold-at-all-costs mandate. We can blow Ginger and get out of here. Next stop, Hungary. I'm told he'll send us off on two weeks' leave and have us reassigned to the Western Front with the rest of Two Fallschirmjäger. You may still die, but it won't be by a Russian bullet, just a shiny American one from Hollywood or someplace like that. So do your goddamned duties. And if anyone sees Bober out there, send him in to me. Now do it, quick quick quick."

An hour or so passed. The men in the woods on picket rotated so they didn't get too bored. Wili Bober arrived, and Karl briefed him on the situation.

"So, catch this woman and we can get home in time for Christmas, eh?" Wili said. "I guess blowing up the bridge, plus all the other jobs, the seven Russian strong points, the railroad yards, the T-34 refueling yard, and several other things weren't worth it, but this gal sniper wins us the class prize."

"Wili, I can't figure out how their minds work. Why this one is so important to them and they didn't even notice the bridge is pretty mysterious to me, too. It must be some spy shit or something."

"I guess for once, the game is working to our advantage."

"I want to get you out of here before the SS

sends you to Dachau. You've been daring them to for years. Sending people to Dachau seems to be the order of the day ever since that guy blew up the Austrian."

At that moment both involuntarily flinched. Screaming came across the sky.

They turned and, from their vantage point four thousand feet up, could see the exhaust flames of seventy-two Katyushas rising from a point of the horizon, a fleet of radiant darts sent howling to the accompaniment of the banshee scream each emitted as it rose, and in the next second the whole horizon seemed to light up as the sound of thousands of the things hurling airborne filled the sky.

"Here they come," said Karl. "Vacation's over."

"They're still a long way away," said Wili.

"We'll be engaged by nightfall, if I don't miss my guess. Through Yaremche and straight down the Yaremche road to Ginger. And if they get here, this is where we stay."

"I hope the boys catch the White Witch. She's our only chance."

"I better talk to my new boss, the great and wise Captain Salid."

Karl ducked into the commo tent, interrupted the signalman reading *The Brothers Karamazov* in the original Russian, and waited as the appropriate connections and protocols were made.

"Zeppelin Leader here, hello, hello."

"Hello, hello, Zeppelin Leader."

"Von Drehle?"

"Affirmative. As you have no doubt noticed, the Russians are coming. I have no idea how long they will take, but I wanted to inform you that if I have to, I will recall my men to defend my position. A maximum effort for one girl is militarily unjustifiable."

"That woman must be caught!" said the voice on the radio.

"Catching her does none of us any good if we can't get her anyplace because the Russians control this position. Surely you understand something that elementary."

"Von Drehle, the Reich has set its priorities. The woman contains secrets of utmost importance. Whether a few Red tanks get through a gap in the mountains is largely meaningless. I will call the brigadeführer and he will set you straight."

"I expect the old boy is rather busy now. He's got a battle to fight. All of us have a battle to fight except, it seems, you."

"I am fighting the real battle. Keep your men on picket duty until otherwise informed. I speak for the brigadeführer."

But something caught Karl's eye. He looked hard and then spoke into the phone. "Well, Captain, it's everybody's lucky day. We just broke the bank at Monte Carlo."

456

Five figures had just emerged from the woods across the road. They were two Green Devils and three captives with their hands clasped behind their heads. One was a woman.

"You have them?" said the captain, and Karl could feel his excitement from miles away.

"A woman and two men. From here the woman looks to be something out of a French glamour magazine, except you don't know what a French glamour magazine is."

"Keep them alive. All of them. They are everything."

CHAPTER 53

The Carpathians
Natasha's Womb
THE PRESENT

They could see the helicopter orbiting the crossroad before the narrow passageway that had to be Natasha's Womb. All the housekeeping had been taken care of, the Stens ditched—"Damn good piece when it counted" was Swagger's verdict—the phone call to Jerry's backup team, via Jerry's own phone, which was then quickly abandoned. Swagger took care of the Enfield No. 4 (T), meaning somehow to get it to the partisan museum.

So now it was a matter of a few minutes. And then Reilly's phone buzzed. She fished it out of the bag, read the number, and said, "D.C."

"No rush," said Bob. "The chopper ain't going nowhere without us."

"Hello," she said, and then, "Hi, Michael. Oh, actually very well. Long story, when I see you, I'll tell you. I do, yes. Very interesting, and it seems to me you'd want to be involved. Oh, really? Oh, great, yes, yes, let's hear what you have."

She listened intently for several minutes, nodding. The smile on her face did not change at all, but at the same time it changed totally. The smile ceased to be a reflection of mood and became some kind of external edifice, supporting the face, which, three layers beneath the skin, in the deep subcutaneous tissue, went taut and hurt. She went from a smiling woman to a woman with a smiling mask on.

"Yes, yes, well, we knew it all along, and it's the best ending under the circumstances. Yes, we'll be back in Moscow in eight hours, I'll call you, we'll set something up. I agree, very good news, oh no, I had help, believe me, I had help. It wasn't all me, not by a long shot. Okay, talk soon."

She turned to Swagger and issued a total blaze of a smile, radiantly insincere. "Okay, all set. Let's go."

They walked to the Womb, where at last the chopper could put down.

Swagger said, "I'd say you seen a ghost, but not even a ghost would smack you as hard as whatever just did."

"Yeah," she said. "Not bad news, not really. Good news, you'd say."

"You don't believe that any more than you've made me believe it."

"I had held out hope. And so had you. It was a one-in-a-million chance. But now it's gone."

"Okay, tell me."

"Long boring background: in 1976, someone was interviewing Jewish survivors of the war. He never got around to writing the book. All of the transcripts went to the Holocaust Museum archives in D.C., where they were read and indexed. One of them was a recording of a guy who'd survived not only the concentration-camp system but then the gulags."

"The Holocaust Museum in D.C.? How does that come into it?"

"Another long story, along the lines of old newspaper friend who married the national editor of *The Washington Post*, who becomes an executive at the Holocaust Museum. Small world, no? But absolutely true. So I called him. That is, my friend's husband, a few weeks ago, to see if the museum had anything in its archives about Groedl. That was finally the response."

"Okay," said Bob. "I copy."

"So this interviewer, remember, recorded a gulag survivor who'd been in Siberia. In the barracks was a man known to have fought with the partisans. The two became friends. Maybe both were Jews, though that's not said anywhere. So our man passed on to the interviewer what the ex-partisan had told him about being in the forest with a woman Russian sniper, who had killed a big Nazi criminal."

"Any verification?"

"He said Ukraine, July 1944. I didn't tell that to Michael, that's independently from the inter-viewee, circa 1976, recounting what he'd been told in 1954. Because someone guessed it was Groedl, a copy of this part of the interview went into the Groedl file, which is why Michael's people found it."

"That's the first outside verification that Mili wasted Groedl."

"There's more to the story."

"You better hurry and tell me."

"He knew what happened to Mili."

CHAPTER 54

The Carpathians
Ginger's Womb
JULY 1944

Von Drehle walked over and examined the captives. They were scrawny, filthy, exhausted, shiny with sweat.

The two men were uninteresting. A fellow in glasses, mid-thirties, with perhaps too much intelligence in his eyes that he tried to mask. A Jew, possibly. The other, big, one of those hearty Ukrainian peasant types.

"Karl, the skinny one had this," Deneker said, handing over a small Hungarian pistol.

Karl dumped the magazine, which was full, then pulled back the slide, so the chambered cartridge popped out. "Sir," he said in Russian, "this could get you into a lot of trouble." He tossed the magazine one way, the pistol the other, into the trees. "Okay, I want to talk to the legendary White Witch now," he said.

The men led the two males off to the trenches for some food. Karl gestured the woman to the grass margin by the road and indicated for her to sit. Yes, goddammit, she was a beauty. From somewhere in his forgotten education—

Flaubert: "Beauty can cut like a knife."

She had cheekbones like doorknobs, which pulled her cheeks taut, almost concave. The lips, however, were full, if grim. The nose had an aquiline perfection, but nothing matched her eyes, which were as blue as summer lakes and as big as winter oceans. They, too, were grim, but somehow calm and capable of holding a stare without revealing a thing. But one knew that the irises could dilate into expressiveness, even warmth, in split seconds. Her eyebrows were dark in contrast to her tanned but still-soft skin; the tawny-dark tendrils of hair hanging down across her forehead achieved not messiness but perfection. Whatever happened to this woman's hair, it would always seem perfect.

"Cigarette?" he said, holding out a Merkur for her.

She took it, watching him carefully. Beauties were usually calm, because they understood bad things would not happen to them. That extended to the White Witch in German captivity. Even though she understood, at least abstractly, that very bad things were about to happen to her.

He lit her cigarette and one for himself.

A new barrage opened up, preceded by the howl of the Katyushas.

"As you can see, your people are on their way," he said in Russian. "I would advise you against false hopes. They're not going to get to this position until nightfall, several hours away. Our business will be concluded by that time, and you will be on your way."

Her eyes settled on far distance, focusing on nothing. Then she said, "My name is Ludmilla Petrova. I am a Sergeant, Sixty-fourth Guards Army, currently on detached duty. I forgot my serial number. That is all I am going to tell you."

"I'm not asking anything, Sergeant Petrova. The SS is on the way, and they'll have plenty of questions. They want you very badly. I'll see that you're fed. I'll give you some cigarettes. Nobody will rape or molest you. We're not that kind of German. My advice is, give the SS what they demand. What does it matter, this late in the war, which you've basically already won? They get very unpleasant when they are defied. Maybe that will earn you a swift execution, which is all you can reasonably expect from them. After all, you killed one of their heroes."

"I would do it all over again, knowing that it would turn out this way. My death means nothing."

"You're vastly superior to me. My death means everything, particularly to me, and I don't care to have it occur today. When I turn you over to them, my men and I get out of your lovely country for good. We may even survive."

"Congratulations," she said. "By the way, I've

never seen that funny helmet. What are you supposed to be, a mushroom?"

"It's a parachutist's helmet. We're the famous Battlegroup Von Drehle, on detached duty with Fourteenth Panzergrenadier, Army Group North Ukraine, Major Karl Von Drehle at your service. You know, we jump out of airplanes. A daredevil like you would enjoy it. I'd take you along if you weren't otherwise occupied."

"What does 'Kreta' mean?" She pointed to the embroidered strip around the cuff of his bonebag. "Is it a kind of cheese?"

"That's 'feta.' Kreta is a Greek island in the Mediterranean. We jumped into it in 1941. They fired at us all the way down."

"Perhaps if you hadn't been invading their island, they wouldn't have been shooting."

"I understood their point of view and the military necessity involved. I didn't take it personally."

"My husband, Dimitri, was a pilot. He didn't jump out of his airplane, he burned alive in it. German incendiary bullets."

"That was nothing personal, either, even if you and Dimitri take it personally. I have many comrades buried under wheat and snow, so I may know something of grief. Who are these men with you?"

He gestured, and both looked across the road to the two captives ravenously devouring German rations.

464

"These are simple men, a schoolteacher and a peasant. Subtleties are beyond them. They are ignorant."

"I can't let them go. The SS wants them, too."

She said nothing. The sun lit her face, which was fair and calm. She took another puff of her cigarette, inhaled, exhaled, utterly impervious to self and circumstance.

"The SS is on its way to pick you up. Yet you remain calm. Quite impressive."

"I never expected to survive. I've accepted my own death. I killed Groedl and nothing else matters. No one is left in my family, so I will join them in heaven, if there is a heaven. Look, Major, you appear to be a civilized man. May I ask you—may I beg you? Please. I accept that I am your trophy and will earn you some prizes. But let those two men go. They're nothing but refugees. I'm your ticket to survival. They're harmless. Ask yourself the same question. What difference does it make?"

"I really hate you noble, heroic types. See that fellow over there feeding your friends? He's even got them laughing? That guy's noble, too. It's sickening. He has six wound stripes and a seventy-five-engagement badge. Seventy-five! That covers him to about 1942, but they don't make bigger badges. For political reasons, the SS would kill him if they could. They know his subversive tendencies. I'd like to get him home;

465

he's earned it. My other fellows, too. They've earned it. And if I don't give your friends to the SS, Wili doesn't go home, and this little group of boys who are pretty much my family, they don't go home. They die here on some godforsaken mountain. For nothing. So that does matter, and that is why I can't help you, much as I might want to. If I have to weigh your friends' lives against Wili's, and it appears I do, then I'll choose Wili's every time. I tell you this so you know my motives aren't malign, even if they have, from your point of view, malign results."

"It's nothing personal."

"To be honest, it feels personal, and I don't like the feeling. But duty is duty."

"I appreciate that the young officer listened to me and treated me civilly."

"I appreciate that the sniper sergeant behaved well. It's a mark of good breeding."

An hour passed. The three prisoners ate a last meal. The other men remained in casual battle positions, with two recon posts half a mile down the Yaremche road to report on the arrival of either the Police Brigade panzerwagens or the Russians. Karl sat in the communications tent with Wili, monitoring developments over the radio.

He smoked and thought. He decided what the hell and finished off the last of his English pipe tobacco. It brought a rich, heavy buzz to his head. The sound of the shells, the scream of the rockets, was constant, though it varied in intensity. It rose, it fell. Still, no small-arms fire could be heard, which meant the battle was too far off to matter.

His reverie was interrupted by his signalman. "Karl, Horst on telephone."

"Yes, yes," said Karl, taking the receiver. "Hello, hello, Karl here."

"Karl, I see them. Still a few miles out. Three SS panzerwagens coming down the road."

"Fine, I receive you. Can you give me an estimate on arrival?"

"I'm guessing at least half an hour."

"Good work. All right, get back here, in position."

"Yes, Karl."

"Leave the phone. Don't waste time respooling the wire. One way or another, we won't be needing it."

"Got it and end transmit."

"End transmit," said Karl.

He rose, summoned Wili to him. "Can you put together a bread bag full of actual bread instead of grenades for a change? Some vegetables, maybe, some clean water in a water bottle."

"Karl, what are you thinking?"

"Wili, just do what you're told. I'm still the officer here, remember?"

"Yes, Karl."

Karl went over to the three captured bandits, now in a trench together. "All right," he said. "I've decided to let the two men go. Wili is putting together some supplies. My advice is to go through the canyon here, then cut right and find a cave or a glade some miles away from the road. You don't want to be on this side of the crest because there may be a battle here, and a lot of sloppy fire will be going all over the place, maybe mortar rounds as well. There will be a large explosion when we seal off the road. Stay over there for at least twenty-four hours after the shooting stops. Then walk in, hands high, to your own people. They're trigger-happy, so it's best to wait until you see an officer or NCO in charge. He will keep things calm."

He turned to the woman just as Wili arrived with two bread bags and a couple of water bottles. "I cannot do the same for you, as I have explained. Use the next few minutes to make your good-byes. The SS will be here shortly, and after that, I can do nothing more for you."

"Karl, are you—" Wili began.

"I am sure."

"But weren't the orders explicit? The woman *and* the men with her. It could be just what they need to turn against us."

"Possibly. But I think they're going to be so happy to get the female sniper, they won't care about anything else. On top of that, I'll make a big deal over the imminent arrival of the Ivans. Believe me, Ali Baba won't like that. He'll be in a hurry to get down the road to Uzhgorod and behind our new lines. I guarantee you, the last thing this Arab wants is to be stuck in the middle of a battle between two forces he despises equally, the Red Army and Twenty-one Para. We'll blow Ginger, and then I'll go straight to Muntz, if he's still alive, and tell him the men were near death, and there was no point in sending them further. He'll have to accept that, and again, he will be happy to have sent this woman to Berlin with whatever secrets she has."

"Yes, Karl, if you say so. We've never doubted you. But Karl, we have it all now, and it seems—"

"The men are meaningless, Wili. There's a reason the SS gets the woman. There's no reason for it to get these two idiots. They won't even notice, I assure you."

The Teacher and the Peasant, rested now and plied with bread bags, passed through the canyon passageway, turned right, and found a high trail deep into the woods under the crest. There were no Germans here, as all had fled. They were safe.

They hurried down the rocky cut in the forest. Then they both stopped.

"I have to see," said the Teacher.

"So do I," said the Peasant.

"You should go on. There's nothing to see."

"No, I must—"

"Your head must be made of marble. Now go, you have officially survived, remember what the German said, take your time, don't jump at the Red Army, they will shoot you."

"I will not go. I must see, too."

"You could easily die."

"So it happens."

"Come on, then."

The two rushed back until they reached the chalky canyon wall. They slithered closer and closer and finally came to the spot where the edge of the rock afforded visibility into the little German fortress.

The Teacher quickly noted the three SS panzerwagens, dappled in shades of forest brown and green, churning heavily on great gnashing treads up the dirt road. The three vehicles came ahead almost on sheer determination. A man stood like a ship's captain in the cab of the first one. They were a few minutes away.

The Teacher shifted his view, came back to the fortified zone, saw nothing, and then—

"Look," said the Peasant. "It's Mili."

"It is," said the Teacher.

She walked with the young officer back along the road a bit. She was smoking a cigarette.

"What is he going to do?" asked the Peasant. "Is he going to let her go?"

"He can't let her go. He would be executed."

"Then what—"

"It will seem cruel," said the Teacher. "But it is not. It is the only happy ending possible. It will probably cost the officer his life, but he cannot turn her over to the SS for torture. Like the two of us, he is in love with her."

"I don't—"

"Watch, Peasant. The drama has a wonderful ending. Think about it, and in time you will understand. You will also understand that the German is a decent man, possibly a hero."

"We could—"

"No," said the Teacher. "No, we couldn't."

They reached a sunlit place. She took a last puff on her cigarette and tossed it away. He walked around behind her and withdrew his pistol.

"He is probably killing himself as well," said the Teacher.

The two watched. The officer put his pistol to the back of the head and fired. She dropped to her knees, then toppled to the earth. He walked around and again placed the muzzle to the back of the head and fired. Then he put his pistol in its holster and walked back to his men.

CHAPTER 55

Moscow

THE PRESENT

It hit harder than he'd thought it would. You can't predict. But this one hit so hard. All the way back he was stony, silent. He just stared ahead, paying no attention when she fished out her laptop and started writing—this story, another story, who knew? The cabin of the helicopter was dark, and the screen lit her face. He didn't look at her, he just looked ahead or out the window.

They landed close to midnight, and Will was in the private terminal, waiting for Stronski's jet. He hugged his wife, and they exchanged jabber and pleasure at each other's presence in the way old-marrieds the world over do. Swagger made a big show of meeting Will for the first time, and obvious jokes were exchanged, all of it a kind of social theater that Swagger wasn't really into. But the conventions demanded, and he delivered; he owed it to both of them. Finally Will drove them into Moscow, unaware that a car full of Stronski shooters rode hard a few lengths behind, just in case. Stronski's idea, approved by Bob.

They got to the apartment complex and pulled in to a lot in the interior of a space between six-story apartment buildings, which rose on either side like walls of a canyon, sparsely lit because of the lateness of the hour. They headed toward the one that housed *The Washington Post*'s bureau on its top floor, and provided a living for Kathy and Will, with an abundance of spare bedrooms. Bob had seen it before; it was a cool place.

"You go on up," he said.

"What?"

"I'm going in there."

"What?"

He had pointed to a neon sign blazing at ground level in another building. It said in bright neon orange COCKTAILS, and next to the word was the universal symbol of the beast itself, a tilted martini glass with a smiling olive inside.

"You're kidding," said Reilly.

"Nope. Never been more serious."

"Swagger, I'm down, too. But we knew. We suspected. It was a war. It was the best ending possible. It's no reason to go off the wagon."

"No, that ain't it. It's a debt I have to pay."

"What are you talking about?"

"It occurred to me on the flight. I put it together. It took him ten years, but he got it done."

He took a breath.

"I don't know who he was, professional or amateur. But the NKVD records prove that one guy figured out what happened to Mili, and he tracked down Krulov and made him pay. Krulov, top of the world, and someone knows it ain't right, takes him down and cuts his tongue out, and sends him for a swim without it. Maximum insult. The way you kill a traitor. So I have decided, goddammit, I will drink a toast to that man. It's the one little shred of right that happened in the whole story of Mili and all the powers who got together to destroy her. He's the one guy who stood up for her. He deserves a drink, whoever he is, and it ain't worth staying on the wagon to deny him that gesture. He'd get it, even if no one else would."

"I think we'll join you," said Will.

CHAPTER 56

The Carpathians
Yaremche
JULY 1944

The Peasant and the Teacher hastened along the high trail on the far side of the crest. They had not gone a mile when, back at the canyon, they heard the Russian attack. It was a sharp, harsh firefight, all kinds of automatic fire and explosions. They paused, listening, as behind them men fought and died. It seemed to last forever, but in reality, it was only seconds.

"Who won?" asked the Peasant.

"I don't know. If enough Germans survived to blow the passage, I suppose they won the battle of Natasha's Womb. If the Russians killed all the Germans, the passage stays open, and it's another glorious victory for Stalin."

"If they blow it, that should be a show."

"If you like seeing things blown up, yes, it should be. Come on, I'm sure we're safe now, but we should move as far as we can, anyway."

They continued, following the track through the ragged forest trees. To their right, the mountains stiffened considerably, almost unclimbable, until they towered above. To the right, through an occasional hole in the trees, they could see more mountains, a sea of mountains stretching away limitlessly.

The explosion was loud even when it reached them, over two kilometers away. Both turned, slightly adjusted their position on the track for greater vision, and watched as a mushroom of hot, gritty gas rose, then drifted apart in the wind.

"The Germans are very good at blowing things up," said the Teacher.

In time, as the dust settled, and through a gap in the trees, they were able to see three tiny vehicles move down the road to Uzhgorod, then disappear, swallowed by trees.

"The SS swine," said the Teacher. "Why does God favor the wicked with such luck?"

They continued another few kilometers, until full dark.

"I think this is far enough," said the Teacher. "We should be safe here."

They went off the track, slipped another half-kilometer into the woods, and found shelter where two giant boulders lay together. Fiercely they attacked their bread and carrots and smoked the German cigarettes they had been given and fell into silent sleep. If nightmares haunted either, he was silent about it the next morning.

"All right," said the Teacher, "now we head back to the passage to see if our troops are in command. Or maybe, after it was blocked, there was no point for them to stick around, so they went back to Yaremche. In that case, we shall have to walk there to find somebody to report to."

"Yes, yes," said the Peasant, rising.

"Wait, I must talk with you before we go. Sit down."

Obediently the Peasant sat.

"We may be separated when we report. For various reasons. Look, let me tell you something that will help you."

"All right."

"You love her, I love her, she was a hero, she deserves to be remembered forever. But under no circumstances should you tell anyone of your time with Mili Petrova."

"What? Why—"

476

"There are politics here. You do not understand them. It would take to the end of the war for me to explain them to you. But it may have developed, by certain realities, that she is considered a traitor. Trust me. I know it's wrong, but it can't be helped at this time. So instead of being applauded for assisting the White Witch, you might be interrogated and executed for it. Do you see?"

"She killed the monster Groedl. She—"

"It doesn't matter. All that matters is: who is in charge? And whoever he is, he will seek to eliminate anyone who had close contact with Mili. That is how it is. Furthermore, please do not claim membership in Bak's army. If the Soviets see him as a Ukraine nationalist, they may decide you were criminal for being with him. Who knows, perhaps they were the ones who killed him. I'm only warning you, that's the way they work. Do you see?"

The Peasant, it was clear, did not.

"Trust me, my friend. I want the best for you. Your story is that you were hauled off by the Germans as conscripted labor. Somehow you ended up in this area. When the big offensive came, you made your escape. You hid in the forest for a few days, and now you are back. That is your story, you know nothing about Bak or about Mili, and you stick to it. Do you understand?"

"I suppose," he said, even if he did not.

· · ·

In the town of—or rather, the smoldering ruins of—Yaremche, the Soviet army set up a clearance center to which all unassigned or nonlocal citizens, uprooted by the carnage of war, had to report, for categorization and permission to return to their own lands or, worse, some dark fate unknown. The lines were long, and the Peasant waited patiently for his turn, while the Teacher was just behind him.

In the distance, Red Army investigators pawed through the burned wreckage of the town and caused a great sensation when they discovered 135 burned bodies in the ashes and charred timbers of the church. Meanwhile, at least temporarily, a tank company had taken up residence, primarily as support and logistics for the NKVD processors who ran the clearance center. A tent city grew, where those released by NKVD were sent to recover their strength before beginning their return home. It was the Soviet empire reclaiming control after the German occupation, a rough bureaucratic procedure. A small field hospital took care of the wounded; a small field kitchen prepared the food, none of which could be considered memorable; a few political officers supervised.

Finally the Peasant presented himself to a young officer at a table; he wore wire-frame glasses, was overworked, maybe a little drunk.

The Peasant was very nervous, for talking to authority was not an ordeal he had much practice with. No matter that the Teacher had told him, just before it was his turn, to be calm, to be relaxed, to cling to his story. He gave his name, presented his tattered papers.

The young man did not bother to look up. "Explain your presence," he said as he examined the paperwork, a flyblown red-covered pamphlet enclosing his ID card.

"I was rounded up by German soldiers two years ago. I have been working as a laborer over that time, building roads for tanks, laying wire, digging trenches. When the offensive came, there was shelling and confusion. I managed to make it to the forest, where I have remained for a week or so."

He went on haltingly.

"Stop, stop," said the young man. "Now, I ask you, sir, are you familiar with a partisan group in this area run by a man called Bak?"

"I have not heard of any Bak, sir."

"You did not fight with his partisans in the mountains?"

"I did not."

"All right, tell me this. Have you ever heard of a woman called Ludmilla Petrova? Also called the White Witch. She was with Bak's partisan army."

"I have never heard of Mili Petrova," said the Peasant.

"Excellent," said the young officer. "Now I see clearly. Show me your hands, please."

The Peasant put his hands out.

"No, no, you idiot, palms up."

He turned them over.

"Explain, please, why after two years of hard labor under German conscription, you have no calluses? Your hands, though filthy, are soft. You haven't touched a shovel or a hoe in years."

"I, I—I have never heard of Mili Petrova," said the Peasant.

The officer nodded to two soldiers, who walked over, grabbed the Peasant, and pulled his shirt open. Tattoos covered his chest. The soldier pointed to one, a design that featured a mandolin flanked by outward-facing R's, though all of a single line.

"That is the tattoo of the Trizubets," said the officer. "It is the Ukraine national emblem, it is the emblem of Bak's Ukraine National Army. You lied to me; you were a soldier in that army and thus a traitor to the Soviet Union. You may well have aided the traitor Ludmilla Petrova, who is on a death list. Only someone intimate with her would know that her nickname is Mili, not Luda, unless you read of her in the magazines years ago, and I doubt that you can read."

"Sir," said the Teacher, "may I speak for the man? His tongue is clumsy."

The officer looked up at the Teacher. "Who are you?"

The Teacher raced forward and handed over his document.

The officer examined it. "So, a teacher."

"Sir, this man is—"

"I ask the questions here. Were you also conscripted? Are you with him?"

"These peasants get tattoos all over their bodies. It amuses them. They have no idea what the tattoos mean. I am a teacher here. I know this."

"I asked you, were you with him? Were you conscripted?"

"Sir, I am only pointing out—"

One of the soldiers hit him in the stomach with his rifle butt.

"Teacher, fool, I ask questions. You do not explain. I am not one of your children. Show me your hands."

The soldier who had hit him dragged him to the table, turned one hand over to show the officer. "Another man at labor with soft white hands. Yours are even clean. I doubt you have tattoos because you consider yourself refined, but you speak for him, you lie for him, you attempt to evade Soviet justice. Take them both away to the—"

"Sir, if I could show you but one thing."

He was hit hard across the neck and went to his knees. The Peasant stepped in to intervene, was clubbed equally hard, and went down, blood leaking from his skull.

"Get this vermin out of here," said the officer. "I'm done wasting time with criminals."

"Sir, I beg you. Just let me show you my papers. I believe you'll find them very interesting."

"I have no more time to waste," said the officer, holding up the Teacher's document.

The Teacher squirmed free, grabbed it, twisted it, and with his deft fingers separated the rear cover into two halves. A card shook out. He handed it to the young officer.

The officer looked at it; his face went white, his jaw dropped, and he began to gibber.

"Major Speshnev, I apologize, sir, I was hasty, I had no idea, sir, sir, please, I was only trying to—"

The Teacher stopped his yammering with one raised hand. "Listen to me, Lieutenant, if you don't care to spend the rest of your life building a road to the North Pole on the off chance that The Boss decides to go for a ride up there. You will do exactly what I require, and you will do it instantly."

"Yes sir, of course. I had no idea—"

"You have caused me to blow cover on an important operation. Let me just say that you will never uncover the missing Bak. I have already done your work for you, and now you expose me. Do you see what I could do to you?"

"Yes sir. I had no—"

"I did so because this man here is my bodyguard and has done extraordinary work in service to NKVD and the security of the Soviet Union."

"Yes, Major Speshnev, my God, everyone knows of Major Speshnev, of his activities with the partisans all over the occupied zones, of his—"

"Get him the highest clearance so that he may return home as the hero he is. I will move paperwork shortly to award him the medals he deserves."

"Yes sir."

"As for me, I require air transportation to Moscow at my earliest convenience. Do you understand?"

"It will be done."

Speshnev went up to the Peasant. "All right," he said, "they will treat you well now. Go home, my friend, live well, have many children."

"Sir, you will speak for Mili? Make them see—"

"It is not time yet. Politics, as I have said. Much needs to be unraveled. I will try. Vengeance is a different matter, however. Now get out of here. Return home. Have more children."

"I will name them after you."

"It's of no importance. If you have a daughter, name her after Mili. That would be something."

The bad news was that the satellite had filmed imagery of six tractor-trailers, each with ocean-going containers, leaving the Nordyne site and transporting their cargo to a Iranian freighter in the Astrakhan harbor. The trucks completed loading. The ship was ready to go. What was holding it up?

"It's Russia. Paperwork."

Cohen explained: "The Russians run their import-export very tightly. Nothing goes in or gets out without close examination. That's why this puzzles me. Those containers will be examined, that load of extremely hazardous material will be discovered, and there will be an immediate emergency. Any kind of damage could set that stuff off, and there'd be a huge tragedy. The Russians will have to disassemble it very carefully."

The eureka moment. The banging of drums, maybe the ringing of a doorbell, maybe just a weird tremor, brain to toes. Gershon experienced it at that second. Dots all connected. "I have it," he said.

All eyes went to him.

"The minister of trade can issue arbitrary waivers on the inspection process. *That's* why he wanted the job."

Silence in the room.

Gershon summed up: "We now know that Strelnikov was the son of the traitor Basil Krulov, who was himself a student of the insane Dr. Hans Groedl, may he not rest in peace. It's a straight line from the coils of Groedl's infected brain to that ship full of Zyklon B sitting in a Russian harbor, waiting for shipment to Iran and then, by means yet unknown, to Israel. The boy Vassily idealized his father, Basil, and wanted to be just like him, wanted to continue his work in the holy war against the Jews. Now he's elderly and absurdly rich and feeling disappointed that he hasn't done enough. So he uses his wealth to set up this insanity as a tribute to his father's wishes. Now all that's left for him to do is to sign the documents and sit back and enjoy the fun."

"When does he become minister of trade?"

Gershon looked at his watch, calculated Moscow time from it, and replied, "In about twenty minutes."

"Options," the director asked.

"Limited, I'm afraid," said someone. "We have no military assets in the area. Even if we did, attacking something in a Russian harbor would be a policy disaster. The ship will be vulnerable for the eight hours it takes to travel from Astrakhan to the Iranian harbor. We could hit it with Phantoms if we could get permission to meet them on the way back in someone else's air space with tankers for refueling. Even then we'd catch hell for bombing a ship in the Caspian, and if there were consequences of the gas, we'd catch hell for that. Not the makers of the gas but us, the Israelis, as usual."

"Once it's unloaded in Iran, we've pretty much lost it," another executive continued. "Our only responses are defensive. Heightened border and air security. A posture of readiness. A suspicion of any large-bulk transport near our borders. All reactive, not proactive."

"Gershon, you're the genius who came up with this. Tell us what to do."

"Everything just mentioned. Prayer would also be an excellent idea."

"Strelnikov will sign the documents, the ship will leave, we will watch it disappear, and then we'll wait for the inevitable. We—"

"Sir," said someone.

"Please don't interrupt," said the director. "I'm trying to—"

"Sir, please. Look at the monitor."

All eyes went to the silent newsfeed on the screen of the television mounted in the corner.

"Mystery blast in Moscow," ran the crawl under the image, which depicted the common sight of first responders working a site of excessive destruction while red lights flashed.

Someone turned the sound up.

"—have confirmed that the limousine contained

the controversial Vassily Strelnikov, on his way to the Kremlin to be sworn in as the new minister of trade. He is among the four dead on the scene outside the Strelnikov mansion in this fashionable section of Moscow. Just who is responsible—terrorists or Russian Mafia figures or other actors—is unknown at this point but—"

"Nice work, Gershon," said the director.

"I had no idea I was on such good terms with the Almighty," said Gershon.

"He doesn't even go to synagogue," said Cohen.

CHAPTER 57

Idaho
Outside Cascade
THE PRESENT

MILI GOT HER MAN: NEW EVIDENCE SUGGESTS DISCREDITED RUSSIAN SNIPER MAY HAVE KILLED NAZI WAR CRIMINAL, by Kathy Reilly and Will French, *Washington Post* Moscow Correspondents, ran as a three-part series, debuting on a Sunday on Page 1 under digitally enhanced photos of both Mili and Obergruppenführer Groedl across six of the newspaper's eight columns. It got more Web hits than anything in *Post* history for a single day; it sold fifty thousand extra paywall subscriptions; and it is a front-runner for the upcoming Pulitzer Prize in Feature writing.

For Kathy, it meant a munificent book contract to develop the series into a book. She took a six-month book leave, right after she and Will wound up their coverage of the assassination of Vassily Strelnikov on the way to his swearing-in as trade minister, while Will alone went to Astrakhan to cover the mysterious "abandoned freighter loaded with poison gas" story.

For Swagger, there were numerous pleasures. When he returned home, Miko was back from her riding camp in the East, and father and daughter and mother had a good three weeks of family. Nikki flew in from Washington for a weekend, and the next, Ray and Molly, who was pregnant. It was a good time.

Still: they went home. Then fall arrived. October turned out to be the cruelest month. Swagger's children went back to their lives, his wife back to her office and the business, he theoretically to his rifles, his 6.5 Creedmoor project, his long rides, the things he did that he enjoyed. But he was alone again, not with ghosts, not with regrets, but with—what?

"You're in love with her, too, you crazy old coot." Reilly had yelled that at him, and though he never would have put it in such naked words, he supposed it was true. He couldn't stop imagining Mili, whose face he'd never seen except in the 1943 magazine blow-up, in the circumstances she'd deserved: Mili with her kids. Mili goes out to dinner. Mili on the job. Mili in her life, a good life, a life both loved and loving. As if Swagger were some kind of screwball angel in some screwball '40s movie. Yet the images gave him such comfort. Even if they'd never happened, they *should* have happened, not because she was beautiful, brave, a warrior, but because she was one of the lost millions who got in the way of madmen and, all these years later, had been largely forgotten.

He thought: The least I can do is help the world remember her. And maybe we did that. It's not much, but it's something.

He was an old man in a dry month. He was hard, stoic, isolate, unmelted. He rocked on the porch, closing hard on sixty-eight, and watched as frost came and took the land. The green grass turned colorless and stiff, the trees went threadbare, the piles of clouds seemed to gray with age as they sped over the landscape trailing shadow, and a chill came into the air. Dead leaves rode spurts of breeze this way and that, and migratory fowl beat wings southward, trailing a forlorn racket.

"You need a mission," Jen said.

"I am out of the mission business," he said. "Here I sit. Call the crematorium when I stop rocking, and that'll be that."

"It's the girl, isn't it? Bob, what did you expect? It was a war. You know war better than any man alive. When you can't fight in someone else's war, you invent your own, because you need to feel alive in the strange way your head is wired. But ever since your first tour, you've known the terrible part of it: good people die all the time. So it goes in the cruel, cruel world."

"I know. Get over it. Wish I could. Jen, it ain't just 'Okay, now I'm all better.' It's not like that."

"I know it. It's clinical depression. It's a disease, like cancer or mumps. You need to see someone or take something."

"I am fine. It will go away."

"Stubborn old goat. Looks like Matt Dillon himself watching the town he tamed turn to hell, and nobody realizes what he went through to get the place livable."

"It's called progress."

"Maybe not progress. Maybe just change."

"I'll be okay, sweetie."

"Go for a long ride. Get some air in those lungs, feel the wind, watch the deer and the antelope play. Maybe the skies will not be cloudy all day. Get some stimulation, that's what you need. Something nice and mild to get you operational again. Take up photography, Chinese checkers, decoupage, quilting, adultery, but *something,* for God's sake."

"You're the best," he said.

"You say that to all the girls," she said.

So one day he found himself riding the rim on a horse called Horse, a good bay gelding, with spirt and more stamina than he had and a tendency to comment in horse on everything. Even Horse seemed to be telling him to get over it. Or get over himself, maybe that was it.

The cliff below was about thirty feet, and Horse wouldn't go near the edge, a sound policy, but cantered along jauntily enough. Bob enjoyed the wind, which was cold, the distance to the blue mountains, which was immense, the architecture of the clouds, like ruined castles or damaged dreams rolling this way and that in unmeasurable complexity. He felt better. He felt okay. Next week he was flying to England to Jimmy Guthrie's vintage sniper match at Bisley, and he knew a lot of old boys and a lot of active-duty younger guys would be there. That would be fun, that would be a toot. Then, Jen was going to meet him in London and—

His cell rang.

He pulled up on Horse, fetched the thing from his jeans pocket, slid it on, and saw a strange number come up. Who the hell? Only a very few people knew his number, and none of them ever had a number like that.

"Swagger," he said noncommittally.

"Bob!" It was Reilly.

"Where the hell are you?"

She was laughing. "I'm in Australia."

"Australia! What are you doing there?"

"I'll tell you. But where are you?"

"I'm a cowboy, remember? I'm on a horse in the middle of nowhere. That's what cowboys do."

"Well, get off the horse."

"Why? What is—"

"Trust me, Swagger. Get off the damn horse."

"Okay, just a sec."

He unlimbered from Horse, let the reins go. The gelding was well trained and would not go far.

"This better be good."

"Oh, it's good, all right."

"Let's have it."

"The story isn't over. There's one more chapter."

CHAPTER 58

The Carpathians
Ginger's Womb
JULY 28, 1944

As Karl walked away from the woman, Wili joined him. "Nice shooting," he said.

"I thought so," said Karl.

"You missed her by what, two, three feet?"

"Hmmm," said Karl. "Was it that obvious?"

"Yes. What's the point, may I ask?"

"I'm not sure."

"What is your motivation, may I inquire?"

"No motivation at all. It just turned out I couldn't do it. I told her to drop when I fired. She did."

"She's a much better actress than you are an actor. Her fall looked quite authentic. On the other hand, every single thing about your performance was insincere. I would stick to race cars after the war. Forget about the movies."

"Do the fellows know?"

"I'm sure they do."

Karl yelled at the first two Green Devils he saw peering over the rear of the trench at him. "Get a shelter half and pick up the dead woman and move her to the trench."

"Suppose she wants to walk, Karl?"

"I'm sure she'll cooperate."

"Sure, Karl."

And off they went.

"I know you have a plan," said Wili.

"Not exactly."

"What do you intend to do?"

"Improvise, I suppose. I improvise brilliantly."

"No, you don't. You have no gift for improvisation at all. I'm the improviser. All the good ideas come from me. You're just the symbol."

"All right. Can you come up with something?"

"It would help if you'd alerted me earlier."

"I didn't know earlier."

"First problem: what do we do with these assholes?"

He gestured, and Karl turned, looking down the road. All three SS Sd. Kfz 251s, mud spattering their dappled forest camouflage, their treads grinding through the soft earth, their MG-42s ominously scanning the horizon, lumbered toward them. In the first, recognizable even at two hundred meters, stood Captain Salid, like a statue above the rim of the armored driver's compartment.

"He looks like Nelson at Trafalgar," said Wili. "Resolute, heroic, triumphant, rolling toward his date with destiny, his triumph."

"I see now I am not going to give him the woman," said Karl. "He is going to be extremely irritated. Wili, tell the guys to be ready for anything. I don't trust these characters, especially Sinbad the Sailor there."

He reached down and unsnapped the flap covering the Browning pistol on his hip. His thumb lingered inside, found the knurled spur of the hammer, and eased it back until it cocked.

"Okay, Karl, I'm going to nonchalantly mosey away as if nothing has happened. But I'm on you the whole way. We'll play it as it breaks."

"First to hairpin takes the flag," said Karl.

Salid ordered himself to be calm as his vehicle lurched along the road to the canyon. As they came into range, he could see the parachute officer standing alone in his baglike camouflage smock and ludicrous helmet, complex chin straps unconnected, waiting with a somewhat disinterested look on his face. These bastards weren't impressed by anything. They had to let you know in every single way they could think of how much better than you they were.

Salid did not see the woman. Presumably she was tied up in the trench complex they had built to the right of the road, a little nest of canvas-roofed machine-gun positions behind sandbags, barbed wire stretched on wooden struts, and other camouflaged men in those stupid helmets bent over their weapons. But even he could see there weren't very many of them. What did they expect to do against a Soviet army?

He leaned over to his radio operator, seated before the transmitter. "Signalman, connect me to the Luftwaffe base at Uzhgorod."

"Yes sir."

The signalman consulted his codebook, diddled through channel finding, reached up to turn the diamond-shaped aerial to a more propitious angle, made his contact, and turned the microphone and headset over to Salid.

"Elephant, Elephant, this is Zeppelin Leader, are you there?"

"Hello, hello, this is Elephant, yes, Zeppelin Leader, acknowledging your call."

"I am about to pick up the package. I want the aircraft ready to fly. This is high-priority SS, as per instructions of Lieutenant General–SS Muntz, area commander, and RHSA, Berlin, do you understand?"

"Zeppelin Leader, you are acknowledged, the aircraft is on the runway."

"I worry that when the Russians get here, with artillery, we might be in range. Berlin demands this shipment, so please accommodate."

"Zeppelin Leader, we are briefed and prepped at this end for immediate takeoff."

"Very good, Elephant. Zeppelin Leader, end transmit."

"End transmit," said the Luftwaffe operator, and Salid handed the earphones and speaker back.

He looked, saw they were even closer, and turned to Ackov. "I'll get out to talk to him. I want you on the gun, covering me. On him, so he feels it. I want the men in this track and the other two ready to deploy. These bastards have it in for us. And remember, we've got the vehicles out of here and the Condor waiting to fly us to Berlin. They've got to stay and hold this pass until no more Germans are coming, then blow it. They could be hit by Reds at any time."

"Yes sir," said Ackov, and got on the radio transmitter to instruct the other two vehicles to assume combat readiness. Then he said, "Captain, are you anticipating a firefight?"

"With these arrogant bastards, you don't know what might happen. If it happens, I want to be ready with maximum firepower. If they fuck with us, we'll destroy them. They're basically traitors anyway."

The three panzerwagens pulled into the clearing just before Ginger's Womb, and Karl watched carefully, noting a gunner at each MG-42 mounted in each cab. He saw that the men in each vehicle wore helmets, and no gun muzzles were visible over the rim of the armored beast, signifying that the troopers inside carried their weapons unslung in hand, ready for action.

He heard the clank of the heavy door opening on the far side, and a second later, Captain Salid, his eyes burning with intensity under the rim of his helmet, his SS camouflage tunic bright with dots and flecks of forest coloration, as if he'd washed it last night for a ceremonial function, stepped around the big vehicle. He carried a Luger in his right hand. That was not a good sign.

As he approached, the gunner in his command wagon pivoted the machine gun onto Karl and jacked the cocking handle, pulling a round into the chamber. The man was not visible behind the double gun-shields.

"Heil Hitler," barked Karl, throwing his arm up and out in perhaps the best salute he'd given in two years.

"Heil Hitler," returned the Arab.

"I am glad you are here. We need the firepower. I want your people on the left line, and I think it best you move the panzerwagens to the right of the road so your field of fire—"

"We are not here to fight a battle. The woman, Herr Major. You know that is why I am here, and I have my orders."

"I have a military responsibility first. Intelligence matters can wait until after we have repulsed the Reds and allowed the maximum number of German staffers to escape via the passage code-named Ginger. Then we'll blow Ginger. Then and only then will I release the woman."

"That is not your option. You are not making decisions here, RHSA is, through me. Rank is immaterial. I knew I'd run into business with you, Von Drehle. You think yourself superior."

"No, I think I have a battle to fight."

"Where's the woman? That's what I need to know."

"Oh, the woman," said Von Drehle. "That's right, SS is making war exclusively on women and generals these days."

"I am not going to banter with you. Von Drehle, I grow impatient and have obligations to superiors. Have your men—"

"She's dead," said Von Drehle.

Salid looked at him, eyes wide open. His jaw may have trembled. Something between rage and panic flashed through him, draining the color from his face. "You were explicitly ordered—"

"Yes, well, she tried to escape, and rather than run after her, one of my men shot her. All German military units are under orders to execute bandits and have been for three years. It was a snap shot, very well placed. I could not blame him. So it goes in battle zones."

"I demand to see the body."

"We let bandits lay where they fall. Care to come into the woods with me, Herr Captain? Although we may run into Red guerrillas."

"You are lying. She is a witch, her beauty is legendary, she cast a spell, you now protect her. You are weak and soft. I demand that you get her. Get her or there will be terrible consequences for you. We represent the armed righteousness of the Reich, you are mutineers."

He leveled the Luger at Karl. "Do not test me, Von Drehle. I will shoot you and my men will wipe out your detachment. You are traitors, as is well known."

"You're getting a bit melodramatic, aren't you, old man? I have had many weapons pointed at me, so I do not find it frightening. As for death, I accepted mine years ago. If it comes today, it comes today. Put the pistol down and get your goddamned vehicles out of here. You can use the ride to Uzhgorod as a chance to think up invective against me for Muntz and prepare the arrest documents. Meanwhile, we'll stay up here and fight to the last man. I'll see you in Valhalla. Oh, wait, I'll wave to you *from* Valhalla as you're on your way to some kind of Arab hell, where the women *don't* wear veils."

"*Infidel! Infidel!*" screamed the Arab as his face went red and his eyes hid behind slits. Spit flew from his mouth. "You insult God. You will be consumed in fire, I swear it."

"Almost certainly," said Karl, "but not before I watch you burn."

"You swine," said Salid.

And then he was fire itself.

Wili Bober hit the SS man with a compressed-nitrogen-powered spurt of blazing Flammol-19 from the Flammenwerfer. The flame took everything. His hair burned, his face burned, his eyeballs burned. His eyelids burned, his nose, tongue, palate, and esophagus burned. His chest and heart and lungs burned. His bones burned. His loins burned, his muscles burned, his legs burned, his feet burned.

Even his boots burned.

The incandescence of his immolation filled the space, and the overhanging arches of the trees captured it, turning full green where the dullness of the day had kept them a kind of lusterless gray.

The flaming apparition took two or three ghastly, lurching steps, screaming something unintelligible, before it toppled to the ground.

A moment of silent horror followed, and then Ackov pivoted his MG-42 to the right to cut Wili in half, but he was a second slow, as Karl had drawn his Browning and shot him expertly from thirty meters under the rim of his helmet but over his shoulder, through his left ear.

Almost at once the 21 Para weapons opened up. A front of pure firepower blew in heavily. The supersonic bullets pelted off the camouflaged armor, the sound of high-velocity steel striking static steel like some kind of lead sleet against a tin roof. Some expert athlete tight-spiraled an egg grenade perfectly into the second Sd. Kfz, and it detonated, taking the fight totally out of that cargo of Police Battalion soldiers, a piece of it severing the spine of the MG-42 gunner, who went down with a finger on the trigger, so that his gun ate a full belt, though the rounds went straight up to descend, presumably, somewhere in Czechoslovakia.

The parachutist FG-42s and STG-44s hammered the opening armored doors of the big vehicles, ripping up clouds of metallic jet spray, lashing against the troopers who tried to disembark to get into action. They went down as the spitzers scythed them, plunged into the compartment, and ricocheted off the heavy armor. Wili was already adjusting his aim on the long nozzle that was the flamethrower's snout, and he squeezed another half second's worth of oxidation off, this gust to shroud the third vehicle in the same cloak of burning, and those poor devils, screaming, flaming, tumbled over the rim of the machine and landed, ran, and went down, smoldering and still.

Suddenly there was nothing to shoot. The stench of burned fuel and meat filled the air, and a cloud of grimy smoke hung over everything. The captain still flickered away on the ground, as his flesh had not all been consumed.

"Comrade!" came a call from inside the second panzerwagen.

"We will throw more grenades next, then burn out the rest of you. Leave your weapons, come out hands high. If we do not see palms, we fire. Quick, quick, quick."

The Serbian survivors emerged from each vehicle; they were searched and led to the road and ordered to sit, hands still up, hands always up. Parachutists with their STG-44s circled them.

Wili dumped the fifty-pound apparatus, which was almost out of fuel anyway, and walked over to Karl. "Well," he said, "I don't think this is the battle they had in mind, but we won it nevertheless."

"Interesting development, isn't it?"

"Good shot, by the way."

"Yes, I did better this time. Now what? Have you figured anything out?"

"No, I've been rather busy."

"I know this is hard to believe, but I have an actual idea myself."

"Amazements never cease."

"I note we have two basically undamaged panzerwagens at our disposal."

"Some bodies inside. But they're easily attended to."

"I note also that if we strip our prisoners, we have, what, fifteen or twenty, whatever, enough SS jackets and helmets to cover us all."

"Yes, we do. I think I see where you're going with this."

"We have *Die weisse Hexe,* our ticket to that FW-200 now on the tarmac at Uzhgorod."

"Yes."

"Let's put on the SS tunics. Let's release the SS boys, who, naked, will be of little harm to us. They can walk out of the mountains in any direction they choose. Then let's take the young woman. Let's blow Ginger. That's our mission, after all. Let's drive to the Uzhgorod airfield. Let's board the plane."

"So far, so good," said Wili.

"Then let's fly to—somewhere we won't be executed, as will happen if we fly to Berlin."

"This plane has great range. We can fly low, so no radar will read us. I'm sure our pistols will convince the pilots to cooperate. After all, they benefit, too, assuming we can find the right airfield."

"I'm open to suggestions."

"I don't want to go to prison, either," said Wili. "It involves being locked up, I understand."

"Well," said Karl, "that means Moscow's out. Russians. Rome's out. Americans. Alexandria's out. Brits."

"Hmmm," said Wili.

Karl jumped into the trench. She sat in a corner, no longer guarded, and looked at him.

She had shaken her hair loose, so it tumbled down, tawny and complex. Her blue eyes were wide open, her cheekbones sharp, pulling her tanned skin tight, almost concave. There was no panic in her, only a kind of languid intelligence. She wore the peasant smock over a white blouse, with a bright scarf around her elegant neck. He had not noticed these details before.

"Care for another cigarette?" he said.

"That would be nice. By the way, who got killed?"

As Karl got out the cigarette, and one for himself, lit them both, he said, "They were from Police Battalion, attached to Thirteenth SS Mountain Division, called Scimitar, which is a kind of sword, I'm told."

"One of those curved things, is that right?"

"Yes. More dramatic than effective. I suppose it has symbolic meaning to certain people."

"Since you're alive and I don't see any

lightning flashes about, am I to assume you shot it out with the SS?"

"I suppose we did."

"Odd, you don't look insane. But now you've killed a batch of your own people, so it seems we're both going to die."

"Not exactly," he said. "On that 'your own people' remark, I think I would disagree. But more important for now, I have a plan. It's quite good, even if I was the one who came up with it, and my plans are usually pretty awful. It seems you're our ticket to a perfectly good airplane, and I hate to let a good plane go to waste."

He told her what he intended.

"It sounds risky."

"It is. But it's better than being worked on in a cellar by SS."

"I understand. But let's be practical. This isn't the movies. You can't just fly away."

"Actually you can."

"Where are we going to go?"

"I thought we'd try . . . Switzerland. They have excellent cheese."

CHAPTER 59

Idaho
Outside Cascade
THE PRESENT

S witzerland!" Swagger said.
"And that's what they did. They hijacked
their own plane and landed in Bern. All of
them. They seemed to be some kind of paratroop
outfit—very small, commandos, I guess—but
evidently they'd had enough of the Nazis. They
took her and they went to Switzerland. Some
officer figured it out."

"Jesus Christ," said Bob, standing on the lone
prairie like a movie cowboy.

"Not only that, here's the twist. Oh, what a
twist. He married her. His name was Karl Von
Drehle, some kind of aristocratic war-hero type,
dashing, from the pictures. He looked a little like
Errol Flynn. After they got out of internment,
they decided that since Europe had tried so hard
to kill them, they'd go someplace sunnier and
emigrated to Australia."

"That's why you're in Australia."

"Her son Paul called me from Sydney. Everything he said checked out. I flew, I've been here a
week with the family, looking over all the

records, looking at the photos. They had four sons and a daughter. The daughter, by the way, was a big Aussie tennis star in the '70s. And now the granddaughter is on the tour as well."

"What happened to Mili?" said Swagger. He was almost afraid to ask. Something tight and dry in his chest.

"She died at the age of eighty-four, a few weeks after Karl, surrounded by children and grandchildren. She became a professor of math at New South Wales University, where she was much loved, if the obits are telling the truth. Everyone thought she was German; no one suspected she was Russian."

"Ain't that a kick in the pants," said Bob.

He couldn't stop imagining Mili in the circumstances she'd deserved: Mili with her kids. Mili goes out to dinner. Mili on the job. Mili in her life, a good life, a life both loved and loving.

You're in love with her, you crazy old coot.

"Karl brought his wartime sergeant over," Reilly continued from Australia, "and the two of them went into business. Ever hear of Volkswagen? Karl and Wili became the first Volkswagen dealers in Australia, and the second and the third and so on. He and Wili got rich. Oh, God, Swagger, after all the shit they went through, all the murder and mud and slaughter, they had such good, decent productive lives. It shows there is life after hell.

It's amazing. I cry every time I think about it. Are you crying?"

"Cowboys don't cry," said Swagger through some goddamned prairie grit that had come into his eyes.

Acknowledgments

My first thanks must go to my dedicatee, Kathy Lally, whom I have cleverly disguised as Kathy Reilly (while her husband, Will Englund, goes forth under the fiendishly altered nom de guerre Will French). Kathy, who currently shares the job of Moscow correspondent of my old rag *The Washington Post* with Will, was majordomo of my trip to Ukraine and most things Russian. Because of her, I got to depend on the kindness of friends, not strangers.

Two of those friends we nicknamed "The Two Vlads." Volodymyr Bandrivskyy was our translator and guide, and despite the tragic history of his nation, he was a merry jokester the whole way. Volodymyr Bak (don't have a cool name around me or I will steal it) was our historian, who had salient and necessary information at his fingertips or, if not, the next day. Both were boon companions and made the travel—especially over the liver-pulverizing Ukraine roads—a pleasure.

On the home front, Gary ("Gershon") Goldberg was instrumental, particularly in the "Interlude in Tel Aviv" subplot. Like Vlad II, if he doesn't know it now, he'll know it tomorrow. Besides, he is a way-fun guy, and at certain points in any novel, a writer needs to have some way-fun. Gary is my go-to on way-fun. Through Gary, Dr. David Fowler, the medical examiner of the state of Maryland, looked at my anatomy lesson on Senior Group Leader Groedl. Gary also had his friend Larry Baker take a look at the MS, which was helpful.

My little circle of advisers also was of great help in this one: Mike Hill, Lenne Miller, Jay Carr, and Jeff Weber all issued astute advice.

In the professional gun world, Bill Smart, a great friend from *Post* days, connected me with the great gunscribes, writers Mike Venturino and Rocky Chandler. Rocky, a novelist himself, set me straight on the absolute necessity of zeroing at a thousand for a thousand-yard shot. Barrett Tillman, the great aviation historian, had lots of smart stuff for me. On my own, I found Martin Pegler, author of *Out of Nowhere*, who was of particular help with regard to the Enfield No. 4 (T) with No. 32 scope. Dan Shea, another good friend and owner of Long Mountain Outfitters in Henderson, NV, let me have a hands-on experience with three of the few remaining FG-42s.

I should also list the dozens of books, films, and websites that were so important to this effort, but I'm too lazy to copy the titles, and you probably don't care that much anyway. I'd put them on my website except I don't have a website. I would have read them on my Nook,

Niche, Wombat, or Blazer 9, except I don't have any of them, either. I'm just a book guy, I bought a lot of books. The Amazon bill was mind-boggling. So let me collectively thank the dozens of writers, historians, screenwriters, and directors who've tried to keep the memory of the horror and the scale of *Ostkrieg* alive. It's too profound to be forgotten, too influential even now to be ignored, and too painful to be suppressed. This book is a humble attempt to be a part of that memory process.

Finally the publishing professionals—agent Esther Newberg, editor Sarah Knight, and publisher Jonathan Karp—oversaw and sustained the project; all manned up and did duties as required. And finally my wife, Jean Marbella, zeitgeist of Baltimore journalism, coffee- and martini-maker extraordinaire, and all-around best chum, provided a rest stop each night and a hot cuppa each morning. Couldn't have made it to the end without 'em.

As usual, none of these fine people is responsible for errors in fact or spirit; I alone am the root cause.

Center Point Large Print
600 Brooks Road / PO Box 1
Thorndike ME 04986-0001 USA

(207) 568-3717

US & Canada:
1 800 929-9108
www.centerpointlargeprint.com